SERVANT OF SLAVES

*A Biographical Novel
of John Newton*

NOVELS BY GRACE IRWIN

Least of All Saints
Andrew Connington
In Little Place
Servant of Slaves

William B. Eerdmans Publishing Co., Grand Rapids, Mich.

Grace Irwin

SERVANT OF SLAVES

*A Biographical Novel
of John Newton*

PHOTOLITHOPRINTED BY CUSHING - MALLOY, INC.
ANN ARBOR, MICHIGAN, UNITED STATES OF AMERICA
1962

To my brother

JOHN C. W. IRWIN

ACKNOWLEDGMENTS

To the late Dr. Donald Grey Barnhouse I am incalculably indebted for his suggestion that I write a novel on the life of John Newton.

For the kindness of Mr. Bernard Martin I can never be sufficiently grateful. Not only has his fascinating biography: JOHN NEWTON, re-issued as AN ANCIENT MARINER, been a rich mine of information, but he has been most generous of help and advice in relevant minutiae, lending me much Newtonia acquired by his own scholarly research.

My thanks are also due to Miss Katharine Bull, descendant of Newton's friend, for her repeated hospitality to me while I read the Log of his voyages; to the Reverend J. N. Bacon, direct descendant of the famous sculptor, at whose home I was privileged to view the original pastel of Newton; to Mr. Bernard Honess of *The Independent Press,* who introduced me to Mr. Martin; to the Reverend R. S. Hopkinson, then rector of St. Mary Woolnoth; to Mr. T. T. Radmore of the Olney Museum; and to many others who, during my stay in England, went out of their way to assist me in my search.

I should like to thank my close friends who have been fed an uninterrupted diet of Newton these past three years; and my sister, Mrs. W. H. Clarke, for her appraisal and constructive criticism of the manuscript.

Finally I must express my gratitude to my friend and secretary, Miss Laura Powell, for her patient loving labour in reducing to orderly type the illegible chaos of my longhand.

—Grace Irwin

Toronto, 1961

PREFACE

JOHN NEWTON's life was stranger than the most improbable fiction. What has happened in the past century to his reputation is as strange and disparate as his life.

"The evil that men do lives after them," observed Shakespeare candidly. But for the evil that a man did *not* do to be attributed posthumously to him in defiance of fact contravenes all sense of justice. "De mortuis nil nisi bonum" may be an outmoded sentimentalism. "De mortuis nil nisi *verum*" should be an axiom of scholarship. It is only to say: "Fair's fair!"

My interest was aroused in Newton when I first heard the slander current about him in religious circles. He was cited as a striking illustration of the gulf between Christian belief and practice: a man who could write beautiful devotional hymns unperturbed in his captain's cabin while, in the stench and darkness of the hold, the slaves on whose trade he fattened groaned and died. A little honest investigation revealed a very different story. Yet the slander has become so popular that many of its propagandists seem resentful rather than happy to have it dispelled.

Many years later a stranger suggested that I make Newton the subject of a biographical novel. I had scarcely begun to read the related material when I discovered another slander, held and spread in literary circles with the same almost crusading vigour. This calumny lays obliquely or squarely on Newton's shoulders the blame for William Cowper's obsessive melancholy. The phrases: "uncomprehending and uncompassionate friend", "the dreadful glassy eye of the fanatic", "the Calvinist bully", are taken at random from modern surveys of the "gentle poet's" career. Any objective reading of the life histories of the two men, their correspondence, diaries and other available documents proves such terms false to the

7

point of absurdity. Amusingly enough, now that John Wesley has become a fashionably sanctified legend, the charge against him of "preaching people mad" is turned upon John Newton, who in his own day was criticized as too gentle, too familiar, determined to avoid controversy and threatening.

On the other hand many apocryphal stories are told and written about Newton, no more lurid than the facts but contrary to them or quite without foundation. From every available source I have sought to discover and present, if not the whole truth which would run to volumes, at least nothing but the truth. There was need of selection rather than of invention. I found unexpectedly ready to hand one of the beautiful love stories of all time — recognized as such by its protagonists and rather deplored for its excess by their soberer friends — with such abundance of evidence as made embellishment unnecessary. Elsewhere, too, incidents needed only to be dramatized. There is scarcely an invented character in the book, though a few required names. Newton's own writing or recorded conversation appears on almost every page. The reader may be assured that if he finds anything unbelievable of adventure or coincidence, anything excessive, either sensual or spiritual, anything improbable in emotion or devotion, that part of the book is provably factual, even understated.

Regarding the physical appearance of John and Mary, I have drawn my conclusions from careful reading and the close scrutiny of available pictures. No portrait or detailed description of Mary seems to have survived. Her personality breaks through her own few letters and her husband's innumerable letters and references to her.

The baffling, exasperating, heart-warming complexity of John's developing character cannot be reduced to the pat terms of a psychological case-history. I have wrestled with the warring facts and tried to present something of the elemental greatness of the man. In small return for the enrichment which I have received, I should like others to know John Newton: melancholy and delinquent, rebellious and pathetic, thoughtful and headstrong, ribald and driven, sensual and sensitive, foul-mouthed and poetic, capable in many fields, scholar, leader of men, above all a great and worshipful lover: but to the end in his own estimation a chief of sinners, even when, in the judgment of a shrewd contemporary, most "heavenly-minded."

1

THE muffled rhythm of a horse's slow-trotting hoofs broke the winter silence with reassuring sound. The creaking of breeches against saddle leather occasionally betrayed a slight movement as the rider shifted position, but for the most part he sat his horse curiously inert, with a familiar security which enabled him to withdraw from concern about his locomotion as remotely as if seated in a sedan chair.

There was, too, an air of withdrawal, almost of sullenness in his whole demeanour, so that a stranger approaching would have been disconcerted to find the face, or what was visible of it between buff-coloured muffler and broad-brimmed hat, a young face, the face of a boy well on the youthful side of twenty. It was almost eleven in the morning and his journey had begun two hours before, with a rift of sunlight thrusting faint long shadows aslant the furrowed fields, and a blackbird singing from a not yet leafless beech tree; now the gray sky hung close from vanishing point to vanishing point of sight and no bird called. So in the immobile face, its fine skin unexpectedly tanned and weather beaten, and in the heavy-lidded blue eyes there was a suggestion that sunlight and birdsong could evoke response; but a winter's gray had settled upon it and it seemed frozen to indifference of either joy or sorrow, ambition or fear.

A close observer might notice, however, slight indications that this habitual indifference was being disturbed by some inward struggle. In fact a crisis was approaching, a decision had to be made, and the very lethargy with which the boy viewed the alternatives made the necessity of choice repugnant. He raised his head at more frequent intervals, scanning the road for landmarks. When the horse's ponderous trot slowed to a walk, he made no effort to quicken its pace. The gauntletted left hand which had been thrust into the breast of his high-buttoned coat now moved restlessly to the pommel of the saddle, to his knee, to the capacious pocket where it found a letter, half drew it out, then thrust it back with irritable indecision.

There was no need to scan the letter again. He knew its contents by heart. Why had these Catletts written to him at all? For ten years they might have written, and a letter would have been welcome. How glad he would have been of this letter ten years ago when the news that his Mother had died in this very home now hospitably opened, had reached him, a forlorn seven-year-old, tolerated in the house of strangers, and awaiting with more fear than longing the still distant return of his father from sea. How welcome it would have been a year later, when that father's arrival and second marriage gave him a residence in which his physical needs were generously supplied, but his small, shy, groping person disregarded. And how thrice welcome it would have been during that first year away at school in Stratford, when the brutality of both head-master and sports infected the long hours of lessons, until he who had been reading easily and avidly since his fourth year lost almost all relish for books.

John stopped his recollections abruptly, drawing a curtain furiously across the hatefulness of that year which still haunted him in dreams. But of what use this letter now? In three days he would be on the coach, bound for Liverpool. Within a fortnight he would sail for Jamaica. He would not set foot in England again for five years, if then. Why go to meet strangers who might think his ways awkward, himself dull and uncouth?

The visit would keep him from proceeding immediately home. That was a point in its favour. With that in mind he had asked and easily gained his father's permission to make it. Not that his father and stepmother ever indicated that he was unwelcome. But they were so absorbed in their own affairs, in each other, in young Billy, in the new child, that John always felt the unspoken relief of their farewells. They had thought him so agreeably off their hands in Spain. Even dread of his father's anger had not subdued the devil of half-resentful mirth within him at their crestfallen disappointment, when his summary dismissal from the comfortable position at Alicante, which the Old Gentleman's Spanish connection had secured for him, had forced the question of his future to be faced afresh. Yet his father had been surprisingly soon pacified. Whether the sight of his strongly built son after some months of absence made him realize that this young man was too old to be thrashed like a child, or whether the boy's very undefending silence had reminded him of the quiet, serious-minded wife whose place had been so soon and satisfactorily filled he was not likely to reveal. Certainly he had contented himself with a brief austere lecture, amplified when he received the report from John's erstwhile employer regarding his "unsettled behaviour and impatience of restraint" — a lecture in which the phrases "these degenerate days", "lack of self-discipline", "my education in Seville", "gross and intemperate insensibility of the benefits bestowed upon you", recurred. "O tempora, O mores", John had summed up the speech as he listened, standing in his father's presence with every mark of respect. The phrase recurred to him now, one of the few tags of Tully which remained from his second, comparatively happy, year of schooling. Yet he had topped the class in Latin before his tenth birthday, catching avidly up in a study begun with his mother when he was six.

His mother! Perhaps he would go to the Catletts after all. He would like to hear and talk of his mother to someone who had known her. Odd that she should have learned Latin. Perhaps Mrs. Catlett had learned it too when they were at school together. Most women, even those with leisure and money, had little formal education, he knew. Certainly his young stepmother, though the daughter of a prosperous grazier, could do no more than write a letter in her own tongue, although she embroidered beautiful samplers and played the spinet well enough. He would ask about his mother and perhaps would hear if she had talked of him, if she had wanted to see him again before she died.

No! He would do nothing of the kind! For, with the thought of his mother came other thoughts which he had put

11

out of his mind lately whenever they recurred: verses of Dr. Watts's hymns which he had learned and recited almost as soon as he could speak, questions and answers from the catechism, verses of Scripture, invariably unwelcome and pointed verses: "The eyes of the Lord are in every place beholding the evil and the good." "Be sure your sin will find you out." "Every idle word that man shall speak he shall give account thereof in the day of judgment." He would go home after all. The three days would soon pass. Perhaps his stepmother would let him take Billy to visit a ship, where he could unravel to the child's admiring eyes the enigma of the rigging and air his knowledge of the mysteries of the waterfront. Or, failing that, he could ride into the City and see a play. *A Bold Stroke for a Wife* would suit his mood if, as he had heard, it excelled Centlivre's other witty farce *A Wonder! A Woman Keeps a Secret,* which he had lately seen in London.

The instant, almost automatic redress of balance, which had saved young Newton many times from being shaken like an insect from a lurching spar into the leering sea beneath, saved him now from shooting over the head of his stumbling horse. So far the road, mud-crusted by recent frost, had been tolerably good in a country where travellers at this time of the year took to the fields for safe journeying. But as this stretch wound through a low-lying soggy country, an attempt had been made to drain it by making a high, barrel-shaped crown, flanked with ruts a foot deep in mud. The horse, picking its placid preferential way along this crown, had dislodged a loosened stone too near the steep curve. Its right foreleg slithering off into the rut, it sprawled head first and John, surprised from his interminable debate, swore sharply, disentangled his left leg from the stirrup and dismounted to examine the damage.

Miraculously there was little. The horse, stroked and reassured, floundered for a moment, then, braced by the hind legs which remained on the road, staggered upright. John ran his hand down the sturdy leg, found with relief that she could walk with only a slight limp, and soberly led her for a hundred yards or so before remounting.

He was rather ashamed of the oath which had been surprised from him, and felt a secret relief that he had sworn in

12

Spanish. The words seemed less blasphemous, somehow, in a foreign tongue.

They had come over the rising ground to a long slow incline. Against the sky in front a weathered signpost recalled him to the need for immediate decision. Suddenly almost frantic, he searched his mind for an escape from the responsibility of choice. If chance could decide it for him! Should he toss a coin? Even as he was reaching for his leather wallet an idea struck and amused him. Let the horse decide for him. The road was almost level now, the ruts only moderately deep. Presently when they neared the turn he would leave the reins on her neck and take the road she chose. Since they had come this way she would probably return to Rotherhithe. Well, that suited him. The nearer the prospect loomed of making himself known to strangers the more he shunned it. But it was fair enough. She *might* turn right on Watling Street into Chatham. In any case the decision would not be his.

So the two jogged on towards the approaching signpost, John riding loose-reined, apparently given up to his former indifference. Actually his heart was beating faster and he was annoyed to find himself shivering. This was not the philosophic calm, the Raillery and Humour towards accidentals enjoined by that great mind, Lord Shaftesbury. Surely leaving his decision to chance, instead of fretting his soul, was in keeping with the imperturbable calm of the author of *Characteristics,* a prized copy of which was even now in his saddle-bag. Discovered at a book-stall in Holland, it had opened his eyes to a new world of thought. He quoted to himself a favourite sentence: "The central powers which hold the lasting orbs in just poise and movement must not be controlled to save a fleeting form and rescue from the precipice a puny animal". To preserve the aloof serenity becoming one who had imbibed such sentiments, he watched the rhythmically nodding head, the sensitive ears of his mare. What was going on inside that head, he wondered. Was she pondering her recent fall? Did she know how near she had come to a broken leg and subsequent extinction? Had she any idea that her master's movements for the next day or so depended on her whim? Unorthodox perhaps to attribute such potentialities to a horse, but Shaftesbury had shown clearly the necessity, the privilege, of

13

free speculation. John found himself — because his heart and nerves were harder to control than his mind; the one would pound, the other quiver — setting the situation to rhyme. On his recent voyage he had discovered in himself a decided turn for doggerel, though not all the verses which formed themselves behind that apparently stolid face were suitable for publication.

The face, in fact, told little of the duality within. From an occasional straight searching glance of eyes habitually veiled and dreamy, from the well-defined mouth at once bold and sensitive, some guess might be made: at the curious mind which fed eagerly upon books, storing and pondering what it read; at wayward passions which mutinied, capitulated and did resentful penance so that he had already forsaken and several times returned to the strict piety in which his mother had trained him. Sometimes, as now, verse-making relieved the endless tension.

> *John has no will to chart his course*
> *To Chatham or to Rotherhithe;*
> *He leaves decision to his horse.*
> *With the beast's choice he will abide.*
> *The creature cares than he no less,*
> *But makes conclusion without stress.*

His conscious invention bridged the last few yards to the sign-post. Sitting rigid, almost unbreathing, he felt the animal plod stolidly ahead to the crossroads, oblivious and undisturbed. Arriving where Watling Street met the Maidstone road at an angle, she hesitated, waiting for the guidance of curb. Feeling none, she was about to take the natural deflection which led across the Medway to Rochester and London. At the same moment John Newton, roused unaccountably from inertia, seized the reins, tugged her head sharply to the right and urged her into a trot down to the main street of Chatham.

2

IF he regretted his sudden impulse as he stood a few minutes later at the Catletts' door with the reverberations of its heavy iron knocker sounding impertinently loud in his ears, he was given little time to repent. The door was flung open; the bustle of welcome and cheer and solicitousness and question, which drew him into the house and removed his muffling wraps and settled him by the fire, the focal point of interest for a seemingly endless number of new acquaintances, was such a change from his solitary ride, such a change from his customary arrival in his own home, such a change from anything he had known in his seventeen years, that he could scarcely speak, and felt as if the few sentences he did utter were spoken in a dream.

"Now are you sure you are comfortable, dear John?" Mrs. Catlett returned from her trip to the kitchen, the ribbons on her cap fluttering with her haste. "Jack will be back shortly. I've sent him to help Dickon see to your horse's foot. The lad means well but he wants any skill in such matters. Jack will not be long, I promise. He is overjoyed to have a friend of your age in the house. And we must hear all your news. You are under no need to be away for a good while?"

John opened his mouth to say that he must leave the next day, but closed it again. Mrs. Catlett had not waited.

"We shall show you the town and our famous windmill. Not that it is a great town compared with your London, but it is busy these days, with Admiral Mathers in charge of the Dockyards. Indeed you know more of such things than we do. What a travelled young man! To Spain you say you have

15

been? And Italy? Mr. Catlett, could we not have a stick more wood on the fire? John has ridden all morning in the cold."

"A mug of cider is what the young man needs." George Catlett obliged good-naturedly with the stick of wood, however. "Have Jane fetch some up. And dinner will warm him more than a fire. Can not Polly hurry it on?"

"Polly has gone to her aunt's on an errand for me. She should be back by now. Jack, fetch a jar of cider from the cellar. I shall give a hand to Jane myself. Sue is busy at the mangle and cannot put it by. Eliza, child, you may lay the table. Show Cousin John what a little woman you are."

The words, the bustle, the warmth of fire and feeling were blurred for young Newton like the unreal consciousness of a dream. The home-brewed cider had settled long enough in its wooden cask to be heady. It warmed his throat, and the second mug loosened his tongue to give more than monosyllabic replies to the questions asked by Mr. Catlett and young Jack, who talked with his mother's affable garrulity. Dimly he was sorting out the household and absolving Mrs. Catlett from the guilt she was so evidently feeling because of her neglect of her best friend's child. The ten years which had seemed age-long to him must have been full for her. Mistress of a solid capacious house, with a household of nine counting the three servants and the baby — no, there was one, Polly, whom he had not seen yet — to be fed and clothed, she would have little time to think of him. Even nursing his mother as she died of consumption must have been a heavy addition to the labour of a woman, then bearing her third — or was it her fourth? — child. The great spinning-wheel and the full spindle beside the hearth spoke of recent employment. . . .

"I envy your travels," Jack was saying. He was like his mother in appearance, too, with bright brown eyes and crisp dark hair. "I'd like to make the Grand Tour when I finish school before I go to be articled in London. But Father won't hear of it."

"I should think not indeed," grunted George Catlett, but in spite of the grunt young Newton was aware of a bond of affection very different from the formal distance at which his father always kept him, even when they had shared the cap-

16

tain's cabin voyage after voyage. "The Grand Tour makes havoc of the morals of too many young men these days. English ways are good enough for you, Jack. John here can tell you what these foreigners are."

The appeal, the suggestion of his superior knowledge and experience, increased John's feeling of trance-like well-being. He was for the first time companioned by those to whom he seemed — with his knowledge of the ocean and Mediterranean ports, of the way of a ship upon the sea and of those who do business in great waters — a man of the world. Kept for the most part under his Captain-father's surveillance, he had still seen — and heard — more unabashed ribaldry, more bawdy talk and foul language than Jack and his fellows at the Rochester Grammar School could dream. And, although the vestiges of his strict belief, the fear of an angry God and of the hell which awaited a sinner at every turn of an uncertain earthly life had kept him from giving rein to the lusts of the flesh, his unsupervised months in a Spanish sea-port town had made him cognizant of every form of vice. Such things could not be spoken of in this gentle home, with youngsters lingering by to watch him in wide-eyed friendly curiosity. But it was pleasant to smile wisely and shake his head in agreement with Mr. Catlett and see the questioning admiration in young Jack's eyes — Jack who had been to school while he had been at sea, Jack who knew far more Latin than he had forgotten and was familiar with the Greek which he had never learned.

He was conscious, even as he answered a question concerning his father's latest cargo, of Mrs. Catlett's voice raised in excited explanation in the passageway. His chair had been drawn by the fire so that his back was to the passage door, yet words came gaily to him before she swept in, or swept someone else in, without stopping their flow.

"A surprise for you, what do you think? He had no need to tell his name. I knew him before he spoke, though how I cannot think for he favours his poor mother very little —"

She had told him not to rise but he did, in awkward imitation of his father's stately manner, and turned to face her and the new arrival.

"Here he is, Polly. Bid your kinsman welcome after all these years. John, this is our Mary."

17

The dream, the trance-like unreality melted. John Newton, standing in the dim low-raftered parlour, had a sudden sense that all his life, all his other experience, had been a trance compared with the acute significance, the portentous reality of this moment. The experience was physical; his whole body tingled with quickened vitality. It was mental; his mind, roused from sluggishness, seemed capable of any effort, any solution. It was beyond both; time was suspended and he had a sense of being present at Creation. The morning-star's sword piercing the dawn light on a waveless sea; the rain-washed green of afterglow from a summer hill-top; the awful unplumbed depths of black sky lighted by the Aurora Borealis; the sharp-edged timeless hush of Aveley village, etched in snow of a rare winter morning: he had entered into them all, perceptive of natural beauty to a rare degree. This experience was of that quality but personal, intimate, foreordained.

In a world where sensation was now sharp to the point of pain the Real object stood before him, so near that he could feel the breath of cold from her red cloak and loosened hood. Mary Catlett had come forward modestly but without shyness, and her smile was spontaneous, not merely obedient. She curtsied as smoothly as any lady at the Rochester Assembly Room, and held out her hand.

"Be sure you are very welcome — Sir," she said. Then, with a questioning glance at her mother, "We have been hoping you would visit us — Cousin John."

John's step into Reality included himself. Gone was the man-of-the-world, exchanging quips with Jack, and commercial news with Mr. Catlett. Hulking, ungraceful, he hesitated to extend a weather-roughened hand to look larger and more shapeless than it was in contrast to the little pretty one which awaited it; and when he did, the touch bereft him of the words he was trying to utter. Even in his state of exaltation he was not deceived. Her hand was firm, the palm and fingers capable and hardened by household work. But it was her hand, and right, as the rest of her was right, would always be right, no matter what surface alteration should ensue. Loosely waving brown hair, dishevelled by her hood, small imperious nose, level eyebrows which turned up, not down at the corners: these his first glance took in entire. But her eyes

18

— he must look longer at her eyes, and the curve of her obstinate little chin, and the flow of shoulder to arm as her cloak fell back and she caught it with her free hand. Meanwhile he must say something. They all must think him foolish standing there dumb, and though he cared nothing that they should know what had happened to him, it was a shame to cut such a poor figure before her.

"Thank you." Did his voice always sound like that, like the bark of a stray seal which they had caught off the coast of Holland on his last voyage? "I am glad I came, Miss —" What should he call her? Mary, her mother had said surely, but Polly was the name he had heard before. And should he have called her Cousin in return? He swallowed frantically and realized that it was too late to bring out either name. The sentence in its unwinning clumsiness was out. It could not be recalled.

But it was part of the lovely hospitality into which he had entered that no notice was taken. Six-year-old Sarah, indeed, scarcely waited for the introduction to be completed before bursting forth with her query.

"Why does Polly call him Cousin, Mother? Doesn't a cousin have to belong to uncles or aunts? Is John's father our uncle? Why don't we ever visit him? Or why doesn't he come to see us?"

"No, John's father isn't your uncle," Mrs. Catlett spoke with some constraint. "See if you can forward the serving, Polly; there's a good girl. John's mother and I were distant cousins. Her great-aunt was married to my great-uncle, if you can think so far back, Sally. But Jack and Polly used to call her Auntie. That was before you were born. And so I have always thought of her son, John here, as my nephew and should like him to call me Auntie and your father, Uncle, if that is acceptable to him?" She spoke to the child but the words were for John.

"I should esteem it a privilege, Auntie." How easy it was to speak with the courtesy becoming to him, now that Polly was no longer in the room. Yet, though he was more comfortable in her absence, he longed for her return. If only he could be near to watch her and hear her, without committing any more blunders to make him look ridiculous in her eyes!

Her eyes. He glanced over as often as he dared, when presently she sat by her mother at table and slipped back and forth to the kitchen helping Jane with the serving. What colour were her eyes? The effect of their smiling glance had rendered him momentarily colour-blind. He wondered how old she was and what she did and what she thought — most of all what she thought of him. He was thankful that, in the genial atmosphere of the table, his stammering awkwardness did not return. In fact he talked more than he had ever talked, expanding to the interest of his audience, countering Jack's Latin tags with phrases of Spanish and the occasional sentence in French. He hoped these would impress Polly that he was not the uneducated barbarian he felt in her presence; then wondered, heart sinking, if she would see through his clumsy attempts and be disgusted at his vanity.

If she was, she gave no indication of it when, the next afternoon, she and Jack took him for a Sunday stroll to the Dockyard to see the new sixty-gun man-of-war nearing completion there. He had contrived to sit beside her in church that morning and was almost entirely oblivious of the gabbled service and the short, pedantically read sermon, amid the crowding sensations and racing thoughts occasioned by her near presence. In spite of Mrs. Catlett's motherly efforts to make him comfortable, piling on his bed an extra comforter filled with down from their own ducks, and putting heated bricks between the sheets — fussing which recalled memories of his mother — he had lain sleepless half the night with the amazement of what had happened to him.

It was as if he had never seen a girl before. He had taken a volume of Shakespeare on his last voyage and repeated to himself Ferdinand's words to Miranda, envying his facility of speech. Yet he had seen many girls, though he wished a different name could be given them to distinguish the whole species from the Unique Girl. The tavern wenches, the girls who hung around sailors near the docks at home and in Mediterranean ports: there had been little to appeal to the stiff, shy boy, who for the most part ignored their occasional advances, only to have thoughts of them assail him in the wild

20

secret imaginings of his heart. And the girls whom he had met at home, farmers' daughters of his stepmother's connection, seemed gauche, colourless in retrospect, as they had been quiet and dull in reality.

"Yon ship will be a fine sight when she is finished," observed Jack, nodding at the great skeleton lying below them. "You've never sailed on one, John."

"And I hope I never shall."

"Not if we fight the French, after all?"

"The French will be well advised to keep clear of a ship like that. Or of our new frigates. I boarded one at Tilbury last week. The French are bigger still but ours are faster sailing."

"How old were you, Cousin John, when you first went to sea?"

"Eleven. We took a cargo of grain from Southampton for Spain."

He thought of a way to obtain information. "You, Jack, were lying in a sturdy bed each night while I rocked on the Bay of Biscay. And you, Polly, what were you doing then?"

"I — let me see, I was seven, nearly eight, learning from Mother to read and to spin. I have never been to school."

"Tell us more about the sea, John," Jack interrupted, just as Newton had swiftly calculated Mary's present age as almost fourteen, and marvelled, not the first man to marvel, at the early appearance of grace and self-possession in woman. "Have you ever been in a terrific storm — one where they cried, 'All hands to the pumps'? Or fallen overboard from a slippery deck, or —?"

"Jack, why do you want to hear all the horrid things?" said Mary. "I'm sure if John ever has been in danger like that, he'd sooner forget it."

"But never can." For the first time John was moved to an uncalculated remark in her presence by the surge of painful recollection. Brother and sister looked at him and he hastened to explain, wishing that he had not spoken.

"Just that I can't forget such things. I've never been in particular danger abroad, Jack — that I know of. But here at home I've had two narrow escapes."

21

"Go on," urged Jack with brotherly disregard. "Don't mind Polly. She is stronger than she looks."

Newton decided to compromise.

"There's nothing to distress you, really," he assured her, wishing that he could look into her eyes long enough to settle the question of their colour once for all. She kept them fixed on the river, however, and he continued. "I was just reminded of another man-of-war. I was going to visit it with a friend one Sunday afternoon but I was late reaching the quay and he went without me. I was angry as I stood watching them," — he did not think it necessary to tell of the furious curses with which he relieved his rage as he saw distance widening between the shore and the boat — "when suddenly a squall came up and overset their craft, throwing them all into the water."

"Oh John! Were they —?"

"My friend was drowned and three others. I should have been if I had come five minutes earlier. I cannot swim."

He saw Mary's eyes now. They met his steadily, warm with comprehension, and he forgot the sobering recollection at the sight. He had thought them like pools on the grass in sunshine and their colour was as uncapturable: clear iris that looked green or gray or topaz in different lights. And her height was right too. He was not tall, though a trifle taller than Jack and much broader in the shoulder. But she would always look up to him like that, and he would protect her — how he would love to protect her — against all the world.

"Let's persuade Father and Mother to go to the Assembly Rooms on Tuesday, Polly. John should see our Assembly Rooms. We can have a game of cards."

"We are taking tea with Auntie Hammond tomorrow. We can play at cards there."

"Cribbage, yes. We can play whist at the Assembly. Do you play at whist, John?"

John hesitated. His father had occasionally unbent during the long hours at sea sufficiently to play a game of cribbage with him. But the only whist-players he knew were the common sailors. Jack laughed.

"I believe you are like Aunt Hammond, who says that whist was a servants' game when she was young. Why, John, it is sweeping the London coffee houses and the Assemblies now. We country folk have to tell you the London fashion! Do you know that a man named Hoyle has published a book this year, *A Short Treatise on Whist,* which sold out its first printing in a week? Do —"

"Jack, do stop showing how much of a beau you are," interrupted Polly. "I don't care much for whist. But I should love to go to the Assembly. Mother promised we might for my birthday and she will certainly let us go for John's sake. Do you dance, Cousin?"

"I could learn." John overcame his fear of appearing awkward in anticipation of having Polly teach him. Now was the time to declare that the Warrington coach would leave London on Wednesday, that he could not possibly stay till Tuesday night. But he did not speak.

He still had not spoken, either about missing his coach or about missing the ship from Liverpool or about his father's plans for him in Jamaica, when, after New Year's day almost three weeks later, he forced himself to take leave. The first coach he had missed, realizing that he would still be in time if he took the next. But long before the next was due, the thought of leaving Polly, of abandoning all hope of seeing her again for five years, of coming home and finding her married to someone else, had become intolerable. He did not tell Mrs. Catlett, for she would have insisted on his departure, though probably adding the whole scheme to her weight of disapproval of Captain Newton. He did not tell Mr. Catlett, who would have considered it an excellent opportunity — "Management of a plantation in the Indies at your age, found for you, just found" — and the young man who crossed his father in giving up such advantages, under compulsion of calf-love, no fit suitor for his daughter, even when she was old enough to have suitors. He did not tell Mary because, in spite of the way her eyelids dropped when she found him staring at her — and this she did far more often, he knew, than politeness should have permitted — she behaved with a gaiety and composure which made him tongue-tied on the rare occasions when they had a moment alone.

So, day after short winter day, week slipping into week with a speed unknown before, he had stayed, repaying their hospitality in the best coin he could of grateful acceptance and eager acquiescence in all the plans made for his entertainment. He and Jack had helped and hindered in the kitchen where preparations for Christmas went forward on a scale he had never seen or imagined. He had yearned to stay for Christmas, and had clumsily allayed Mrs. Catlett's regretful certainty that his father and his stepmother "would not hear of his being from home." He had tried his hand at stirring the plum pudding and mincemeat to spare Polly, for Mrs. Catlett supervised the baking with a jealous eye and only the elder of the maids was allowed to have a share in it. Christmas was evidently the jolliest time of the year at the Catletts, and religion seemed to have little to do with it. They did sing carols Christmas eve and decorate the parish church for the service, which they all attended on the wintry morning, before returning to a round of eating and drinking and merriment, which ended with country dancing in the parlour and mulled cider around the dying yule log.

They had gone to the spinney to cut holly and had found, after some searching, a heavy-berried growth of mistletoe stifling a wild apple tree. Jack had laughingly cut generous quantities of it and teased John — for all the family by this time made sly occasional jokes when Polly was not present — about the chances he would have by staying for the Christmas festivities. The very thought stunned the young lover into silence which occasioned from his friend more ineffectual raillery. To kiss Polly! The mere touch of her hand, gracefully given, duly withdrawn in the measures of the Sir Roger de Coverley at the Assembly, had turned his knees to water and his whole being into an eager anticipation of the next touch; but he had not dared press it for fear of arousing her displeasure. And though Jack availed himself of the hanging mistletoe with several guests and neighbours, and though Mr. Catlett saluted a young niece and an elderly cousin with dutiful gallantry, John would not have ventured such a liberty with Mary, even if she had not serenely, and without apparent contrivance, avoided passing or pausing beneath it.

He had never thought much of his appearance. Now he wondered if she found him ugly, and envied Jack his neat

24

features, his crisp tractable hair, his slender figure set off
to great advantage in the knee-breeches and fine green coat
which he had worn over a canary yellow waistcoat to the Assembly. Young Newton, narrowing his blue eyes to stare in
the glass, thought despondently that there was nothing to
attract a girl like Mary about his large head with longish
hair coarsened and bleached by sun and salt spray, his face
with its dominant nose and massive chin. His clothes too,
though of excellent cloth, were not modish nor intended for
such a formal occasion; he had watched guardedly the resplendent young men, some with short wigs and long coats
cut away in front after the new fashion, who succeeded him
in the privilege of dancing with Mary. The knowledge that
they would be on hand to dance with her, to please her with
the courtly compliments which he composed by the dozen
in the night and could never utter in the daytime, lent poig-
nancy to his necessary departure.

Now he must go. Dickon had brought his horse from the
stable. All the family were at the door, heart-warmingly regretful at his going. He took leave of them in turn, taking
care, and not caring that his design was patent, that Polly
should be last. The winter cold had given way to mild sunshine which had brought a white rose to bloom in the garden
and Mary out of doors without cloak or shawl. Her morning
dress, with its laced bodice and loosely flowing skirt, was of
green wool and there was a reflected green light in the smiling
gray eyes which looked up into his.

"God give you good journeying, John." It was the first time
she had omitted the formality of Cousin. "See that you don't
forget your friends in the country."

John, almost helpless in the surge of tenderness and longing
which swept over him, was about to stammer his protest at
such a suggestion, when Jack interposed cheerfully.

"Nonsense, Polly. Do you think John will waste a minute
remembering you with all those girls he meets in foreign
ports? But you had better write to me, my friend. Young
men of my parts are not so easily met with."

"Nor with so high an opinion of their parts," countered
Newton swiftly, realizing, in the midst of his annoyance at

Jack's interruption, that it had saved him from leaving Polly an impression of himself as a speechless boor. He rode off down the street, hoping that she would think that at least he sat his horse well, and looked back to see only one hand in the flutter of friendly waving.

Thoughts of her as he rode to Rotherhithe relieved his sullen growing apprehension at the interview ahead of him. Thoughts of her, wrapped around his heart, warmed him through the chill of his stepmother's greeting, the cold rage of his father's rebuke. John knew that their disapproval was more than justified. Not only had he frustrated arrangements made at considerable trouble and expense, but with complete irresponsibility he had not even sent word of his whereabouts, so that his father, though reasonably sure that news of a mishap would have reached him, had been about to institute inquiries. After a day's ostracism during which he remained in his own room to avoid the disapproval of family and servants alike, he was summoned to the Captain's private sanctum. There he stood, answering question after sharp question with formal courtesy and suppressing any reference to the real cause of his defection. What astonished him was the speed with which the Old Gentleman — a title half-ironical used surreptitiously by the officers of his ship — again abated his anger. Quite suddenly at the end of the inquisition, he tossed down the quill with which he had weighted his words, leaned back in his chair, the skirts of his blue coat spreading to the floor on either side, gave his truant son a long enigmatic stare from blue eyes sharper and smaller than his, and said with cutting finality:

"Well. Since you lack the judgment to prevent you from squandering your opportunities, there is little chance of my words making you sensible of your loss. I cannot approach Mr. Manesty on your behalf again. What he will think of your conduct I can well imagine. Let be, let be. I must find something else and I think I have it. Captain Yeats of the *Dolphin* told me yesterday he lost three sailors from smallpox while on shore, and wants others in their room. His ship has been scrap'd and painted and he hopes to begin loading next week. His voyage is to Lisbon and Venice. I shall speak to him tomorrow."

"But, Sir" — young Newton was not sure that he had understood his father's words — "how shall I sail?"

"Before the mast. How else? Do you expect always to share the Captain's cabin?"

John infinitely preferred his father's anger to his sarcasm. But he persisted.

"Sir. You do not mean I should go as an ordinary seaman?"

Captain Newton leaned forward and brought his fist down on the heavy carved desk so forcibly that the model brigantine there leaped and quivered unsteadily as in a heavy sea.

"I mean just that, Sir. I made a better opportunity for you and you threw it away. You have no qualifications for a higher post nor should I seek one for you if you had. Perhaps next time you will think twice before you flout my authority. Now go, Sir. And no more words on this subject. I shall ask Captain Yeats to keep an eye on you, if he can."

Summarily dismissed, John sought the fields and woods of Surrey to weigh this unpleasing prospect. All his seafaring, however devoid of comfort or companionship, had been accompanied by privilege. Insignificant to the officers and disregarded by his father, he had still been the Captain's son, under his direct command. An ordinary seaman had not only the roughest of lives — better, certainly on a merchant vessel than on a man-of-war — but no station and no prospects of betterment. What chance would he have of fulfilling his ambition to present himself as an acceptable suitor for Mary? He seethed with impotent pride, on the verge of open rebellion.

Yet it was the thought of Mary which kept him from revolt. In spite of the boundless horizons of his dreams the mind behind those dreamy eyes was keen and self-analytical. The depressing facts were unavoidable: he had neither education nor training to gain, by his own efforts, any position commensurate with Mr. Catlett's requirements for a son-in-law. Everything depended on his father's favour. Without this, even if a miracle should endow him with money, it was doubtful whether such parents would consent to their daughter's marriage. Twice he had strained the Old Gentleman's patience to breaking-point. Fathers had disowned sons for less, and young Billy was increasingly the apple of Captain

Newton's eye. At all costs he must avoid the rupture which open defiance would certainly occasion.

Once this decision was reached he was able to consider the prospect more calmly. The turmoil of his mind had taken long to subside and he was surprised to find that he had retraced his steps on the Chatham road as far as Blackheath. From where he stood, the mass of Shooter's Hill loomed against the eastern sky and he was strongly moved to climb it that he might gaze off at the horizon beyond which his beloved lived. Prudence restrained him. Already the short winter's day was closing and he had six miles to cover. Nobody at home wanted him, but it might be the part of discretion not to absent himself too long again. If he gave satisfaction on this voyage his father would probably exert himself again on his behalf. Meantime, since he could not be with Mary he might as well be away from home. He began to look forward with secret pleasure to a voyage without his father's constant supervision. The experience would be maturing; perhaps he would feel less awkward the next time he met Polly. Strange that a girl so young could exercise such absolute power. His father had hoped the voyage might make a man of him. So did he.

3

WAS this what his father had meant? thought John on Midsummer afternoon, as he prepared to man an oar of the ship's boat amid the cheerful hubbub of half a dozen shipmates, overjoyed at the prospect of a day and a night ashore. Surely not; for the Old Gentleman, though not given to religious observance, had kept a restraining hand on the shipboard practices of his crew and had supervised his son's time ashore, forbidding all excursions except under the eye of an officer.

This trip was a test for which John's half-hearted asceticism was poor preparation. A Mediterranean trading-voyage was for Englishmen the least dangerous and the most pleasant of all the busy sea-tracking in which they were engaged and the crew, numbering eighteen before the mast, was composed chiefly of experienced and inveterate sailors who had chosen their calling in preference to a life of drearier labour and poverty at home. But if life in a captain's cabin was by no means luxurious, life in a crowded foc'sle was the most rigorous — apart from his school days — that young Newton had yet known. The rough labour sharpened his hunger even for coarse, abominably cooked food. There was no privacy for reading or religious exercises and the crew, scenting an alien in their midst, had bent their concerted and by no means skilless efforts towards 'making a man' of him according to their own concept of manliness.

At first he had made the tactical error of revealing his father's connection with Captain Yeats; but this and the Captain's perfunctory efforts to fulfil his promise of keeping an eye on him roused such resentment that John's life was made miserable by a series of inexplicable disasters: disappearance of essential articles of clothing; unexpected location of slop pails where he would step in them or, on one occasion, to discharge its odorous contents over his hammock; the spilling of his platter by a plausible accident which all other dinners survived. His youthful boasting also called out their best powers of mimicry and his voice, his accent, the vocabulary which betrayed his wide reading, were burlesqued until Newton, finding all Shaftesbury's counsel to philosophic calm as unavailing as natural discretion, challenged his chief tormentor to a fistfight. Out of this, his driving rage and superior size answering to his opponent's trained hardiness and veteran experience — he was twenty-four — John had emerged bruised, bleeding, but accepted as a member of the crew, an acceptance gravely indicated by the boatswain ("Lookee, young fighting-cock, belay. You've drawn blood and showed you're worth your salt. As for you, Tim, you'll fall foul of the Cap'n if be he sees the youngster mauled. All hands'll be needed, d'y'see, at dawn to heave the cargo.") and confirmed in a ration of rum, which they drank to him with plenty of good-natured suggestions regarding the next steps in his education.

So far, in spite of the opportunities which presented themselves at every port and his companions' importunity — they had smuggled women aboard in the Captain's absence at Lisbon and been so pressing in their offers of accommodation and instruction that John had retreated to the crow's nest, out of reach of all but their derisive laughter — he had resisted the most obvious temptation. Outwardly, however, he was relaxing more each day from his spate of formalistic piety, the longest of his periodic attempts at reform. It had resulted from the shock of eye-witness of his friend's drowning, the realization of his own casual escape, the unsoftened reminder, black draped, skull-and-crossbones adorned, of the funeral procession, all this working upon a mind early stored with Dr. Watts's *Children's Hymns* and Bennett's *Christian Oratory*. He now sought rather than shunned the sailors' company, disregarded the Lord's Day, laughed at and passed on, sometimes with clever embellishment, the wittier ribald stories, and seasoned his speech with salty and varied profanities. The germs of doubt which Shaftesbury had glorified into virtue rationalized his occasional prickings of conscience. And lewd conversation, excesses described with relish of detail, lingered in his mind with persistent attraction.

Meanwhile, in curious paradox, his infatuation for Mary persisted as the motivating force of his being. For three months after their meeting he dreamed of her every night, and scarcely a waking hour passed without conscious thought of her. He looked forward to night-watches because then he could utter aloud, repeating it in a variety of tender cadence, the name and nickname which he would not profane by mentioning in the hearing of his companions. Then he could hold interminable conversations in which he was never at a loss for words, dream golden dreams of acquiring enough money to propose for her, follow these with delirious mental pictures of a hasty courtship and early marriage — and when the moment of possession had come and his blood was pounding with desire, Mary's idea, as he called it, would suddenly vanish, and some other image take her place. For though the feeling she had awakened was not merely romantic knight-errantry but compulsive physical passion as well, it yet was love; though its frustration and seeming hopelessness of realization rendered him an easier prey to lust, not in imagination, not even in dream, could Mary be the object of a lustful act. So his thoughts of her remained as a dark fire locked in his breast, intensifying his pain.

This afternoon, however, all circumstances conduced to pleasure. The Mediterranean blue mirrored the Mediterranean sky, the boat raced over the water, pulled easily by arms to whose strength an undercurrent of excited anticipation gave willingness. Tim and Nathan had come aboard the previous night with some addled talk of a great festival to be celebrated at a village across the bay and William Wainwright, the boatswain, suddenly recollecting a former voyage, launched into a highly coloured narrative which ended amid planning for to-day's expedition. Newton had been trying to read on deck, but the sudden dropping of the sun, the racing stride of southern darkness, had involved him in the discussion of schemes more hazy in detail than in intention. It was his turn to go ashore but the disappointment of the watch was so keen that he had almost offered to change places with one of them. Almost, but curiosity and a beckoning sense of adventure, and something more — a deep restless response of the blood to the pulsing summer weather and the unknown shore — made him more than usually vulnerable to the suggestions of his companions: "A chance for our fighting cock to show his spurs," the boatswain had said. "It's a religious rout, d'y'see, we'll need you with your Spanish lingo to keep us hove to," Tim had contributed with a portentous wink. But in their own pleasurable anticipation they had forgotten him, and by the time the boat's nose crunched on yellow sand in a little cove, across the bay from the white gleaming houses of Malaga, John was just one of a dozen ill-assorted English sailors ready for any fun that offered.

That the village nestled in green countryside amid undulating hills, that the countryside itself was in fiesta was obvious from the first sight of its flower-hung houses, the first throb of music, a steady alluring rhythm which still vibrated in the sun-drenched streets. The streets themselves, though empty as at the hour of siesta, seemed by their strewn flowers to have been recently inhabited and still appeared to be peopled; for outside every house, every pueblo hut were ingeniously contrived dummies, stuffed figures so obviously representing the male and female that John, in spite of his new sophistication, looked away, only to find himself staring at yet another, the phallus even more flagrantly displayed, the woman's outline more suggestively swollen.

His comrades were not equally embarrassed. Uninhibited, jovial, they exchanged obscene comments and swung with their unmistakeable nautical roll in the direction of the luring, departing music.

"Como se llama esta fiesta?" John lingered behind to ask a grave old man who sat outside a whitewashed hut, solitary as a sea-creature left on the sand by a receding tide.

The ancient looked at him surprised, whether at the ease of his Spanish, or at the Alicante dialect or at his ignorance.

"La vispera de San Juan. L'a procesion acaba de pasar."

"Procession?"

"The Saint blesses all things with fertility — the soil, the crops, the fruit, the men and women."

"Where are the people now?"

"Gone to the fields for the blessing. Then dancing and feasting begin. Go and join them. A stranger is from God on this day."

John overtaking the others found the old man's opinion shared by the entire populace. The image of the Saint, robed and brightly painted, was duly lifted in benediction over the fields, while appropriate chants interrupted the music of guitar and tambour. Then the procession, attenuated to ecclesiastics and a few elders, moved back to the village and the festivities began in earnest. The English sailors, many shades lighter in complexion than their hosts in spite of exposure to sun and wind, were made welcome by signs and actions which had little need of words. Young Newton, able to communicate in fragments of recollected Spanish, shared the symbolic circular loaves and cheeses, drank the thin wine of the new vintage and sat, watching the already dancing children, the colourful dresses and gay shawls and elaborate coiffeurs of the women, as they prepared to dance. Characteristically he was turning over in his questioning mind the puzzle of this new experience, for which nothing in Protestant England had prepared him. Even the Maypole and other festivities, restored to country life after their banishment under Puritan regime, had no resemblance to this overlay of Christian terminology on something that was rooted deep in a primeval and pagan past. The tie between Puritanism and morality in which he was reared left no room for a suspension of ethic, a moral moratorium condoned perforce by the Faith. Yet for such a lapse into incontinence the words of the songs, the symbols and fetishes, the seductive mime of the dances now being enacted were evidently preparing the company. Apparently too, from remarks made and imperfectly understood, the welcome to strangers originated in ancient superstition that at such a festival gods descended, in the person of strangers, to answer the prayers of the barren. For the season at least all possessiveness, all jealousy, all continence was sacrificed on the altar of fertility. John, in his stalwart youth, with his eighteenth birthday still a month away, was a heaven-sent instrument to renew and continue the strength of a race which had absorbed vitality through many an invader from Hamilcar to Tarik.

33

Something of this communicated itself to him as he sat watching, not sorry that his possession of a few words beyond the easily acquired phrases by which sailors made their wants known, had separated him from his associates. For this event he preferred to be isolated. For this event he waited, while the children and the very young girls were carefully escorted back to the village; while the dances became more voluptuous and the music lascivious. Suddenly the picture of Mary came before his mind, of Mary as she approached him in the courtly movement of an English dance, gay, modest, a little aloof with all her warmth — and even as his heart cried for her, he put her idea from his mind. In this event Mary had no part. She belonged to another world, in a sense to another John Newton than the one who waited, outwardly controlled, but calculating behind veiled eyes the length of time before the sun rolled its splendour to the rim of the distant hills, the one who was deliberately set on the course of conduct before him, yet whose mind irrationally soothed itself with the sanction of religion disguising that course. Mary belonged to Protestant England, to the eighteenth century, to the scent of lavender and roses, not to air heavy with orange and mimosa. This was a different country, a different race, a different age . . . in a sense a night lifted from old magic and prehistoric custom, an intercalary night for which there was no preparation and no consequence and no anniversary, Midsummer night.

The tempo of music, the movements of the dancers, became more frenzied as the sun touched the hills. Somehow John and the others who had not yet taken part were drawn into the dance, though only to stand while the sinuous arms and swaying hips and dark-eyed faces and blood-stirring clack of castanets swirled dizzily around them. The sun plunged. Swathe after deepening swathe of violet gloom wrapped the valley. The music faltered. Features and figures blurred. Movement gave place to touch. The moment came which John had anticipated and rehearsed many times in feverish and waking dreams, under many circumstances, but none so strange as this; and when it came, with an unknown woman panting in his arms and his uncontrolled desire incredibly sanctioned as obedience and charity, he found himself not unequal to it.

Was it the sudden light or the sudden sound? John did not know which woke him from the short night's heavy, pre-dawn slumber. He was lying in the field. No woman was near him, though he knew he had held more than one in the ritual madness of the warm unrevealing dark. Shivering slightly, he raised himself on one arm, fastening the ruffled shirt which he had worn when his companions put on their bravest array for the festival. The scene of last night's revelry was deserted except for the recumbent, inert or stirring figures of his shipmates. The well-trodden earth of the dancing-floor, crushed and dying flowers testified to the fact that he had not dreamed it all. But of the villagers and country-folk there was no trace.

The sun had leaped out of the sea, restoring the light as swiftly and completely as it had been removed. Simultaneously, or so it seemed to Newton's clearing mind, had come a sound, sharp crackling which swelled and filled the air; and with the sound came the pungent, pleasant smell of burning. John stood and stretched himself.

"What's up, lad?" Wainwright the boatswain, unkempt and bleary-eyed, but with an old tom-cat's air of rowdy triumph, sat up as he passed. "Did I not promise you the night of your life? Ye look fit as a cockerel and I warrant —"

"What's burning in the village, d'you think?" John interrupted to cut him short. He did not want to discuss the night with anyone or for the moment to recall it too vividly.

A few minutes later the two men stood in the angle of an adobe wall, looking down a street alight with fires. Then they understood. From house after house the fetish figures were being solemnly lifted and cast into flames which had been kindled at the exact moment of the sun's rising. A solemn chant accompanied the action, a chant in which vengeance and penitence were strangely mingled. It struck the sailors as odd that, although the villagers passed and repassed, they gave no greeting, no sign of recognition or of acknowledgment. Puzzled and abashed, they retreated to round up their sleepy fellows and head for their boat. As they skirted the village where by this time ashes were being ceremonially gathered, a word in the chant caught John's attention.

"Judas," he said to a small boy who came sleepily out of

the last house, too late for the fun of the fires; "who is this Judas? And why are they burning him?"

The child looked in round-eyed wonder at the heretic.

"Judas el traidor. El merece morir asi," he said with righteous scorn and, sighting his mother, ran from the stranger to join her.

Down the steep path to the shore, over the sands to their beached boat, across the awakening harbour to their ship John walked and pushed and rowed in silence while the stream of uproarious reminiscence flowed past, thickening in filth with recounting. Even with the feeling of triumphant well-being, of added stature and assurance which the night's physical release had brought, even with the half-defiant sense of having made an irreparable break with his confused but consistent past, even with the secret desire to be alone and recapture in mental imagery this experience so momentous yet so swiftly commonplace, he still pondered the puzzle of the festival and its ritual. What had Judas Iscariot to do with John the Baptist? Why should the name of either be associated with a fertility rite as old and as pagan as Rome or Carthage? Where in the blending of Midsummer night revelry with a Saint's day did the prototype betrayer find place? And why should the betrayer be identified with the obscene fetishes first held in honour, then destroyed? There, perhaps, lay the answer. The night's license demanded expiation, the lapse into idolatry must have atonement. The strangers welcomed as divine visitants under pagan rite were the betrayers of chastity under Christian revelation. So, in the burning in symbol of the Great Betrayer, all memory of their betrayal was blotted out for another year. Today would be kept with solemn purification. His sober face relaxed into an ironic smile at the inconsistency of such belief and practice.

Sprinkling the betrayer's ashes on the fields in blessing as the procession had been preparing to do? John gave up the puzzle, swung himself up the ladder and was glad enough to be deprived of leisure for more thinking in the bustle of hoisting sail for Italy.

4

JOHN was alone on deck. There was a strange ominous quality in his aloneness, as if he were alone on the ship, alone between the indigo sky and the velvet water which scarcely lapped the motionless hull. He could not have said when his watch had begun but he was sure it was mid-watch and he was pacing the forward deck, his eyes turned towards Venice with her magnificence of palace, dome and campanile ghostly outlined beyond the spars and rigging of the crowding ships in her harbour. Suddenly he was not alone, but the man unexpectedly beside him was a stranger. Oddly young Newton had no inclination to challenge him or to rouse the ship. Something about the man — strange, for he could discern neither his face nor his clothing in the star-light — dispelled alarm.

"I have brought you a gift," he said and the abrupt commencement of the conversation did not seem unnatural nor did his action in opening his hand and disclosing a ring. The hand was dim but the ring shone brightly. "This is no ordinary ring, John Newton. While it is in your possession you will be secure and successful. Keep it carefully, then, for if you lose it or give it away you must expect nothing but trouble and misery."

"I can take care of it, and I shall. Have no uneasiness on that score," said John eagerly.

He put the ring on his finger, thinking, as he did at every turn, of Mary and of his luck in obtaining so good an omen. He turned to thank his unknown friend but could not find him. Presently he caught sight of a figure approaching on his other side, but when the figure came closer he perceived that it was another stranger, though this time with a faintly familiar aspect. Once again, although this person's presence did not impart the same sense of well-being, he felt no alarm and no surprise at the other's knowledge of him and immediate interference in his concerns.

"Where did you get the ring that you are wearing?" Though the words were blunt, this person's manner was polished, his bearing suave. Somehow he managed to make John a little ashamed of the way the ring had come into his possession.

"It was given me just now — by a friend."

"May I examine it?"

"No — by your leave." John drew back, though unwilling to give offence. "You see, this is a ring of special virtue and I am forbidden to part with it."

"Indeed? What special virtue? Or may I ask?"

The words were courteous and indifferent but they made John feel uncomfortable and very, very young, as he explained.

"So long as I do not part with it I am assured of happiness and success. If I lose it, my prosperity goes with it."

"And you believe that tale?" The polite incredulity of the tone made the statement interrogative.

"I have no reason to doubt the person who gave it to me."

"Of course not. Who is he? You have known him for some time, without doubt?"

"No — I do not know his name," John stammered but recovered himself doggedly, "and I have seen him only once; but I feel sure, perfectly sure that he told me the truth."

"As you wish." There was a suggestion of brushing dust from a glove in the other's detachment. "So many charlatans these days deceiving so many credulous fools. I had thought better of you. But like the ignorant wretches who cannot aspire to the glory of the life of reason, you prefer to depend on a fakir's amulet for security which a man should find in himself alone. How can a bauble — what man would give gold to a chance stranger? — ensure success? How you would laugh at such superstitions in another! Haven't I heard you making fun of these Venetians with their charm medallions around their necks — a survival of pagan fears of the evil eye? But a ring, forsooth, is different! That is a charm worthy of an enlightened Englishman."

"But —"

"Employ your reason, my friend. Believe me, my concern is only for your best interests. So many I have seen depending on such worthless toys, and with what result? A chance disaster, and life is wrecked, because the ground of their confidence has been swept away. You were not meant to be one of them. You are of the strong who can depend on self."

"But" — John thought of a compromise — "suppose that what you say is true. How will it harm me if I keep the ring?"

The stranger turned away as if any further association was unendurable. Then, apparently mastering his scorn, he spoke, but coldly:

"We shall speak no more of this. I have mistaken you, I see. One is deceived at times. I thought you had been an honest mind, to search for Truth and Virtue, but I perceive it is otherwise. You would mock or pity to see a man with straight legs leaning upon a crutch; or a man with sound eyes wearing a patch over one. There can be no fellowship between a man of reason and a superstitious coward."

"I am no coward," said Newton angrily.

"Not physically. I am aware of that. Not at all, I had hoped. Come, then, put it to the test. You are sailing in this ship. You have no ring. Do you really believe that the Eternal Reason by which the winds and waves and stars are held in equipoise will disturb the course of nature and bring about a destructive storm on your account? How many men, without such a ring, make a successful voyage every year. Come, let me throw it away for you."

"No." John twisted the ring uncertainly on his finger. "What I do with it — if I do anything — I shall do myself."

"Good! That is the spirit I expect of you. Be rid of it then and of this base fear. You love someone, I know. Is she likely to be won by a boy who trusts a childish gew-gaw or by a man who is master of his own circumstances?"

John took the ring from his finger and, with a show of carelessness which concealed his reluctance, tossed it into the water. The circle glimmered in the starlight so that he saw where it fell, but scarcely had it disappeared when light and sound broke upon him from another quarter. Beyond Venice the distant mountains had burst into flame. The sky was lurid and the sound was as clear as though Venice itself was burning.

There was no need to ask the reason of the conflagration. His cry of fear and regret was drowned in the contemptuous laughter of his companion.

"Deluded young fool! What easy victims such creatures are! Appeal to their vanity or what they call love and they give no further trouble. Come, young man. All the mercy God had for you resided in that ring. You threw it away of your own accord. Now you are to come with me to those burning mountains."

He held out his hand and John knew that he must take it, knew too that in taking it he was lost. The agony, the remorse, the despair which racked him were intolerable. He felt suffocated and struggled as if he were drowning, in a dual effort to plead, though he knew pleading to be useless, and to resist the force that was moving him slowly, mercilessly towards his tormentor and his torment.

No word, no sound could he utter. But suddenly he was aware that another had joined them, another — or surely it was the same man who had given him the ring? The magnetic pull of his tempter's imperious hand lessened, but John stood utterly confused in the presence of his benefactor.

"What is the cause of your distress?"

"I am." In such a moment John had no desire to evade or shift the blame. "I doubted your word. I threw away the ring. I deserve my punishment."

"Assuredly you do," said the other serenely. From the sinister figure still close to John there was no word, no movement, only constrained and baffled watchfulness. "I am glad you admit it. I suppose, however, that you would be wiser, if you had the ring again?"

"I cannot say — it is impossible — the ring is gone —" cried John and stopped. Without waiting for an answer his friend had plunged beneath the water at the exact spot where his treasure had vanished, and presently he re-appeared on the deck with the ring in his hand. With his coming a great silence fell and the sudden peace of ceasing pain. Looking up,

Newton saw that the mountains were no longer ablaze. He was alone with his deliverer. He tasted relief like food, moved as though freed from fetters, and full of inarticulate gratitude approached the other, stretching a remorseful eager hand towards his property.

"No." His benefactor shook his head gravely. "This you cannot have. If you should be entrusted with this ring again, you would very soon bring yourself into the same distress. You are not able to keep it, as you have shown; but I will preserve it for you, and, whenever it is needful, will produce it in your behalf."

With the words he disappeared, absorbed in the night, and Newton, straining to see where he had gone, steadied himself to keep from falling and woke in the close stale darkness of his sleeping quarters, clutching at the sides of his swaying hammock. His forehead was clammy, his body shook, and the dream in its mingled horror and joy had been so exhausting that it was scarcely a relief to find it but a dream.

Even when he dressed and emerged on deck in the fresh morning breeze which filled the sails and darkened the Ionian sea to purple, he was held almost in a trance. Under its spell he somehow stumbled through the duties of the next two days, scarcely eating, and lying awake even in the short hours of his broken rest, for the equinoctial gales were approaching and the westward passage around Sicily gave more than usual trouble. The prickings of conscience which had occurred, though less and less frequently after each deviation from the path of piety, he had blunted with reading, occupation, or thoughts of Mary Catlett. The circumstances of his fall from chastity had made it easier to reconcile with Shaftesbury's explanation of Virtue. A mixture of fastidiousness and shyness had kept him from another lapse. The frank venality of wharfside amours was distasteful, and he was arrogant enough to prefer some distinction between himself and his present associates.

The remembrance of the dream — a remembrance less like recollection than re-enactment — was so inescapable in its revelation of his insecurity, his helplessness, and his doomed condition, that even thoughts of Mary afforded him for once no escape. Instead he saw or felt her as an additional instrument through which he could suffer, an equally vulnerable pawn whose helplessness increased the anguish of his own. But he was homeward bound. His health was good and he had a purpose in living, as he had lacked one the previous year. So his spirits recovered and in a few days the dream and its effects had passed.

Meanwhile, with no more than the incalculable vicissitudes of weather and wind which made the termination of even so prosperous a voyage as this one impossible to predict within a month, Captain Yeats steered his ship through the Straits, tossed up the coast of Portugal, navigated the dread Bay of Biscay and early in December, having found the Channel as difficult as all the rest of the voyage, brought her safe to rest in the Pool of London.

5

THE Channel in wind, the coast through rain, London in mist, Rotherhithe and home, all were welcome to John only as stages on his way to Chatham. Captain Newton, satisfied with his son's appearance and account of the voyage, had no wish to keep him idle near London when he was anxious to spend his time with a respectable family in the country. Perhaps he felt responsible for the fact that the home to which he had willingly retired from sea-faring was no home to his first-born. He approved the Catletts, in spite of the coolness which had sprung up between Mrs. Catlett and himself over what she had considered his neglect of his first wife and his undue speed in re-marrying. (These landlubbers think we have as much time to sit ashore, observing punctilio, as they have. George Catlett might delay less, if he had a ship with her crew and cargo to fit out and look after and his income depending on the voyage, instead of coming in comfortable from the Dockyard mills!) In any case, he raised no objection when his son, after one day at home, made his request.

"You are sure of your welcome, I hope."

"Sir, Mrs. Catlett told me to come whenever I had the opportunity. Jack will be home for holiday when Court adjourns at the end of Michaelmas. I should like to see Jack again." He dared not breathe the real reason for his urgency. He could not trust himself to mention Mary's name without betraying his state to his father's shrewd eyes. Though there was little sympathy between the two, the younger Newton had considerable respect for the elder's good sense and great knowledge of the world.

"No doubt. Well begone then. But harkye! I shall busy myself presently to find you another opportunity. Idleness is no good for a young man of your years. Be back within a fortnight without fail. D'you hear?"

"Yes, Sir." John dutifully took his leave and with a speed foreign to his usual leisurely dreaminess was soon mounted and on the road which led by Blackheath and Shooter's Hill to Mary.

The Catletts' home was as he remembered it. By the time dinner was over he might never have been away, except for the added inches of the younger children and the eager interest of the family in his recent travels. Jack, now articled to a London firm, assumed city airs for their amusement and told casual incidents in pompous legal phraseology. To match this, Newton mimicked, now the captain, now the boatswain, slipping from quarter-deck to sailor lingo and carefully expunging all lurid epithets from his account. Mrs. Catlett was affectionate and motherly as before, though pale and thinner from a recent confinement which the child had not survived.

"And what we should have done in this house without Polly I shall never know," she told him fondly. "She took complete charge of the house like a little woman. I should have been a great deal worse if she had not relieved me of all anxiety about the family. A better manager than her mother, Mr. Catlett says."

"Mother — please have done," begged Mary, and John, taking the occasion to look full at her, as he did whenever he dared, realized that she was more adorable than ever in her confusion.

Adorable, that was the word. She was all he had pictured her to be in the long months of separation, only lovelier, more womanly, gay, full of unexpected repartee — unexpected because she was not talkative — and of unconscious grace of movement and pose which at times made it almost impossible to conceal his yearning. There was nothing, he vowed to himself, that he would not do for her sake, no danger that he would not brave to protect her, no hardship that he would not undergo to win her.

In fact, all he did do was avail himself of every opportunity of being in her company and behave like a stricken calf at

44

the moments when he might have put in a good word for himself. Acutely aware of the poor figure he cut among the Catletts' sociable friends, he tortured himself with fears that she would be disgusted with him and attracted by one of them. Fortunately he was popular enough with the family, whom he had remembered with small but individually chosen souvenirs of his Mediterranean voyage — for Mary, a neckerchief of Moorish silk which she wore tucked in her best bodice, to his literally speechless delight, when they went to the Assembly. They saw him in his more relaxed moments and tolerantly overlooked the devotion about which Mary's friends were already teasing her. Jack rallied him several times on the folly of what he called his "faulty methods" of courtship; but he found John, when free from the spell, so amusing and controversial a companion that he preferred to leave his madness to consume in its own fire.

Not so Mr. Catlett. A year earlier he had dismissed the affair as childish. Now with his eldest daughter almost fifteen, a not uncommon age for marriage, and John a man in appearance, he felt his responsibility.

"You sailed to Venice before the mast, then," he asked suddenly one night when the rest of the family had retired.

"Yes, Sir." John hoped that he would not ask the pay of an ordinary seaman.

"H'm. And what are you intending to do now?"

"I — I am not certain, Sir," said John, realizing that the answer was far from satisfactory and wishing that Jack would interrupt. But Jack had lighted his bedroom candle and was reading. No help forthcoming from that source, he felt a further explanation incumbent upon him.

"My father is looking for another opening as soon as possible."

"On a ship, you mean?"

"Yes, Sir."

"Before the mast, again?"

"I trust not, Sir. My father felt that the experience before the mast would be good for me. Sailing as I had done with him, I could have had little knowledge of the whole business of a ship as I have now." But it was unconvincing and he knew it. The Catletts were not county people but good yeo-

45

man stock, their prosperity increasing steadily. In the ordinary course of Polly's life she would never meet a common seaman. Mr. Catlett was not likely to be impressed by specious pleas of 'gaining experience'. All the experience his daughter's suitor needed of a ship could be gained from the quarter-deck, as Captain Newton himself had gained it. He would certainly not permit his Jack to engage in such menial service.

"Well, that is Captain Newton's business, not mine." His disapproval was so evident that John was inclined to come to his father's defence by relating his efforts to establish him in the counting-house at Alicante, and in Jamaica. He stopped himself in time, recollecting that such defence was his own condemnation. But the atmosphere was not propitious for even the most delicate reference to his feelings regarding Mary, and he changed the subject in hope of erasing the bad impression from her father's mind. He would wait, wait until fulfilment of one of the grand projects which his imagination conjectured nightly made him able to approach Mr. Catlett with easy assurance and ask permission to pay his addresses. And Mary . . . ?

He did wait, in fact, postponing the possibility of embarking on any project as long as he could be daily in her company. Finally, after three weeks, very shame and lack of invitation to remain again over Christmas (Mr. Catlett had evidently curbed his wife's motherly propensities at this point) succeeded in forcing him back to Rotherhithe, where the subsequent interview with his father shook him out of day-dreams and stirred him to genuine alarm.

Never, even on the comparatively rare occasions when he had flogged his son, had Captain Newton been so angry. Never before even on shipboard had John seen him white-lipped and unable to control the voice in which he uttered his scathing diatribe. And although the Captain's speech was not free of the vigorous oaths which punctuated the speech of all but the pious, he had never before expended on his son the wealth of a vocabulary which, had the occasion been less serious, the boy would have heard with shocked admiration.

"This is the end of my patience with you, the end, d'you hear?" He had been pacing the room, the better to free himself of the whip-lash sentences reviewing John's failings since

46

childhood, and had twice brought himself up short before the slighter figure of his son, as though about to strike him. Now he paused in the narrow window and stared out over the river. "D'you think I have no pride, to be made a laughing-stock among my friends on account of a despicable young lout like you? My father would have flayed me alive if I had forced him to go, hat in hand, as I had to go last week to tell Captain Oakes you were not here to fill the place I had obtained for you. We'll see how you'll fend for yourself, you blasted young mutineer! Too good to sail 'fore the mast, were ye? So I bespoke a petty-officer's berth for you. Jamaica was too far, forsooth. So the voyage was for Holland and the Netherlands, where I had minded to entrust some business to you. Which if you had handled it well would have turned out much to your advantage. That's gone. No son of mine will gull me thrice. Son of mine! So help me, young Billy shows more responsibility, and not yet eight. It's to him I must turn for any pleasure or pride. I've done my best for you. I defy you before God and man to deny it. You've forfeited your rights. You'll admit the justice of that? Hey?"

He swung around with the words, the query jabbing like a goad. John, groping in horror for his meaning in the last ominous sentences, found words expected from him. But words always deserted him in moments of fear and he was afraid now, as no merely physical fear could make him afraid, afraid of the suggested possibility which would ruin his life and remove all hope of Mary.

"Father —", he began, instinctively using the unfamiliar title.

"You'll call me Sir," Captain Newton cut him off. "Father! Must you remind me that I've begotten such a ne'er-do-well? As for your mother it's well for her she died before you broke her heart, poor woman —"

He broke off abruptly, looking hard at John's face, bloodless beneath the quickly faded sunburn of his voyage. It had been strained and haggard under the verbal lashing but, at the mention of his mother, the mobile mouth quivered suddenly and it was a boy's face again. Aware of his father's dislike of emotion, he tried to disguise the weakness by speech.

"You mean, Sir, I'm not — I am —" he could not bring

himself to utter the dreaded word, as though mere utterance would translate the word into fact.

"No. I'll not disown you — yet." Captain Newton sat down for the first time in the interview, and almost faint with relief John recognized the gruffness of his tone as a sign that his anger was temporarily over. "I had made up my mind to it, and, hark ye, the next piece of disobedience will be the last I'll put up with. But I'll not look out another prospect for you. Food and lodging I'll give you here — here, mind, and the Lord pity you if I find you in any mischief. By the time you've cooled your heels in idleness a while you'll set better value on a father's influence, though I much fear idleness has no terror for you. Ah well! You've no taste for drunkenness, that much every one says for you. As long as that is true we may see you reformed yet."

6

SEVENTEEN-FORTY-THREE passed into seventeen-forty-four, January of that year slipped into February and John Newton, recovering from relief, found the idleness to which his father had consigned him doubly irksome. Once, given freedom to roam the fields and woods of Blackheath and Limehouse Poplars and unlimited time for reading, he would not have minded, for his delight in the country was unimpaired by lack of a like-minded companion and he had until lately preferred books to people. But his meeting with Mary had expelled much of the old lethargic dreaminess and replaced it with desire for action and with vague undirected restlessness. Besides, when he could not be with her he spent his time scheming to be with her again, and every week without employment postponed not only the blissful agony of that next meeting but the hope, to which he clung tenaciously, of ultimate marriage. No position which would further this aim was obtainable without his father's assistance. A few young men were leaving home and amassing a fortune in the Indies or in Africa, he knew, but that prolonged absence with its almost assured loss of her he could not force himself to undergo. Even if he could ask her to wait for him — how charmingly she had parried his few clumsy efforts to lead the conversation into personal channels — even if an opportunity like the one in Jamaica should open up again, he could not bear the thought.

Meanwhile he possessed himself of what patience he could until his father, anxious for a settlement which would benefit him as well as his son, should again exert himself on his be-half.

"Have a care where you show yourself in that garb, John." Meeting him at the door Captain Newton eyed his check sea-man's shirt with disfavour. "Press-gangs are busy these days and you'll get short shrift if they spot you near the docks."

"Thank you, Sir. I plan to walk towards Blackheath. But I shall be careful."

Captain Newton entered the house without further speech and John hesitated a moment, eyeing the sky. The morning sunshine had encouraged him to make his weekly pilgrimage to Shooter's Hill from which eminence he could look to the horizon beyond which lay Chatham and Elysium. Indeed he had gone there twice a week in December and early January, sighing his soul, as Troilus had done, towards the place where his love lay. Now he was undecided. The blue sky, prema-turely spring-like, had darkened with clouds driven by an east wind. To walk six miles in the teeth of it, and possibly in a deluge, would be a small thing if Polly were at the end of the walk, but it was no day to stand on Shooter's Hill and meditate before a six-mile walk home. Besides it was later than his usual time and roads were none too safe after dark. For want of alternative, however, he set out on the road.

He had not gone more than a mile or two when the rain came down in wind-driven sheets. The false spring had en-couraged him to leave his great-coat at home and he was glad to remember that there was a tavern nearby. To be sure, the tavern was on the Deptford Road near the Greenland docks, but he made his way to its shelter and remained until the rain's sharp fury had abated, drinking his ale very slowly and listening to the cross-currents of talk which flowed past him. The main news was the sighting of French warships off the Nore, the main theme, speculation of the wildest sort as to the probable action of Admiral Matthews, and the effect of such action on shipping outward bound. John wondered how it might affect his father's new interests in the African company and his consequent influence towards obtaining a business opening for him in England. Beggars could not be choosers, he reflected, but he did hope that there would be no more seafaring.

50

When the rain ceased to beat against the leaded panes, he buttoned his short jacket and went out into the gray afternoon. It had grown colder and the wind blew icily from the river. Turning up the collar of his woollen shirt he followed an uneven course across the docks to shorten the disagreeable homeward journey.

Suddenly he was not alone. The man who came towards him around the corner of the long shed which he was passing was a naval man, an officer from the cut of his coat, the cock of his silver-laced hat, his air of command. He stopped and John knew that he had seen him before, though he had paid little heed to the others in the tavern.

"What ship d'ye serve on, m'lad?"

Resentment preceded realization by seconds but in those seconds his chance was lost. Opening his mouth haughtily to refuse an answer, he thought for the first time of his father's warning and at the same time saw the other signal. Aiming a quick furious blow with his stick, he began to run. His interceptor feinted and recovered with a swift thrust of his cudgel in the boy's path. Young Newton sprawled on the wet boards, and before he could rise, three more were upon him. Arms pinioned, he was jerked to his feet and hustled, in spite of his shouts and furious struggles, across the wharves to a waiting tender. With the same impersonal disregard they raised the grating of the hatchway and shoved him unceremoniously down into the hold where, blinded by the change from semi-day to total darkness, he felt and smelt the bodies of too many human beings.

Above him the hatch was fastened. The lieutenant's voice snapped out familiar orders. John's shouts for a hearing brought no answer from the deck and a flood of filthy imprecation from his fellow-victims. Sickly he heard the too familiar sounds as the tender loosed moorings. Stunned by the swift reverse of fortune, his head throbbing from a cudgel stroke, his spirit chafing at his impotence, John Newton clutched at the thought of Mary, and the thought cleared his mind to scheme for succour.

Afternoon, indistinguishable from twilight, blackened into night — a long, cold, hideous night of pitching on the choppy waters amid the stench and slime of unseen filth. By noon

51

next day when the hatch was opened and they were ordered up on deck, John, gulping the fresh sea air thirstily, was too resentful at his sufferings to feel any concern for the worse conditions of other wretches, some of whom had spent a fortnight in such confinement. His attempts to speak even a word had been futile the night before, when ship's biscuits and an indefinable mess had been shoved down to them by lantern light; but in the morning, calling through the grating to a sailor, he had managed to bribe him with one of the few coins which he had removed to an inner pocket to bear a message to the lieutenant.

So when the unkempt, scared, sullen assortment of pressed men was lined upon the *Betsey's* deck for a brief period of air and exercise — the sailors' cutlasses and cudgels, the lieutenant's pistols, and the open waters of the estuary sufficient assurance of their docility — the officer came to run an appraising, indifferent eye over his haul.

"Which of you men is called Newton?" he demanded sharply.

"I, Sir, Lieutenant Rubin." John's speech had never been more careful; much depended, with the sorry spectacle he now presented, on the impression made by the few words he could utter.

The lieutenant's ear recognized the distinction.

"You wish to speak to me. If it's for release, save your breath. There's an invasion expected and every able-bodied man is liable for service."

"It's not for release, Sir."

"Then speak and be quick about it."

"Sir, my father is Captain Newton, late of the *Hind* in the Mediterranean service. May I send a message to tell him where I am?"

The lieutenant hesitated. He had carried out his orders and no action could be taken against him. But sons of commanders were not usual victims of impressment. What if he refused and Captain Newton happened to be a friend of Captain Cartaret? Besides, he felt no ill-will towards a youngster who had behaved only as he would have behaved in similar circumstances. Pressing men was a necessary, not an agreeable part of his business.

"Where does your father live?"

"Rotherhithe, Sir."

"I'll see to it." He turned on his heel with a curt order and John had to be content.

Contentment was the last word for his mind in the grim days which followed. Another day or two he fumed in the hold of the *Betsey* while she moored at any likely wharf and half her crew of thirty went prowling for prey, not too successfully, since only one victim was added to the seven already on board. Then the tender headed for her ship and John was driven up the side of H.M.S. *Harwich,* riding at anchor in the Nore, to serve in the lowest capacity in its crew of three hundred and fifty. No amount of experience in merchant ships could adequately prepare a man for the lot of an ordinary seaman on a man-of-war in wartime. Yet even in this lot gradations in treatment obtained, of which recently impressed men had the harshest. Given the hardest, vilest, most dangerous tasks, the poorest accommodation in vermin-infested quarters, without recourse in private quarrels, and liable to the rope's end for the slightest tardiness or surliness, they at least served a temporary purpose of giving the regular crew the illusion of superiority.

So week after week Newton, whose natural arrogance and quick temper, sharpened by a sense of outrage, made him a target for vindictiveness, scraped the masts, scraped the decks, scraped the boat's sides, suspended precariously and soaked by spray and dashing waves in the keen gales and snow from the North Sea. Day after day he ate small rations of food which made him for the first time homesick for his father's table, and lived with one hundred men in quarters which rendered the foc'sle of his recent ship with its twenty sailors seem palatial by contrast. And each succeeding longer day as the work neared completion, he paid the masts and sides of the ship with rosin and tallow and carried loads up companionway ladders, dreading that the *Harwich* would be readied and sail before relief could arrive from his father.

If his father had heard? He dared not doubt Lieutenant Rubin's word which the latter had with considerable asperity confirmed when John, after several day's contriving, forced an opportunity to ask him. If, having heard, he washed his hands of the whole matter? That too was a possibility which his son refused to contemplate. Even if his father had no affection for him, even if he felt — justly enough — that his own unheeding carelessness was fairly punished, John rested his hopes in his knowledge of the Old Gentleman's pride. Merchant skippers were continually at loggerheads with Naval officers, whose high-handed methods they resented. Also it would be a reflection on his father's prestige to have his first-born forcibly impressed into the lowliest service afloat.

How well he read Captain Newton's mind he never knew. Whether in time of peace he would have secured the boy's discharge or not, the state of crisis in national affairs put such action out of his power. But in March, almost a month after his capture, John was summoned before Captain Cartaret, told succinctly of his father's intervention, warned sternly against entertaining any idea of privilege and received upon the quarter-deck in the rank of midshipman.

That evening Newton entered the gunroom in a state of well-being which even his shyness could not diminish. With the scanty facilities available he had scrubbed himself clean, removing as much as one effort could achieve of oakum and tallow. A remittance from his father and the help of the purser had fitted him out with a somewhat eclectic garb, similar enough to the others of his rank — there being no compulsory uniform — to make him pass muster. A quiet boy, rather younger than he, had been ordered by the Captain to show him the junior officers' quarters, have his hammock slung, and initiate him generally into his duties. His friendliness in acting as guide, and in chatting until summoned to run an errand, was an added drop in John's almost overflowing cup. During the brief period he had to himself in the cockpit he began an ecstatic imaginary conversation with Mary. He thought of her as Mary and addressed her, both in person and in imagination, as Polly. It was not as beautiful a name but it made her seem more attainable. Then he suddenly remembered that, though he had prayed repeatedly during the past month, wild desperate bargaining prayers for release from his degredation, he had completely omitted to return thanks for the change, which at last gave him a position in which he might one day be acceptable as her suitor.

His thanksgiving prayer was propitiatory. He realized that even perfunctory prayer — apart from the agonized demands of recent days and compulsory attendance at Sunday service — had been badly neglected and, while neither Bible nor other books had been available since he came on board, it might well be that his long, previous neglect of the former had brought about his punishment. So with a half-hearted resolve to pay his storm-made vows by being more 'serious' in the future, he decided to write a letter to the Catletts and went up to the gunroom to see where he could obtain writing implements.

The very appearance of the low, sparsely furnished compartment, bigger than any comparable room on his father's merchantman, thrilled him with its indication of the world of difference between his recent situation and his new dignity. He cared very little at that moment whether anyone spoke to him or not, but his new acquaintance, Job Lewis, looked up from a game of draughts and beckoned him over.

Several men were smoking pipes over the 'tub of water' required by naval regulations. One of them, glancing up as John crossed the room, favoured him with a long discriminating stare. Then, as though he had drawn his conclusion, he shook out his pipe, hung it in its place on the wall and came forward.

"A new recruit? — though, egad, your face is familiar. Your name, friend?"

"John Newton."

"Miles Cleaver, Sir, at your service." He was a handsome, assured young man, taller than John and with an air of unlimited self-possession and experience. "Forgive my curiosity but surely I have seen you before today? Pray enlighten me."

"If you saw me," said Newton without pretense, "it was in such condition that you took no notice of me. Lieutenant Rubin and his crew on the *Betsey* pressed me, a most reluctant recruit, I assure you, into His Majesty's service almost four weeks ago."

Miles Cleaver whistled, questioned and heard his answers with flattering interest.

"So 'All's well that ends well'," he pronounced and the quotation conveyed the impression of reference to Shakespeare rather than to a trite proverb. "Fortune is a fickle jade, as I am not first to observe.

'hinc apicem rapax
Fortuna cum stridore acuto
sustulit, hic posuisse gaudet.'

But this time the whimsical goddess has placed the crown on you without robbing anyone else to do so."

John tried to think of an apt quotation and gave it up.

"I can't cap your Latin, though I believe it is Horace," he said frankly. "And the little Virgil I learned at school I lost long since. However, as Ben Johnson tells us that Shakespeare had 'small Latin and less Greek', I claim the precedent without the genius."

It was a pretentious speech and he knew it, but there was a compelling attractiveness about Miles Cleaver's assurance and he was unwilling to seem dull or slow-witted before him.

"Well said! And welcome to our mess. We'll make some flip at supper and drink a toast to your future. Meanwhile have a smoke. Or have you your own pipe?"

"No." John took the long-stemmed clay while his new friend struck flint and steel in his tinderbox, waited patiently till the pipe drew, and puffed it with gratitude, for it allayed the pangs of hunger which were becoming acute. His summons to Captain Cartaret had come when noon rations were being dispensed in the forecastle and in the business of his promotion he had missed dinner.

So the poorly cooked food of the junior officers' mess seemed like a banquet. It was carried in and the table laid by two of his quondam associates, whose gaping astonishment at beholding him so exalted almost made them forget their business and earned them a cuff from Cleaver. Far more than increased physical comfort John rejoiced in his exemption from the contemptuous domination of the quarter-deck. For himself he had resented it bitterly; but more deeply he had felt that it demeaned him as Mary's lover, and had showed his resentment on several occasions to his own hurt. Now he need never endure it again.

"Messmates, a toast: To John Newton, Fortune's new favourite," proposed Cleaver, when his skill had produced a can of the best flip John had yet tasted. He sat embarrassed but pleased while the rest, who had followed Cleaver's lead in accepting him, drank the toast and struck up a fairly tuneful rendition of "Down Among the Dead Men". The phrase which each man had repeated as he drank lingered in his mind, and later, when they met on deck and stood in the April air for a few minutes before turning in, he referred to it.

"Fortune's favourite is not quite accurate in my case, is it?" he said, forcing a laugh lest he should seem too serious.

"Why not? You are, you know."

"In view of your remarks on her fickleness, I should expect a reverse and that is not a prospect I face with equanimity."

"No? for shame," said Cleaver who had never suffered any hardships in his life greater than the cramped quarters of his present berth, which he was enduring for the minimum time before succeeding to a commission already secured by family influence.

> " '*Aequam memento rebus in arduis,*
> *Servare mentem nec secus in bonis,*
> *Ab insolenti temperatam,*
> *Laetitia, moriture Delli.'*

But I forget your unfortunate lacuna. Construe, Lewis," — Job Lewis, on his way to his watch, had joined them.

" 'Memento' — remember," said Job, obligingly and in the sing-song of the school-room, " 'aequam servare mentem' — to preserve an even mind, 'rebus in arduis' — in hard circumstances — 'nec secus in bonis' — nor otherwise in prosperity — 'temperatam ab insolenti laetitia' — a mind guarded from overweening joy — 'moriture Delli' — Dellius, doomed to die."

"Well conned, Lewis," Cleaver praised him with mock school-master condescension. "Horace has the word for every occasion, and so prettily put."

"Yes, but," persisted Newton in whose ears the words "doomed to die" had obscured the 'prettiness', "surely it is questionable how much control what you call Fortune actually has. In accidentals probably she seems to have much, but what of the omnipotence of God?"

Both hearers were affected by the word but differently. Miles Cleaver darted a keen glance at him — there was a full moon and the deck was bathed in almost day-like brightness — and Lewis made a small murmur as of approval. When the

57

former spoke he was evidently choosing his words with care.

"Ah there, of course, we have the ultimate Mystery. Who can answer such a question with glib certainty? Yet in view of the unlovely wrangling of churchmen on such matters, it is perhaps well for men of reason to restrict our speculations to the observable phenomena.

'Know then thyself; presume not God to scan,
The proper study of mankind is man'."

"Granting that," said John, still feeling that his recent benefits demanded a return of gratitude, "I fail to see any impersonal fortune in my case. I sent a message to my father, my father interposed on my behalf, Captain Cartaret made the restitution in his power, and here I am."

Cleaver's shrug was a charming, not an offensive gesture.

"All true. We must not ask then what you owe to Fortune that you have an influential father, as presumably those others, poor creatures in the foc'sle have not, or that your father's message arrived before we sail — which I hear strictly sub rosa we shall do tomorrow — or that, when it arrived, you were still on board, unlike the wretch who dropped from the yard arm yesterday or the other who succumbed with ague a week ago. With all respect to an over-ruling Providence, can you say with certainty that you are more worthy than they, or even that they did not send up as many prayers as you?"

"Shaftesbury sees no discrepancy," said Newton, falling back on his mentor, "in holding orthodox faith and employing all the powers of reasonable speculation."

Cleaver changed an incipient whistle abruptly into speech.

"So you know Shaftesbury. What a relief to meet a man who reads widely. Job, there is a good fellow." He nodded graciously towards Job's retreating figure as he went to walk his watch. "But his mind is stocked only with his school texts, commonplace orthodox books and the Bible, which he also has conned by rote. And the rest care for little but rum and cards and the prospect of a wench the next shore leave. Whether you like the expression or not, I bless Fortune who sent you my way before I died for lack of companionship."

7

HE companionship flourished during the stirring and strenuous months which followed. The War of the Spanish Succession, which had been unofficially and spasmodically recognized since the abortive French invasion in February, was duly and solemnly declared on April the third. Amid watchful manoeuvres to guard the British coast and prevent collusion between Jacobites within and French without, the task of the *Harwich* was to escort merchant shipping on its lawful but hazardous occasions. Up the East Coast to Scotland, across to Norway, to Denmark, to Sweden, she headed her convoys and returned. Once she gave chase to a small enemy vessel and fired a warning shot; once she fired a shot across the bows of an English trader in order to exchange three worthless sailors for three able merchant seamen; once she had a brief spirited engagement with the French man-of-war, *Solide,* and, though the enemy struck her colours and the *Harwich* lost only one man, the thunder of guns and the crash of shot, shredding sails, and falling timbers gave John his first experience of war.

These moments were sparsely scattered over long periods of uneventful arduous routine. Meanwhile Cleaver, Lewis and Newton spent their off-hours together. Miles Cleaver applied himself to the task of enlightening his young friends — and to Lewis who was eighteen and Newton whose nineteenth birthday occurred while the *Harwich* was at Elsinore, his twenty-one-year-old knowledge passed for profound wisdom. Job Lewis had read Hooker and Butler and William Law; John knew Milton and Addison and Bacon as well as Shakespeare, and had tasted the heady speculations of Shaftesbury; but here was a daring soul who had at his tongue's end the mordant wit of Voltaire, the ponderous works of Locke, the free-thinking of Bolingbroke and the scepticisms of David Hume. From the moment in which he convinced Newton that he had missed — as indeed he had — the subtle teaching of *The Characteristics,* John became a willing and eager disciple, and as first one fetter of prejudice, then another, was struck from him, he could not be satisfied until he had brought Job to a similar emancipation.

Re-reading Shaftesbury, he felt as if scales had fallen from his eyes.

"How could I have failed to see his drift and thought he was an orthodox Christian?" he marvelled after reading Palaemon's speech on miracles.

Miles Cleaver smiled.

"Most of us read into a book what we wish to believe. Your upbringing compelled you to think that none but orthodox Christians were good or intelligent or amiable. So when you read a book, the author of which is evidently good and intelligent and amiable, he must be an orthodox Christian! Besides, Shaftesbury, realizing how revolutionary his thinking is, wisely veiled it in language which would not shock his readers. He recognized that the meaner sort are better with the curbs and restrictions of orthodoxy. We pity the ancient pagans. Yet Lucian and Lucretius discovered the weakness and inconsistency of their religion and were acclaimed. If our writers claim an equal freedom, religion would have them in the pillory."

"Not all," said Newton determined to be fair. "Milton pleads eloquently for freedom of opinion and press — and he was an orthodox Christian."

"Though accused by the orthodox of Arianism," conceded Cleaver.

"But according to your interpretation," said Lewis, who had been listening silently, "nature is perfect and man is perfect. I don't pretend to be a philosopher but the falsity of that is patent. Consider the devastation caused by last summer's tidal wave. Look at the offscouring of the gaols we have on board or our own mates, Gillies and Roman, or for that matter ourselves —"

60

"We don't contend," broke in John eagerly, identifying himself for the first time with Shaftesbury and Cleaver, "that men are perfect. We do say that they are born in a perfect state, that their instincts are noble and good, that by example and training . . . and by fear and domination they become evil. And as for the universe being imperfect, Shaftesbury contends that such teaching argues imperfection or impotence on the part of the Creator; that what seems imperfect to us is because we cannot view the whole in perspective, even as a man who was perpetually confined in the hold of this ship and caught only a glimpse of an isolated spar would have no idea of its function or performance in the motion of the whole — it would seem an ugly and useless appendage."

"But the Bible teaches that man is totally depraved and incapable of good," persisted Lewis, his native Devonshire becoming more apparent in his speech with earnestness, his dark eyes fixed on Newton as they were in every discussion. He seldom looked at Cleaver or addressed him directly, feeling insecure with his raillery and light condescending manner; but John without effort had won his confidence. The words awoke an echo, though a faint one, in John's conscience and it was Miles who answered.

" 'The Bible teaches,' you say." The quotation marks were gently inserted in his cool smiling voice. "You talk as if the Bible dropped from heaven, printed in English and bound in Paternoster row! But there again, my friend, you come to the Bible, not with an open, much less an enquiring mind, but with one already barricaded and bolstered with the teaching of your childhood. Have you never realized how many people, if you asked them why they believe and act in what you consider a wrong and ridiculous manner, would give that same reason? 'The Bible teaches' the Papist says, careful not to call himself a Papist, but a believer in the Old Religion. 'The Bible teaches' the Quaker says, and would greet the French on our shores with: 'Thee is welcome, friend.' 'The Bible teaches' say the followers of Luther and 'The Bible teaches' thunder the disciples of Calvin, at one another's throats. But 'The Bible teaches' cry the Anabaptists and decry your baptisms as a pagan superstition. And 'The Bible teaches' cry these mad enthusiasts called Methodists who preach the ignorant deluded rabble into fits and trances and orgies, the excesses of which they doubtless explain by a text. Ah, but, you say, what we say 'The Bible teaches' is right — and so all the wretched and barbarous persecutions and wars which have racked Christendom these many centuries! But a thinking man does not, cannot, if he is to have self-respect, limit his thinking by such a cant statement — unless he is prepared when the Jew says 'The Torah teaches' to become a Jew, or when the Mohammedan says 'The Koran teaches' to become a Mohammedan. And truly," he concluded, "judging by the number of wives Mahomet conceded to the devout, and the tangible delights of his heaven, I think that last step might be an advantageous one for a man to take."

The others shared his laugh but Job's square plain face settled back into its habitual gravity. John, whose mind was racing ahead to the unexplored possibilities which such liberty opened up, felt the drag of his reluctance.

"The Bible itself contradicts what you say about man, Job. Wasn't your namesake called 'a perfect man and upright'?"

Job's troubled eyes came back from the green waters of the North Sea, but before he could answer, Cleaver spoke again.

"If we ask ourselves — holding our creedal prejudice at bay for a moment, if we can — which concept is more honouring to the Author of Being, surely there can be only one answer. Man made in the image of God (as the Bible teaches, Lewis) and to have dominion over all the works of nature (as the Bible also teaches) a wretched, depraved, helpless, cringing creature doomed to grovel or be damned: or man the rightful lord of creation capable of self-knowledge, self-expression, self-realization, in fact bound, if he is to be a whole man, to be true to his nature, unafraid of his instincts, enslaved by no super-imposed taboos."

"Yet," murmured John, conscious of where some of his instincts would lead, "Shaftesbury enjoins Virtue and condemns Evil."

"I think," said Miles, and somehow, though not smiling offensively, he conveyed the impression of suppressing with difficulty a smile which might give offense, "we must re-read his discussion of Virtue. Shaftesbury is too good a Latinist — your pardon, John — to forget for a moment that Virtus is manliness and that as virtue for any creature is the full expression of its nature, so Virtue for man is the complete expression of his manliness. To you it consists of suppression, of denial, of mortification. Remember his use of the word Balance which we use in such terms as Balance of power among nations but never think of in connection with a Balance of power in our proper nature. What orthodoxy has blessed as Virtue the philosopher censures as Evil — a warping and spoiling, an atrophy of part of man's real nature, which is essentially good."

There was a pause. Was there then a truce possible in the struggle between desire and conscience? Could the flesh be at peace with the mind? Cleaver pressed his advantage.

"We are talking as men. But what happens when you feel the natural (and, if we observe nature, what is more in tune with her benign sway?) urge of man? You act like boys, and frightened boys. You, John, immediately consider a course of artificial emasculation, refraining from meat or drink; you, Job, betake yourself to grovelling prayers. And if these do not serve, you are visited with remorse. Is it virtue, is it either wisdom or courage not to be master of your own thoughts, your own actions? Ah, time for dinner." Miles had a fine sense of the right moment to stop. "That is if such stuff as we are served — at which I assure you my father's good Herefordshire hogs would look askance — can be called dinner."

8

OHN awoke one morning, with a peculiar sense of lightness, to realize that he was at last a Free-Thinker. He had been nurtured in the fear of God; under His righteous law he had been unequivocally condemned all his rational life. Now this God had been removed in location from a position directly overhanging his guilty head to a region indefinitely remote, and in nature from a tendency to preoccupation with John Newton's personal affairs and intimate thoughts to an impassible unconcern for the worlds He — or it — had set spinning in space.

The previous night, having argued himself into a state of mental rejection of the old and acceptance of the new, he had put his assumptions to the test. Deliberately he had broken the rule of continence which he had not transgressed, in overt act, since that strange pagan night in Spain. They had gone ashore at Ostend and Cleaver, who had some acquaintance among the senior officers, overcame John's scruples by introducing him to a place of pleasure to which the common sailors could not aspire. Job Lewis, whom they invited, had refused at first, then joined them just as they were leaving the ship. He had taken his pleasure sadly, and his gloom on their return journey had rather damped the frolicsome mood of the other two.

Newton had feared that his own mood would not survive dawnlight and the dying of the wine within him. Evidently his reading from Miles's library and from the books which he had purchased wherever a book stall could be found in his visits ashore had done its work. Swift and Voltaire, Bolingbroke and Hume, Boccacio and Rabelais had obliterated the vestiges of *The Family Instructor, Christian Oratory* and Dr. Watts's *Children's Hymns.* It was a strange feeling, pleasant chiefly in its sense of relief, like the empty lightness which sometimes succeeds bodily pain in illness. It was not happiness. Certainly it had no relation to the ecstasy of disquieting emotion which attended the presence, or even the thought of Mary Catlett.

On that one theme John remained independent of Miles Cleaver, in spite of every effort made to alter him. He knew of Mary, though John was reticent in his talk of her before this gallant, to whom by his own admission all women, physical charms apart, were much alike. But the state of excitement and apprehension into which he was thrown in June, when the *Harwich* cast anchor in Margate Road would have drawn the attention of a less acute observer than Miles. His pride was piqued, too, by John's complete indifference to any plans for leave except his own: which was to take horse for Chatham within minutes of leaping from the longboat to the shore and stay so long that he had to be smuggled aboard on his late return, Cleaver lying blatantly and Lewis uncomfortably to cover up for him.

The same thing happened later in the summer when the *Harwich* lay at anchor in Sheerness harbour. The time allotted for his leave expired and he was called for his watch on deck. Job who had just served his four-hour turn prepared to do a double stint. Unfortunately the Captain required Job's presence on the bridge and the substitution was discovered. It was well for John that, when he came on board some hours later, he was able to plead that his horse had fallen lame and to refer Captain Cartaret to the stable owner in confirmation. John did not find it necessary to make clear at what stage in the journey his mount had been disabled and in the rush of preparation for a new project the Captain did not press the question.

Cleaver, however, seized upon this delinquency to rally his love-sick friend more seriously on the unphilosophic excess of his attachment.

"But leaving philosophy aside, what good do you get by feeding this affection?" he continued. "It has a double disadvantage: first, unfitting you for practical concerns, it cannot but present you to her family in an unfavourable light; secondly it renders you unable to appear before the lady herself with the assurance and polish which the fair creatures love in a man. Shaftesbury, you remember, warns against the false elevation of the sex which is prevalent in this Island. Believe me, women are strangers to the absurd delicacy of thought and feeling which you attribute to them. They are much like us, only inferior in capacity, and the man who treats them so is most favoured by them. I have seen a girl like Mary —"

"Blast your eyes!" said Newton explosively, "You've never seen — her — nor can you have seen anyone like her. You're not capable of appreciating or distinguishing her and I'll thank you in future to keep her name off your polluted tongue."

With this he flung himself out of the presence of his friend, who showed his philosophic temper by refusing to take offence. Thereafter Mary's person was omitted from discussion but Miles renewed the attack indirectly with anecdote, quotation, and light animadversion on the women with whom they came in contact.

Here, at least, John recognized the facts too clearly to make them subserve theory. Neither reason nor self-interest could weigh in the balance with his passion for Mary and the power she had exercised over him, present or absent, since he first saw her. What was worse, and the underlying cause of his petulant outburst at Miles, was the fact that neither argument nor endeavour freed him from the numbing self-consciousness which constantly prevented him from appearing to advantage in her company. Only the joy of being near her, joy which drugged him into physical inability to tear himself away in spite of consequence, compensated for the disappointment of his last two visits. He had been pleased and proud as he hurried towards Chatham after his preferment, sure of his newly acquired ease of manner and man-of-the-world assurance, full of wittily rehearsed anecdotes regarding his recent experiences. But of what use a fine blue jacket and a happy gift for a well-turned phrase, if the form inside the jacket froze to log-like awkwardness, and the phrases which impressed others halted on his tongue whenever he addressed his idol? Meanwhile Polly, graceful and at home in the gay, easy-going society of her acquaintance, was quite evidently attractive to others. Perhaps she would find one of them attractive, another smooth-tongued, handsome Miles Cleaver with no heart to realize the priceless value of hers and no will to make and keep her happy. And such a villain had all the advantage of being constantly at hand while he would be doubly handicapped, for word was circulating through the crew of an imminent twelve-month cruise for the *Harwich*, and John's self-depreciation exaggerated the extent of the mockery which his awkwardness aroused among Polly's friends.

Obtaining leave again, he rode to her home, determined to safeguard his hazardous hopes by a tentative proposal. To his dismay, though the family greeted him, Mr. Catlett with somewhat less warmth than formerly, Mary was not among them. Mrs. Catlett relieved his misery before he found courage to ask.

"Polly is staying with the Soans for a few days. The eldest Miss Soans is to be married on Saturday and Polly will be one of the bridesmaids. She will be sorry to miss your visit."

John had no intention that she would miss his visit. He despatched a messenger to Rochester forthwith asking for an interview. The messenger returned and Jack Catlett, riding down from London and stopping in Rochester on the way to see his sister, came Tuesday evening with the same message: Would John please not come to Rochester? She was obliged to come home on an errand and would be there on Thursday.

"It's your own fault, John," said Jack with the frankness of assured friendship. "Polly's friends all joke her because of you. Why do you let everyone see how you feel about her? Believe me, no girl likes to see a man act like a sheep at shearing time."

" 'He jests at scars, that never felt a wound,' " said John, thankful that his tongue was never tied where Jack was concerned. He recognized the truth of his friend's words and the likelihood of forfeiting even the short time of this precious interview. So he anticipated their meeting by sending a letter in which he wrote carefully some of the things which he would probably be unable to say when he saw her: his regret that she had been exposed to raillery on his account; his inability to make a serious proposal with his present prospects; his desire and unwillingness to elicit any answer from her lest it should be unfavourable; his plea that "if, as I doubt not you will (or have) from your appearance in the polite world, meet with proposals from others better skilled in the arts and nicetys of making themselves agreeable," she would "suspend your final decision for one twelve month and remember that there is one absent who in sincere affection and desire to make you happy will at least equal and (I think) far exceed any you can meet with." And he subscribed himself "Your most affectionate and faithful admirer."

These written sentiments were all he was able to impart. The meeting, though Mary came to it alone as requested, was so spoiled by his awkwardness and so soon interrupted (of design he felt sure) by Mr. Catlett, that it gave him little satisfaction in retrospect.

His next attempt to clarify the issue had at least one definite result. By December it was generally known that the projected voyage of the *Harwich* was to the East Indies and the thought of several years absence goaded Newton to a renewed effort. Christmas found them anchored in the Downs while the ships for the convoy were gathering. Newton, forcibly reminded by the contrast of the happiest Christmas of his life two years before, performed all his duties with an alacrity and show of cheerfulness calculated to impress the Captain. Whether or not sufficient impression was made, on the twenty-ninth shore leave was granted, but for a day only.

A day was of no use to John. From Deal, where he parted with his comrades, to Chatham was almost forty miles, but without deliberating he took horse and, urging it on as fast as the road permitted, came by way of Canterbury and Maidstone to Chatham at sundown.

The Catletts were all at tea. Introduced by his admirer, three-year-old Georgie who had run to the door at the sound of horse's hoofs, John, taking a quick inventory of the familiar room, felt his heart give a great thud of relief as he saw Mary. Then he plunged into the explanation which Mr. Catlett's evident surprise seemed to demand.

"The *Harwich* is lying in the Downs, Sir. We are due to

sail almost any time now for the Indies. The voyage will take at least three years so they say." His eyes sought Mary's face but, though she was looking at him with distracting brightness of courteous interest, he could not read there any sign of distress.

"Ah well, at your age three years will pass like so many months," said Mr. Catlett with middle-aged forgetfulness of the long days and weeks of his own youth. His wife showed more sympathy.

"It's easy for you to talk, Mr. Catlett, with poor John facing the hardships of the seas — and the dangers of war as well. You've never been away from England in your life."

"No more I have, and thankful I am for it," said her husband comfortably. "No, a seafaring life isn't my choice for myself — or my family," he added rather unnecessarily, and John, considerably shaken, sat down to tea, wondering if the last remark was a deliberate warning against any presumption he might entertain. The rest of the family were friendly and talkative, however, and, though Mary's Aunt and Uncle Hammond, who liked John and made him feel at home, came for cards in the evening and he was not able to see her alone, he went to bed so full of the soothing delirium of being again under the same roof with her that he gave no thought to Captain Cartaret's displeasure and little to Mr. Catlett's.

George Catlett had no ill-will towards the boy who had adopted his family, but he did not share his wife's sentimental pity. John had a father and home of his own and, if he had been more dependable, could have been settled in business away from the sea. This much he had learned from Jack's inadvertent chatter. Also from Jack he had gleaned the gist of much of the friends' conversation, for Newton had passed on, with all the ardour of a convert, the arguments and discoveries of his new philosophy and had found Jack a most receptive disciple. Mr. Catlett was not a deeply religious man and he detested 'enthusiasm'. But he was a conservative member of the Established Church and associated free-thinking with revolution and the corruption of public morals.

Still he did not attach too much importance to the chatter of nineteen-year-olds. What concerned him more was the young man's persistent, undisguised and undisguisable devotion to his Polly. And though, he would say it for her, Polly was behaving with a composure and discretion which would do credit to a matron, there was no knowing what effect such whole-souled admiration might have — the boy was personable enough and a good talker when he was not transformed by emotion into an awkward and risible piece of formality. Such nonsense as a basis for marriage! He was not going to have his fifteen-year-old girl under any commitments to an unstable sailor who would shortly be away for three years — though Mr. Catlett had his doubts about that, for if ever a boy had a way of turning up it was young John Newton.

And Newton! That was another point! Captain Newton had made no overtures in spite of their hospitality to his firstborn. No certain prospects, no parental approval, no self-control! George Catlett snorted and hoped to Heaven that Newton's extraordinarily obliging Captain would not grant him another leave.

Meanwhile he did his best to see that John and Polly had no time together. In a busy household like the Catletts' this was not difficult. Mary alone could have arranged an opportunity but Mary was bafflingly obtuse. Without any apparent consciousness she was always on her guard. She would neither understand his hints nor give him a chance to come to a direct explanation, as several times when only Elizabeth or little Georgie was present, he tried to do.

The thirtieth of December passed and the morning of the thirty-first. Even in John's bemused mind it became clear that there was a limit to the self-granted extension of his leave.

"Polly," he said desperately, waylaying her in the passage by the simple expedient of leaving the room when she came in to fetch a special platter from the dresser and waiting until she re-emerged, "Polly, I must get back to the ship. I — I was given a day's leave only and I have taken three already —" She started with dismay and he pressed his doubtful advantage. "Don't distress yourself. I have done it before because I could not bear to leave you. But you are too generous to send me away without even a moment. May I not speak two words to you without" — he thought of the play they had seen the night before — "without interruption from the groundlings?"

She remained still for a blessed moment, her lovely mouth

70

relaxing into gravity after the quick responsive smile. John stood adoring her, caught again from anxiety and depression into the charmed circle of their brief communion, the inevitable ordained rightness of their being together. Mary was always the same but always new: he had not seen her arms at just that angle, the full sleeves falling back as they clasped the platter; the rise and fall of her breast, surely swifter and less rhythmical than usual, was accentuated by the movement of her burden clutched to it.

"You must have dinner before you go, of course," she said in her ordinary tone and John realized with a thrill that for the first time she was indulging in duplicity. Her voice dropped, although its quality was still deceptively conversational to any casual listener. "It isn't too cold for a turn in the garden afterwards — as far as the sundial."

At dinner John announced his departure for that afternoon. He would push straight across country and try to make Canterbury by nightfall so that he could rejoin the *Harwich* on New Year's morning. When the meal was over he went up to his room, refusing Jack's offer of assistance, and almost immediately descended. Slipping on his great-coat, he emerged quietly by the garden door and made his way to the sundial. Once there, he smiled at Mary's wisdom in appointing this spot, for a holly hedge on one side and the kitchen garden wall on the other screened it from view of the house.

So, though his being was strained for her coming and he heard her quick footfall on the garden walk, she came, her familiar scarlet cloak against the glossy green spikes of holly, quite suddenly upon him. In spite of his desperate determination, for a few moments he could only look at her, speechless, like a shipwrecked mariner sighting landfall.

She waited for him to speak. For all her outward composure she was nervous. Granting an interview to this "ardent and faithful admirer" who had not obtained her father's approval was not, she knew, what she should be doing. But he was going away, so far away, and although she did not understand the feeling which made him so annoyingly — and ludicrously — dumb in her presence, she was so sorry for him!

"I do hope, John," she said at last, feeling that someone must begin, "that you will have a safe and successful voyage."

71

All John's world was present in the slim figure beside the sundial, head bent as her finger traced the stone-cut motto: 'I mark only Sunny Houres'. And between them presently a waste of seas and dragging years would roll.

"I can't go, Polly," he said wildly. "I can't leave you for so long. I —" As usual, words deserted him and Mary rose to the occasion.

"You can and you must, John," she said a little coldly and sounding the older of the two. "You have done wrong already in overstaying your leave. And what is to be gained by remaining here?"

The cool womanly practicality of her words restored a measure of his dormant good sense. There was nothing to be gained by remaining, and everything to lose. He could make no serious proposals and by what other sort could he seek to bind the beloved who had no answer in her clear unawakened eyes for the passion which tormented him. How could he expect it? "I do not so much as presume," he had written to her, "that a love so ill expressed and conducted as mine can have inspired a return." What he had most to dread, if he persisted, was that he would arouse her anger and draw from her an answer which would leave him no hope. Anything was better than the finality of despair. After all, her consenting to this meeting was in his favour. He knew that her generosity of nature would not grant him even that modicum of encouragement if she despised him. Better to leave the situation as it was, perhaps, but —

The small capable left hand, pink with cold, stopped tracing the silly words and flattened out on the dial with a curious uncertain movement of the fingers. It was nearer to him than the rest of her and its attraction proved suddenly irresistible. John caught it up in both of his and, murmuring inarticulately, went down on his knees — he thought afterwards that they had collapsed under him — and buried his face in its palm.

For a few seconds they remained so. Mary knew that she should snatch her hand away but the experience was new and her warm young heart was moved, though with vicarious pain. Instinctively she let the captured fingers move slightly, as she would have caressed a distressed child, but it was a man's face and mouth that felt the touch and recaptured the sensation months and years afterwards in delight and anguish. Then the beauty was broken.

"Polly," said her father more sharply than he had ever spoken to her. "I thought you had more sense of what becomes you. Your mother wishes your help in the house immediately."

John did not remember releasing her hand or stumbling to his feet. When he faced Mr. Catlett, angry that Mary should incur any blame on his account, they were alone.

"Now, young man," said George Catlett, "let us understand each other clearly. I have nothing against you. You've been welcome here and treated like our own whenever you pleased to come. You'll not deny that?"

John could not deny it.

"But I have my daughter to consider and my position. At first we took no notice of your hanging around Polly. You would be over it by your next visit. But you aren't, it seems. She is too young to know her own mind even if she thought she favoured you. But you seem quite sure of yours. And I won't have any more of such conduct as I saw just now. You have no prospects, I don't know your father's mind in this, and I will need to see a great deal more steadiness in you before I trust my daughter's future into your keeping."

"Sir," began John, but Mr. Catlett was determined to finish what he had begun.

"So I am telling you — and make no mistake, I've intended to tell you for some time back, even if I had not come upon you here — you are not to come to the house again under these conditions. No, don't protest. I should think your pride would keep you away if your common sense doesn't."

These, except for a formal good-bye, were Mr. Catlett's last words to him. John had hardly regained his room before Mrs. Catlett entered.

"John, my dear boy," she began, but, overcome by pity for him both because of his dreary expression and because what she had to say would make it drearier, she put her hands on his shoulders and stood on tiptoe to give him a motherly kiss on the forehead.

"You are my dear boy, you know," she went on earnestly, when John, still angry and embarrassed, made no response,

73

"and I feel as I should feel if I had to say the same things to Jack. But I should want the same things said to him if he were in the same case."

"I know what you have to say," interrupted John sullenly.

"Perhaps you do," she rejoined gently, so that he knew he should be ashamed of his ingratitude, but was not. "But I thought perhaps my way of saying it would pain you less. John, I have not the slightest objection to an engagement between you and Polly, if it comes about at a maturer age that you have prudent prospects. But as things are there is no peace for her or satisfaction for you. Mr. Catlett has told you not to return to our house. He means, of course, unless Polly is away or unless you will give up your pretensions to her, or assure me that your father expressly gives his consent for their continuance. Moreover," she continued, reading in his face the unlikelihood of compliance with these conditions, "I think it only fair that Polly should not be troubled by letters from you. I know you will regard my wish in this matter as if it were put as a strict command."

Perhaps it was well for Newton that disappointment, resentment, endearing recollections of his brief moments with Polly, the thrilling mental re-enactment of her touch, kept his thoughts tempestuously busy so that the prospect of Captain Cartaret's wrath was only remotely disturbing. His summons to the august presence was delivered to him before he came alongside and repeated gleefully by several seamen with whom he had been unnecessarily officious. Mary's faithful, if dejected, admirer had enough wit to obey the command instantly and to bear with an expression of humble remorse the tongue-lashing which his outraged commander dealt him.

"A week in irons is the least you deserve," he growled finally and Newton, feeling that his surroundings were unimportant since he could not be with Mary, was resigned to the decision. But the orders did not come. Captain Cartaret was a disciplinarian but he was also short-handed. Inquiries from Cleaver and Lewis when John's absence could not be hid disclosed that his tardiness was always due to the same cause. Presently when they left England this effect of infatuation would at least not disturb shipboard routine. Meanwhile twenty-five men were ill either in the cockpit or ashore. Newton had more naval experience and intelligence than most of the crew; he was not a drunkard, and he had some ability to command. Besides, putting an officer in irons was not good for discipline on the fore-deck.

"On second thoughts," he snapped, "you'd probably enjoy mooning in idleness, and there is too much work to be done on board. You'll perform double watch the next three weeks instead. But remember: this is the last time I put up with any nonsense from you. Step over the mark once more and you'll take the consequences, if your father were Admiral of the Fleet. I'm a man of my word and I'm at the end of my patience. Do you hear?"

"Aye, Sir!"

"Well, let's have some evidence of it." And John, uncertainty once removed, had little gratitude for the leniency of his treatment.

9

DAWN over Plymouth Sound on a calm March morning
should have been a grateful sight to any member of
the *Harwich*'s crew, or indeed of the other warships
and merchantmen which lay there, some damaged but all safe
after battling a day and a night with terrific gales off the
Cornish coast. But to the young midshipman lingering on
deck after his watch, relief at preservation was swallowed up
in a fierce renewal of longing, and the gracious beauty of
Devon's rolling hills beyond the tranquil bay accelerated the
corrosion of his surface resignation.

He had thought himself resigned. He had indeed written
to Mary, disobeying her mother's prohibition within three
weeks of their last meeting, to the effect that, since her father's
officiousness (which, he said, he was determined never to forgive) would keep him from seeing her, all countries were
nearly alike to him. He recalled the pains he had taken
with that letter, the phrases which he could not utter in her
presence coming so happily from his pen: "All the tender
emotions and pleasing inquietudes of a heart actuated by so
sincere and strong a passion as mine. . . . There is I know not
what within me that bears me up and assures me I shall certainly come home again; but whether it will be to any purpose, whether I shall be happy in you, or no, is what I long
to know, yet should dread to be resolved in. . . . The first day
I saw you I began to love you; the thoughts of one day merit-
ing you roused me from a dull insensible melancholy . . . and
pushed me into the world. My designs are now bent to one
point, this voyage which I seriously believe will make or marr
me . . . my hand has wrote nothing but what my heart dic-

tated, a heart incapable of Artifice and which I value only for its sincerity and unbounded passion for you. Could I write or speak less feelingly I perhaps might more engagingly. But I have tryed and find it impossible to assume an indifference in what is of so much importance to me. . . . I could run on to a volume but it would be quite needless, for it is not in the power of words to express with what ardency I am your most devoted. . . ."

She had received the letter without her mother's interception, his design having succeeded of sending it to her Aunt Hammond with a covering note in which he threw himself upon that kindly relative's mercy. She had not, it is true, acceded to his request for "a blank sheet of paper (if I could obtain nothing farther) directed to my father's house at Rotherhithe in your own hand"; but Mrs. Hammond had written an enclosure with a pair of knitted hose, hinting delicately that she had acted as messenger and Mary "was not at all displeased." The parcel had reached him just before the convoy set sail from the Downs and the exhilaration of its arrival had tided him over the finality of leaving England.

But now they were in England again, or so tantalizingly near that the opportunity seemed to be dangled by a whimsical fate to see if he had the courage to grasp it. Since his emancipation from religious belief, he had come to attach considerable importance to chance and omen. Even numbers were lucky for him. His birthday, July twenty-four, Mary's birthday, January twenty-two, December twelve, the day of their first meeting, the two dates of his escape from certain death he contrasted with July eleven, the day of his mother's death. He had been impressed on the *Betsey* on an uneven day and had been received on the quarter-deck on an even one. He suddenly realized that this morning was March the tenth and his feeling of restiveness increased.

Why had they put again into English waters? Once on their way down Channel, talk on the quarter-deck had been freer and five years was the term now mentioned as the probable duration of the voyage. The news had thrown John into a state of depression in which he felt like a caged creature and even Miles Cleaver forbore to rally him. Five years! In five years Mary would be twenty and what chance was there that some personable beau, some polite scoundrel would not have prevailed upon her father with wealth or upon her unsuspicious nature with devotion? And what opportunity after all did this voyage offer? The weekly pay of a first-lieutenant was only a guinea a week and the chances of his arriving at that exalted station on the *Harwich* was remote. Promotion depended on outside influence but also on the favour of his superiors and he had no delusions about the loss of favour which his impatience of restraint and his resentment at subservience had occasioned.

Then the unexpected had happened. The wind which had wafted the flotilla steadily down Channel past Hastings, the Isle of Wight, and Portland Bill, changed overnight and blew so strongly that the fleet took refuge in Tor Bay until it came round again next day, though blowing harder than before. Several ships of the Royal African Company, which had joined the convoy at Spithead, were driven on rocks as they tried to leave the harbour, and others, badly damaged, limped back into the bay for repairs. The *Harwich* with the rest continued on its course; but a black night of storm between the Eddystone Rocks and the Manacles caused such havoc, ship ramming ship in the seas' confusion, that with the coming of day Admiral Medley gave orders for the entire fleet to put in at Plymouth.

That had been yesterday. Exhaustion from a sleepless night and relief from hands and face nearly frozen in biting wind and cut by icy sails had left John numb and moving automatically. But a few hours of sleep in a steady hammock and the long watch while stars wheeled and faded in the dawning sky had brought his mind and heart to life again; and as thawing members feel exquisite agony so the resurgence of pain bit more sharply after brief anaesthesia.

He would *not* go to India. The resolve took sudden form in his mind and ran as a steady undercurrent to his thoughts as he performed the regular duties of his station and the unpredictable tasks which the lieutenants could impose at will.

"I just heard something that will interest you," said Job Lewis, joining him at dinner-time.

"Me or Cleaver?" asked John indifferently, his mind still groping for a way out.

"You. I was aft when Lieutenant Quayle came aboard to get some spare rigging for the Admiral's ship. I got a couple of tars to fetch it from the hold and heard a good deal of the talk. It seems Jenkins of the *Gray Doe* rode over from Tor Bay yesterday and they happened to mention your father's name. I pricked up my ears and sure enough, he has come down to see the damage — report on it to the African Company, most like."

His father was at Tor Bay. If he could see his father! Suddenly the scope of his determination widened. He would not go to India. But that was negative. That threw away the position and experience of this last year and left him farther than ever from Mary. He *would* go to Africa. The African ships were bound for the Guinea coast, a much shorter voyage. A merchant ship offered far more opportunity for a fortune-hunter than a man-of-war. He *would* go to Guinea. His father had been pleased with him of late. He would surely exert himself to obtain his son a transfer to the merchant navy. But how to see his father?

"I'd like to go ashore," he exclaimed, breaking a silence which had lasted since he finished eating and came out on deck.

"Do you think I shouldn't," grunted Lewis sweeping the horizon with a proprietory eye. "Not that this is my corner of Devon — but with luck I could be in Bideford in two days. It's a long time to be from home."

"But you wanted to go to sea," objected John who had pity for no one but himself at the moment. "And you have no — no — special reason to keep you here."

"I know," said Job equably. "It was the sea or farming and I'd like to see the world. But I never intended to see service on a man-of-war and the sooner I get off on a merchant-man once this trip is over the better I'll like it."

"Do you think the Captain would give me leave?" mused John.

Miles Cleaver would have become profoundly raucous at the speculation. Job looked at his friend sorrowfully.

"I am afraid that after your last default the Captain isn't inclined to grant you favours."

John cursed the Captain quietly but with thoroughness of coverage and an unusual juxtaposition of offensive epithets.

"Mr. Newton!" Both men jumped at the bark of command as if John's tirade had been overheard.

"Aye, Sir."

"Report to Captain Cartaret in his cabin at once, Sir."

"Aye, aye, Sir." John raised questioning eyebrows at his equally surprised friend, and obeyed.

"I'm sending a boat ashore," said the Captain almost before he entered. Philip Cartaret was a small thin man with a thin mouth and a thin voice. His success in the Royal Navy was due to uncompromising self-discipline — he had a weak stomach and invariably became sea-sick in rough weather — as much as to family influence. Whether his suffering broadened his rather narrow sympathies, he was on the whole a humane man and unusually considerate of his crew. "And I am obliged to send you with it."

"Aye, Sir," said John automatically, wondering if he were dreaming.

"Well, look alive, man! This is no evening at Ranelagh!" snapped Cartaret. He had done well by John Newton and felt a strong sense of injury that he had secured no domination over him either from fear or from obligation. Miles Cleaver's cynical assurance, the roistering behaviour of his second lieutenant, the scrupulous dignity of Lieutenant Rubin, these he could understand; they fitted into known patterns and were subservient to self-interest. But this young man with dreamy eyes which missed nothing, with a sardonic mouth which always spoke politely, this young man who acted incalculably and from no discernible impulse gave the impression of insubordination while he was completely subordinate. Captain Cartaret disliked mysteries and, understandably, had no time, if he had had inclination, for psychological study. But he recognized seamanship when he saw it and had admired several exhibitions of Newton's ease and skill. Moreover, though again the inconsistency irked him, the haughty quondam foremast-hand put up with no nonsense in his dealing with his inferiors and seldom had trouble when in charge of them.

"There are fourteen cases of shot at the dock, salvaged from

80

H.M.S. *Trelawney*. Mr. Snelling will take charge of the boat and bring it aboard. I'm sending you to keep an eye on the men while he's busy. One of them could give him the slip and with this trip ahead they may be restive. Keep them working. You should be back inside two hours."

"Aye, Sir. Mr. Snelling has his instructions, Sir?"

"Boat, men, and all. See that you bring them back. That is your one purpose in going."

It was not John's one purpose.

The ship's boat swept along the dock. John sprang from the bow and superintended its mooring. The bosun led his crew to the designated shed, the officer bringing up the rear, outwardly casual, inwardly tense. He had no use for deliberation. His mind had been made up from the first mention of shore, but his senses were alert for the chance of fulfilling his mind's design.

The last of the men disappeared inside the shed. John heard Snelling identify the cargo and apportion the men to their loads. Walking quietly and as of set purpose, he stepped from the busy quay to the lazy street and took the first turn to put a row of buildings between himself and the men in his charge.

Nightfall found him still walking, exultation at his escape gradually gaining ascendancy over the strain of watchfulness, which had made his stomach rise and fall with every sound till he got clear of Plymouth, and which had beset him with an almost irresistible desire to look over his shoulder, until miles of unimpeded travelling convinced him that he was not yet pursued. He had not dared to stop or hesitate or even ask the way. Fortunately he had a general idea of the country and the promise of a fair day had been abundantly fulfilled, so that he could walk in comfort and see without difficulty long after sunset. When he finally ventured to enquire, the man assured him that the road led to Dartmouth in a dialect so broad that John was glad of his initiation, through Job Lewis, into Devonshire idiom. Reassured, he continued in the starlight, only stopping after midnight to snatch some rest under a hedge and noting, as part of his luck, that spring had come early to the south and that he was able to sleep for two hours before the cold awakened him.

Mid-morning found him almost hilarious. The sky was

gray, but relief made the unfamiliar country more beautiful to him than when it was warmed with sunlight and he was chill with apprehension. He was hungry, for he had not ventured to enter the few inns he had passed and the supply of hardtack hastily thrust in his pocket before he left the ship was poor provision against twenty miles of vigorous walking. But, calculating his distances, he expected to be in Tor Bay with his father within two hours and with his goal in sight weariness and hunger were weightless. That his father would be angry, that he would refuse his request, that he was not closer — by years — than at the same time yesterday to achieving the summit of his hopes in Mary, his sanguine mind refused to consider. As for his broken trust — apart from amused speculation on the dismay of the boatswain and the baffled rage of the Captain he did not give it a thought. The red Devonshire earth, the blue Devonshire violets, the sweet Devonshire air all spoke of Mary to him and for the first time in months his spirits were gay.

A bend in the hedge-hidden road, one of many — but this bend revealed a party of redcoats, their officer on horseback advancing towards him. Either the full-throated chorus of birds had drowned the sound of their approach or his ear had lost its vigilance, but he was in full sight before he saw them and to turn would be disaster. So he kept on without a moment's variation of pace, head up with a swagger he was far from feeling, and hoped, in desperation which would once have found vent in prayers but now had no refuge, that they would accept his salute and pass by.

They came abreast on the narrow road.

"Halt," cried the lieutenant and John halted and saluted, looking him in the eye with an attempt at disconcerting hauteur.

"Your name, Sir, and ship?"

"John Newton, Sir, Midshipman of H.M.S. *Harwich* at anchor in Plymouth Sound."

"Whither bound?"

"To India, Sir, on escort duty."

"Not the ship," barked the lieutenant rudely. "You, Sir."

"To see my father, Captain Newton, at Tor Bay."

The officer hesitated, impressed in spite of suspicion by

John's manner and quick replies. Unfortunately his squad, sent out to round up deserters from the Tor Bay ships, was less easily impressed and more observant. John controlled his eyes and to some extent his voice, though it was higher than usual, but he had clenched his hands and the shock, coming upon his tiredness and hunger, made him short of breath. The men exchanged appropriate comments.

"Me father's Admiral Medley. Fair glad ter see me, 'e'll be."

"Yers. Too bad 'e didn't know you was coming. 'E'd have sent 'is horse for you to ride."

"Silence!" said the lieutenant, but he profited by the suggestion. "Yes, my man. Where is your horse?"

"I — I couldn't procure one, Sir."

"Shortage of 'orses," murmured the first humourist. "Orl the men got leave to see their fathers. So there wasn't any left."

"Where did you stay last night?" continued the officer sharply, by this time convinced that his foray for deserters was not to be unfruitful.

John was no liar and quick invention was beyond him.

"About turn. Back to Plymouth with you."

"I have told you the truth." John made a last effort. "My father is in Tor Bay inspecting the damaged ships of the Royal African Company. I am on my way to him."

"We'll see about that," said the lieutenant, who had ceased to believe in Captain Newton's existence. In the unlikely event of a midshipman's being granted leave when the fleet was virtually in passage, he would not walk twenty-five miles, still less if he were on an errand. "Now start walking, without any more argument. I make you one promise. If we find you've told the truth and we've inconvenienced you, I'll apologize. That's fair enough, isn't it?"

The men found the suggestion highly entertaining but there was nothing entertaining in their manner of falling in around Newton or in the business-like prod from the butt of a musket when he hesitated. His dream blackened into nightmare. Travel-sore and heart-sick, full of indignation, shame and fear, he was marched the next evening like a felon through the streets of Plymouth and, the officer's action found amply justified, was confined to the guard-house awaiting instructions from the ship.

Mercifully exhaustion claimed its due and the night passed in slumber, though a slumber not oblivious of misery. Somehow the next day dragged by and the next night, no word from outside breaking the interminable suspense; the harsh discomfort of cold cell and wretched food were almost unnoticed in the harsher discomfort, the deeper wretchedness of his thoughts.

The third day after his return he was led out, handed over to Lieutenants Rubin and Bowser, marched by the Sergeant at Arms to the quay past a curious idle throng, and put into the boat, the same boat over which he had held brief command. Sharply and unceremoniously, when they came astern, he was ordered up the ship's side and down into the hold, where he was handcuffed and left in pitch darkness and foul cold air and the lonely anticipation of unknown fate. Unable to stand upright, he felt out his length amid the casks and chests and lay, hand clasping clamped wrist, crying tears of bitterness and rage.

In spite of his isolation, the familiar though muted sounds of shipboard life, and the routine which gave grudging concession to his barest needs enabled John to measure the dreary passage of days. The seamen who brought rations of ship's biscuit and water attended to their duties without addressing him a word, and after his first questions met with no reply his pride kept him from inviting another rebuff. They were, surely by design, men who had some grudge against him, and their caustic comments and dark hints to each other while they moved briefly about by lantern light were not intended to raise the prisoner's spirits. Yet the appalling darkness, when light was removed, and the bleakness of his solitary thought made their coming a relief.

The darkness! How he hated darkness and had since childhood, when it had meant the withdrawal of his mother's presence, the loneliness of the house upstairs. All his life he had spent little time indoors when daylight and open country were available. But this was worse than any darkness he had endured. The hold of the *Betsey* had been lighted through a hatchway grating; the cell in the guard-house had marked

84

the day with a gray light through a barred slit in the stone
wall. This was the darkness of unbroken night and the darkness of captivity. The arrogant spirit which had fretted
against all restraint, craved absolute self-dominion, and recently exulted in release from all restrictions of belief, was
enslaved in a helpless, manacled body weakened and inwardly
cringing with fear.

Fear — he put what he had to fear out of his mind, and
again and again it seeped through the defence of his resolution as foul water slowly seeped through the bilge immediately below his prison. Light and liberty had been taken
from him at a stroke, but that he could have endured better
than the dark fire in his breast when he thought of Mary. The
dread that he had forfeited all hope of her love made him so
frantic with mordant recrimination that he wondered if he
would go mad. He who had craved only to love and to be
loved by one person, was pent here in the darkness, hated and
outcast and, with one exception, hating everyone.

He hated Lieutenant Rubin, the first cause of his present
distress. He hated the officer who had arrested him, the men
whose witticisms had confirmed their leader's wavering mind,
himself for his stupidity in showing confusion. The answers
he now rehearsed pitiably in the blank, stretching hours would
have convinced a major-general and set him free on his way
to his father. He hated his father, even while he pinned an
occasional fluttering hope on his interference to save him now;
hated him for not providing him with other business, hated
him for the lack of reconciliation with the Catletts which had
fatally jeopardized his position there, hated him for failing
to obtain his release from the Navy, hated him for taking a
small boy to sea, so that he was unfitted for other employment, hated him for all the slights and disappointments and
failings which surge up from the subconscious mind of a lonely sensitive child to feed an unsated hatred. He hated Captain Cartaret, the arbiter of his fate; and here his hatred was
mingled with gnawing fear. Surely a week or two in irons
was sufficient disgrace for a midshipman, he tried to convince
himself, and knew in the sinking pit of his stomach that it
would not be. Surely there were extenuating circumstances
which he could plead, he thought, refusing to remember the

repeated kindnesses he had betrayed. He would have hated God, but there was no God, only the memory of a constantly outraged Being who would have joined the rest in hating him.

The end, when it came, came suddenly. He had been dimly conscious, since the piping up of all hands which marked five a.m. of another day, that there had been unusual movement, an interruption of the rhythmic harbour routine. At first he thought they were under orders to hoist sail for departure but his experienced ear waited in vain for indicative sounds. Foreboding that they would hoist sail with him still caged on board led to such a resurgence of gloomy meditation that he lost interest in what was happening above deck. Then came a regular march of feet down the ladder, a dim lantern lighting the faces of the Master-at-Arms and an escort of marines. A spasmodic convulsion of his body produced the impulse of nausea without its relief. He stood, stooping under the low beams, at their challenge. His fetters were removed.

"Strip and put on these." The Master indicated some garments which a marine held out. Using his numb hands with difficulty Newton divested himself of the bedraggled breeches, waistcoat, hose, and jacket in which he had lived for a week and donned the pair of wide knee-length trousers and checked shirt of a common seaman. The square broke to take him into its centre, the command was given and the party moved ladder by ladder to the upper-deck.

The morning sunshine, the lovely land scent of a gentle offshore breeze striking his weakened senses after foul-smelling darkness, made him stumble. His escort jerked him upright and their march carried him across the deck to an appointed station where they stepped one pace back and left him, again alone but no longer hidden.

The deck had been so quiet when he emerged from the hatch that, blinded by the sun, he had thought it deserted. Now he saw, without raising his heavy eyelids, that the entire ship's company of over three hundred were ranged opposite. He straightened, thrusting out his chin in a determined and difficult effort to keep his head erect. He did not know how long he stood, the sun beating on his uncovered head, the deck unfamiliar to his bare feet, before the hatchway leading to the Captain's cabin was opened and Captain Cartaret, resplendent in blue and gold, with four other epauletted constituents of the court martial, appeared and took their seats at the table prepared for them.

Through the brief preliminaries John stood and moved and listened and gave the one or two fixed answers as in a daze. He heard his crime propounded and had a copy of the accusation thrust into his hands: "wilfully and of design . . . in open neglect and betrayal of trust . . . after frequent pardon and stern warnings for lesser offences. . . ." He heard section sixteen of the Articles of War: "Every person in or belonging to the fleet who shall desert or entice others so to do shall suffer death or/and other punishment as the circumstances of the offence shall deserve and as a Court Martial shall judge fit." And in a hush so deep that the breathing of three hundred and fifty men might have been suspended he heard . . . "whereas the court has been pleased to recommend mercy instead of the death sentence within its power . . . eight dozen strokes of the cat . . . after which. . . ."

He did not hear the rest. One will, one purpose, one thought alone was left him. Since there was no way out — and he had glanced sideways to estimate his chance of a dash to the side and a leap overboard, glanced and realized that he could not escape the vigilance of his guard and that if he could, the calm harbour would not cheat them of their prey — since there was no way out, he would endure in silence. If Mary heard of this — and the thought of her twisted his heart — she should not hear that her lover screamed and shrieked as he had heard men scream at the rope's end and under a dozen lashes.

At the order he removed his shirt, was led to the place of punishment, his feet tied to a grating, his arms lashed over the top of another on which he leaned. He was out of the daze now, the cherished flesh shrinking from its coming agony, the mind bent to master it in grim endurance. He heard Snelling, the boatswain, step forward to give the first dozen. It was coming — now!

The thudding blow with its nine-fold cut knocked the breath out of him — but he had not screamed. It could be borne, he told himself, clenching his teeth. He had taken it at school, flogging after flogging. Well, perhaps, for him that his first master had been notorious for brutality. Such pain, such pain, such pain he had survived when small, he could surely bear now. There, the first dozen was over, and a tiny respite from the pain-on-pain while the boatswain's mate took his place.

He would count — add — subtract — something to fix his mind on — something to remind him that this would pass, that every stroke — counted — would come no more and left one less to endure. His school-day floggings were left behind. He had never felt pain like this. Another dozen. There was respite too — he must think or he would die — in the last few strokes of each dozen, as the flogger's arm tired before another came fresh with the first unendurable blow. How much pain could one endure? Spartan boys, he had read somewhere, had submitted to be flogged to death without crying, for the honour of a prize. It was a Spartan boy too, it was, who suffered a fox to tear out his vitals rather than reveal that he was concealing it. So could he, so could he, so could he.

In the midst of agony he felt wetness on his chin and tasted blood. He had bitten his lips till they bled, but what was that to his torn bleeding back? He became conscious of a new sound, a strange, dull yet whistling echo of each thudding blow, a sound like a trapped animal gasping its life away. It was, he found with numbed surprise, his own breathing, forced from him in long shuddering gasps. Suddenly he was angry with a wave of murderous, strengthening anger which enabled him to hold on and out while once again the instrument of torture changed hands. For its brief duration the pain was swallowed up in rage at the indignity; and he inwardly cursed and cursed and cursed everyone who had a part in this needless wilful breaking of wholeness, this defacing and lacerating of a body which had been intended to know and protect and love Mary.

Mary — he seized on the name which he had put out of his mind lest it be defiled by association with this beastliness and horror. It was his talisman now, and from it came the thought which carried him when he thought he could no longer resist the relief of venting his anguish in moans. If this were for Mary, if he were bearing this to keep her from pain, *then* he would endure. So in a way it was; it was for her that he had incurred it. Mary, Mary, Mary, Mary, he breathed her name with every blow; he had lost count, he could not think, he was no longer a man, merely a throbbing agony, a blur of exquisite pain.

He did not know when the Pipe Down came, when he was untied, caught as he fell, covered with a piece of sail and carried below. He did not know that a young marine had fainted or that his stoical endurance was the subject of many covert admiring comments, or that the Captain, on retiring to his cabin, had taken three glasses of wine to recover from the ordeal. Philip Cartaret did not enjoy inflicting this type of correction. Since it had to be, he was glad that in this case the victim was John Newton, for whom his rebuffed kindness had turned to implacable anger. But the latter part of the long-drawn torture had been a sickening time and anxious, for he did not want the boy to die. Several times he had thought of calling a halt, and each time his pride and sense of out-raged justice had prevailed. But he was glad that this phase of the punishment was over. The rest would be hard on Newton, but not on others.

Down in the cockpit the marines deposited John on the floor, called the surgeon and awaited his orders. A new and pressing case of illness had at the last moment excused this hard-working official from attending the performance on deck and he came, stooping under the close-slung hammocks of two dozen men, and lifted his lantern to examine his new charge. A small, stout, anxious man, new to the service, he took one look, dropped on his knee to feel the patient's pulse, shook his clenched fists at the ceiling and evidently committed the ship's command to the infernal powers.

"Here, Mr. Robinson," he said wearily at last. "Come and tell me what we shall do with this. It's enough to drive a man mad! Twenty-five we've had to send ashore to hospital and as many here in conditions not fit for pigs — and as though we hadn't enough to heal, they go and break them to give us more work."

"Why didn't they hang him from the yard arm and be done with it?" growled Robinson.

"Well, it's not for us to say. But I hope it doesn't happen again or when the ship's at sea," said Mr. Dene. "Look you, we can't put him in a hammock. Lay a pallet there. Now lads, heave him over gently. And keep out of mischief or it'll be one of you next."

John was too strong to be fully unconscious even at this stage. The pain of being turned on his side to have a dram of rum poured down his throat, the rum itself, the stinging agony of liquor applied to sterilize his flayed flesh, brought him effectually from the stupefaction into which he had been beaten to acute suffering. For days he lay face downward, falling asleep in snatches to be awakened by a new twinge of sharper pain as an inadvertent movement awoke a dormant muscle or opened a half-healed sore. Fortunately his body was proof against the germ-laden air and fought its way stubbornly back to the life for which he had no desire. In little more than a week his scars were in healthy enough condition for the surgeon to dismiss him from hospital where the wretchedness of others accentuated his own. Then he entered upon a prolonged wretchedness unshared by anyone else on board.

The final words of the Captain's sentence, obscured by the shock of impending punishment but rising to his consciousness in the long days and nights of convalescence, had decreed that he be stripped of his rank and degraded to his original position on board. Later his former associates had been strictly forbidden to have any communication with him at all.

At first, John had been as indifferent to the surgeon's rough pity as to his mate's callousness. But as, day after day, he was unvisited even by message or inquiry, he became incredulously bitter and when, receiving orders to report for duty on the forward deck, he was passed without a word by three midshipmen, two of whom were Lewis and Cleaver, he was furious to find that his suffering could be increased. The rude reception accorded him by the sailors, his reintroduction to duties and surroundings which seemed worse by contrast with the privileges he had recently enjoyed, could not move him to such desolation as the defection of friends.

That night he was standing on deck by the bowsprit, staring down into the black water which lapped the ship's nose. Sleep in a hammock was still impossible and the crowded foc'sle a place of loathing. For the first time he was thinking of suicide, not with the wild fleeting impulse of fear or dis-

90

appointment, but in the grim seriousness of settled despair. A step behind him he thought the step of the larboard-watch, and prepared to answer if challenged.

"John," said Job Lewis in a whisper. "John, how are you? I —"

"You weren't interested this afternoon," returned John contemptuously. "And I'm not interested in friendship that is ashamed to show itself before the world. Keep it."

"John, I'm sorry. You don't understand. The Captain has ordered all of us to have nothing to do with you, not even to speak. He threatens, if we do, it will be worse for you as well as for us. You don't think we — I enjoy it, do you?" He changed the pronoun out of honesty, remembering that Miles had declared himself completely through with a fool who would bring such a fate on himself. "Most of us felt sick about it."

It was not balm but it was one hurt less.

"Thank you, Job." Both men kept their voices to the lowest possible murmur, scarcely distinguishable from the night sounds of the heavy rigging as the ship rode the harbour swell. "Have you heard any news? Does my father know? What talk of sailing?"

"In a day or so, I think. One piece of news but nothing to cheer you. Admiral Medley came on board yesterday to inspect. I was on the bridge when they were talking and heard your name; so I made myself scarce and listened. He'd had the report of the court martial and asked if the Captain would consider transferring you to another ship. Cartaret refused point-blank, though he was most deferential. 'I certainly will not', he said, 'if you leave the choice to me, Sir. That healthy young whelp has recovered already,' he said, 'and if he gets a transfer, it's what he set out for in the first place, and what is my position with my crew? I'm not a hard commander, Sir, but I will be obeyed or I'll give up my ship. Newton or no Captain Newton, I don't play favourites, and that young man will learn it, if it's the last thing I do.' Medley didn't press the point. 'You are Captain of the *Harwich*, Mr. Cartaret,' he said and that was the end. I must leave now. Cheer up, John. Remember what Horace says about Fortune. And don't forget how I feel when I have to ignore you."

91

Neither Horace's philosophy nor Lewis's reluctance shed any ray of light on the darkness of John's mind when some days later he saw the English shore receding from his view. The intervening time had been unpleasant enough. Those who felt sorry for him dared not show it; but nothing hindered the others from showing ill-will. Taunts about his disgrace, infliction of labours which his scarcely healed stripes made an agony, a hundred little deprivations and needless insults made life the more unbearable because he had no recourse, not even one friend to hear a complaint.

But all faded into insignificance as, seeing the rolling water steadily increasing between ship and shore, he felt that he was being forcibly torn from his beloved. The prospect had been bad when he was an officer; it goaded him to the mad attempt which had borne such evil harvest. Now it was more than likely that he would never see her again. As midshipman he had had access to the ship's log and had a clear idea of the high mortality rate aboard a man-of-war on shorter and less hazardous voyages. Even if he should return, his present condition and its hopelessness of improvement guaranteed the failure of his aspiration.

The green hills had imperceptibly lengthened and straightened into a soft blue band; it blurred into haze and was gone. Gaunt with yearning John looked down at the sea furrowing steadily out from the ship's side and felt helpless against the impulse to throw himself into it.

"Mr. Snelling!" A crisp formal voice behind him carried instant recognition with it. Lieutenant Grossmith, he thought dully, keeping still to avoid the pointed discourtesy of a junior officer whom he had never liked. "Captain Cartaret requests me to inquire how much longer Newton is to consider himself a mere passenger on board. He seems to have time to do nothing. The Captain suggests that you find some task to keep him from his present boredom. He needs to practice his seamanship after his enforced idleness."

"Lieutenant Grossmith, Sir," said Snelling, "I shall carry out the order with pleasure. Newton, you bloody young swine, turn around here. And salute when you're spoken to." John turned a livid face to the supercilious stare of his former associate and the pleased officiousness of the warrant officer, and in default of alternative obeyed. "Stop malingering there or I'll give you a reminder with a rope's end. You hear what the Captain says. Let's see how your sea legs are. Up the maintop-gallant masthead, right to the cross-trees, instanter."

The task under normal circumstances was a light one. John had been up the masthead any number of times as sailor or midshipman. But the needless imposition, the public taunt under amused eyes of quarter-deck and forecastle roused him from grief to unappeasable fury. Climbing was torture. It called into play all the bruised muscles of back and shoulders, and, in increasing giddiness, he discovered for the first time since he was dismissed from hospital how deep-seated were the effects of shock in his system. But he made the ascent, past the maintop, the maintop-masthead and stopped at length, not daring to look at the dizzy drop of one hundred and forty feet, and clinging with a determination at complete variance from his near embrace of death a few moments before. He would die, on that his heart was more than ever set, but at his own time and by his own means, and not — the decision, long nascent, had come to birth during the climb — until he killed Captain Cartaret.

10

JOHN stirred in his hammock, turned, and deliberately
settled himself to sleep again. He knew he should be
up. The boatswain's piping and the scrambling of
others into their clothes and up to the deck had awakened him
from a vivid, satisfying dream in which he had watched the
death-throes of the Captain. That it was still a dream and
not a reality was due neither to a change of his attitude nor
to an improvement of his condition. The weeks of sailing
to Madeira, the days moored there in Funchal Road while
the convoy took on provisions and conferred with the Commodore, had been a time of unrelieved gloom. The pleasure
unhappy men seek in a butt for ridicule was not likely to abate
when one was provided whom they could bait or blame with
impunity; and nothing in Newton's sullen demeanour or
smouldering resentment was conducive to conciliation. De-
spising his messmates, detesting his former friends, hating the
Captain, he was prolonging his own existence merely with a
view to revenge.

But revenge was not easy. His mind, corroded with venom,
planned simple or elaborate methods of murder only to find
a flaw in each. He planned it with a cutlass, with pistols (to
be stolen when the time was ripe), with a club. He fixed
times and watched movements until he could give the daily
schedule of everyone on board. But the great hindrance was
the uncertainty. The blow or shot or stab *must* be fatal and
administered in such circumstances that he could jump overboard before being seized. He would *not* undergo punishment for a simple act of justice. He would not suffer again.

Once in the sea he would not come to the surface, not, that is, until it was too late.

So far, in spite of vigilance, the opportunity had not presented itself. And on occasion, although he had no compunction or fear about the deed which he committed repeatedly and with satisfaction in imagination, nor about putting an end to his own intolerable existence, he was held back, as by a restraining hand, by the thought of Mary. Not that he had any hope of winning her — the physical and mental pain of his punishment had eclipsed even the ignis fatuus which sometimes outlasts possibility — but she would, he was sure, eventually learn how he died. And she would, he was equally sure, think such a death somehow mean and ignoble. He could not bear that she should think badly of him when he was dead.

These melting moods usually led his mind into other channels. The eager desire which the very recollection of her person aroused in him had been generally tolerable while he hoped to possess her. Now, cut off from all companionship and interests, treated with contempt by offscouring of jails and wharves, he was driven within for some satisfaction, some ground for self-esteem. Not unnaturally his maltreated body, regaining health and vigour in spite of itself, recalled and re-enacted the sensations of its delighted acceptance by women, and imagination tantalized the passions that it fed.

John turned again in the hammock, glad that the foul air was a little lighter since his companions had departed. He was in no hurry to face another dreary day on the ship and he had been refused even the task of rowing to shore in cutter or yawl to fetch cargo. He would probably be punished for this infringement of rule but, good or bad conduct being regarded alike in him, he had made no effort to do good service and was calculating in disobliging the officers without actual insubordination. Only alone like this or on deck at night could he find any respite. And tomorrow they were weighing anchor for the Cape of Good Hope, a euphemism if ever he had heard one.

There was a brisk exchange of voices overhead and a step on the forecastle ladder. John lay still with eyes closed, even when the intruder made his way through the lines of ham-

95

mocks still unstowed, for it was not yet seven-thirty, and stood beside him.

"Time you were up, Newton." It was Miles Cleaver and John refused to open his eyes at the good-natured asperity of his tone. "Come," he repeated, "I know you're not asleep. You never liked early rising and you haven't changed. Hurry, I have no time to waste."

"Go away, Miles." The familiarity was John's retort for the other's assumption of authority. At least his instructor in free-thinking and philosophy would not find his spirit cowed by circumstance. "You have enough underdogs to bully. Can't you leave me alone?"

There was a moment's silence in which John thought he had gained his point. Then Miles spoke again, the good-nature gone from his voice.

"You're no philosopher, Newton. You'll never learn."

His knife cut through the lashings at the foot of the hammock and John fell with it to the floor.

"Now," he went on, "you see I mean business. Too bad you always ask for proof. Get out on deck before I have to carry the complaint higher up."

Seething but powerless, John stood up, catching at the covering to hide his naked back with its shameful scars from Cleaver's uncaring eyes. The latter turned curtly and went up on deck and John, once more reminded of his hateful position, presently followed.

Standing for a moment in the morning sun, half-expecting a reprimand or imposition for his tardiness, he was suddenly aware that a jolly-boat was lying alongside and that Joe Hogg, a seaman who had recently occupied the next hammock, was dropping his belongings into it.

"Where are you going?" he asked, catching the man's arm as he brushed past to re-enter the forecastle.

"Leaving you for the Guinea ship over there. Two of their men for two of ours. Commodore's orders. Lucky, eh?"

He disappeared. I will *not* go to India; I *will* go to Guinea: John heard the words he had uttered at Plymouth. Shocked into action, he looked around wildly. Lieutenants Rubin and Bowser were standing amidships. No other emigrant sailor was in sight.

"Hold the boat, hold it for just ten minutes," he called hoarsely, and ran to the lieutenants. No pride, no sullenness, no stoical composure mattered, and somehow the desperate longing of his soul overcame their indifference and dislike.

"Lieutenant Rubin, Sir, Lieutenant Bowser, I beg of you. Two men are required for the other ship. Let me be one. Intercede with Captain Cartaret." He hesitated, casting all his new hope on the efficacy of his plea. "It's nothing to you. It is everything to me. Put yourselves in my place, I pray you, do."

Rubin looked at him, then at Bowser. He had never had occasion to like John since dodging his blow on the Surrey docks, but he had a strong sense of caste and shared with some of his fellow-officers regret that John's punishment had lowered his class before the foremast rabble.

"Might as well go as another?" was all he said and they strode off with no little dignity, leaving John rooted to the spot in fearful hope.

He had not seen the Captain on the quarter-deck but, following the officers with his eyes, he tried to read in the exchange of salutes, the gestures, the pose, as they stood talking earnestly, the signs which would decide his fate.

It was over quickly. Rubin returned and did not leave him in suspense.

"Captain Cartaret consents," he said, not unconscious of magnanimity, for he had pleaded strongly. "He is sending your dismissal at once. Be ready in ten minutes."

"In less, Sir," said John and found some words to express gratitude, the first such words that he had required or wanted for many weeks. Still unbelieving, he was afraid to spend any time below lest the boat leave without him, and accordingly snatched only such belongings as came quickly to hand. Before his written release arrived he had taken his place in the jolly-boat of the Guinea ship.

What Philip Cartaret's thoughts were, as he saw the small craft bearing his stormy petrel out of his ship and life, John never knew. Perhaps the implacable resentment, which had rejected Admiral Medley's request at Plymouth and expressed itself repeatedly in inflicting shame or hardship whenever John crossed his path, had sated itself at last. Perhaps the disagreeable consciousness of John's steady hatred was a strain on a man who in general did his best for his crew. Perhaps he welcomed a chance to dispose, without loss of face, of a potential trouble-maker. The all-important fact was that he had yielded. Why, John did not care.

His own thoughts during the short passage to the Guinea merchantman were startlingly clear, as if the flood of relief had washed away the rusty residuum of unexpectant lethargy which had weighted them for so long. He was free, and so suddenly free that there could be no sobriety, no moderation in his consideration of his freedom; free from the scene of his captivity and disgrace, free from the comrades of his prosperity and his misery, free from the particular bondage which had made him the victim of every vicious whim and from the general discipline against which he had chafed, free from the lengthy nightmare absence from England, free for the shorter voyage he had craved.

He took one last backward look at the *Harwich* and ran an experienced affectionate eye over the *Pegasus*. A Snow, slightly more capacious than his last Mediterranean vessel, she would carry a crew, he estimated, of twenty-five. There would be room after the crowded fore-deck of the warship, and not a soul on board knew him. Apart from Hogg beside him, a quiet harmless lad, he was free of his past. Free — the advantage flashed suddenly to his mind and increased his gloating. All the taboos, the superstitious fears which had been his when he boarded the *Harwich,* all the vestiges of his ascetic control: they had been swept away when he cast off his old religious beliefs; but some sense of shame, of not indulging openly in the practices he once condemned, had kept him under an odd sort of conventional restraint. Now he was free, free to do what he liked without control. Shaftesbury might be surprised to find how literally he intended to take his injunction to discover for himself what Virtue was. He was glad Cleaver had explained the real meaning of Virtue — how thankful he should be, not to but for Cleaver, as an instrument of fate. But for his high-handed act in cutting down the hammock! John shivered with the delight of actuality. He glanced down at the small bundle of clothes and read the title of the single book he had snatched in his haste. Barrow's

Euclid! It had caught his eye in the book-stall in Portsmouth just before the *Harwich* sailed, and with his usual curiosity he had decided to master it. Not the book he would have chosen perhaps. His Shakespeare, his Milton, his Shaftesbury, his Voltaire, all left behind. Still — nothing could dull the beauty of the present and the future. Even Euclid might be useful.

11

CAPTAIN Guy James Penrose of the Guinea Snow, *Pegasus,* was standing on the quarter-deck when the men climbed aboard. John was conscious of observation, but even the fleeting wish that he were still in his midshipman's jacket and rank could not quench his exhilaration. A second-mate carried their credentials to the Captain, who glanced at them without much interest. Captain Penrose was feeling aggrieved. Usually the business of sending men aboard a man-of-war was a relief, even though the goods received in exchange were seldom of first quality. The threat of being sent aboard a warship was always a powerful deterrent to men of the merchant fleet and those disposed of in this way were usually proven trouble-makers. On this occasion, however, Sir George Pocock, giving precedence to the needs of the *Harwich,* had ruthlessly commandeered two good men, one of them a carpenter, from the *Pegasus,* and the Captain, with months of sailing ahead, felt their loss. War was on and duty was duty, but Penrose felt that the action was high-handed and somehow reflected on his dignity. His feeling was aggravated too by the bad impression he thought it might make on his passenger, Mr. Clow, who had acquired quarter interest in the ship and was returning on her to Africa.

"Send the men to me, Mr. Bates."

"Aye, Sir."

"John Newton." Captain Penrose looked from the chit in his hand to the gaunt but stalwart sailor before him. "I knew a Newton some years ago in the Mediterranean, Captain Newton. I scarcely suppose *you* are related."

"He is my father, Sir."

The Captain's pleasure in discovering a friend's son and a skilful seaman, his willingness to overlook what John could not conceal of the reason for his demotion and to assist him within his power, were of short duration. John was pleased with the recognition, more pleased with the predisposition to leniency which such recognition betokened. But his recent treatment made him look askance at friendliness. It was no part of his exuberant sense of liberty to confine his propensities in order to curry favour with his superiors; and he regarded the *Pegasus* and his sojourn on it less as means to an end than as a small stepping-stone to other means. The Captain, a fussy man of uncertain temper and no settled standards or convictions, was not likely to inspire him with a desire to please. And when he observed shrewdly, during the comparatively leisurely days at sea and the novel business of trading, that he was largely dependent on the first-mate for initiative, and anxious to make a good impression on his employer-passenger, John regarded him with indifferent contempt.

A much greater factor in determining the bent of his conduct was his popularity with the crew, a heady popularity without any precedent in his career. When he thought about it at all, he realized that on all previous occasions his relationship with such a group had been subject to restriction. At school first cowed, then precocious, on his father's ship under surveillance, in later voyages half-ascetic, half-arrogant, and during his vicissitudes on the *Harwich* never mentally or physically his own master, now for the first time he came among strangers completely indifferent to their opinion, completely unhampered by scruples. These two sure qualifications for social acceptance were enhanced by the super-abundance of animal spirits which marked his release from bondage. Always a good talker with an audience, he spiced the mess-talk of men tired of one another's company, and the mind in which profanity had been stored since childhood with horrid fascination produced it now in unabashed profusion.

In fact, now that God and the fear of God had ceased to exist, John found an excessive, but not irrational pleasure in showing his independence by blasphemy. Oaths merely to bolster a weakness of vocabulary he despised, as he did the weak-mindedness of Joe Hogg, who was horrified by his atheism, and yet blasphemed the God to whom he admitted praying. Newton, his memory stocked with Scripture verses, catechetical questions, and stanzas of children's hymns, amused himself by composing parodies on the phrases which had once filled him with fear, and soon discovered that his uninhibited tongue was regarded with admiration by his profane associates. Proficient seamanship and foolhardy daring — for with his change of fortune had come the sense that he bore a charmed life — joined with unresting ingenuity in promoting some escapade, soon made him the acknowledged leader.

This leadership and his irresponsible use of it could not fail to bring him in an unfavourable light to Captain Penrose's attention and in a still less favourable light to that of Josiah Blunt, who was first-mate and the martinet that his commander would never be. The Captain did not expect his sailors to be continent. On a long voyage, the most trying part of which was still to come, he took for granted that they would seize opportunities for normal indulgences. He himself, although he confined his attentions more strictly to Mrs. Penrose while he was in England than did many husbands, regarded the marriage vow of "cleaving only" as automatically suspended when the act of cleaving was rendered impossible by distance and time. He recalled Captain Newton as an austere and formal man, but he was not surprised to find his son sowing a record crop of wild oats, and cared little for that or the snatches of gaudy blasphemy which he overheard, as long as the boy's conduct did not impair his own efficiency or that of the crew. But when young Hogg lay dangerously ill with fever for days after a drinking contest which John had promoted — acting as umpire himself because he knew his limited capacity for liquor — and when half the crew escaped with minor cuts from a brawl in which infuriated natives almost succeeded in firing their boat, he reprimanded the ring-leader sharply, and gave him a week's double duty, the only result of which was to arouse his resentment and determination to be avenged for the slight. Blunt urged that he be put in irons, but short-handed, with illness a constant factor and with slaves daily coming aboard, to have a white man, a healthy and popular one, confined, appealed to the Captain as neither diplomatic nor practical. Also Mr. Clow advised against it.

Amos Clow had been, almost from the time of Newton's arrival on the *Pegasus,* the only person who commanded his attention. A great barrel of a North Country man with a red rugged face and sharp calculating eyes, he was perhaps twice John's age and a personality to be reckoned with. From observable facts and highly coloured rumours on the fore-deck John soon pieced together a story which made him tingle with admiration and envy. Clow was obviously a favourite of Fortune. From nothing, they said, and certainly his speech betokened no formal education, he had become a virtual potentate and lived farther down the coast in conditions which seemed to the English sailors like those of the Arabian Nights. In John's moments of sober reflection, when the never-absent thought of Mary became an ache and not a goad, he dreamed that he could do what Clow had done but with a different end in view. It was not in his nature to scheme; he waited instead for the turn of Fortune's wheel in the arrival of opportunity.

Meanwhile, as the *Pegasus* pursued her undulating way past the Canaries and down the Guinea coast towards Gambia, John was introduced to the strange fumbling business of buying human beings. With the actual purchase the sailors had nothing to do. Sometimes three or four were brought aboard; sometimes the Captain went ashore to inspect a dozen offered for sale by other blacks with some knowledge of lingua franca, more often by white or mulatto traders.

On the first of these trips, John with seven others manned an oar in the barge which bore the Captain and Clow to shore. It was almost a pleasure journey over a friendly sea with the commodity brought within a stone's throw of the landing. Half the crew remained at the water's edge. John and three others carried a keg of brandy, several chests of gunpowder, and a bale of cloth to the village square, and stood back to watch the procedure.

New impressions crowded on him more thickly than his mind could deal with them: the slaves — seven men, four boys, five women — stood, bound and naked, strange, wild, sullen or terrified creatures, while the chief who had them for sale

103

talked volubly and Clow interpreted laconically. John, with his smattering of French and Spanish, his few phrases of Italian, and his quick ear for language, listened avidly, guessing at and storing up the meaning of repeated words accompanied by elucidating gesture. Much bartering was involved. His curious mind noted the varying prices and he glanced at each slave selected to ascertain the standards of evaluation. At first he had comprehended them in a single glance, with the same passing stir of pity because of their fetters that he might have felt towards a chained dog. Now he regarded them individually, endeavouring to see them, not through the eyes of the Captain but through the eyes of the successful trader whom he felt a vague desire to emulate.

"Not that one," he heard Clow say, after a quick negative remark to the chief, who threw up his hands and responded with a torrent of refutation. "Long-breasted. Fetch far less at Antigua. Never take a long-breasted woman except as fill. Now this next one is worth —"

Newton noted the deformity and let his eyes pass to the next, puzzled by a new note in Clow's tone. The second was young, taller than the others, the bronze body and supple throat faultless. Suddenly he realized, wondering that to him so susceptible the realization was late in coming, that these items of exchange were women. A glance at Clow's face and at the hungry eyes of the other sailors informed him that they had realized it long before. And something in the pitiful eyes of the girl and of the other women huddled beside her told him that they recognized in the expression of these terrifying white monsters an unmistakable Esperanto.

Any faint scruples concerning the double difficulties of women slaves vanished from John's mind with habituation. As they continued down the Windward Coast they fell in with other ships bent on the same trade. Rivalry ran high and trips in the long-boat, usually under the first or second-mate, sometimes lasting a month, were attended by dangers and difficulties which made the immediate existence of slaves on board a slowly filling ship by no means pitiable in comparison. Drenched by the dews or the rains, in an uncovered boat, exposed to strange reptiles and insects, often ambushed by natives who were avenging an injury done them by the last

104

London crew — they would never punish an English boat for the wrong of a French one and even distinguished nicely between English ports — involved in fights because of the sailors' reckless lust: scarcely a crew returned without illness aboard.

On the *Pegasus* the women and boys were segregated from one another and from the men — that is from the black men. But sailors, told off to bring them daily up on deck, to wash, shave, and anoint them in order to keep them as valuable as possible for market, found ample occasion to carry out the design for which they had marked down their prey as soon as they were brought aboard.

Some few ship captains, John knew from current gossip, restrained the conduct of their crew on board and maintained a strict and difficult discipline. Captain Penrose was of the majority. Several of the choicest specimens, including the girl whom Clow had so highly appraised, were kept as servants and interpreters on the quarter-deck, and the sailors' comments on the duties performed for the officers were many and ribald.

From this aspect of lewdness John at first kept aloof. Opportunities on shore were numerous enough to allay, if not to satisfy, an appetite which grew with feeding. Besides, whenever he touched a woman he thought of Polly, and though the idea of her never kept him from indulgence, yet somehow for her sake he tried to be as gentle as his headlong passion permitted. The helplessness of these victims, the hopelessness of either refusal or resistance, put any thought of solicitation, except in rare cases, out of the men's minds; and several sailors were given a round dozen with the cat, not for moral turpitude but for devaluating items of cargo.

"Cargo!" said John, revolted. "You talk as if they were animals."

"So aren't they?" asked the boatswain's mate, Hugh Black, nettled. He had a smattering of theological jargon and argued interminably against John's free-thinking principles. "Or if they're human we're doing them a favour. It says in the Bible that the twain become one flesh. Now if these poor heathen become one flesh with us Christians they may have a chance of escaping hell. Of course, you don't believe in hell but you'll find out when you get there. So lay off preaching."

Preaching! The idea was anathema to Newton and the bare-faced speciousness of Hugh Black's argument, received in a roar of applause, was amusing. But the women were safe from violation while under his care and, when he found one of his mates molesting a ten-year-old girl, he first ordered, then hauled him away, and, as the man proved ugly, fought him into unconsciousness.

As Clow was still on board, bent on seeing that the ship in which he had invested his money carry a good cargo, and as the long-boat journeys were trying and perilous, Captain Penrose was content to leave most of the shore trips in charge of the trader and the mate. When they reached the Benanoes, however, Clow invited the commander to pay a visit of several days to his establishment there. The party set out in the long-boat and John, delighted that his curiosity was at last to be gratified, manned an oar.

They were already within a little natural harbour in sight of the landing place when a small boat hailed them. "Yellow Jim, Captain Penrose," commented Clow. "Bringing you some slaves, by the look of it."

The boat came alongside. It contained the mulatto recognized by Clow, two blacks at the oars, and two slaves, a fourteen-year-old boy and a remarkably perfect woman, his sister, some years older. Their father and her husband had both been killed in a feud, Yellow Jim explained by way of credential of his right to sell. He was giving Mr. Clow's captain first choice.

The boats rocked side by side while Penrose and Clow conferred. It was a good buy. The price was set, the haggling finished. Penrose glanced over his crew distrustfully till his eye fell on Newton. His dislike of this assured youngster was growing, but, although the young man did as little work as he could and that with annoying reluctance, he was honest. Amid all the petty pilfering which went on aboard and in the ship's boats John had been free of accusation or suspicion. And he was capable of holding authority.

"Here, Newton."

"Aye, Sir." John realized what was coming and his expression belied the willingness of his words.

"Go back to the ship with Yellow Jim. Pay him off. The purser will deal out the goods. Ours are stowed away here. Take special care of those two — they are expensive. I put them in your charge. Fine, Mr. Clow. Dougall, take Newton's oar. We needn't interrupt our trip."

John's face, as he swung himself wordlessly into the small boat, indicated that the solution was anything but fine. He had waited for this day and hoped to find some opportunity of speaking to Clow. Now, out of all the crew, he was sent back to cool his heels on the ship.

He began to swear before the boat was well out of earshot and continued at intervals without repeating himself until it reached the ship, much to the admiration of Yellow Jim, whose knowledge of English was fragmentary but who knew a round and vigorous vocabulary when he heard one. The blacks rowed stoically, deftly managing a boat not designed for the open sea. From the woman and her brother crouched again in the bow there was no sound.

The business on board ship was soon transacted. Yellow Jim bowed himself quickly over the side and the boat began its bobbing way to land. John was alone with his charges. With half the crew ashore and some eight-score slaves to be tended, the second-mate, who was in charge, made no effort to interfere with his orders.

He hesitated a moment before untying the rope which fastened the two together. Somehow he was unwilling to take the woman below to the boy's barricade to see him fetter her brother there. It was even less desirable to take the boy into the women's quarters. Neither could be left on deck alone unless stapled to the ring bolts. He opened his mouth to hail someone to assist him and closed it with sudden decision.

There were three cabins empty on the quarter-deck. Driving his charges before him he motioned the woman inside the first, which happened to be Mr. Blunt's, and knotted the rope through a ring on the lid of his big sea-chest. Then he took the boy below deck and, with a half-ironical "Lemmi" to the wary group already there, fettered him hand and foot, glanced sharply over the boys to see that nothing untoward was in progress, looked at his captive again, said the Sherbro words for "bring food and drink" and turned abruptly away. The look on the boy's face brought back the memory of a boy he had seen when he was last in London, a boy of the same age standing with others in a cart on its way to Tyburn. At least, he told himself, this boy wasn't going to be hanged — and if he was flogged occasionally, so had he been and thousands more like him.

The woman did not move from her seat on the sea chest as he entered. When he told her to stand she obeyed and he saw that she was crying. His hands fumbled, untying the rope, and touched her. She shivered at his touch and he did not think the shiver was of loathing. The tears and the shiver changed her from an unwelcome charge into a woman, changed him from an irritated boy into a hungry man with food unexpectedly in sight. Captain Penrose, he thought a few minutes later, when he could think again, would doubtless not include this treatment — at least not on his, John Newton's part — as strictly within the meaning of "special care." The Captain be everlastingly cursed! He was justified in taking — and giving — the compensation within his power.

The crew of the long-boat, returning two days later, brought glowing accounts of the elaborate style of Clow's temporary quarters and fantastic stories of the mistress of the establishment. The trader was planning to move, it was rumoured, to the Plantanes but meanwhile the riches of his table, even the food provided for the foremast hands, made the mouths of their ship-bound companions water. Nor did their description of fresh fowl, fruit, and wine sent aboard for the Captain's table do anything to add contentment, when a dismal, meat-flavoured concoction of dried beans made its way for the third time that week to their mess. John looked at it in violent disgust, rose to his feet and made the sign of the cross backwards.

"What are you up to now?" asked Hugh Black.

"Saying the infernal grace for you ungrateful Christians," retorted John, and contined, intoning, "Glory be to the Captain, and to the mate, and to our Holy Clow — for this mess at it was in the beginning, is now and ever shall be, world without end. Amen."

The roar of applause was out of all proportion to the wit and John knew it, but it encouraged him to fresh effort.

"It's a hard life, the Captain's. We shouldn't complain. Think of the weary round of social activity while he has to drink till all hours on the other ships —"

"And we have to wait up till 'e gets 'is blooming foot aboard."

"Fie," went on John reprovingly. "Could you sleep, uncertain of your Captain's safety? Then think of his anxiety when the boats are up the rivers trading —"

"'im sleeping on board nice and cozy and us without a dry stitch about us for six days on end."

"Think of the arduous task of selecting slaves —"

"An' selecting the best of 'em to sleep with."

"Shame on you! The best is none too good for our Captain, of course! The best is hardly good enough for him." The last sentences fell into rhythm just as he said them and the final words were almost sung.

"That's good, lad, sing it again," cried several, and John fitted it to a raucous but catchy melody and sang it again while the men joined in with cheery irreverence.

"Make up some more, Newton. Never knew you was a poet."

"Didn't know myself." But the couplet sang itself into his mind and by supper-time he had the song ready. The tune was a blend of snatches from the *Beggars' Opera* and forgotten melodies, but it was singable. If some of the words were new to men most of whom could not read, they admired them the more, repeating them after their fashion, imitating and broadening the author's intonation and gesture as he mimicked the Captain. At first they joined only in the chorus but presently they were all singing it; and John felt the pride of a composer when he heard it hummed and sung all over the ship:

In London Pool they found a Snow, the oldest in the nation.
The Flying Horse, that was its name — misleading appellation.
They didn't wish to sink the tub and clutter up the River;
So they sent her on a cruise instead beyond Gual' de Quiver.
It's the best that we can do with her, my bully lads, said they.
And the best is hardly good enough, said they.

They chose to be commander of this obsolescent whaler
An officer, a gentleman, but certainly no sailor.
When storm's above, he lies below, but O when danger's
   shoreward
He loves to stay and pace the ship both quarter-deck and
   forward.
For the best is none too good for me, my jolly tars, says he.
Yes, the best is hardly good enough for me.

His crew so love this connoisseur they sweat by night and day,
Content to take his leavings and to serve in any way.
For bed and board he can afford the choicest life can offer.
And profits from our labour find their way into his coffer,
For the best is none too good for our captain, we agree.
And the best is hardly good enough, says he.

Even the second-mate and the ship's doctor found themselves whistling the air and the chorus became a catch-word, hastily repressed on occasion when the Captain or first-mate appeared.

"You are a young man of talent, I hear." It was the drawling intonation of Amos Clow's voice, and John, who had been thinking of him, as he leaned against a bulkhead wiping his forehead from the heat after stowing the men slaves for the night, started to find the trader regarding him quizzically. It was the opportunity he had watched for and he tried to collect his thoughts for the all-important speech. Clow continued blandly:

"Aren't you afraid that witty tongue will get you into trouble?" John shrugged wordlessly. "Mr. Penrose might think that the *worst* is none too bad for you, you know."

"Sir," said John boldly, feeling that boldness was the right tack to take with Clow, "there is nothing in the ship's articles about singing. I felt it my duty to cheer the ship's company."

Clow roared with laughter.

"You've done it, I grant you! But what about your duty to please your Captain. Hey? You're less successful at that."

"Sir," said John smiling, "perhaps I do not please him because I do not intend it."

"So you could if you wished. Is that it?" Thus encouraged, John was about to voice his request when Joe Hogg appeared at his elbow.

"Mr. Blunt's compliments to Mr. Clow, and there's a boat alongside with a message for you, Sir."

Clow turned on his heel without another word and John, cursing the unfortunate Hogg, resolved to make another opportunity the next day. The ship's business was almost completed. She had sailed to the Plantanes and unloaded the purchases Clow had made in England for his new domain. The tale of slaves was made up and the Captain was anxious to embark on the Middle Passage without further delay.

His opportunity did not come the next day or the next. And on the fourth day, while Clow was still on shore, Captain Penrose, who had returned to the *Pegasus* one evening in a feverish condition, died, after thirty-six hours of illness.

The effect on the ship's crew was sobering. Death itself they had seen often enough; so far on the voyage two of the company and seven slaves had succumbed to fevers and fluxes. But though the Captain had inspired neither respect nor much affection, he had been easy-going. They stopped singing the song, ceasing guiltily when a bar or two broke from their tune-burdened minds into an audible hum. And their breaking-off was not entirely a tribute to the Captain's memory, but an indication of their new commander's temper.

As for John, the succession of Mr. Blunt, and not the decease of Captain Penrose, was of primary importance. He had no compunction about the song which he had composed or the possible discomfort it had caused the object of its mild ridicule. The Captain had ceased to be. He was not, in John's opinion, a considerable person and the loss was one which the world in general and he, John, in particular would sustain easily. But a voyage under the absolute command of Josiah Blunt was little to his liking, if he had nothing more to fear. From comments overheard by the crew, and from the new Captain's grim way of eyeing him, he was reasonably sure that, once the difficult Middle Passage was completed and the ship relieved of her human freight, the raucous ring-leader would be returned without thanks to the first man-of-war within hail in the West Indies, a fate to which death was preferable.

The funeral for Captain Penrose was held with naval honours on shore, attended by the crew decorously banded in black, by the captains and crews of two other merchantmen lying off the coast, and by the few European traders in the

111

vicinity. Mr. Clow came on board after the ceremony and was in conference with Mr. Blunt while the boat sailed up coast to the Benanoes. John, waiting an occasion and not finding any, finally took the matter into his own hands and went to Mr. Clow's cabin late in the evening.

Clow glanced up and, if he felt surprise, he did not show it. Control of facial expression had saved him from death several times and contributed greatly to his successful trading with the natives.

"Well, you've not come to sing me a new song, I suppose," he drawled, leaning back from the chest-on-chest which formed a desk and surveying the evidently purposeful young seaman good-naturedly.

"No. And yet perhaps yes," said John and, given his cue, put forth his plea with an eloquence which he could seldom muster when in need of it.

Clow heard him through without change of expression. He needed competent assistance in his growing trade, immediate assistance for his projected building. This twenty-year-old was healthy, intelligent, and so eager or so unbusiness-like that he never mentioned terms. There was nothing for Clow to lose under such an arrangement, perhaps much to gain. And it would be a relief to have a fellow-white to talk to, an amusing companion who would yet be completely at his disposal.

"You seem more anxious to work now than you have been on the ship. And in a foul climate too, rather than return to England," he observed, probing. "Come now, what is in your mind?"

John told him with wry candour.

"Sir, I doubt I should get back to England on the *Pegasus*. Captain Blunt has no affection for me and I doubt intends to retain my services if he has opportunity to transfer me elsewhere." Clow nodded. He was of the same opinion. John resumed resolutely, embellishing the text of his speech, as Clow had done, with vigorous and appropriate profanities. "And I am resolved to die rather than to let that happen. Besides, Sir, I see no future in seafaring. Surely there are prospects in trade on the coast. I promise you will not regret your decision. At any rate take me on trial until I prove my worth to you."

"You seem sure that I can obtain your release."

John's eyes met the trader's so frankly that the flattery of his next words lost any suspicion of hypocrisy.

"Sir, if I may be permitted to judge, there are few things you cannot do if you set your will to them."

Clow gave a sound between a snort and a laugh.

"Well, in that case you may consider it done."

And John went to pace his watch and make rosy calculations of the length of time in which he could amass enough money to return to England and sue for Mary.

He never knew whether argument or authority prevailed upon the ex-first-mate. A sailor, who had survived a boat wreck up river and made his way back to shore to find that his ship had sailed, was available to supply Blunt's need of a man in John's place. There was no graciousness in his words of dismissal; if he had looked forward to John's dismay at being handed back to the Royal Navy it must have been hard to see the boy getting his own way.

"Here," he said curtly, signing his name and handing over the statement of release. "You'll draw no pay. This is a bill upon the ship-owners in London for the time you've served with us, and I cannot say I'm sorry to see the last of you. An ungrateful young dog and a bad influence with the men. However, if you don't mend your ways you'll get short shrift from Mr. Clow. Dismissed."

"Thank you, Sir," and John, resentful rather than abashed, went to give a perfect imitation of his speech to the crew in the forecastle; then with a mock prayer and benediction he took up his few belongings, including the neglected Euclid, and flung himself into Clow's boat which was waiting to take the two ashore.

12

ND who is this?" The words were uttered in the same liquid voice which had greeted Clow but there was a sibilance — was it in the words or the tone? — which struck a faintly ominous note. John had stepped back, his mind a maze of impressions, his eyes keen while seeming incurious, to let Clow greet the mistress of his home.

So this was P.I. of whom the sailors had spoken. The daughter of a petty king, she had saved Clow's life, when at the beginning of his penniless career he had fallen among a group of her father's people who were seeking vengeance on a white man for an outrage committed by the last European trader. As the king's son-in-law he had obtained trading privileges with kindred and friendly tribes to the south and east. So much John had heard, and that, however dissolute Clow was elsewhere, he brought no other woman to question, even as concubine, her absolute sway. Dressed elaborately in an English afternoon gown of green muslin, with rows of lace around the low neck and flowing sleeves, a great ivory-handled feather fan spread in her slim black hand, her small feet in rosetted European shoes, she did not reveal the feline grace and ebony harmony which were hers. Yet no discerning person would miss the strength of character, the intelligent determination patent in the fine eyes, the full resolute mouth, the proud flaring nostrils. And any woman could have learned from her adept alternation of pride with yielding, of storming with softness how to keep her ascendancy with a man like Clow.

"My dear, this is John Newton who has come to live here and assist me with the building and later with trade."

"You not tell me." There was no doubt now about the harsher quality in her voice. She was looking at John with no sign of welcome in face or hand.

"Not know till now. Very quick plan. Greet him, my dear." Clow put his great arm around her erect shoulders and lapsed into native dialect. Her face cleared.

"Good-day. Come in," she said briefly and John followed the strange couple into the comparative coolness of a palm-shaded room where a table was elaborately set, European fashion, for two.

The strange white man obviously presented a problem. To have him constantly at table with them would infringe, John gathered from the vigorous colloquy which ensued, on her unique position as co-regent. For him to take his meals with the slaves would, Clow pointed out delicately, endanger the white prestige which must be maintained. For the moment matters were settled by placing him alone at a small table some distance away where Newton, more than content, ate the best dinner he had seen before him since he left England and felt that once again luck was with him.

On Christmas day John leaned against a palm tree, smoking his pipe before dinner and surveying, in unwonted leisure, the result of their two months of labour. Before he had become accustomed to the comfortable, but ramshackle dwelling on the hilly island in the Benanoes, most of the menage had moved to temporary quarters on this long, low Plantane island twenty miles to the south-east, taking advantage of the cessation of the rains to build Clow's new house. All the hot long days Clow had not spared himself or his new assistant or the blacks who did the heavy work under their command. P.I. had insisted on joining them in spite of her husband's protests before there was adequate shelter, John thought to keep a wary eye on him. She alone did as she pleased, and since she was both capricious and imperious the work was not facilitated by her presence.

Now it was sufficiently complete to permit Clow and Newton to leave in a few days on their first up-river trading trip. John, looking at the wooden structure, a pretentious imitation of the comfortable English houses which had impressed his employer in his straitened youth, was swept by a wave of nostalgia for Mary. Three years ago he had spent Christmas with her. How many years before he would be welcomed under her roof at Christmas again?

He shook out his pipe and wished that he could shake the mood out of his system as easily. What was the matter with him to feel depressed, when his prospects were brighter than they had been since he rejected his opportunity in Jamaica? He was tired, he told himself, from constant driving work in the constant unsparing heat. Also he was hungry. Clow was celebrating the day with a special feast and John was to sit at the table with him in honour of the occasion. Of Clow's treatment he had no cause to complain, except that his own clumsy efforts to broach the matter of wages resulted only in vague promises for the future, when he should be sufficiently initiated into the mysteries of up-river trading to take over that hazardous branch of the business. Meanwhile he reminded himself of his misery on the *Harwich* and his uncertainty on the *Pegasus,* and decided to wait until he had more definite news before sending another letter either to his father or to Mary.

The banquet to which he was presently summoned was lavish and appetizing. P.I. had accompanied her husband on trips aboard European ships, had been entertained at captains' tables, and was skilful in imitating and varying dishes which had specially pleased him. John's hunger had left him by the time they sat down but he forced himself to eat and was glad of the excellent wine which enabled him to continue, when refusal of one of the many concoctions would have given offence. As it was, P.I. was endeavouring to be gracious but found it difficult, especially when Clow became absorbed in talk of England. Sitting in a pink brocade dress with a gold chain on her neck and gold bangles on her wrists, she poured coffee from a pewter pot as she had been taught to do, her black inscrutable eyes fixed on the young, light-haired white man, who could use big words and twist his mouth when he told stories so that her husband laughed and forgot that she was there. John, conscious as he had been from the first of her dislike, was completely obtuse as to its cause. Aggrieved, he felt that he had seldom tried so hard to be ingratiating when ingratiation was little to his taste.

116

That P.I., who had attained a state of power and influence unique among her black sisters, could be jealous of his status with Clow did not once occur to him.

The wine carried him through dinner. After dinner he feared it would carry him too far; yet he kept drinking, partly on Clow's insistence, partly to counter the strange feeling of illness that kept recurring. The trader was determined to celebrate this festivity between the achievement of one goal and the quest of another. It was good to have one of his own kind to share the celebration and, although P.I. stubbornly refused his suggestion that she behave like an English lady and leave the men to their drink — a suggestion which she evidently viewed with the deepest suspicion, he soon disregarded her presence altogether.

"Let's have a song," he suggested. "You have a good voice, Newton. How does that song of yours go? 'For the best is none too good. . . .' What's the verse? Come on."

He joined in snatches of it while John sang, fighting the waves of heat and cold which passed over him.

"Let's have another. Know any carols? 'Deck the Halls'? I was a wait at Christmas once — used to go carolling Christmas Eve. Forgotten the words now."

John had lain awake the night before, harassed by longing for Mary and angered that the words of carols he had sung at Chatham kept repeating themselves in his mind. To avoid the recollection he had idly composed some parodies, one of which he recalled now.

> *"Unto superstitious fools*
> *Christ was born of Mary,"*

he sang, to Clow's great amusement.

Further witticisms were received with roars of approval. John was proceeding to explain the superior wisdom and the practical advantages of his free-thinking position when he had a sudden sense that he had caught fire. He rose unsteadily to his feet, saw on turning twice around that the fire was not outside him, wondering how the man across the table could sit so calmly, caught the malevolent eyes of P.I. fixed on him, and turned hastily away.

117

"Sorry, Mr. Clow." He heard the words but did not recognize the voice. Then he saw the floor rushing up at him.

A long nightmare of pursuing Mary across parching sands, of catching up with her and seeing the face of P.I. turn to look at him over Mary's shoulder, of being fastened on the deck of the *Harwich* waiting for the stroke of the cat and knowing again the pain without feeling the blow, of putting fetters on the woman slave who had wept in his arms and finding, as he looked back from the foot of the ladder, that he had left Mary chained there in the darkness. . . . a nightmare interspersed with moments of dreadful burning consciousness, when after an age of craving for water — he could not have said if he called for it or not — some would be put to his lips, only to let the dry parching recur more stiflingly than before.

During one of these periods he saw Clow beside him, but at a careful distance, and P.I. standing in the doorway. His eyes burned too badly to keep them open but words drifted to him.

"Can't put off the trip any longer. Too late now. May pull through. Take care of him. . . .?"

It was after this that his yearning for water never seemed to be gratified, that he could call and call — he knew now that he was calling — and no one appeared. After this his thirst became so frantic that he rolled off the bed and, unable to stand, crawled half way to the door before he collapsed. Somehow he was put back on the bed and one of the slaves brought him water. Then, for how long he could never tell, he lay wrapped in a black, heavy, oppressive sentience.

When he opened his eyes it was to the sudden knowledge that his fever had passed, to a sudden awareness of strange surroundings. When the new house was finished he had been given a small room in it; now he was back in one of the huts which had served them as temporary shelter and were being kept for the slaves. His bed was one of the chests in which the effects of Clow's Benanoes' menage had been brought to the island. A straw mat was spread on it and a log of wood under the matting was a sufficiently hard pillow. Evidently fear of contagion or the annoyance of his delirious moaning

118

had influenced Clow's mistress to have him moved. John lay weakly, watching the shadows moving on his floor as the wind stirred the palm tree outside the entrance, and wondered what day, even what month it was.

Presently he became impatient. The feeling of extreme weakness he identified with the only other cause of weakness, except extreme pain, which he had known. He was hungry. He wondered how long he had gone without food and how long it was since anyone had come to look at him. He lifted a feeble hand and was amazed at his growth of beard. Quietly at first, then querulous with weakness, he began to call.

The young black girl who appeared momentarily in the hut opening stared at him in astonishment; then, paying no attention to his request for food, disappeared. It seemed to John a long time before P.I. arrived, and at his weak, clear greeting entered the hut and stood looking down at him. Was there disappointment in those black velvet eyes?

"So," she said at last, "you are better."

"Better," John tried to smile but his head swam, "or shall be when I have some food. Food," he went on urgently. "I am very hungry."

She turned with an impatient remark in the Sherbro tongue to the girl who was standing behind her. The girl disappeared, and P.I. was about to follow.

"Tell me," begged John weakly to keep her, "how long I've been sick. What day is this? Mr. Clow, where is he?"

"Sick two weeks. Your master gone Rio Nuna. You no help him on his trip. Get well quick."

She was gone and in time her servant arrived with a small measure of rice on an iron plate and a mug of water. John looked at the unappetizing stuff with disgust.

"What is this for a half-starved man? Have you nothing better?"

The girl looked distressed.

"Please, Mrs. P.I. say this all. Say you weak, not want much."

In vain John protested then and later. He never knew if his futile threats were carried to their mistress. The rations which were brought irregularly to his hut were so sparse and unsuitable that he became convinced she did not want him to

119

live. The slaves evidenced by their manner that they were under orders to give him as little attention as was consistent with the cleanness and consequent safety of the establishment. Sometimes when his ravenous returning appetite made him devour the scanty meal more desperately than usual, one of them — the same one was never allowed to come regularly — would return furtively and silently place a portion of food on his bare plate: rice or fruit or the baked root of a potato-like plant which grew on the plantation, evidently saved from a none-too-generous meal. One day, a day on which he thought that he touched the depths of degradation, a man-servant, whose bearing when working under John's supervision had held a covert insolence, appeared as the food-bearer. The plate in his hands was not iron, but pewter, and there was nothing covert now in his insolence.

"Mrs. P.I. send you her plate," he said, putting it on the floor beside the chest with a contemptuous gesture. "She had too much. Can't finish."

Fury heated John's body like the fever which had so recently left it. With an effort he leaned over to pick up the plate and fling it with its contents in the man's offensively smiling face. The forced slowness of movement gave sight and smell an opportunity to work on his famished senses. Half a breast of boiled fowl, obviously bitten into, a diminished portion of curried rice still warm, some spinach, part of a baked plantain. The hand to which rage had given false strength for the throw hesitated, trembled. Niceness was no match for weakness and the desperate craving of an empty stomach. Without raising his eyes, John uttered a curt dismissal which the man obeyed, deliberately unhurried, and restrained himself till he was alone before devouring the despised and despiteful food.

P.I., apparently pleased at this novel assertion of her power, repeated the experiment, always when he had been kept waiting longer than usual. It was on the day following one of these humiliating beneficences that she stooped under the low frame and favoured him with her inscrutable stare.

"Still abed, lazy," she said sharply. "If your master here you be about and working."

John flushed hotly.

"I am ill and half-starved," he said, making his voice as firm as he could. "If you gave me decent food and treatment I should soon be better."

P.I. laughed harshly.

"You get all the food you will lying idle. We work here for food. I said to Mr. Clow when I saw you first day: 'He bring us no good.' And now he will say me right."

John sat up, supporting himself on emaciated arms.

"Madam, that is a lie and you know it. I worked to Mr. Clow's satisfaction and approval. He left me in your charge and you have done your best to kill me —"

P.I. turned to her slaves, speaking rapidly in Sherbro, then swung back to him.

"So you sit up when it pleases you. I thought. Try hard now and you can stand. Come. You never walk lying still."

John raised himself on unsteady legs so that his head touched the low ceiling.

"Outside," commanded P.I. "Not room here to walk."

John made his uncertain way to the door. If he could walk, all the better. If not, she could not tell Clow that he refused to make the attempt. The heat of the sun struck him, almost blinding his weakened eyes, and he staggered a step or two and leaned against the hut wall for support.

P.I. crowed with laughter and her attendants dutifully laughed too.

"See him. Walk like him, Mamba, Jodi," she ordered and the boy and girl, hearing the note in her jesting voice, staggered a few steps and threw their arms across their eyes with clever mimicry, to the delighted amusement of the rest.

John was past caring. The glare of the sun, the strength of the air on his enfeebled body, made him almost unconscious of their presence. He groped blindly for the opening, missing it and turning dizzily to feel his way along the wall. Something struck him and fell to the ground, another round missile and another. He did not know that they were limes, one a little stone which struck his arm with a small sharp pain. But nothing mattered except the imperious urge to seek asylum, the frantic compulsion to be once more prostrate. He found the opening, struck his forehead trying to enter, felt his way

121

inside to what seemed total darkness, lowered himself to the floor and crawled till he found his bed where the last wave of darkness engulfed him as he collapsed.

Up to this time John's body had been fighting alone for survival. The inroads of fever and weakness on his mind had made him incapable of sustained thought or feeling. Now resentment and determination to endure until Clow's return, to give the lie to P.I.'s accusation and to prove himself an able and valuable assistant: these encouraged the instinctive struggle to health of his resilient flesh.

It took a dogged determination to combat the equally dogged determination and unequal advantage of his enemy. Baffled in her hope that death would remove her rival, just unsure enough of her power with Clow to be unwilling to risk his discovery that John had died of absolute neglect, P.I. was obsessed by a heady sense of power and by the conviction of her own animal strength that his weakness would make him contemptible in her husband's eyes.

She repeated her experiment of making him walk, threatening to cut off food altogether. And her servants, though when she was absent they treated him with pity, soon learned that her favour depended on their joining her in scorn and mimicry, while one or two were by no means averse to this whimsical opportunity of pelting a defenceless white man with limes or stones.

He had scarcely managed to walk twice the length of his hut, when a message was brought to him that if he wanted food that day he must come to the house and receive it from P.I. herself. He was sitting when the messenger arrived, waiting for the poor meal to supply him with energy to walk a little farther. The back of the house across the compound seemed an endless distance away. He continued to sit there, calling down a rich selection of curses upon his tormentor's head and realizing that he was postponing the inevitable.

"Needs must when the devil drives," he muttered as anticlimax and set out, deliberately conserving his little strength, from one palm tree to the brief support of the next until he reached the house. He paused briefly on the back stoop; then, remembering that on the last occasion he had been treated as an equal there, he made his way through the hall to the living-room.

P.I. received him with a smile of triumph. Dining alone at a table covered with dishes, she felt like a queen with this white man coming at her summons. Several attendants stood behind her chair. There were no other chairs at hand or John would have sunk down on one, risking her anger and rebuke. Instead he steadied himself, flattening his body and the palms of his hands against the wall, for he was shaking after his exertion. He waited a moment.

"You sent for me, I think."

"Yes," the sibilant sound was always in her soft voice when she addressed him but it was less noticeable in her good-humoured insolence. "I know you come far as you need to get food. Food! All you think of." She surveyed the table slowly, took a spoonful of yams and put it beside a half-dressed portion of boiled pigeon on her soiled plate, broke a small cake made of rice flour and put part of it in her mouth, eyeing him amusedly, added the remainder to the melange and held the plate out to him with her most regal air.

John silently vowed an awful vengeance on her and came forward to take the bounty. The pewter was heavy. In spite of his efforts at steadiness, the plate dropped from his feeble, eager hand and the contents scattered on the floor. P.I. screamed with laughter and, looking at John's white face stunned with shock and disappointment, she laughed again till the servants laughed with her.

"Get down and eat it," she said at last sobering, for John stood, exerting all his power to remain standing, and the thoughts which made him many times a murderer stared at her through his steady eyes.

"Will you give me more?" His glance left hers to sweep the table with its plentiful variety, and for a moment he estimated his chances of seizing food if it was denied.

"No! Stupid and wasteful! You cannot have more. You can eat what you have." And she pointed again to the floor.

But this John would not do. Reduced to utter extremity, he would not add by this ultimate servility to the satisfaction he had already given her. Walking carefully as though on a slippery surface, he made his fruitless way back to the cabin, lay down on the chest exhausted, and found himself shedding tears, not so much of rage as of utter desolation.

The sun set and he had not moved when a slight rustle told him that someone had entered the hut. Against the comparative light of the opening he discerned the outline of a female figure. She raised a cautioning finger to her lips as he stirred.

"Sh-h," she said softly, then drawing out a small bundle twisted in a plantain leaf, she laid it in his hands. Hers touched him timidly in the action for a second and she murmured an unknown word in native dialect. Then he was alone again.

The leaf contained food, part of the monotonous daily ration of the natives, not the experimental blend of European and African delicacies prepared for the master's table and doubtless finished by P.I.'s personal favourites. John ate it slowly, a finger of warmth penetrating the cold armour of his ugly wretched thoughts. He had identified his recent benefactor as a 'slave on the chain', not one of Clow's household. Half a dozen such captives had come in the trader's way too late for the slave-ships and were being kept for the ensuing season, meanwhile working on the plantation. He lay in the darkness, eating the last of her scanty bounty, and reflecting that he had intended at the Christmas feast to ask Clow if he could have her for the time being. He could not use his employer's property without permission. Now, by a strange reversal, she was ministering, instead, to the physical need which superseded the other, that other for which weakness had removed desire, except as the feverish comfort of his imagination.

That same night, the meagre food serving only to create a craving for more and to give enough strength to enable him to go in search of it, John made his cautious way to that part of the plantation where a tuber had been grown for domestic use. Often served in place of potatoes on Clow's table it was the only edible article within his reach. Perhaps it would alleviate the constant gnawing of hunger from one poor meal to the next.

The island night was thick with fog. Fortunately he possessed an accurate sense of direction and, after a lengthy and devious route, found himself amid the furrows of light soil, ran his hands over the familiar plant leaves, and pulled up one root after another, carefully thinning the clumps so that appearances would not betray him.

He must eat on the spot too, he told himself, disposing of the leaves as he could not do in the compound. P.I. would certainly punish him as a thief for taking an infinitesimal part of what was owed him, and Newton's grim determination to denounce her made him resolve to give her no occasion for further abuse. Besides he was too ravenous to wait. Hardly delaying to brush off the earth, he chewed and gulped down half a dozen of the cold, almost tasteless vegetables, considering bitterly in his dark clear mind how quickly hunger reduced man to a level with the beasts. If Mary could see him. . . .

He had eaten all he could force down and had completed about two-thirds of his return trip, feeling his way by the landmarks of the partly planted lime orchard, when without warning he was doubled up with retching pains and rendered dizzy with nausea. His whole body broke out in cold sweat and, after an attempt to stagger a few paces further, he collapsed and lay writhing on the ground, until the emetic effect of the raw food found devastating relief. It was dawn before he recovered strength to crawl back, empty as he had gone, to his hut.

13

I N mid-February Clow's shallop sailed with a following wind into the little bay and anchored just off shore. The new slaves were left aboard while Clow was rowed to land by the black who had been his chief assistant. He greeted P.I., who went down to the water's edge, as Newton, in spite of her efforts, insisted on doing, and gave a long whistle when he caught sight of the white-faced emaciated figure standing nearby. John had not yet mustered strength to divest himself of his heavy growth of reddish-brown beard. His food ration had scarcely been increased and, though almost every attempt to repeat his experiment with the raw tubers had the same result, necessity had driven him to it again and again.

"Newton is it — or your ghost?" cried Clow. "Man, I'm glad you survived."

It was John's opening and he had no intention of being diplomatic.

"If I have, it is no thanks to the one in whose charge you left me," he said boldly, indicating the impassive P.I. "I have been housed like a slave and fed far less, in what I fear was a deliberate attempt to let me die before your return."

P.I. began to speak but John's raised voice quelled her protest.

"I am sorry, Sir, both to make this accusation, and to greet you in such a weakened state. My fever was severe for two weeks, but I could have been in good health now, and much better able to serve you, if I had not been starved."

Clow who had listened in uncomfortable astonishment turned to his mistress.

"Surely there is some mistake. What do you say to this, my dear?"

P.I. drew herself up.

"Which you believe, me or stranger? I starve him? Food I send every day. Every day he lie and lie, will not get up, will not try to get better, but eat — oh yes! And come much way for food. Idle I tell you and I told you. Lazy. He work only when you here. I take care as you order. These will tell you."

Her dark glance went from one to the other of the household who nodded assent.

"Look at me, Mr. Clow," said John earnestly, unable to believe that his wrongs of six weeks could be set aside. He had a sudden inspiration: "If she obeyed orders, come and see my hut. Did you command that I should be housed in the compound with the slaves?"

P.I.'s face was a mask of virtuous surprise.

"He had fever, shout, scream. Others maybe catch it. I put him in hut. After —" she lapsed into rapid Sherbro but John from a word here and there, as well as from her intonation and expression as she laid her arm on Clow's and looked into his eyes, deduced that she was avowing her unwillingness to let any white man sleep beneath her roof in her lord's absence.

He began to speak but Clow interrupted with the finality of a man who has made up his mind what he wishes to believe.

"Come, Newton. You've had a bad bout of fever and you are not used to the climate. Natives would have died or recovered quickly. She doesn't understand a long convalescence. And I must say you got out of all the work you could on the *Pegasus* by your own admission, didn't you? Come," he said again, as John hesitated, feeling that this ending of a bad dream was more baffling than the dream itself, "we shall all feel better after dinner. Direct Hwoy and Ize to bring the load ashore. You will dine at your table, of course."

The subject was closed and John realized it, realized too, when he could force himself to think of the situation without personal bitterness, why this was so. Not only was Clow, in spite of moral laxness elsewhere, infatuated with his mistress-wife, but too much was involved in her influence and tribal connection to risk her anger, much less to repudiate her at the accusation of a friendless adventurer. P.I. could be left in charge of such a settlement as this; she was fertile in schemes for expanding trade; she represented stability, security, and all Clow would ever know of home-life unless he became wealthy enough to retire to England; and he would never live there in the kingly luxury which he would presently command here. John had tried in a struggle not of his own choosing, and lost.

It was a good sign that Clow bore no ill-will to his assistant for the trial. Perhaps he believed more of the complaint than, for his own interest and domestic peace, he pretended. John was restored to his previous status as if nothing had happened. If eating in the room where he had been mocked and turned from a full table was at first an unreal experience, the excellent food consumed added daily to his strength and compensated somewhat for the sight of his enemy, her word vindicated, asserting her feminine sway over Clow after his long absence as skilfully as any famous courtesan over a returning monarch. After all, he thought savagely, to have failed in her effort to get rid of him and in her attempt to demote him, must cause some discomfiture beneath the mask of alluring devotion. Whenever Clow addressed a remark to him, the restless rolling glance of her black eyes testified her unease.

By the beginning of March, Clow had the shallop prepared to sail, this time up the Sherbro. An English and a French ship had taken all his available slaves and he was impatient to visit a tribe in the interior which had just made war on its neighbours and would doubtless have an enriching number of prisoners for sale. These tribal wars, always frequent, John learned, were now often deliberately fomented to obtain the coveted goods from Europe which made up the bars or currency units paid for captives. Free blacks were seldom, if ever, taken by traders, as he had thought before his personal acquaintance with the trade. He had never given it serious thought, accepting it as part of the "whatever is", not perhaps

128

right but inevitable, and certainly less distressing to him than the brutal public punishments meted out in English cities and villages to men and women — punishments to which ducking stools and stocks, public gallows and begging hands through the bars of prisons were a constant witness. He was interested in Clow's talk of Sherbro customs and institutions — according to him it was a far more enlightened section of the coast with respect to law and order than the rest of the Windward Coast — and waited eagerly for the voyage to begin.

The first days and weeks passed pleasantly. The rainy season was not due for a month and might not, if they were lucky, begin until almost May. They crossed the leagues of open water to the mouth of the Bagru and made sufficient speed with their single mast up its tidal estuary. They played endless games of cards, not for stakes, at first because John had none to put up, then because Clow seldom won. Insects were a nuisance on their shore excursions and on hot windless nights up the rivers — for the Sherbro was, properly speaking, a sound fed by several large rivers; but Newton had become accustomed to the unwelcome attention of parasites. Crocodiles and reptiles kept them alert and wary, and because of wild beasts they were careful to be on board or in a native town at night; but the experience was exciting and, after the benumbing misery of his recent existence, it fed John with hope.

His thoughts of Mary once again became constructive. He tried to be active in Clow's interests — in spite of the fact that he was coldly determined some day to revenge himself on Clow's wife — and availed himself of every trading-hint for future use though, as honesty was the only remaining quality of his good upbringing left in him, he viewed some of the trader's methods of cheating the natives with distaste. He knew that his former messmates had drawn off and diluted liquor, taken gunpowder and inserted false heads to make the kegs look full, cut yards of cloth from bales near the centre where the deception would escape notice no matter how the cloth was displayed for exhibit. Clow, as he depended on the continued good will of these natives for his livelihood, did not resort to the more obvious practices, but brought to the art of cheating a finesse worthy of a nobler end. He was careful, however, to avoid any transgression of tribal law and briefed his companion on varying customs as they approached each village.

"Keep those lecherous eyes of yours off the women," he warned, as they distributed loads to their bearers in preparation for a visit to the king of the largest town they had so far visited.

"Even granting that my eyes are more lecherous than yours," retorted John with some additional remarks complimentary to Clow's proclivities, "why this particular — and most disappointing — caution?"

"Because we are in the realm of the Purrow, and those who belong to the Purrow have their rights more carefully guarded than yours are in England. That's why," said Clow sententiously. "Any theft which can be repaid in kind is so paid. . . . if the thief is discovered. But for injuries which are not repayable — bodily injuries where 'an eye for an eye' does no good to the man who has lost his eye in the first place — they have a different system. The complainant, even if he is a poor man, as long as he belongs to the Purrow, may demand anything that the offender has and keep on demanding until he says he is satisfied. I've seen one of the wealthy men of this tribe reduced to slavery on my next visit by this pleasant custom which, please God, Christian countries will never adopt."

"But could the rich man not bribe the judges? Are these people free from chicanery?"

Clow shrugged. "They are human. But you forget they belong to the Purrow — a sort of initiated brotherhood. It is to their interest to keep a law which protects all equally."

"But where," asked John, returning to a subject which was of more pressing concern to him, "do my eyes come into this?"

"For both our sakes I hope not at all," grunted Clow. "Adultery ranks among the injuries for which there can be no recompense in kind. It is common enough, naturally, because they are polygamous, but if it is discovered, the cuckolded husband can claim all the cuckolder's property. Most of the women you see will be somebody's wives. However, cheer up. The king will undoubtedly put a woman at the disposal of each of us. I'm warning you against making your own selection, that's all."

"I shall be quite satisfied with the king's hospitality," said John, and he was.

He was impressed also by the dignity of the king, or patriarch, for age and not wealth or heredity was revered in these tribes. He had already learned enough of the language to address courteous remarks and to follow the gist of the conversation. After a ceremonious dinner some of the king's grandchildren stood staring at the new white man. As Clow was deep in negotiations, John beckoned to the hesitating youngsters and, picking up the gourd out of which he had been drinking, proceeded, with the aid of some twigs and twine and a strip of cloth which had been torn from the sleeve of his shirt as they came through the jungle-growth, to fashion a river-boat complete with mast, sail, and ballast. The children laughed and John laughed, thinking of his young brother Billy for the first time in months, then of Georgie Catlett, then inevitably of Mary. The grave king smiled, his chief wife smiled, the slaves clearing the feast away smiled, and Clow looked surprised and a bit disconcerted.

Perhaps in consequence he struck a good bargain with the king.

"He told me that they were all convicts, not prisoners of war," he drawled, "so from now on we shall have to keep watch. You will stay on the boat if there are any over-night trips."

"Did he tell you their crimes?" inquired John, watching the rope-bound single file on the well-trodden path in front of them.

"I didn't ask. For some cases of theft, if the owner can't be satisfied, the thief may be sold. The man and woman both in adultery, if the husband chooses. Not that they treat slaves badly. The Purrow does not allow individuals to shed blood, even to draw it from a slave."

John thought of his own flogging and cursed Captain Cartaret almost automatically. Then he laughed.

"No, they don't treat slaves badly — or visitors. I suppose the accommodation we received comes under the head of domestic service."

Clow was beginning an appropriate reply when a call from

the vanguard who had just reached the river bank interrupted him.

"Look, Master. Another boat."

They saw it at the same moment, a larger shallop weighing anchor near theirs. Clow's sharp eyes narrowed against the river-reflected sunlight.

"Lewis Keating's boat," he observed. "Well, he won't find any pickings where we have been. Serve him right. Last time he sailed the river ahead of me he took off the entire crop except in some towns where they know him for the cheat he is."

"Bird of a feather." The remark slipped out involuntarily and Clow did not think it funny.

"That tongue of yours is too quick for your good," he snapped and was silent while they were rowed out to the boat.

John, who had seen his moods before, was not greatly disturbed and by the time Keating came aboard to visit, Clow introduced his young assistant with a certain satisfaction. The two traders greeted each other with surface cordiality and, if John was not drawn to the wiry, monkey-faced little man, whom he caught watching him warily while they supped, he thought very little about him.

Next morning they hoisted anchor and proceeded up river, Clow in high good humour, having induced Keating to make a trip to their recent calling-place in quest of some slaves whom he had rejected. Two nights later Keating's boat caught up with theirs and from that time the traders were often together, talking business, narrating experiences, watching each other distrustfully, but bound in a fraternity of interest and colour against a dark and dangerous continent.

John, if not happy, was reasonably contented. He had found Clow difficult to pin down to terms but something had been said about a commission and he was satisfied that he had proved his worth. Returning health made him sanguine and he trusted Clow to weigh the value of his assistance in general and in particular instances: once where his quick intervention had saved his employer from a leaping lynx, and again where he had detected a carefully concealed disability in a slave which the other had been about to purchase. So when the blow fell, it fell with stunning force.

One evening Clow returned to the shallop from a day's visit ashore with Keating. John came on deck to greet him and was completely ignored as the trader came aboard, growled an order or two to the bearers — he had come back empty-handed — and descended to his cabin. Disconcerted, John saw that the boat was lashed secure, made sure that all was in readiness to sail with the incoming tide which rose eight feet far up the Bagru, and went to his bunk, wondering at activity by lantern-light in the next cabin.

Early the following morning when Newton, who had been up long before dawn to supervise the departure, had stretched himself out again for an hour's rest, he heard his name bellowed in Clow's most intimidating tone. A minute later he was facing a look which the trader had never turned on him before and a bewildering barrage of accusation and inquisition, where the questions were purely rhetorical and his answers completely disregarded.

"So you thought I was blind, eh? You thought I'd notice nothing?"

"Sir, I am at a loss —"

"Oh, no, you aren't! I am at a loss. And should have been mulcted still more, if Keating had not warned me. Wanted to make your fortune, didn't you? And at my expense. Why, you castaway mutineer, if I hadn't begged you off you'd be back on a man-of-war, by this time getting the treatment you deserve, instead of roistering here in my absence, making free with my wines and slaves, pilfering my goods when I leave you in charge, and undermining me when I take you along."

John stared at him, blinking in astonishment. His tongue always failed him when he most needed it and the sudden charge, multiple yet amorphous, left him without resource.

"Sir, I swear —"

"You do. That's true enough. Far too much." In view of the profanity which had punctuated every accusation, John, too harried to be amused, felt that the reproof came from a peculiar source. "I should have known that a blasphemous tongue like yours would lie as quick as it curses. And I took your word — against my better judgment, against my wife's. Well, from now on I'll know better."

"Sir," said John, raising his voice to match the other which could be heard all over the boat. "What do you accuse me of? I have the right to know."

"Right — if you had your rights in this country you'd join the slaves over there. You're a thief."

"That is a lie," said John, angry in spite of his danger. "There's not much else you can accuse me of that I shouldn't admit. I'm no hypocrite. But I have never defrauded you, never been false to your trust. I can't swear by God because there is no God to swear by, and those who swear by Him break their oaths. But I am speaking truth."

"So you say," retorted Clow, "and I say you're a lying sneak thief."

"But are you condemning me without evidence?"

"Evidence enough," said Clow, beginning to shout again as a man does when he is unsure of an action on which he has determined. "I've the evidence of Keating and his overseer, of the boys on board and of my own calculations. They've told me of your behaviour on the boat when I was away. I can see how much wine I have left. I've been counting up my stores and reckoning them against the bars we've paid out. What you've done with your little cache I haven't found out yet. Perhaps you've used it to bribe some of these native officials you have been cozening up to. The next voyage you'll be on your own, you think, and doing a bold stroke for yourself — on my boat, with my hard-earned goods. Well, it's your first and last trip. I don't trust you out of my sight again. Now get up on deck and do the one job you're fit for — sailor."

John had a wild impulse to fling himself at Clow's massive frame in a mad attempt to force him to listen. Only the cold sad certainty that he was no match, even in full health, for the other's giant strength restrained him, that and dread of consequent physical humiliation especially under the eye of Muni, his former overseer, who had stood by throughout the interview and who, he suddenly realized, might have corroborated Keating's slander.

Furious but impotent, he gained the deck, still unable to

believe that such injustice could be done or that Clow would persist in his attitude without proof. Careless and profligate though he had become, he was essentially simple and straight-forward. He could understand and share every vigorous, gross, passionate vice; but the subtleties of meaner motivations were an insoluble puzzle to him; they found him unprepared and undefended.

So for days of increasing wretchedness he pondered Keating's attack. The sight of a prosperous rival, now advantaged by an intelligent white assistant, had bent his crooked mind in search of this scheme to discountenance him. The other witnesses, whatever they had said, had been threatened or bribed. But Clow himself? How could he cast aside his companionship on a lonely voyage, his practical help and his potential value, on the improbable falsehood of a distrusted rival?

That was where John, elementally simple in motive and ac-tion, was at a loss. Against Amos Clow's pleasure in his com-pany and assistance was set the deep-seated mistrust of others ingrained in a ruthless man who has made personal gain his only goal. The qualities which made John a valuable assist-ant made him also a possible rival. Clow was incapable of genuine affection and the boy's free witty tongue, though amusing, had often pricked his domineering arrogance, even as had his contempt for shady practice, which had not been too carefully concealed. Beneath it all, scarcely recognized by Clow himself, was a craving to justify his former cowardice. He had not believed P.I.'s accusations. In his heart he had felt that John's charges were true; and his compromise for the sake of peace had lowered himself in his own estimation, showing not only his mistress, but John and his slaves that he was completely under her capricious sway. By a tortuous process more primitive than reason, he seized on Keating's untenable propositions to defend his failure to vindicate P.I.'s victim. John was learning through experience what the in-genuous cannot otherwise credit: that distorted pride and self-interest can force a man to believe a demonstrable lie: worse, that having chosen to believe it, he becomes implac-able towards its victim.

Even if Newton had understood this, the stark misery of

his situation was beyond the reach of philosophical comfort. Banished from Clow's confidence, society, and table, rationed to a pint of rice a day and occasional scraps from the fowls killed for his master, he was still unready for the next indignity and, even when it came, had little idea how much more than humiliation was entailed.

The boat was anchored the third day after his condemnation near a small plateau where the thatched roofs of a village could just be seen, built providently on ground out of the reach of flood waters. John heard orders being given. Clow would be ashore for the day. The trader came on deck, inspected the boat which John had made ready, then turned to him, blustering slightly, perhaps to hide embarrassment.

"Come over here, you blasted nuisance! Curse me if I take pity on a discontented tar again. As if I haven't enough to attend to without having your excess weight on board just now. And I can't even trust you when my back's turned." John had followed him without realizing what was coming. Now he felt someone behind him but, even as he turned, Muni had slipped the fetter on his ankle and he was chained to an iron ring in the deck. Clow had regained his composure and sneered at his incredulous fury.

"Why are you complaining? Nothing to do and a pleasant deck to lie on. Food to hand, too." Muni placed a bowl of rice beside him, they descended to the waiting boat, and John was left in the maddening desolation of captivity.

That day was the precursor of many more. Its pains of hunger, heat, and despair were keener because of the freshness of their attack. His body, recovering from prolonged weakness and fever and taxed by constant activity, had developed an enormous appetite and the pangs of hunger were as severe as a recurrence of illness. His chain prevented him from availing himself of the bars of shade which moved slowly from the furled sails across the deck and his unsheltered body blistered under the unrelenting sun. For the turmoil of his thoughts there was no relief in the variegated colours and splendours of river and shore in which he had previously taken delight: the iridescent whirring of innumerable kingfishers, the gold tiaras on the crowned cranes' black velvet heads, the incessant chattering of little red-and-green love-birds and long-

136

tailed parakeets, or of baboons swinging in the wild coffee shrubs and baobab and palm-oil trees on shore. Arguments in self-defence, schemes of revenge, dreams of Mary agonizing in their hopelessness, were slowly dulled by sheer physical suffering. And when, late in the day, a gust of wind blew his cap off his head and overboard, he hoped that sun-stroke would put a quick end to his misery.

Two days later he was to think of the sun with longing. Clow, cursing him for a careless fool, had grudgingly handed out a handkerchief to be knotted into a cap, and before his next imprisonment on deck John had taken from his bunk a strip of cotton about two yards long to cover his exposed neck and arms against the sun. But several hours after the boat had gone to shore, squatting with eyes closed against the glare, he was suddenly aware first of coolness, then of shadow. A glance told him that the rain, which never fell in January and February and which seldom became incessant until May, had come. Almost with the realization it fell and continued, intermitted with squalls and chilling gales of wind, all that day and night and part of the next. Clow and his party were delayed by it and by their trading. When they returned, John, soaked and starved and numb with cold, too spent to complain or curse, limped below to the comparative comfort of his bunk and the fitful sleep of over-exhaustion.

That evening, when he was ordered on deck to rig the sails for departure, the servant who cooked for Clow was cleaning a fresh-killed fowl from the master's pen. John had a sudden inspiration.

"Could I have those?" he asked, pointing to the entrails for which he did not know the native word.

The man looked uncertain.

"The master — " he began, but just then Clow came up from his cabin. John turned to him.

"Mr. Clow, he is throwing the entrails overboard. May I have them?"

"To eat?" asked Clow amused.

"To fish with."

The trader shrugged.

"Give him the offal," he instructed carelessly, and to John, "I don't care which way the fish get it."

John sank still lower in his own estimation when he bit back the retort in which Clow's own entrails were consigned to a like fate, for fear the miserable, but all-important grant would be rescinded. If hunger and his body's determination to survive had been less compelling, he might have wondered more at the hardness of the man he had faithfully served. His own vices were for personal gratification and he could not understand how wanton cruelty could contribute to Clow's. An utter lack of the imagination by which a man puts himself in another's place, the corrosive effect of deliberate commission of injustice until the victim appears the aggressor — these were subtleties beyond his experience or comprehension.

From that time on his sole sustaining interest was in fishing, his only relief — so great as to constitute pleasure — the tremulous excitement of feeling a fish on the hook, and the fish itself, carelessly broiled and usually half burnt, devoured without salt, sauce or bread, a meal so grateful as to seem delicious. Most of the day, incoming tide or swift current made the fish seek the river depths. Only at slack water there was a chance, and at slack water John fished assiduously, sometimes rewarded, sometimes forced to sleep away his disappointment if he could, while constant exposure for twenty, thirty, even once for forty hours, to changes of excessive heat, rain, wind, and cold made this quest a strange means of preserving some degree of sanity.

Two months after their departure they sighted the island to which John had hoped to return vindicated and valued. Clow's trade was not merely in slaves. He traded also for gold dust, ivory and beeswax, and had designed his plantation on the Plantanes to furnish provisions of limes, vegetables, bananas, for the ships about to make the Middle Passage or to return to England. On this expedition he had succeeded admirably. There had been no trouble with the slaves. Captives, who had escaped the dreaded fate of being eaten, they had heard attractive tales of salt-eating plantations on the coast and had no conception of their ultimate destiny.

So it was with self-applauding gratification, which was his substitute for genuine pleasure, that he greeted the watchful P.I. And if the undisguised delight and the added warmth of her greeting when she saw John's situation was not a reward of virtue, it was the nearest approach to it that Clow was likely to experience. After the first "I told you, I told you," she suppressed her inclination to crow over her husband; but the contempt with which she ordered John to his former hut, and the assiduity with which she thought up tasks for him which no white man had hitherto performed on the coast would have made him more miserable, if such things had not almost ceased to affect him.

In fact the combined effect of disappointment, illness, hunger and exposure had robbed John of spirit and of resolution. After his flogging on the *Harwich* his mind had burned with plans for revenge; now, though he hated Clow and his mistress, he was too apathetic to plan and hopeless as to the result of any plan which he could conceive. A dismal sense of failure sapped even his powers of reflection. Nothing that he had done had succeeded; the chance occurrences which he had hailed as omens for good had led to more grief; he had been unable to win a good opinion from anyone; he could not impress Clow with his one remaining good quality of honesty. The ambition for which he had brought this train of disaster upon his head was now utterly impossible of attainment. Escape from the island was useless. If he had not succeeded with Clow, who else would want his service? Escape to a ship would, at unlikely best, return him to England in far worse state than he had left it. Why go to England if he could not go to Mary. . . . to Mary. He wondered if she had received the letter he wrote before he set out with Clow. Probably not. Letters changed ships and hands, and many ships were wrecked.

But he wrote again, several letters, and wrote to his father, filling up the paper which he had obtained from Clow while in his favour and found untouched between the pages of his Euclid. Usually he left his task and hid in the woods when boats visited, but on occasion Clow had him row with slaves or provisions to the ships; and on these occasions he summoned up courage to beg any friendly-looking sailor to take his letters in charge. The letters to "My dear Polly" hinted at his misery but stressed his undying devotion. To his father he was more explicit, but resolutely asserted that he would not return home unless expressly sent for. But what chance that his father would receive them or be interested in reclaiming a son whom he had threatened to disown, and who was now a servant despised by slaves? And was Polly still alive, and, if alive, unmarried?

"So here is your partner, Mr. Clow." He did not turn at the well-known voice. P.I. and Clow had stopped beside him as he planted the young wands of lime trees in their new orchard.

"Yes." Clow's harsher voice was heavily sarcastic. "Who knows, young ambition, but by the time these trees bear, you may go home to England, obtain command of a ship and — who knows? — return to reap the fruits of your labours? We see strange things sometimes."

P.I. crowed with laughter. John said nothing and the two sauntered on.

Month succeeded month. Even the thought of suicide, which had crossed his mind frequently at first, recurred seldom. He had first put it away, rather from the same dim sense that it would seem mean to Mary Catlett than from any fear of death. Later it seemed too much trouble. He sometimes wondered at the completeness with which any thought or fear of a deity had vanished from his consciousness. Even granting that such a being had existence only in the imagination, he might have expected superstitious phobias to recur in the difficulties and dangers he had met and in the weakened state of his body, but they did not.

A single pursuit partly escaped this atrophying numbness. Sitting disconsolately in the door of his hut one evening, while the slaves some little distance away were chanting in a strange barbaric rhythm, he found himself idly tracing a triangle on the hard earth of the compound. He hesitated a moment, then drew another triangle, labelled the angles, and slowly recalled the proof of the proposition of Euclid which he had memorized while on the *Pegasus*. This finished, he glanced around for his book and with it, walking casually lest he be noticed — although it was no little part of his humiliation that he was almost completely disregarded — he sought a sandy cove on the west shore. Here he took off his single remaining shirt, washed it as best he could, and hung it on a

140

bush to dry a little before he should finish drying it on his back.

Then, with the nearest approach to interest he had known for weeks, he opened the book and began, in spite of difficulty in concentration born of weakness and long disuse, to draw a diagram on the sand and, muttering the hypothesis, to work his way through the next proposition. This diversion, which he could indulge only on the rare fine evenings of the rainy season when he was not summoned for some extra task, became the one dignifying interest of his existence. Slowly, ploddingly, he completed the first book, then the second; by the time the rains were over in October and he could seek asylum more regularly he was master of the first four books and well into the fifth.

14

BEFORE the rainy season was well over, Newton became aware that Clow was not to be left longer in sole possession of an island so advantageously situated. The continued presence in harbour of a sizeable cutter, which at first sight he had taken for a visitor from a man-of-war farther up the coast, then much unloading and clearing at the far end of the island brought it to his consciousness that another trader was establishing himself within a mile of the original plantation.

At first it did not occur to him that the change could have any personal significance. He wondered how Clow and P.I. would be affected and concluded indifferently that the companionship of his own kind would please the former and antagonize the latter. For himself it meant only the embarrassment, which was still an acute discomfort, of trying to keep out of sight of a white man, or white men, for this Mr. Williams — a name which suffered strange things in w's and l's on the tongues of the natives — was evidently a more prosperous trader than Clow and employed several Englishmen in charge of his affairs.

Employed? The idea took root and germinated, though not quickly as it would have done earlier. Some days passed before he acted upon it.

"Mr. Clow," he said, after listening to detailed orders about scraping the shallop's keel, "may I have your consent to ask Mr. Williams for employment?"

Clow swung back on the heel which had already turned away.

"What makes you think Mr. Williams would take you? Have you asked him?"

"No, Sir. But he employs other white men. And you have no use for me here."

"That's not for you to decide," said Clow sharply. "And it's neither here nor there. I have no grudge against Mr. Williams that I should palm off a dishonest loafer on him. Now get off to the boat."

Newton went perforce, cursing Clow with a horrible thoroughness for which he had not recently felt the energy. The germinal idea had scarcely been a hope but he felt its blighting almost keenly. The keenness dulled as days went on and he took little further interest in the building and activity down the island.

One clear evening a few weeks later, John stood, glancing from the book in his hand to the rather involved polygonal diagram of the twentieth proposition on the sand before him. Book Six had interested him more than the others but bodily weakness induced such weariness by the time evening came, that it was difficult to summon enough concentration for its requirements.

"An unexpected place to find a student of Euclid."

I must be getting deaf, too, thought John, not to have heard anyone coming. He knew who his visitor was without glancing up. Abashed, he tried to speak and failed. Mr. Williams took the book from his hand with an apology.

"Book Six. I'm afraid I gave it up at Book Five," he said, still pleasantly. "Tell me — Newton is your name, I think — Mr. Newton, why are you pursuing mathematical studies?"

It was the first "Mr." addressed to him for half a year. John lifted his head and his direct blue eyes met the equally direct gaze of his questioner.

"Sir, it is the only book I have, the only thing which — which takes my mind —" he stammered and looked away again.

"You do not, I take it, like your present situation?"

"Like —!" John caught himself in time. His glance was eloquent.

"I see." Mr. Williams was silent for a moment while John's stick made of the careful diagram something Euclid had never dreamed. "Why do you remain then? Mr. Clow has no legal hold over you, has he?"

"Where and how could I go?"

"I could use another man. Would you come to work for me?"

Words tumbled over one another.

"I asked Mr. Clow if I could — some weeks ago, I think — apply to you. He refused —"

"Can he keep you from coming?"

"Would you take me without his consent?"

"No. I see your point." Williams meditated. In the struggle for survival the few white men on the fringe of the Dark Continent had for self-preservation to maintain at least a show of amity. However John had come into Clow's possession, he was his servant and to break the unwritten law of property was to invite reprisal. Mr. Williams had noticed and asked about the strange white slave. He had, in fact, heard of him before he came to the Plantanes, for gossip flourished where news was scarce and, although Clow could have killed a white man in a duel or quarrel, he was regarded vaguely as lowering European prestige by degrading an Englishman to John's position. Clow's excusing accusations had not impressed the new settler, still less when P.I. had joined in with unconcealed vindictiveness. Morals mattered little to Williams but he was a shrewd judge of character and felt that he could trust this emaciated, dispirited boy farther than his master. Besides he had a strong sense of caste.

"I think perhaps I can overcome Mr. Clow's objections," he said at last.

John spoke bluntly.

"You must know that Mr. Clow accuses me of dishonesty — of making free with his goods and pilfering them while I was left in charge of his boat."

"Is it true?"

"No," said John simply. "But you have only my word against his. I would have you ask him for proof, however. He refused to give it to me. Beyond that you must judge."

"That I shall. Good-day, Mr. Newton." Mr. Williams was not a waster of words.

John watched his unassuming but confident bearing till the

144

furze-tufted bank hid him. Then he sat down on the sand, shaken between the sensation of feeling like a man again and the sick dread of conceiving another doomed hope.

Mr. Williams was not a waster of time either. John never knew what he said to Clow of reason, cajolement, polite request, suave warning. He did not know whether Clow himself, having kept him to satisfy P.I.'s childish vanity, was glad of an excuse to conform again to established practice. All he knew was that two days later he received at the hands of Muni a written release from Clow's service, with the additional information that Mr. Williams expected him to report at sundown.

The time on the instructions was not irrelevant. Mr. Williams, when he committed himself to any course, committed himself thoroughly. He was taking Newton on trust; that trust should be absolute. He was treating him as he believed a white employee should be treated; therefore it was unwise for those whom he was to control to see him looking less cared for than one of themselves. What those in his service already knew by hearsay he could not help; but they should see nothing to lower John's status of a trusted junior manager.

Accordingly the unpretentious roomy house was empty when John arrived, except for Williams himself and an English-speaking Fullam woman who acted as his housekeeper. John was given warmed rain-water and the forgotten luxury of soap — a homemade soap compounded from palm-oil but cleansing and soothing, producing the first lather for his shave that had spared his skin for many months. Williams's own clothes were the right size for him, though generous for his present thinness. In them, and with the unaccustomed feeling of shoes on his feet, he came to dinner with his employer, where his shrunken stomach and his ravenous appetite were at such enmity that he could eat very little without agonizing discomfort.

His hardy constitution threw off this impediment to recovery after a few judiciously taken meals. In the days when his strength was rapidly returning he spent hours with charts and maps of the coast, while his new employer showed him the location of his several factories or headquarters for trade, with special reference to the new situation on the Kittam river well over a hundred miles to the south. He discussed terms

145

and wages frankly, so that John could look forward to immediate satisfaction and to lucrative increase. And, when within a fortnight Mr. Williams went on the cutter to transact business in the Benares, leaving him in charge of the estate which comprised, slaves, buildings and goods included, easily a thousand pounds, John was almost intoxicated with well-being.

Any doubt that this state of things was too good to last was dispelled when Mr. Williams returned, was satisfied with the progress of work in his absence — a ship had called and John had traded advantageously — and introduced another of his employees who, with him, was intended to take charge of the Boom Kittam factory. In spite of his twenty-seven years, six of them on the coast, McCaig had a round fresh face above a rotund but muscular body and looked younger than the twenty-one-year-old sailor. John, isolated and condemned for so long, was disposed to find any comradeship congenial. By the time the two set off in a shallop up the Kittam they were well-pleased with each other's company.

The swing from hunger to plenty, near nakedness to adequate clothing, disgrace to responsibility, loneliness to friendship brought such surging animal spirits to Newton that for the first time he considered himself happy. Not happy as he could be with Mary — there was no doubt of that in the mind which seldom in his waking moments let an hour pass without some thought of her — but able to enjoy the mere fact of living with gusto. Mr. Williams's only fear, as he saw the two aboard, was that his new recruit's exuberance might lead to excesses which would make him susceptible to tropical fevers. Otherwise he was pleased with his decision. The young man was not addicted to drink; he knew his weakness in that respect and could stop — an odd but desirable virtue in an otherwise intemperate constitution. His tongue was witty and its profanity was at least not monotonous, though its calculated blasphemy sometimes made Williams raise his eyebrows. Not a passionate man, he was realistically tolerant of the passions of others.

"As long as you attend to business and don't antagonize the natives, you may live as you please," he said indifferently.

"He means it, too," McCaig said, when Newton reminded

him of this in extenuation of his participation at a three-day native feast. "But I've been longer in this country than you and have buried three or four who couldn't mix the climate with dissipation. It's a good thing to know the time to stop."

"I do. Or I shall when I come to it." John stretched comfortably on a hammock slung on bamboo poles in their living quarters. "Don't be afraid of burying me. Did I tell you that Karfa found an adder coiled in my pallet just before I went to bed one night? Or that a leopardess leaped at me near a water hole and he got it with his spear? The devil wants me at large a while longer. 'I must work the works of him that sent me. The night cometh when no man can work.'"

"Mr. Newton, I beg you to desist from that in my hearing." McCaig, who had been reared among Presbyterians, looked as severe as his round face would let him. "I make no pretence to be a religious man but I'd be afraid to mock the Scriptures as you do."

"Why, if you make no pretence?" It was a source of endless squabbling in which John always felt the superior logic of his attitude. "Once I was blind — like you — now I see. When I was a child I thought as a child — like you. Now that I have become a man I have put away childish things. You haven't. Why be afraid to mock what you call the Scriptures if they are no truer than the Koran? And if they are true why behave as if they aren't? 'Thou shalt not take the name of the Lord thy God in vain. Thou shalt not commit adultery. Flee fornication.' There are strong words on drunkenness and carousing. Yet I saw you —"

"Have done, have done!" said McCaig, laughing at the singsong in which John, finger-tips together, lips pursed and head solemnly bent, intoned the last sentences. "You may laugh on the other side of your face some day but it may not give me any satisfaction if I'm not one of the elect either. You are wrong about one thing though. You've never heard me mock the Koran — to a Mohammedan at least."

"Now there's a religion I might adopt with enthusiasm, especially the diluted form some of these natives have," said John idly, thinking of Miles Cleaver and the shocked admiration with which he had heard much the same remark from him. "Compare its tenets with the milk-and-water teaching of Jesus. Say a few set prayers five times a day, fast till sunset one month a year and eat all night to make up for it. . . . do without wine — bad for you in a hot climate anyhow — and go to hell as you please, you'll end up in heaven. And what a heaven! Besides allowing four wives with extras on earth!"

"A good system, I'll admit. And it keeps women in their place," agreed McCaig and wondered at John's sudden abstraction.

Thought of Mary, pain at the idea of Mary, which drove him to the nearest pleasure at hand to quell his longing, was the only drawback to this period in which nature rioted after her long suspension. It was beautiful weather, the peak of the dry season. Brilliant colours, eye-feasting sights, rich variety of sound from the throb of African music to the harsher musical chatter of monkey and bird, even the dangers encountered and avoided with no more than a casual soon-forgotten thrill: all were for his enjoyment. The authority and independence of his position challenged him. It was a point of pride as well as pleasure to win the confidence of headmen in hitherto unvisited towns, becoming adept at dealing with them, learning their customs, satisfying his omnivorous appetite with strange food, and feeling, on his return to the factory after several successful trips, that he was coming home.

The factory was situated in a "town" governed by a "king" under the law of the Purrow. The west shore of the Boom Kittam, the southermost tributary of the Sherbro, was a long peninsula at no point for many leagues more than three miles wide; the factory on the outskirts of the native community was less than a mile from the sea coast. The king reminded John of the other grave old chief who had entertained him with Clow up the Bagru. This man had some lingua franca and the two were presently able to communicate with a freedom which McCaig, whose gifts were not linguistic, admired without envy. Like Mr. Williams's, the young Scotsman's ultimate goal was retirement to Britain with a competency. To that end, but impersonally, the natives interested him; he could go on

148

among them to the end of his life, as a creature of a separate species.

Not so John. The arrogance of his nature was the undiscriminating arrogance of unsure youth; in his humiliation and ill-treatment, relief and pity had come from black more often than white. Besides, cut off from books, his avid curiosity turned to people, and while some of their customs revolted and others amused him, he was quick to admire the justice and honesty of many natives, particularly those of the Purrow, and particularly those who had not been corrupted or embittered by dealings with unscrupulous whites. When McCaig was away he became accustomed to the fact that, sleeping in an unbarred house full of valuable goods, he was in greater safety than he would have been in London. And more and more he was invited with ceremony to feast with the chief and with his council.

"When you next go elephant-hunting," he said one day, inspecting some ivory which had been brought for sale, "take me with you."

The chief nodded.

"Too late now. Perhaps twelve days. Or another month."

John was disappointed. The idea had just attracted him and he craved immediate action. His mind was too variable to depend on his interest holding until the stated time.

"Why not this week? The weather is fine."

"Past the full of the moon?" The round dark eyes of all present turned on him with such incredulity that his curiosity was aroused.

"Why not?"

The old chief shook his head patiently.

"We make no expedition when the moon wanes. Only evil comes of it. Best for men not to sleep when the moon is above the horizon. At the full moon we feast all night to keep watch."

"What do you think will happen?"

The chief's shrug ran like a physical echo around the councillors.

"Who knows? The dark goddess is hostile to men. Women she fertilizes. Her beams make sleeping men impotent." He

149

nodded sagely at John. "The adder in your bed. Was there no moon that night?"

"Yes — yes," said John recollecting. "The moon was bright late every night, I remember."

"And the leopardess which sprang?"

"It was before dawn," said John thoughtfully. "The moon had not set. But I was saved both times. Good omen, not bad."

Again that ripple of a shrug through the circle.

"Karfa guards you. Karfa keeps watch in the moon's reign. You believe not white men's god, my son. Well. But mock not the moon spirit. We have seen. We have known. She is powerful."

John laughed to McCaig about the warning and about the amulet of "agri" beads which the chief's first wife gave him. He did not throw the amulet away, however, and later at dusk on the day of the full moon he met his partner at the door.

"I'm going to bed," said McCaig yawning. "Up at dawn if I'm to get away early. I think Mr. Williams will be pleased with the month's work. Coming, Mr. Newton?"

"I think I shall wander over to the square for the festival."

"You need sleep more than a festival. And you've not had much these last few nights, have you? Remember my warning — I'm not criticizing your morals. My own aren't above reproach. But —"

"I've been near death too often for you to frighten me with it," said John carelessly. "To lessen your concern I had a siesta today. I am interested in this moon ritual, and may be up river this time next month."

McCaig looked at him curiously.

"You'll grow black, if you continue as you are. They don't do it at your age usually. But you have the chief indications."

"Grow black?" The phrase was new to John. "Like Clow do you mean?"

McCaig laughed shortly.

"Clow isn't growing black. His only distinction is that he is a white man. Rather, P.I. considers that she is growing European. No, the man who grows black becomes genuinely interested in African customs, ceremonies and people. He has no interest in going home. It usually begins with the

150

realization that life here is easier and more carefree, if not more comfortable for him; and from then on he is assimilated to native ways. And you are showing symptoms of the disease."

"Perhaps I shouldn't consider it a disease," said John unperturbed, and went his way to the throbbing drums, the prolonged barbaric conjo, the propitiatory blood ritual, the symbolic shelter of heads from lunar rays, the long-drawn feasting — palm-oil soup, roast antelope and effervescent banana wine — which went on after dawn, until the moon bowed herself palely down the western sky.

He turned the phrase and the possibility over in his mind during the weeks of McCaig's absence in the Plantanes. They had intended to make another inland trip before carrying their gains to headquarters but the accumulation of goods and slaves taxed the factory's accommodation and John's next voyage was postponed until his partner's return. It had been his preference that McCaig should report to Mr. Williams, and even this, his willingness to remain alone among the natives, gave colour to his friend's suggestion. Would he not be better to give up all thought of returning to England and live out his life here? If Polly — yes, this was already February and Polly had turned eighteen in January! — was not already married, there was little hope that she would still be free by the time he amassed enough fortune to go home. She had never completely discouraged him, but neither had she given him any reason to believe that she cared. What chance in the world that she had waited and refused others, eligible and immediate? And if he could not marry Polly, the disappointment was easier to bear here than in England where everything would remind him of her, even if he never saw her again. Remind him! As if he needed a reminder, when every wholesome delight of ear and eye made him long to share it with her and to warm himself in her gay or grave enjoyment.

He moved her idea to the outer circle of his thoughts to return to his consideration of McCaig's remark. Since, without Polly, he had no place and no desire for a place among his own countrymen, why not make the best of what he had found here? Some white men found the climate impossible. His body had survived the worst conditions it would ever meet and was now, in defiance of McCaig's forebodings, full of vigour. He was happy — or would be if he reconciled himself once and for all to the fact that Mary was lost to him. If he deliberately entered into closer engagements with the natives it would help him to gain a feeling of permanence, to allay his restlessness. A wife, in time several wives judiciously chosen, would give him connection and advantage in trade. It would also be preferable in comfort to his present dependence on uncertain and desultory relations with an assortment of slaves, and the constant risk of running foul of some law of the Purrow — although that in itself, he reflected perversely, was not without zest. An establishment of his own, enough women — wives, concubines or slaves — to minister to his comfort and enable him to entertain as he pleased; books — eventually he *must* assuage his long unsatisfied craving for books; unlimited freedom of action for as long — or as short — a time as he had to live. What more, always excluding the One Thing, could he want? And how much less he had recently had!

He was not given to long deliberation. By the time McCaig returned, he had entered into preliminary talks with the chief regarding his daughter by a young third wife, a light Camma girl from the Ivory Coast. John was enormously amused by the gravity of the preliminaries for a wedding in which the bride would expect to share her husband with any number of other women and, even as first wife, be little more than an upper servant to her lord. The ceremonial could not take place immediately, both because of his next trading trip and because the season was not propitious — it was learned by elaborate divination — for marriages. But the chief was pleased and gracious. She was without blemish — and still, by choice, a virgin. Did Mallam Newton object to that? Virginity, though rare, was honoured in his tribe. There were other tribes in which no man would accept a virgin as wife. The detriment could be duly removed before marriage if desired. Newton would, of course, inspect her. And as for price — John, controlling any evidence of amusement, solemnly waived the disadvantage of virginity, and tried to subject his future bride to an inspection as critically appraising and impersonal as he was learning, in spite of temperamental difficulties, to bestow on the slaves he purchased. The girl, perfect from her small shaven head to her small shapely feet, was restive under the scrutiny and showed such evidence of natural modesty that John could not bring himself, though urged, to count her teeth and ascertain the truth of her father's claims as if she were a young animal. Passion was one thing — that overwhelming urge which he had not the power, nor any longer the desire, to resist; but he was not yet sufficiently acclimatized in his thinking to treat this girl, who might bear children to him, as if he were buying horse flesh. He declared himself satisfied, consented to undergo the ritual of blood-brotherhood with the clan and began to make plans for a house near the factory.

McCaig, returning from the Plantanes with tidings of Mr. Williams's pleasure at their success, heard the news without surprise.

"I suppose you've faced the possibility of a complete change of mind in the future? What if, when you make your fortune, you wish to go back to England?"

"I shall go, I suppose," said John indifferently. "Why live in the future as you and Mr. Williams are doing? I prefer to take what is offered here and now."

"I hope your domestic arrangements won't interfere with our pipe and our cards," McCaig observed drily, "though it would be better for my purse to play less often. You must have influence with the spirits, for I've never had worse luck than when I play with you."

"I'm a good hand, as you'd say if you won, and not put it down to luck," said Newton. "Perhaps Mr. Brownridge will join us in a game tonight."

The Mr. Brownridge in question was another trader from Gambia whose boat had caught up with McCaig's in the river. As a white man he had been welcomed to the hospitality of the factory, and dinner was under preparation. His arrival interrupted their conversation now and John was confirmed in the dislike which he had felt on first sight of him. A powerful man, almost equal to Clow in stature, he had an offensively supercilious manner and an unpleasant, knowing laugh. As the meal proceeded, Newton, who was not usually harsh in judgment, wondered why he himself had been subjected to so much ill-treatment in a world which allowed this

153

creature to live to maturity. Repeatedly during the meal a covert sneer or an insolent glance from his light-blue eyes provoked him to a quick retort, and McCaig exercised all his powers of diplomacy to prevent an open breach.

After dinner they played three-handed whist, but again Brownridge's irritating manner and veiled innuendos when Newton won incensed him, so that after one game he pushed back his bench and stood up.

"It's a better game for four or two," was all the comment he allowed himself and, leaving McCaig to entertain the guest, went outside to walk off his annoyance in the starlight.

He had almost succeeded, for the spacious air and the fragrant land breeze from the river were soothing; and he was re-entering the candlelit living-quarters of the factory when the newcomer's voice, strident under the influence of the excellent rum he had been drinking, struck him coldly:

"Growing black? What else can you expect? No self-respecting whites are going to accept Clow's drudge, an Englishman who has licked P.I.'s European boots. Each to his own, I say."

"Mr. Brownridge," — McCaig's Lowland accent was very marked — "may I remind you that you are speaking of my partner and the trusted servant of Mr. Williams? I am bound to resent comments which reflect adversely upon his judgment."

"No offense meant." Brownridge's voice restored the offense which the words subtracted. "You have to make the best of the situation — more honour to you. And for Mr. Williams's sake I hope the young deserter has learned his lesson and won't try any sharp practice on him as he did on Clow. . . ."

"That's a lie," said John coming into the circle of light and loosing his pent-up wrath in a stream of profanity animadversive of his accuser's person, conversation, mannerisms, and pedigree, which brought Brownridge to his feet, the cynical sneer gone. The visitor replied in kind. Newton, without repeating himself once, returned to the verbal attack and McCaig flung himself between them to prevent their gigantic guest from striding over to chastise his partner.

"Mr. Brownridge, remember you are our guest," he protested, "and Mr. Newton had provocation."

"I'm not asking for protection," said John, ungratefully,

though his clear head realized that he was no match for Brownridge with his fists. "It's like a bully's cowardice to malign my character and then provoke a fight with a man smaller than himself." And John's five-foot-eight-inches, even when his frame was more robust, would have been ill-matched with his attacker's massive six-foot and more. "If he is as brave as his words, let us fight it out with pistols."

Brownridge hesitated. McCaig seized the opportunity.

"John, Mr. Newton." He quickly reverted to the formal title. "Think what you are doing. It outrages all the laws of hospitality. It will lower our prestige immeasurably with the natives if you are successful, and if you aren't, consider my position, consider your obligation to Mr. Williams."

Brownridge had also been considering. He had no idea how good a shot Newton was, but in the middle of an exploratory trading-trip he was not inclined to find out. If McCaig had not interfered he could have given the foul-mouthed young blackguard a good thrashing. As things were, he took discreet refuge in McCaig's plea.

"Sorry to forget what I owe you as host, Mr. McCaig," he said, "though no other consideration could make me overlook your partner's insults."

"I am not asking you to overlook them," interrupted John, pressing the advantage which his suggestion had given him. "I challenge you to meet me in the morning — you may have Mr. McCaig for a second and I shall do without. . . ."

"Mr. Newton," said McCaig patiently, "if you have no concern for your own safety, let me repeat what I said about your duty to Mr. Williams and the feeling even of the tribe here. You cannot shoot a man who has broken bread under your roof."

"I will have satisfaction," said John stubbornly, wondering a little at the tenacious anger which possessed him. All the resentment, the bitterness, the implacable hatred which his former harsh treatment both on the *Harwich* and under Clow had engendered, was revived and concentrated on this contemptuous newcomer. "Very well, Mr. McCaig. If we cannot meet now and here will you exact a promise from Mr. Brownridge to meet me at a more convenient place and season?"

This McCaig proceeded to do, eliciting from the trader the

probable time of his return from his visit to the Tong River and an assurance that he would meet Newton after due formalities either there or at the Plantanes. They parted for the night, and if John awoke in the morning feeling rather relieved than otherwise, his relief was due to pride in having maintained his honour more than to concern about the outcome of the duel.

Brownridge went his way, disappearing like a dirty cloud from a serene horizon, and the partners busied themselves with preparation for Newton's next up-country trip. February was well advanced and he was anxious to return before the rainy season. It would take him far inland up a tributary of the Kittam which led directly away from the sea.

"I thought you were bringing more rum and cider," he observed to McCaig, looking over a depleted stock. "Did you not bring any guns back with you? There are only half a dozen here."

"Mr. Williams was short himself," said McCaig.

"Flints," said John, enumerating. "We are low on knives too. It seems a pity to make the trip, lacking those. If we could hail a passing ship we might purchase what we need."

"Go down to the shore and watch for one," agreed McCaig. "Though I cannot say I'm too sanguine. In general those that pass keep well out from shore, not expecting to trade here. Still there is no harm in trying."

John returned several hours later without success.

"Ah, well, we may have better luck tomorrow," said McCaig with the patience of a man who has learned to wait on tides and rains and winds and the haphazard goings of vessels bound by them. He took alternate watch the next day with John, walking the scant mile to the sea and patrolling the firm yellow sand to relieve the monotony of staring out across the unresting blue to the blank horizon.

On the afternoon of the third day, John, who had spent the morning on shore, fire ready for the smoke signal, long canoes drawn by the beach, was entering in his note-book the last items calculated into bars. He was, they had decided, to sail the next morning and to do the best he could with the stock on hand. His prospective father-in-law had sent palm-oil wine, salt meat, dried lotus cakes and shea butter, gri-gris to ward off unnamed evils, as well as several jars of salve and antidote for bites and wounds. John smiled at the chief's concern for his son-in-law and thought instantly, the smile fading, of the man whose son-in-law he wished above all things to be, whose interference he had sworn never to forgive.

He heard his name called and scarcely recognized McCaig's voice, high with haste and excitement.

"Mr. Newton!" The call came again and McCaig came through the trees which fringed the low knoll to the west, flushed and perspiring with exertion.

"You've smoked a boat," said John pleased. "Better, you've been aboard, by the look of you. What luck? Did they have knives — and rum?"

"Both, but that is not the point. The vessel had already passed when I got to the shore and there was a fair wind. However, I thought I could lose nothing by smoking her and sure enough, she came to anchor and signalled. But this is the amazing thing. As soon as I went aboard the Captain said: 'Is your name, by any chance, John Newton, or do you know of him?' And when I told him that you were here, nothing would serve but he put ashore to see you. He has a message from your father. Karfa and I came ahead in the canoe. The Captain says he will not stay or dine with us and I engaged that you would meet him at the shore."

He paused for breath and looked at his friend who stood, as though arrested in the act of listening, the sun glinting his russet-brown hair to gold, his blue eyes dazed, his lips parted for a question that did not come.

"Go, man," urged McCaig. "We can't leave the Captain standing on the beach. I'll be down — Sunli, where are you? — as soon as I can get me a drink and bring Sunli to help Karfa carry the chests. Here, take your hat. Odd that I nearly missed that ship — the first one I ever smoked from here."

Captain Swanwick of the *Greyhound,* who introduced himself fifteen minutes later to the still spell-bound young trader, was a man with a mission. That John Newton should spend the rest of his life on the coast of Africa was, personally and understandably, a matter of indifference to him. But that he, Captain Swanwick, in addition to making a successful voyage for rare and difficult cargo, should succeed in a quest which

157

had been enjoined on him by Captain Newton through Joseph Manesty, part owner of his ship, was a point of pride and worth the trouble it had so far cost him. He had enquired at Sierra Leone and at the Benanoes, but had heard that the young man, if alive, was hundreds of miles away and had abandoned hope of finding him. In fact, he had been of two minds about coming around at the smoke signal, but had no regrets at his delay now.

"My instructions are most definite," he said while John, still inarticulate, stared at him without seeing him. "Your father wants you home. If you have incurred any debts or obligations, Mr. Manesty said — he seemed to think you might be in difficulties — I was to redeem you, whatever the cost, from my own cargo. Come now. Surely you want to see your father again?"

"I — don't know." John did not refer to the prospect of seeing his father, but to the whole matter of his return. If this message had come when he was sick and starving in Clow's service he would have heard it as life from the dead. Now he was curiously indifferent. England had meant restriction, disappointment, heartbreak; the boy whom he thought of with some detachment had been for the most part lonely, frustrated, ill-at-ease. Here he had found acceptance, pleasure, a life made for him with little need to make decisions, no constant belittling comparisons, and almost complete liberty. Why should he give it up? What good had England to offer in exchange?

Mary. Beneath the numbness his heartbeat had quickened with the thought of her as soon as he heard his father's message. For her anything would be worth while. If he were going to her, nothing that he had suffered would weigh against the joy, no suffering to come would keep him from hazarding the attempt. But to go to her penniless, with no prospect of proposing even if she were still free: that was unbearable, and that was more than a risk, almost a certainty. He felt the good soaking warmth of the sun; this was his here, with the flavour of food and drink, the strong incessant colours and untiring variety of things to hear and see, the abandoned freedom of sensual delight, the novelty of discovery, always flavoured with the pungent scent of danger and lurking death. Why give up substance for shadow?

"Surely you believe me," Captain Swanwick continued, the possibility of losing his prize driving him to greater efforts. "I swear" — and he did — "or by anything else you like that I've told the simple truth. I wish I had that packet of letters for you I've mislaid. They would tell you how your father feels." John did not care how his father felt nor did he believe that feelings played much part in his father's action. If he had felt, or cared for his son's feelings, all this suffering would have been avoided. It was one thing to call him home now, lest his deplorable condition under Clow should become known and reflect on an official of the African Company. See his father again? He had long since given up thought of it and without regret.

"There was something more, I was to tell you — though of course the letters would have given the details," pursued the Captain. "About some relative dying and leaving you a tidy sum — four hundred a year. Come, that's worth going home for."

But it couldn't be true, thought John; yet why was he saying it? Great-Aunt Henrietta might have died. He used to dream that she might leave him a legacy though he had seen her only once, when a child. But four hundred a year — unthinkable. If it were true, then he could propose for Polly — if Polly were still unattached. . . .

"I'm not asking you to work your passage," said Swanwick, his voice shocked as though answering an accusation. "Never think it. You'll lodge in my cabin, eat from my table, be my companion and passenger. I can't speak fairer. And I can't wait longer. Will you come?"

The pleasant heat-relieving breeze, the gold and blue and green of the island, the dusky familiar faces of his bearers, and the cloud of dark faces with whom he had cast his lot, all faded. He was back in a winter garden, looking with dumb adoration at a white English face, wind-reddened by the cold, with young generous mouth and green-gray eyes pitiful under brows that turned up at the ends.

"I must fetch a few things," he said.

He did not ask McCaig, who was standing beside him, for

159

his opinion, nor did he give more than a passing thought to his or Mr. Williams's inconvenience. Fortunately, McCaig would have considered the rejection of the offer madness but had been afraid that John was mad enough to reject it. As for the re-adjustments of his and his employer's plans, nothing was sure but change. He might have lost John — he had been reasonably sure of losing John — in an accident up river, in a dissipation-induced fever or in the event of a duel with Brownridge. This in some sense lightened him of responsibility. He retraced his steps to the factory, made up part of John's arrears in wages out of the small trading funds, pledged himself to give satisfaction from the rest to the chief for his defaulting son-in-law and saw him off in the ship's boat, scarcely more than an hour after he had borne the panting message from the shore.

15

THE Gabon estuary spread wide and tranquil under a rising December moon waxy white as a magnolia in the indigo sky. John paced the deck restlessly, waiting for his companions to emerge from the cabin. Captain Swanwick and the second-mate had gone ashore with the long-boat and were not expected back until the next day. The sun had flamed down the western waters with its year-round equatorial punctuality just before six, and night had immediately engulfed the hemisphere. Would he ever become accustomed to the long northern twilights, the uneven northern days? Would he ever reach England again? If he had realized when he committed himself to this blasted tub and its fast-talking Captain that almost ten months later they would still be nosing along the coast one thousand miles farther from Mary than when he embarked — well, what then? He would, he supposed, have done the same thing, though the hope had settled into a grim refusal to despair.

As for his legacy, Swanwick, when accused point-blank, had admitted that it did not exist. "I invented it on the spot, when you were doubtful about coming," he asserted laughing. "I reckoned that would bring you, and sure enough it did."

Not that Swanwick had failed in his other engagements. The only passenger on a busy ship, the Captain's guest had time on his hands and too little to employ his mind. He went ashore hunting or carousing, he took a passing interest in the trade — for the *Greyhound* did not carry slaves and its cargo of ivory, beeswax, dyers' wood, and gold took longer to collect — and an observant seaman's interest in the flora and fauna and sea-changes of the new tropic. At sea there was time to waste. The few books on board were soon devoured; the Bible he ignored, a translation of Thomas á Kempis he dismissed after a glance, as belonging to his salad days. Composing some stanzas to Mary filled an idle hour or so but increased the desire which drove him to mischief.

One such fit was on him now. In consequence he had challenged the first-mate, the surgeon, the purser and one or two others to a drinking bout at his expense. Drinking was still the least of John's excesses; but the restless devil within him enjoyed seeing his friends get drunk, and complete ennui welcomed the prospect of uninhibited hilarity. Besides, the moon was full and, though he smiled rather sheepishly to realize how seriously he had begun to take native superstitions, his emotions were always high-pitched under her unsparing beams.

The others emerged ready for the frolic.

"What's to drink?" asked the first-mate pulling his chair into the circle.

"Geneva and rum," John had both on hand, purchased from the Captain's store and, instead of a glass, a large crater-shaped shell of over half-a-pint's capacity. "This shell is the size of the draught. He wins who holds out longest, drinking alternately."

"Well, you won't win, that's dead sure," said the purser. "Lucky I have a steady head. One of us should be still vertical when the Captain arrives."

John filled the shell with rum and held it out for a toast.

" 'Lay on, Macduff,
And damned be he who first cries Hold, Enough.'

That's Shakespeare. John Newton will amplify it. What's the worst thing that could happen? Ah, I have it! The curse of the moon goddess upon him who starts first from the liquor."

"What's the curse of the moon goddess, you benighted heathen?"

John quoted the old chief's caution.

"Serve you right if it falls on you."

John finished his drink and passed the shell to the mate.

"I'll cancel Mr. Newton's curse," said Hardy. "Women all round at the next port!"

"That's more like it," said the surgeon waiting his turn. "Besides, for all your talk of the moon, she did us a good turn off Cape Lopez last month. Nothing will ever look better to me than that lop-sided moon breaking through the clouds to the east."

"I'll say Amen to that!" said the boatswain as the surgeon stopped for his drink. "And our master-navigator and buffalo-slayer here —" he nodded at John.

"What do you mean buffalo-slayer? I swear it was my shot that got him," growled the surgeon, wiping his mouth and passing the shell.

"Our master-navigator here," resumed the boatswain, "look ye, had carefully marked the place where you left the carcass. So we followed his lead, and what a lead it was!"

"Sometimes on dry land, sometimes to our bellies in swamp, no star showing, the night getting blacker," ruminated the surgeon. "No idea which way we were walking — except that Mr. Newton here has an unerring sense of direction, so he said!"

John broached the geneva and stopped with the shell in his hand to reminisce. The rum had lightened his spirits and he took the ribbing good-naturedly.

"So I have, so I have, but you forget one thing." He tasted the geneva, then drank the measure steadily off, and resumed, "My inner compass is geared for this side of the equator. Naturally it went in reverse down below the line. Simply proves," he went on, growing a bit argumentative, "that I'm not antipodal. Nothing wrong with that, is there? Is there anything wrong with that?"

"No," said Mr. Hardy, handing the geneva on to the surgeon. "It explains perfectly why, when the moon came up, you were headed, the men tell me, due east instead of west."

"And lucky for us it came when it did," grumbled the boatswain. "No light, no food, no arms in dense, god-forsaken woods."

"Whatever kept the animals off, I'll never know," said the surgeon. "Scared? I'm not ashamed to own I was and I've never been worse scared even in a tornado. I expected a tiger to rush from behind every tree."

"The lads were nigh petrified too," said the boatswain,

taking his turn at the geneva. "I'll say for our passenger here he was the only one who showed no fear. Weren't you afraid we'd die, Mr. Newton?"

"No," said John. "I'm afraid of pain, yes, afraid of being clawed or left to starve. Not of death. Why be afraid of eternal sleep?"

"You're going to get one hell of a big surprise when you die," observed the purser disapprovingly. "Not afraid of death! You'll laugh on the other side of your face then, you will."

John held his shell full of rum and proceeded to chant in his deep baritone a parody which he had recently composed on the twenty-third psalm. Beginning modestly enough: "Captain Swanwick is our skipper; we shall not want," it continued with a ribald travesty on his care for the crew which set the rest laughing uproariously, except the purser who tut-tutted disapprovingly, and then hiccupped violently to the renewed delight of his comrades. John kept his seat after this third drink by a determined effort, though he had a peculiar sensation of floating above it. The relentless shell, enormously enlarged, came round to him. He poured the geneva carefully and joined in the raucous chorus of a sea-song begun by the boatswain, laboriously waving the shell in time. The purser shook his head again.

"No cheating, there — spilling it and making out you're drinking it full. I'm suspicious of you — no cheating, I say."

"I'm not cheating." John gulped the geneva down a burning throat. "I'm not sheating. Who saysh I'm cheating? Do you say I'm cheating?" he appealed to the first-mate who became placating.

"Nobody says you're cheating."

"Somebody did," said John ponderously. "I heard him. A nice thing to say. Drinking my liquor and saying I'm cheating."

"I didn't say you were cheating." The purser was goaded to reply by the accusing eyes upon him. "I just said you weren't to cheat. That's different."

John appealed to the mate again.

"That different, Mr. Hardy?"

"That's very different." The mate was the only one of

164

the party so far completely sober. The quart of raw liquor was running through John's blood like fire. He tried to hold the floating chair but his hands could not find it. There was no chair. He could feel no chair beneath him. He had better stand up. He did and heard something crash behind him in a roar of derisive laughter.

"You think I'm drunk," he told them slowly and accusingly. "I'm not drunk. Dead sober. Thash the trouble with us English. We're too sober — thash —" he knew the articulation was important — "that'sh, no thash-t-sh whash wrong with us. Lesht have a dansh. The nashivt's dance. Enjoy selves — dansh all night — dansh moon down the sky. Like thish."

Still with the floating sensation lightening his limbs he began an ijo while the others kept time with their heels on imaginary drums. Their applause stirred him to renewed efforts.

"A dansh you never saw before," — he wiped his brow wet from exertion in the seventy-degree night air — "never saw — saw it myself jush once — a kowi dance — at a Conjo — spinning ball they called it. Spin like a ball. Hard to do."

The spinning on one foot was executed with more ponderousness than grace but the next movements: to dance on hand and foot, then on hands, then on spinning feet again, eluded his most determined attempts. More applause came from his audience. The surgeon had risen also and was executing steps suggestive of a hornpipe rather than a native dance. In the midst of the basic spinning operation John's hat flew off and disappeared overboard. He ran to the side. White on the black water and already some distance away with the swift-running tide floated his lost headgear. There too, below him, was the ship's boat.

"The boat," he cried, "get my hat, back soon." And just as he flung himself over, his left arm about to release its hold, someone caught his clothes from behind.

"Help," shouted the surgeon, hardly knowing what he did but clinging to the struggling hat-hunter. Hardy and the purser dragged him back over the rail to safety.

"You bloody young fool, there's no boat there," said the mate. And Newton, stunned if not sober, saw that the small craft at which he had been hurtling, was riding quietly at the end of her rope some twenty feet away.

"Name of —" he began but Hardy cut in on him sharply.

"Go to bed, all of you. That's a close enough shave for one night." And in spite of John's confused protests the frolic broke up.

The episode soon passed from John's mind, although the Captain, to whom it was related, took occasion to warn him of the narrowness of his escape; for his inability to swim, the strength of the tide, the fuddled state of his companions had made death inevitable except for the drunken instinctive clutch of the surgeon.

John heard him through and turned the warning off in jest as he did Swanwick's remonstrance, not the first, concerning his blasphemy. It had become a point of pride that his newly invented oaths and sacrilegious parodies could make a hardened and passionate man like the Captain squirm. Somehow it marked the measure of his superiority over these superstitious slaves to the fears of a religion they disregarded in practice. The remonstrances too he resented as an infringement of his guaranteed liberty on board; they drove him to more ingenious efforts. These, together with his lurid narrative of past misdeeds and his ready argumentative ridicule of every Christian dogma in the long hours of cabin talk, while the *Greyhound* negotiated with winds and currents on her seven-thousand-mile homeward voyage, made Swanwick shake his head and wonder if he had taken a Jonah on board.

The exhibitionist talk and the finesse of blasphemy were John's outlet for an active mind bereft of food, a vigorous body deprived of activity. He diverted himself occasionally with mathematics; he talked scraps of French to the surgeon who knew less than he; he composed proposals to Mary, and broke off usually in a panic to ask himself what lay ahead if his hopes there should be dashed. Drink gave him little satisfaction; interminable games of piquet, whist, backgammon did not stretch the length of the days from their departure from Annabona at the beginning of January across the South Atlantic almost to Brazil, then up with the trade winds to the coast of Newfoundland by the first of March. It was some

166

recompense for his inner uncertainty, for the imbalance between regret at the security he had left and fear of the insecurity he had invited, to quell the ignorant ranting and the half-digested second-hand beliefs of the few whose talk encompassed any topics other than tall tales and bawdiness — and John was not left behind in that conversation — with impressive arguments concerning a mechanistic universe and a rationalist view of man's place in it.

The Newfoundland banks furnished a half-day's healthy diversion while they fished for cod to vary their plentiful supply of provision. All fishing reminded John of grim days on Clow's shallop. The contrast between this carefree haul of plenty and that gnawing anxiety for one, gave him a brief period of satisfaction, and the knowledge, when they set sail again with a strong westerly breeze pushing the voyage-worn ship steadily ahead, that this was the final and shortest lap of his quest made him almost hilarious. So far, very much so good. Surely the omens were favourable that he would win Mary at the end.

16

THEN our Lord answers: I have taught prophets from the beginning and I still do not cease to speak to every creature. But many are deaf and will not hear, and many hear the world more gladly than Me, and more easily follow the likings of the flesh than the pleasure of God.

"The world promises temporal things of small value, yet is served with great affection; but God promises high and eternal things, and the hearts of the people are slow and dull. Oh, who serves and obeys God with so great a desire as he serves and obeys the world, and as worldly princes are served and obeyed? For a little benefit great journeys are undertaken; but for everlasting life people will scarcely lift their feet once from the ground. A thing that is of small price is many times busily sought; great contention sometimes rises over a penny, and for the promise of a little worldly gain men do not shrink to labour and sweat both night and day. . . ."

A reader's vice is that he must read, and several times in the course of the voyage John had taken up *The Imitation of Christ* only to lay it down after a few pages with a yawn and a feeling of pity for the long dead author of such unreal moralizing. Tonight the close, crowded cabin had driven him to take a turn on deck; but the March wind, blowing almost a gale, had driven him back to the cabin where a game was in progress; so once more he had leafed over á Kempis's volume. The obvious truth of the comparison he had read struck home: he had seen the penny-haggling time without number; and as for taking a great journey, which might bring no benefit at all — what better case in point than this on which

he was engaged? Whereas following the likings of the flesh —
was a man capable of such shrewd observation of human affairs
completely deceived in his premises?

He could not bear the force of the inference. The little
book snapped shut in his hand and he pulled a chair up beside the card players to watch their game.

John never found it difficult to sleep. The most constantly
recurring pleasure of this voyage had been the sybaritic satisfaction of lying in bed recalling the days when he had to turn
out of his hammock at all hours and in all weather. Neither
motion of ship nor howling of wind disturbed his healthy
slumber; yet before dawn on this March the tenth it was
rudely disturbed. A crash like a giant baobab falling in the
Guinea forests woke him, and a deluge of icy water over his
bunk made him spring from it to find himself standing in the
half-filled cabin.

"She's sinking!" The cry from above deck was hoarse and
wild. Newton groped in the blackness for his coat — in the
North Atlantic cold they were sleeping fully dressed — and
felt his way out of the cabin and along to the ladder. The
hatch was open and a heavy foot appeared on the top step.
In the pre-dawn light he saw the Captain.

"That you, Mr. Newton?" he shouted above the confusion
of noises. "Fetch a knife, and for the Lord's sake hurry."

Another giant wave broke over the damaged hull. John
stumbled knee deep along the passage, got his knife and made
for the ladder. Before he reached it one of the sailors swung
up in front of him. Just as he stepped out on deck, and John's
head had cleared the hatch a vast sea broke over them. The
man's feet went from under him, the vessel lurched, and he
was gone.

"My God!" said Swanwick when John, drenched and shaken,
joined him on the littered deck. "Well, it'll be one or all of
us next. Cut away that shroud and then give a hand baling.
She's filling fast."

With ten others John began the apparently futile task of
hurling buckets of water into a sea which returned them fifty-
fold. All his faculties were concentrated on the gigantic contest of meeting water with water, combatting cold with energy,
eluding the powerful cunning blows of the preying ocean. An

169

hour later with the dawn came a slight abatement of wind. John was called to the pumps and lashing himself there kept a steady rhythm of effort amid the hurry of desperate activity around and above him.

In the best of health and reckless of spirit, his recollection of past pain and privation kept him from being much affected by this unexpected mishap. It was one more of those circumstances which made good stories when the hardship was over. Even the disappearance into the icy sea of a man with whom he had chatted the day before left him comparatively unmoved. He was gone, all of them would be in a matter of days or years; meanwhile he was part of the primitive effort to cheat fate, to hold blind-stabbing death a little longer at arm's length. In this mood he found the gloom about him depressing.

"Cheer up, man, cheer up!" he said to the surgeon, who was pumping manfully next to him. The devil doesn't want you yet. In a few days this will be something to laugh at over a glass of wine."

Todd turned a grey face to him and burst into tears.

"No, no," he said wildly. "Don't talk like that. Better admit the truth. It's too late, too late now."

Meanwhile with increasing light the damage became apparent. The sea at the very crisis of the gale had hammered in the upper timbers on one side, and through this breach and the other leaks in the long unrepaired vessel the water was pouring at such a rate that, had not the cargo of beeswax and wood been lighter than water, she would have already sunk. Most of the sodden clothing and bedding was dragged laboriously from cabins and forecastle and plugged in the leaks. Then boards were nailed over these and, when this was done, those at pumps and those with buckets perceived, in an almost imperceptible lessening of the water, a slight return for their killing labour.

But there was no lessening of the strain as the ship staggered drunkenly up and down mountainous waves, her worn masts broken, most of her sails torn away, the cordage, rotted by long months in tropic seas, snapping under the impact of the storm.

"Here, Mr. Newton, let Matt relieve you at the pump," said Hardy, pausing by him at about nine o'clock. "The Captain

170

wants your help at the bowsprit. I'm going to see if I can get at the provision in the hold. The live-stock is all overboard. Come back as soon as you can. Matt must ready some food or the men can't carry on."

John straightened his numb limbs, and realized that he was almost spent with cold and unremittent work. He made his cautious way across the slippery deck, stooping under flapping shrouds and bracing himself for the wash of incalculable waves till he found Captain Swanwick examining the damaged foremast.

"Here man, lend a hand with this," said Swanwick hoarsely. "Think you can get aloft and secure that spar? This is beyond repair, we'll have to let it go."

"If I can splice the rope," said John running an eye over the yard-arm, and suiting action to word as deftly as his purple hands would let him. "Now." He climbed the shivering mast, made the necessary adjustments, caught and paid in the rope which dangled from the broken spar into space and regained the deck. "I think she'll hold now that the wind's down a bit. She'll not take a strain again."

"I hope you're right." But Swanwick spoke without hope. "Back to the pumps. With that sea aboard it's a wonder we aren't at the bottom now."

"Yes." John cast another glance at his work and turned with a shrug. "If this won't do," he said aloud, though the Captain was making his way to the starboard side and could not hear him, "the Lord have mercy upon us."

Had the incessant noise of the storm injured his ear drums? It suddenly sounded muffled and far away, outside the strange inner stillness that fell upon him, a hollow stillness in which his last words lingered, as though an unreverberate echo were prolonging and intensifying their utterance. Mechanically he found his way below and took the pump over from Matt, scarcely noticing that Todd's place had been filled by a more stalwart sailor. The brief respite had given him a renewal of endurance and, lashed to the pump, he began the rhythmic desperate struggle with no visible abatement of effort. But within, in that inner world where something had gone limp that was once taut and impregnable, a strange logomachia

171

went on, over and over, repeating itself with the rise and fall, the swish and gurgle of the pump.

The Lord have mercy on us. Why did I say that? I didn't intend to say it. It said itself. The Lord — I've said that or some such name a hundred times a day. This was different. This was not blasphemy, or ridicule, or even habit. This was simple; not intentional, no, not meaningful, but sober; as if it had meaning. And I haven't uttered a name of God without blasphemy for years. How many years? Why should I do it now? Danger? I've faced death before, time and time again. I've been colder than this. And as wet. And far, far weaker. But I never called on God before. Why should I? There is no God. No personal God, at least. No one who can hear. No one who can intervene. This storm is the working out of natural law. The ship is an accidental victim. What senseless cant: the Lord have mercy — mercy on us — mercy on me. What mercy can there be for me? What mercy — if there were a God of mercy — a God who could show mercy — should there be for me? So be it! I didn't ask. The words were not mine. I spoke without volition. Perhaps they were an echo — a recollection expressing itself in tiredness for lack of anything sensible to say. I've found myself humming tunes I learned in Wapping. Hymn tunes from Watts's book. Not the words, though.

He laughed shortly, thinking of the words he had fitted to those childhood tunes and sung to the uproarious applause of half-drunk companions.

The Lord have mercy. Even if there is a Lord — Thou art the same Lord whose property is always to have mercy — then there would be no mercy for me.

Crash! A cask in the hold shattered against the side of the ship, as she descended into the trough of a mountainous wave with a pitch as seemingly endless as if she would continue to the bottom.

And she will, any moment now. Each of these washing waves, each of these pitchy descents may be her last. Well, the sooner the better, if it's coming. I shall know then — either nothing, if death is the end, or the worst if those things are true, those things I once believed. And I'm past caring. I can't keep this up much longer.

Even his abstraction, his mood of sullen impatience, failed to maintain him after three more hours. At noon he called for relief. He had worked longer without it than anyone else, and when he stretched on the denuded bunk in his water-soaked, plundered cabin, he was too spent to care if he ever rose from it. Polly, Mary: he used her names as a sort of talisman to keep away the thoughts which had breached the ramparts of his indifference, and lay, too uncomfortable to be dozing, too exhausted to be conscious of his surroundings, for an hour until he was recalled to work.

"Can't pump again yet, I'm afraid, Sir," he reported to Captain Swanwick, for he had found his right arm almost too numb to swing him up on deck.

"No." The Captain had been astonished, except that hurry and pressure of catastrophe excluded astonishment at lesser things, at the steady toil which his undisciplined young passenger had already endured. "Think you can take the helm?"

"Yes, Sir."

"Keep her in to the wind, then. It's all we can do."

So began John's vigil, hour after hour keeping the ship lurching up and down the mountains of the sea. Around, below him, the rush and shouted orders and steady combative labour went on. Isolated and remote, all-important yet with dreadful leisure, he tried to concentrate upon the task under his hands, upon the extent of the damage to sails and masts and spars which he now saw for the first time in its entirety. But control of the wheel, even making delicate allowance for the unpredictable rage of wind and water, became quickly mechanical. The disorder of littered deck could not engross his mind, when each plunge of the water-logged ship might put an end to all need of mast or sail. Alone between a most fearsome sea and a grim threatening sky he could not escape thought; and the worst thought from which he could find no refuge was the thought, more than thought, conviction, that, isolated between the yawning sea and the torn grey sky, he was *not* alone.

No more than that; no more than that at first, it was enough, a breach wide enough to widen, as thoughts of which he had been free and undisturbed for years pressed their way

173

through. He knew little, he knew nothing. Yet because he knew nothing he had denied everything as if he knew everything. He could not believe what he had once accepted, accepted on the statement of others; so he had accepted the statement of still others to reject what he could neither prove nor disprove but what was believed by men who knew as much as he. Reject? That was one thing. But he had rejected with oaths and curses — why was that phrase familiar? — he had denied with blatant assurance, he had ridiculed and derided.

And what he had derided! If he was right, if the Scripture was fable, if the universe was at best a vast mechanism ruled by uncomprehended mechanical law, at worst a chance concatenation of atoms, then nothing mattered. But if — suppose it, though he had no evidence to believe and belief was the last thing he desired — suppose that it was true, what things he had refused and made others refuse, holding them up to profane ridicule! The life of Jesus, His rejection of power, His self-expenditure in acts of goodness, His deliberate acceptance of death, the preceding agony, the shame, the torture of that death; and whose death was it? and for whom? What, even if it were only fiction, was there to ridicule? But if true, it was the story of God, of God's Son, of God's mercy — but there could be no mercy for him. The unpardonable sin, that mysterious sin for which there was no forgiveness in this world or the next, he had certainly committed.

Ridiculous! he was talking — thinking — as if the Bible were true. He had no more reason to believe than he had had yesterday, or, for that matter, on those other occasions when he had watched death approach with seemingly sure foot, watched, and seen it turn away, without more than passing concern. But of what use was reason against assurance, argument against conviction? And though the assurance did not extend to the truth of Scripture, it convinced him that there was a God to whom he must answer, a righteous and holy God.

He stirred irritably. The helm twisted with the movement and for a moment he toyed with a diabolical impulse to let the ship swing broadside, capsize, and put a swift end to his doubts and to the dreary anguish of thinking. Instinct asserted itself. His fateful hands steadied the wheel and swung the vessel surely into the wind again.

The hair-breadth escape, the thin edge of crisis, recalled to his mind those other strange occasions when he had been spared or favoured: the span which separated his twelve-year-old body from the sharp impaling stakes of a new-cut hedge when his horse threw him; the five minutes delay which divided him from his friend's capsizing boat; the chance cutting down of his hammock on board the *Harwich;* his unlikely meeting with Captain Swanwick; Todd's wild grasp at his clothing as he went overboard in the Gambia from this very ship. If these occurrences had *not* been mere chance — so many in one short life — if God had been dealing with him, sparing him, giving him opportunity for repentance, what a requital he had made!

There his guilt was unique, there he was in worse case than the rest on the boat, than all the others with whom he had mixed. The holiness of God was just a word to him. The sense that he *was* dealing with an almighty God made him feel helpless, defenceless, strangely ugly and foul, but he had little sense of sin. True, he had indulged in sensuality without limit or compunction, but so did most of the men; if his desires were more insatiate than the average, that was his nature. But his urging of others to unbelief, to profanity, to excess, his restless desire to argue others out of the poor shreds of faith which they retained, his deliberate mockery of every sacred — or possibly sacred — concept, his defiance of God in daring blasphemy, of this he stood convicted. And he had been given opportunities and training granted to few of his comrades. He had read, learned, memorized catechisms, hymns, Scripture verses.

Scripture verses! As if a locked book were opened, those long-forgotten verses stood out in bold print on his mind:

"Because I have called and ye refused, I have stretched out my hand and no man regarded, but ye have set at naught all my counsel and would heed none of my reproof. I also will laugh at your calamity; I will mock when your fear cometh. Then shall they call upon me but I will not answer; they shall seek me early but they shall not find me. For that they hated knowledge and did not choose the fear of the Lord. . . ."

The shrieking of wind through bare yard arms sounded like the laughter of the offended God. John had no word to say in his own defence. He had rejoiced in sinning. He recalled his exultant reflection when rowed from the *Harwich* to the *Pegasus* that he could now be as abandoned as he pleased without any control. No, the justice of his condemnation was unimpeachable. God had offered; he had refused and refused and refused. Even what he now felt was not repentance — just realization, bleak, stark, dismal.

"For it is impossible for those who were once enlightened, and have tasted of the heavenly gift, and were made partakers of the Holy Spirit, and have tasted the good word of God and the powers of the world to come, if they shall fall away, to renew them again unto repentance; seeing they crucify to themselves the Son of God afresh, and put him to an open shame."

Crucify the Son of God afresh — that is, if he was the Son of God. But apart from that premise, the Scripture had no meaning. Could words, John wondered dully, have been written more specifically for him? And where had those words concealed themselves that they came so vividly now to mind:

"For if, after they have escaped the pollutions of the world through the knowledge of the Lord and Saviour Jesus Christ, they are again entangled therein and overcome, the latter end is worse with them than the beginning."

Well, so be it. It might be a biography, so true was it to his experience. He had known, he had escaped — at least outwardly — the pollutions, he had become entangled again, and his latter end was worse, much worse. He contrasted the nobility of his boyish resolution, his urge towards righteousness, the stabs of conscience, his repugnance at foul conversation and cruel or venal practice, his fastidiousness even in fornication during the early days of his indulgence, with his present callousness, indifference to duty, increasingly sordid appetite, insatiate desire to promote in others the mischief and rebellion which he practised himself. It was only human, he told himself. The excuse seemed singularly inadequate on the verge of an imperious Eternity.

He had not heard the mate come up behind him and started to hear a human voice at his side.

"I'll take over while you get some food."

"Food?" John had not expected to eat again.

"Not much variety, I'm afraid. Almost all our casks were stove in. But we're alive to eat. That's something."

Something indeed — and a slow new thought. John went below to find that Mr. Hardy had been understating the case. One small barrel had escaped, containing coarse grain, no longer needed for the hogs to which it had been fed. Their other sustenance was the result of their forenoon's sport off Newfoundland. He ate his share ravenously, gulping down fresh water to relieve the saltiness of the cod. The water butts, fortunately, had been tied in position.

At first the talk, subdued but babbling talk of tired frightened men, seemed irrelevant to him. All the long day he had fought with the rest, but it was with an instinctive desire to go down fighting rather than with any expectation that they would see another sunrise. Now scraps of chat drifted past him; if he took no part, each other man was too absorbed to notice.

"Free of water. . . . coming in slowly but pumps can handle it. . . . worst leaks stopped. . . . just a hundred leagues from Ireland, ... if wind holds steady."

Back at the helm under flying clouds and an occasional cold, peering star, John re-accustomed himself to the possibility of living. His assurance of imminent doom, his half-sullen, half-frantic desire to get it over with and know the worst; this had been so complete that his present hope was exquisitely discomfiting, like the awakening of a sleeping limb.

At first he tried violent treatment. If he wasn't going to die, that was that! Untrue to past experience though it was, his mind *must* have been shaken by fear of death. Now, if luck stayed with them, they would reach Ireland in a few days, and then what a story he could make of the storm when he saw — if he saw — Polly. Polly, Mary — he said both names aloud, fearless in the whistling wind, and tried to realize that he was closer to her than he had been for three years. Surely his luck would hold. Surely he hadn't been brought so far to fail in the one quest which gave meaning to life.

The talisman of her name failed of its magic; more, it failed to weigh his thoughts with the mandragora quality of its repetition. Unwilling, resistant, he was aware that the change in him was unaffected by the removal of crisis, rather that the crisis in himself was independent of outward circumstance. The God — if it was God — whom he had to face after death, he had to face here and now. And refuse to face Him though he might — though he must — yet the terror of His Presence did not depart.

As the evening wore into night, he began to think coherently, to apply to his situation some of the slow logic with which he had approached and bolstered his position as a free-thinker. If there was a God — and in view of the many who believed it was not incompatible with intelligence to admit the possibility — if God somehow, he could not explain how, and it ran counter to all the thinking of recent years, was dealing with him, then this reprieve, this latest of many, was also of His design. No, that was going too far, taking too much for granted; but at least, he might re-examine the evidence, reconsider the doctrines which he had thought finally disposed of.

He wanted to pray, began several times to pray, and gave it up. God, if there be a God. . . . God, if You are there as You seem to be. . . . God, if Thou — the personal thou was surely the better form — but on what grounds could he approach this unknown, this if existent, almighty, this if personal, estranged and justly offended, this if holy, revolted? For Jesus' sake? But that was sheer hypocrisy when he had no conviction that the story of Jesus was true — and *if* it was true, what vulgar mockery he had made of it. The death of Jesus was for sins not his own, true — *if He had so died* — for whosoever should believe, but he could not mock a heart-searching God (and whatever was searching his heart, it was being searched and revealed appallingly to him) by pretending belief. No, he could not pray, not with his mind. The cry that escaped him, repeating the Name aloud in fumbling puzzlement but in deadly seriousness, was as instinctive, almost as querulous, as the cries of the wheeling sea-gulls before they had dropped back several days before from the ship.

But he could do one thing, and he would, if this respite continued. He would search the New Testament, assuming

at least the possibility of its veracity. Then if it were true
— he used the subjunctive consciously — the God who had
arrested would surely enlighten. If it was, as he now half-
reluctantly feared, a fable, then would this disquietude leave
him, this relentless sense of Presence?

17

UESDAY morning, March fifteen. John awoke early with the cold although he had paced the dog-watch. Cold had been the worst of their distresses in the last five days. Food was literally monotonous, salt cod for breakfast, dinner, supper, with coarse bread made from the hog-meal served sparingly. Labour had been heavy with the pumps incessantly in use. But with much of their wood gone, with their bedding and clothes stopping leaks in the damaged hulk, the cold of the North Atlantic gale took more energy to combat than tired undernourished men, recent from a hot climate, could manufacture. Most of them had coughs and Todd in particular looked like a walking corpse. But the wind had continued to push the limping ship towards her goal and the storm had become something to curse as the cause of delay and hideous discomfort, and to congratulate themselves upon having encountered successfully.

"Land-ho!" Had he dreamed it? No, the cry came again, exultant, and the scuffle and tramp of responding feet, the confusion of voices reassured him. When he gained the deck the entire company was assembled, black against a tremulous first thrusting of colour of an uncommonly beautiful dawn, pointing, and laughing, shouting hysterically, embracing one another as they pointed.

"Calls for a celebration." Captain Swanwick's voice rose above the babble. "Time for the last of your bread, Matt. There'll be bread and to spare by nightfall. I have half a bottle of brandy left. Mr. Hardy, you know where it is. This is no time for hoarding. There'll soon be brandy enough."

His proposal was drowned by cheers in which John absently joined. Land at last — over to the east a long hilly coast-line terminating in a promonotory, and just beyond it two small islands low-lying in the sea. The north-west of Ireland no doubt. With any favouring wind they could find harbour by night.

Matt arrived with bread and mugs, Hardy brought the brandy, scarcely more than a pint. The liquor burned John's throat pleasantly. The chorus of gratulation and comment continued, but he was slightly aloof from it as he had been these past five days, full of his own thoughts. Now he noticed that he was not the only one who stood apart from the excited circle. The mate, mug in hand, had not taken his eyes off the sighted haven and John, following the direction of his gaze, became swiftly, inexplicably uneasy.

"Ireland, Scotland, England — as long as it's land!" said the boatswain. "Blowed if I set foot on a ship again. Land —"

"I hope it may prove land at last."

The grave speech and the graver tone in which it was uttered quelled the noise, but for a moment only. Angry disapproving voices were raised until the celebrants realized who had uttered it. One of their own number would probably have been knocked down in their superstitious indignation at the word of ill-omen. But Hardy's authoritative warning communicated gravity instantly to Swanwick and the rest crowded again to the side, gazing in an agony of suspense.

They had not long to wait. Day came on quickly and with its deeper light the surety faded. John's keen eyes were almost as quick as the mate's, but even the most stubbornly astigmatic was convinced when one of the islands reddened in the light of the sun whose great fiery ball presently rose immediately beneath it. Captain Swanwick was speechless with disappointment. Todd's gray face sagged into wordless foreboding. It was left to Hardy to give where he had taken away.

"Cheer up," he managed to say with sufficient conviction. "If it isn't land now, it will be soon. We must touch Ireland in a day or so."

"If we don't, there must be a Jonah among us, that I know," muttered the Captain, less easily restored than the rest.

The mate's cheering words lost their brief efficacy when

the wind died soon after sunrise. That day and part of the next the *Greyhound* rolled sluggishly on a levelling sea, her few sails manoeuvred to catch a listless flap of breeze. The crew, unless at the pumps, spent most of their time on deck, careless of the cheering warmth of sun as they waited fearfully, like children expecting noises in an empty house, for every sound, every rustle that should tell of rising wind.

Before noon on Wednesday, after a few vagrant, hope-raising breezes, the wind came up, came up in earnest, rose almost to a gale, but directly from the south-east. With the sea's first resurgent swell the *Greyhound* heeled over on its wounded side and only swift action, bringing her about to keep her larboard to the wind, saved her from sinking. But this same action kept her headed directly away from port, and as day dragged after day and a week lengthened to a fortnight the famishing sailors saw their ship increasing the distance between them and all known land, heading for unvisited northern waters where no other ship could sight them, where indeed no other ship might ever have been so early in the year.

John led two lives. Outwardly from a privileged passenger he had become a member of the crew, enabled by his former experience to perform almost any task aboard, and taxed like every man to capacity and beyond it in the prolonged agony of keeping the wreck afloat. With them he suffered from cold and sleeplessness and hunger — one half a salted cod was now divided among twelve men for their day's ration, and the supply dwindled with ominous rapidity. With them he saw Todd succumb from hardship, saw his body "committed to the deep" in grim preview of the fate which almost certainly awaited each one, if not a grimmer — for all the men had heard and on roisterous occasions joked at tales of cannibalism at sea, and none was sure, quite sure, to what lengths starvation-induced insanity might drive them.

In this regard John had trouble unshared by the rest. The genial Captain Swanwick who had pressed him aboard with false inducement made no secret of his bitter regret at having done so. *Something* had turned a successful voyage into a nightmare and most of the disasters had occurred after this shockingly blasphemous young libertine joined the company.

182

The earlier and later story of Jonah was unknown to him; but every English sailor knew that some ships had a "Jonah" aboard and the Captain vaguely recalled that a storm had ceased when the original was thrown into the sea. Whether he himself intended to do it, whether the men who heard his repeated forebodings would take the law into their own hands, John did not know. But the constant accusation — for Swanwick was so soured by his distress that he never passed him without some slur — was less than cheering; and his own conscience reproached him with enough guilt to have brought the anger of God upon the whole ship.

Of this change in his inward life no one was aware. Under normal circumstances no one could have failed to notice a startling manifestation: John had stopped swearing. He had not determined upon it, intended it — in a sense he scarcely noticed it. He simply stopped. Not only the calculated impiety, but the vigorous oaths with which every speech had been punctuated had disappeared in the shadow of this awful Reality which compassed him. It was not so much that he did not dare blaspheme; he did not want to blaspheme. The things he used to say were not only ugly but empty, not only daring but meaningless, if God was. And that God was, he knew; of little more, but of that he was certain.

The cleanness of speech passed unnoticed among men too weak for many words, too obsessed by personal misery for attention to others. Besides, in the brief leisure from work and watching he kept to himself. There, with himself, he wondered to find his condition almost uninfluenced by outward vicissitude. The days of comparatively prosperous sailing after the storm, the days of awesome uncertainty and increasing attrition after the false landfall, were alike in their effect — or lack of effect — on his inner being. There, he was riding out a storm of which the Atlantic gale was but a symbol. There, the long rudderless vessel of his life was seeking a compass, a chart, had become conscious of a dispossessed helmsman. There, he was embarked on a voyage so long that the termination of this one — even the manner of its termination — was of secondary moment.

He had set himself to re-examine the evidence. No one missed the Bible from its place and John was thankful for the

183

keen eyesight which enabled him to read it by almost any
light. But his attempt to read the New Testament consecu-
tively was disappointing. Familiarity made the narrative dull;
ingenious argument recurred unwanted at almost every page.
Realizing how much willingness had influenced his jettison-
ing of youthful belief, he had taken for granted that willingness would enable him to believe again. As a free-thinker,
he had despised those who wished themselves into faith. Now
he realized that wishing was not enough. His sceptical friends
would accuse him of being very anxious to find evidence for
the truth of Christianity. He was, he frankly conceded. So
would they be if God had shown to them as He had shown to
him, and having shown, refused to leave him indifferent, the
great fact of His Being and of his own appalling state. How
did he know it was God? they would ask. Let them call it
what they liked: it was Something without which they had
reckoned, and without which there was no longer any reckoning for him, a real Existence, a living Power, outside and
beyond, yet dreadfully impinging upon him. Talk himself,
think himself into faith indeed! Let them try!

Reading at a venture, he came upon a verse which stood out
suddenly from the other verses, as one opened blossom stands
out from a cluster of buds.

"If ye then being evil know how to give good gifts to your
children; how much more shall your heavenly Father give
the Holy Spirit to them that ask him?"

Polly with her new hat, the London hat which her father
had brought her from Rochester — "your brother Jack says
the ladies at Ranelagh are wearing them this season," George
Catlett had said, delighting in her delight. . . . the remembrance carried John's mind away on a flood of longing which
brought him close to tears. Resolutely he re-read the verse.
The analogy was perfect. That was how fathers gave good
gifts to their children. Similarly to those who asked — those
who wanted to become children? — God had bound Himself
to give the Holy Spirit.

If the Bible be true, reasoned John aloud (he was pacing
the dawn-watch as he read) this passage is true. I have need
of the very Spirit who wrote it to understand it rightly. He
has engaged here to give that Spirit to those who ask. I must

184

therefore pray for it; and if it is of God, He will make good His own word. I do pray then. I am asking. I don't believe the gospel. I don't believe this book. I'm not pretending. But I am willing to learn if it's true. If it is Thy promise, fulfil it, I pray. Give me the Holy Spirit.

Other thoughts crowded in on his attempts to pray. What was the other verse he had seen when he was idly leafing through the Gospels and finding little meaning there? He had to read five chapters but he found it at last.

"If any man will do his will, he shall know of the doctrine, whether it be of God, or whether I speak of myself."

That was fair enough. To will to do the will of God — not to do it; that was far beyond him — but to be willing: if this requirement was fulfilled, then the knowledge would come, the assurance. Well, he would put it to the test.

Putting it to the test he continued, without any dazzling light or further horror of great darkness, to examine and think through what he examined. He was not a rapid scholar; the principles of his infidelity were deep rooted. Slowly, ploddingly, he added conviction to conviction, without emotion, without going a step beyond the unavoidable impulsion of reason. God was and God was holy. He, God's creation, was a rebel and a sinner. He had no revulsion at the thought of his sins. His concept of mental and spiritual health was not very lofty; he only knew that he did not possess it and that without it he was estranged and uncomfortable and helpless in the presence of God. He was essentially realistic; for the first time in his life he had no desire to make excuses. In fact, he did not think he had an excuse. God's thoughts, he read, were not as his thoughts, but some comparison could be drawn. Certainly Scripture used anthropomorphic terms because in no other way could God be made real to man's understanding. Was that another evidence of its divine origin?

"If I could form a little creature and make it live," he said to himself with the whimsicality of tremendous earnestness; "if it hated and opposed me, slighted my kindness and took pleasure in displeasing me — more than that, incited other such creatures to rebellion, injured them and vaunted its puny defiance, would I not soon be tired of it and trample it under my foot like a spider or beetle? I know the answer.

Why should God bother with me another instant? But He sent His Son to die — not to reconcile Him to me, but, amazing thought, to reconcile *me* to Him. That is the Almighty Saviour I need. I have nothing to pay my own reckoning. Actually I don't know anyone with a larger reckoning. If this is true there is perhaps some hope. If it is false —" he broke off. Why then could he not return to the security of his former indifference? Surely it would be better than the unfathomable darkness which lurked on all sides of the feeble light in which he moved. Yet he did not want to return to his impervious state. Compared with the life, painful life, but life, which stirred within him, that other John Newton seemed dead, a return to his frame like becoming a corpse.

March, by count of day, but not by change in weather, became April. In spite of the black prospect and the possibility of greater blackness for him as the crisis of complete starvation approached, he could not despair. His body, perhaps inured by far longer privation on the Plantanes, endured doggedly; though weakening daily, he was able to perform heavier tasks and work longer hours than anyone else — a fact which may have counterbalanced the Captain's urge to dispose of him. But their survival day after day, instead of causing him increased foreboding, somehow engendered hope. And when he lingered after his watch on the morning of April the first to see the wind, which had died before dawn, come up gently and around to the very point from which they had desperately wished it, he uttered his first prayer of thanksgiving from an undoubting heart.

18

THE sea was too close to the villagers of Fahan on Lough Swilly and to the citizens of Londonderry to let them treat any strangers snatched from its entombment with indifference. When the crippled *Greyhound* crept into port four weeks and a day after sustaining her wounds, the villagers lined the quayside; and when the men who had shared the last ration of cod that morning tottered to land like incredulous spectres, they were welcomed as the welcomers would have wished their own or themselves welcomed in the same case.

Several weeks later, lying in the clean comfortable bed to which he had become quickly accustomed, John thought soberly of the past and the future. Since he had no position on the ship, which they would yet be a while refitting, he had repaired to Londonderry. The story of the ship's adventures had preceded him, and not only the people where he found lodging but the mayor and officials of the city went out of their way to occupy his time.

For the first packet sailing for England John wrote two letters. One acquainted his father with his misadventures and safe return. In it he wrote also, for the first time and freely, of his regard for Mary Catlett and of the insuperable barrier which the coldness between the two families raised in her parents' eyes. Then he sent it to the only address he knew at Rotherhithe.

About the second letter he hesitated much longer. If he wrote to Mary, what chance was there of an answer, at least of an answer which would tell him what he so ardently wanted to know? And if she was married, the embarrassment and pain, for he could not write to her without declaring his passion, was something which, even in the wave of physical sickness which engulfed him at the possibility, he would not willingly cause her.

He could not write to her parents. The last interview still rangled in his memory, and his state was worse than it had been then. He was older, true, but the years had been utter waste with regard to making him eligible. No, Aunt Hammond was his only possible contact. The letter accordingly had gone to her, containing a Liverpool address for the fateful reply.

In the meantime, while the chief business of his temporal life was necessarily in abeyance, the chief business of his spiritual life claimed the attention which his mind, honest now that it was free from the chains of prejudice and the whip of passion, told him it deserved. In spite of the grossly ungrateful returns he had made for clemency and favours, he was naturally susceptive of gratitude; and his recent experience had given him such particular cause for gratitude as to spur him in his determination to establish a right relationship between this hearing, answering God and himself.

The complete lack of such feeling on the part of his shipmates impressed him the more with a sense that God had placed His hand upon him personally. One or two prayers at wild moments of crisis, one or two mutters of, "Eh, thank God," at landfall, amid a chorus of: "Cheated Davy Jones that time," "If the ruddy fish had got us they'd have eaten solid cod," and, as far as he could see, their deliverance had made no lasting impression. They considered it a huge joke when they discovered that the fresh water of which they had drunk so lavishly had been their last — that five of the six large butts on which they had depended had been inconspicuously damaged in the storm and were empty. John thought of the additional privation which thirst and salt-fish would have occasioned, if they had known the truth earlier, and shuddered. He became thoughtful, too, when, scarcely two hours after their landing, the wind which had blown them gently for seven days increased to a lashing gale.

But the change which had come over him since that careless arresting utterance during the storm was outwardly nega-

188

tive. He no longer swore. He had lost all desire to joke about holy things. The Scriptures, admitted to his consideration, evidenced their power and their wisdom, their accurate presentation of man's heart and state, the utter suitability of their remedy to his need, so that he no longer actively questioned their truth. Determined to put himself in the way of conviction he had read Bishop Beveridge's sermons, finished Thomas a Kempis, now attended prayers twice daily in the Derry church, and had, several days before, gravely intimated to the minister his intention of receiving the sacrament. Making an effort to divest himself completely of his former cynicism he took for granted that what went on in church was right and good. He blamed himself, though not over-much, for finding the Sunday sermon dull and had been disconcerted at the clergyman's evident surprise that anyone should follow the rubric closely enough to signify his "intention" to come to the Lord's Table. Now, turning over in linen sheets with a sensuous enjoyment quite unimpaired by religious convictions, he determined to rise early the next day and prepare himself for the great event.

It was late in May when John reached Liverpool and, finding no letter from Mary's aunt, sauntered uncertainly past the Dry Piers across Pool lane and found himself sitting in Clevelands Square, a stranger with a strange anticlimactic homecoming. This — or perhaps yesterday — was the day Captain Newton was to sail from the Nore for Canada. The letter which had come by swift packet to John in Londonderry was the most affectionate his father had ever written. Delight at receiving his son back from the dead — for the *Greyhound* had not been heard of for eighteen months — had blotted out all memory of his shortcomings. John thought gravely of the son his father would have had to cope with several months earlier and wondered if the affection could have survived the revelation. He was warmed by his father's heartiness and by his insistence that if he reached England in time he should accompany him to his new post, where he was to be Governor of the Hudson's Bay Company. Secretly John had dreaded the possibility, even with the chance of a future thus offered; he had been relieved that delay on delay in the *Greyhound's* repairing, and the lack of space on other boats, made him honestly unable to reach England earlier.

Now he thought dispiritedly that his relief had been premature. To leave England almost before he had seen it again and without seeing Mary had been unthinkable; but to remain in England without hope of Mary was impossible. And what could Mrs. Hammond's silence mean but that Mary was lost to him, perhaps dead, more than likely married, certainly indifferent. He buried his head in his hands as he sat on the iron bench overlooking the Square, and wished that he had never left Africa.

Instantly he regretted his thought. The God whose he had engaged himself to be for ever on that solemn morning in Londonderry had not so dealt with him to leave him desolate. Perhaps, no assuredly, his passion for Mary had been idolatry. She had long occupied the place in his life which belonged to God alone. When he engaged to be His, only His, God had taken him at his word. Well, he would not withdraw, he *could* not withdraw from the covenant. What had God said to Ezekiel?

"Son of man, behold I take away the desire of thine eyes with a stroke."

With a heavy heart he sought the nearest inn, purchased a frank, borrowed a quill and inkhorn, and "troubled" Aunt Hammond for the last time.

"I do not expect to be ever able wholly to conquer my passion," he wrote, and finding his eyes full of tears turned his head lest they drop on the paper. "I will endeavour to keep it within my own breast and never to trouble either her or you any more with it. . . . I believe absence to be the best palliative for my disorder tho I have experienced it to be no real cure. . . ." He would, he wrote miserably, endeavour for a long voyage; since he had given up those hopes that chiefly made him esteem England, he looked upon the whole world as his country.

As if he were interring the body of his love, he sent the letter and continued to pace the streets of Liverpool. Would he be able to keep his word? A few months ago, neither ordinary prudence nor fear of causing distress and annoyance would have kept him from making his way to Chatham. And if he had found her finally unattainable, he would probably have carried out the intention of suicide from which hope of her had many times kept him.

Now, wretched, lonely, uncertain, he was nevertheless under Government, no longer completely tossed by the storms of passion and whim. He knew very little of the God whom he believed. The doctrines to which he had returned with his finding of the Reality of God, or rather, he felt, with God's finding of him, were, naturally enough, the basic beliefs which Christianity had implied for him before it was jettisoned. He found them as he read the Scriptures and the few books on Christian evidences he had been able to borrow; and though more seemed to be contained there, and a state of mind and experience quite foreign to his own, he felt vaguely that those things were goals to be attained by arduous self-discipline and unremitting vigilance. He had needed no argument to bolster his conviction of personal sin or the sinfulness of men as he knew them. What God had done in him had been unasked, undesired, therefore of God's sovereign grace — another incontrovertible fact. He needed an almighty Saviour to mediate and atone, and such a Saviour he found in the Gospels. He had the assurance that his past sins were blotted out. The future, he supposed, was up to him, struggling and availing himself of the means of grace. And at the last, he prayed in the language of the Prayer Book, he might come to His eternal joy.

From it he was certainly very far, as he turned moodily and aimlessly along one street after another. That he was to do something in the world he was sure. Else the Lord would not have so evidently interposed to prevent his being taken out of it. If his conversion was the only object in his being spared, why that amazing occurrence in Derry, the very day after he had partaken of the Sacrament, when his state of mind and spirit had never been more ready for sudden removal? He had been invited to a shooting-party by the mayor of the town; and, as he was climbing a steep bank, his fowling-piece had gone off, the bullet burning a hole in his hat-brim. The men had clustered around congratulating him on his providential escape. Escapes, they might have said — so many and so prevenient. At the thought, John straightened his listless frame and with more resolution glanced around him.

Manesty Lane! The well-known name was like a sign that God was indeed guiding him. Yes, he rationalized, in the ordinary course of things, such a walk as he had taken even in a rapidly expanding Liverpool would probably have brought him to this thoroughfare. But it was an odd coincidence that he should arrive at this very moment when disappointment had driven from his mind the obvious next step for Captain Newton's son in Liverpool.

"Go to see Joseph Manesty," his father had written.

John did, and beyond all reasonable expectation found the homecoming he had lacked, and in the eminent citizen of whom he had heard so long, a substitute for the father he had missed.

19

SHOOTER'S Hill! Had that Rotherhithe ostler rented him the slowest horse in the stable? How lovely the achingly familiar countryside looked and how impatient he was to hasten through the loveliness of its midsummer landscape.

Late June, 1748. He had last seen Chatham — oh, what was Chatham to him? — seen Mary on the last day of 1744. Strange that, after so long an absence, these final few hours could drag intolerably. That he should see her at all was an example of the Lord's exuberant goodness to him. It must, it must presage the fulfilment of his dreams.

> *"His love in time past*
> *Forbids me to think*
> *He'll leave me at last*
> *Without her to sink,"*

he murmured, taking refuge, as he had on the four-day coach journey from Warrington, in composing rhymes. Surely he was not being over-credulous or hopeful. Why else was she still unmarried? Beautiful, gay, sought-after, as her aunt's delayed letter had assured him, in the "polite" society of Chatham and Rochester, how and why had she been kept single — if not for him? And why else had all obstacles been so miraculously removed? For his father to write to the Catletts had been the summit of his daring ambition when he sent his plea from Ireland. That he should have taken the trouble to visit Chatham after long estranged years and make so good an impression that Mary's parents would no longer oppose him as a suitor: this he could still scarcely believe.

Even the mundane business of suitable employment — not ideal nor yet lucrative enough, but sufficient — had, thanks to God as giver and Joseph Manesty as instrument, been wonderfully provided. Now there was only Mary —

In Rochester he hesitated, prudence striving with impatience, then turned into the inn and spent precious minutes removing the worst stains of travel. Before a long pier-glass he stopped, not so much looking at himself as trying to see what would meet Polly's eyes in — he shivered at the thought — an hour's time. The long blue coat to which he was entitled as first-mate was imposing, as was the three-cornered, silver-laced hat. The riding boots hid most of his straight, well-shaped legs and the stalwart figure was thinner than on his last visit.

But the face — he stared earnestly at it, unable to regard it objectively, still less with her eyes. He was too big, he thought disparagingly, not in height, though well above average, but in head, shoulders, features — too big for the classical neatness of visage, the fastidious trimness of figure which was the current mode. His brows were too full, his nose too prominent, his mouth too large — he tried to smile and laughed outright at the deprecating sheepishness of the mouth and eyes which smiled back at him. If he could only tell her — Polly, Mary — half the things he had planned to tell her, a hundredth of the things he had thought about her; if he could depend, not on words alone but on the strength which would be so tender with her fragility, on the devotion which would expend itself in making her happy — and making her love him —

Well, smirking at himself in a glass at Rochester was no aid to winning his love in Chatham. He swung himself astride his horse and, finding the beast responsive and the roads dry, covered the well-known intervening stretch in short time.

The Catletts' welcome reminded him of their first reception almost six years before. Mr. Catlett had apparently forgotten the harsh words of their last interview. Mrs. Catlett embraced him in motherly fashion; Jack, happily on holiday, was ebullient; the younger children were full of excited questions and wide-eyed admiration. Polly was not there.

"She has been visiting with the Soans," said Mrs. Catlett, putting him out of suspense which he made no effort to conceal. "We expect her back tomorrow. I'm sorry that we didn't know of your coming."

John began to say that he should have sent a letter and realized that he could not have done. At the receipt of Aunt Hammond's heartening reply, he had taken the first coach from Warrington. No post could have preceded him.

"I have only a short time," he said anxiously. "Are you sure she will come tomorrow?"

"Let's make sure of it," said Jack, good-natured and with enough experience of the past to know that even a monopoly of John's company would be insipid while his mind was so evidently elsewhere. "John and I can take the chaise over to-morrow and fetch her. It will spare Mr. Soans the trouble."

Next morning they had covered half the distance between Chatham and Mr. Soans's residence at Rochester grammar school when Jack reined his horse.

"Here's Polly now," he said, nodding towards an approaching chaise. "That's Mr. Soans's piebald. We may as well wait here."

John did not answer. The moments which elapsed before the other chaise drew alongside were brief, but long enough to set his heart pounding so that he thought that Jack must hear it, and to loosen all his sinews till he wondered if he could get out of the chaise and stand. Somehow he did. Somehow he managed to wait, holding their pony's head while Jack went gaily forward.

"Aren't I a devoted brother, Mr. Soans? Can't wait for my sister to come home. Or perhaps you think I wished to spare my honoured former master the trouble of bringing her? Well neither is precisely the case. Look who has come to see us, Polly — mind, I say us! Fresh from the wilds of Africa. 'Multum ille et terris iactatus et alto vi superum.' But here he is, in the flesh. Welcome the returning hero, Polly. John you have met Mr. Soans?"

Somehow John acknowledged the school-master's greeting. He heard a voice — her voice — and swallowed to keep from choking at the dearness of the remembered sound.

"Jack, you do put on insufferable airs. I wish Mamma had taught me Latin so that I'd know what you are talking about. Mr. Soans, I am grateful to you. Please bear my thanks again

195

to Auntie and the girls. Jack, my box isn't so heavy and you needn't pretend it's crushing you."

Then she was before him, all that he had dreamed and lovelier and kind, but oh what serenity, what unaffected poise!

"It is really you, Cousin John! We are so glad that you have arrived home safely at last. You have had most dreadful and exciting adventures, I hear."

John never knew what he answered. It had happened again, this unwilling paralysis of speech just when he most needed fluency and wit. He regained enough sense, when she turned away to enter the chaise, to gain her side and assist her. Jack, having stowed her box safely, took the reins, John swung himself up beside her, some skilful manoeuvering was done with the chaises on the narrow road, and their pony headed back for Chatham with such whole-souled approval that conversation was flung out of them in breathless remarks on the flying air.

John was content. It gave him respite from the need for speech, gave him long delicious minutes to accustom himself to the unbelievable fact that he was with Mary, so conscious of touching her that he dared not move his arm in its fine blue coat, lest she became aware that it rested over hers — at least to the elbow where the sleeve of her sand-coloured linen dress flared loosely, lace-trimmed, over her rounded forearm. Out of the corner of his eye John watched her hands folded restfully on her lap, the hands whose cool touch he had yearned for wildly again and again in pain or fever. His own great hard palm still tingled from the brief contact when hers had lain momentarily there before it was coolly withdrawn. He longed to take it in his again, to hold both of them fast, and wondered that his longing was not palpable, so intensely did it move him.

When Jack drew up with as much of a flourish as one black pony could make in front of the house, John was quick to dismount and help her alight. "Gracious God, let me lift her out of carriages for the rest of her life," he prayed silently, steadying her with one hand and feeling the delicious momentary weight of her body on his arm. He wanted to hold the moment, wished there were any excuse for not letting her go, any fright to drive her closer, to drive her to him for protection.

"John's back, Eliza," said George, dashing out of the house at Dickon's heels. "Hello, Polly. Cousin John, will you —"

"I see who is the important person here. I might as well have stayed in Rochester," protested Polly smiling, and turned away. How could the contact which shook him with ecstasy leave her remote, delightfully unmoved? "Georgie, I shall not give you half my syllabub next Sunday. Nor sew a neat patch on your hose next time you tear them on the thorn hedge. Ungrateful!"

"But, Polly, we can see you all the time," protested Georgie. "We haven't seen Cousin John for four years. Don't you know he has been in Africa? Do you know he was nearly shipwrecked? Do you know he's going to sea again almost right away?"

Didn't she know? John wondered, as Fancy, her King Charles spaniel, dashed madly from the door to greet her. Did she care at all that he had come, under the lovely warm interest which was part of her natural generosity? It was all very well to be welcomed again by her parents, to have their approval and his father's support. It was gratifying that Jack enjoyed his company and that he could hardly stir without the admiring and embarrassing attendance of Georgie and young Sarah. Eliza too was all girlish interest. But with the one person who mattered — mattered more than ever though he had not thought it possible — he stood in as great uncertainty as on the first day he saw her.

"Your new Captain was mate on your last ship, you say?" Will you like working under him?"

"I expect so, Sir." John thought that Mr. Hardy at one time would have taken decided exception to working with *him* but he did not find it necessary to say so. He hesitated a moment, wondering if Mary would think him boastful; then plunged recklessly. "I could have had command myself. Mr. Manesty offered me the ship and I found the offer tempting. But after some consideration I refused."

"Oh?" Had his admission presented him in the wrong light, John wondered. Would Mr. Catlett have preferred more aggressive confidence in a prospective son-in-law? He hastened to explain.

"The business of trading for slaves is involved and dangerous. The *Greyhound* was not a slaver and on the *Pegasus* I had no experience of the Middle Passage or the sale in America. In a matter involving much expense and so many lives, I thought it prudent first to take a voyage as second officer." He caught a quick glance of Mary's eyes and almost lost the thread of his conversation. Doubtless the word prudent had struck her as strange in connection with him! "He has promised me a ship of my own for the next voyage."

"Are the slaves hard to manage, Cousin John?" asked Georgie. "Must they be tied up all the time?"

"As soon as any number come on board they are kept chained, yes."

"Why, Cousin John?"

"Georgie, use your brains," expostulated Eliza. "Do you think they like being bought and sold and taken across the sea? They'd up and murder John and throw him overboard or even eat him as quick as think about it. Don't be silly."

"I'm not silly. I only asked. I thought that they were black and wouldn't feel the way we should about being sold. Are they human, Cousin John, I mean really human? Like us?"

"Yes, they are human." A crowd of memories rushed on him. "And in some things at least, very much like us."

"And they would murder you if they had a chance, wouldn't they?" persisted George.

"If you mean that they would murder any white man, no. I have lived among them in complete safety — greater safety with my house full of goods and unlocked than I could enjoy in London. But they never forget an injury and will revenge it on the next white who comes their way if they cannot punish the actual wrong-doer. But two hundred or two hundred and fifty slaves, Georgie, over half of them men, with sometimes less than a score of whites to look after them, are always on the alert to raise an insurrection and take over the ship. So we must keep them in irons."

"I should hate it," said Polly suddenly, "having to keep people against their will, taking away their freedom. . . ."

"They aren't free when we buy them, you know," said John,

198

anxious lest she include him in her dislike of his occupation. "We never kidnap free men or women. It is really just a question of whether they are to be slaves in Africa or America."

"Does the price vary greatly, John?" asked Jack. "I expect the success of your voyage depends on the profit you can make in the Indies. What makes a slave valuable?"

"Physique mostly. Meeting the needs of the market, too. So many men and women are needed as labourers, so many children can be used in the fields to pick cotton, so many as domestic servants. Sometimes one commodity is in great demand because of scarcity. There is no way, from year to year, of knowing. The trade is always a risk."

"Do the children go with their mothers?" asked Polly, again with disconcerting suddenness.

"You mean on the same boat?"

"Yes, and afterwards. Are families, or parts of families allowed to stay together? Or —" she broke off abruptly but the word, hanging on air, demanded an answer.

"I have never been in America at the sale. I have often seen children bought with their mothers. And a brother and sister —", the boy's eyes, the sister's grief, his dealings with her, called themselves back to John's mental vision in his long moment's hesitation. "There is a good chance that they might be bought by the same master in America, particularly the young children, if he is humane."

"I think it is horrible!" said Polly with a passion he had never heard in her. "People have no right separating families like that. Why must they have slaves at all? I'd sooner do all my own work than depend on such traffic."

"A remark of which I shall certainly remind you, Sister, next time Sukey goes to visit her mother," said Jack. Polly, flushed already with earnestness, coloured more deeply. Was she about to cry? Distracted with love and helplessness, John had no words.

"Polly, child," said her father. "There is no use in your upsetting yourself over things that can't be helped. You may be quite sure that the blacks don't mind as much as you would."

"Polly has always been tender-hearted," said her mother

fondly. "She hates to think that there are things which she can't help. Will you ever forget, Jack, the time you put her off eating meat for months by telling her that the baby chicks she was petting would be just ready to eat for her birthday dinner?"

"I still think it was a horrid thing for Jack to do." Polly had regained her composure but John, who had subsisted so long on pictures of his own colouring, stored up the memory of her generous warmth, her tender concern, as authentic tints for their future limning.

This renewed evidence that she was beyond all concept loveable did him little service in finding a time or manner to give that love utterance. The Catletts showed their hospitality by entertainment. Aunts and uncles were invited, games and walks were provided, John was prevailed upon to tell and re-tell his adventures, a carefully censored narrative of which sounded in the ears of the polite inbred Chatham folk much as Othello's "anthropophagoi and men whose heads do grow beneath their shoulders" sounded in the Venetian ducal palace. But Mary, John felt, was less easily impressed than Desdemona and he, John, was no conquering general. He had some skill as a narrator and when she laughed, which she usually did before the rest saw the joke, that spontaneous convulsed laughter spurred him to better efforts. Meanwhile time was slipping past. The very haste which was necessary might prove fatal. What if he should say the wrong thing and she should formally forbid him to cherish any further hopes?

"Why must you rush so?" asked Jack, whose pleasure at their renewed friendship gave John some confidence — that is until he saw Mary again. "You don't mean that you came across England, and are going back again, for three — four days?"

"I should have come for one day — and counted myself well paid," said John simply and Jack, who knew that the compensation was not the sight of him, grunted tolerantly. "But I expected to take the coach back — and that would have allowed me more time. As it is, I shall walk from London."

"Walk — from London to Liverpool?"

"It's a tedious story. If I tell you, will you explain it to

200

Polly — after I'm gone? You see I expected some money in London. When I left the *Pegasus* the Captain did not pay me, merely gave me a bill on the ship-owners in London. I went to their office on my way through, thinking to receive six months' wages. They have gone bankrupt."

"What appalling luck. But surely, Father would lend —"

"No," said John fiercely. "You must promise not to tell them until I have left. It is bad enough to turn up like this, still unable to make a definite offer. But I will not be a beggar or borrower into the bargain. This is one way I can economize. I shall have enough difficulty accumulating a sufficient competency to ask Polly to marry me without spending another fortnight's wage on coach fare. But you see why I must leave tomorrow. Mr. Manesty expects me back for duty by July. The ship is to sail early in August. And —"

"*'Eheu fugaces Postume, Postume*
Labuntur anni —' "

murmured Jack.

"I wish I knew Latin," said John, admiring his polished friend. "I'd give a good deal, first to know what that means and secondly to be able to cap it."

"Oh, don't worry," said Jack comfortably. "After all I know not a word of African."

John laughed.

"That scarcely disqualifies you for London society, as my ignorance of Latin does me."

"True. Latin is taken for granted in a gentleman." Jack became suddenly conscious of his tactlessness. "Rot, John. People would sooner listen to those sea yarns of yours than to Latin quips that anyone can make."

"But it is another awkwardness," persisted John, "and Polly must be conscious of the difference."

"Why don't you speak to Polly?" said Jack. "You'll never be comfortable till you do, nor anyone else. Man, it can't be any surprise. You've made it plain to her — and to all the rest of us — since you first came here. Only be a bit cavalier. That's what a girl likes."

"Polly?" said John doubtfully.

"Of course. What are you afraid of? After all, if she turns you down there are other fish in the sea. . . ."

201

"Have you ever been in love, Jack?"

"A dozen times."

"Exactly."

"Look," said Jack, glad to be the man-of-the-world to the friend who had seen so much more of it than he ever would, "I'm not disparaging Polly. There isn't a girl I'd compare with her, if she is my sister. And I'd like nothing better than to have you as brother-in-law. But your attitude is wrong. It's bad for women to be made so much of. Remember what Shaftesbury says: ' 'Twas as impertinent and senseless as it was profane to deify the sex, raise them to a capacity above what nature had allowed and treat them with a respect. . . . something to the effect that they are the aptest to complain of in the natural way of love'."

"That man knew nothing about love," said John stoutly.

"Hear him, ye gods," apostrophized Jack. "This is the gospel according to Shaftesbury, John, your one evangelist."

John winced.

"Don't, Jack. That's sacrilege."

"How are the mighty fallen! Will Polly's image topple next? Why, you were the first one to talk me out of superstition, drawing all your arguments from Shaftesburian premises. He was your other idol."

" '*My salad days.*
When I was green in judgment,' "

said John lightly. "If I talked you into admiring the *Characteristics,* maybe I can talk you out of it. At any rate, pat theories like his are of no help to me in this — or any — crisis. And Jack — I can depend on your good offices with her when I'm gone? But you are right in one thing. I must speak to her today."

The opportunity for which he asked before supper that evening was made for him next morning. With strange unanimity — not entirely unforced in the case of Georgie — the Catletts had affairs in other parts of the house and Polly and he were left in the parlour. Rather, he was left and Polly came presently downstairs to where he stood before the empty firplace. Quite mistress of the situation, she dropped into a chair and sat reposefully looking up at him, her blue morn-

202

ing dress — had he seen her in blue before? what lovely colour it brought out in her eyes! — flowing from her arms in loose sleeves, and flowing from her waist to the floor, below the white fichu laced across her young breast.

The time had come, the time he had longed for and recently prayed for, the time from which all his past sorrows could be blotted out, on which all his future hinged, the time for which he had been rehearsing until he found himself awakening morning after morning in the very act of uttering one of the ardent, beautiful, inadequate but eloquent speeches he had composed.

"Polly," he said, and could go no further. Too much depended on it, far too much. Not only were all the speeches merged in one vast adoring jumble but there was every danger that part of one, tumbling out of context, would sound ludicrous and annoy or disgust her. She had only to ask what practical proposals he had in his power to make and he would be effectually silenced. And though he trusted that her consenting to hear him was a favourable sign, how could she decently have refused when he had come so far? Reason was no aid. It was all very well for Mrs. Manesty to say that the unknown Miss Catlett was a very lucky girl to have his devotion. She could not see the adored object, as he saw her now, instinctively graceful, beautiful, surrounded by her own atmosphere of radiant maiden sufficiency, untouched except by pity for his incomplete passion. That was the difference between them, he realized desperately, between the male and the female. He was conscious, so conscious of his incompleteness, of his need of a helpmeet for him. She — until she could be shown, until she could be prevailed upon to experience his love and what it would awaken in her — had no such feeling of need. And in this case what could he offer? She had been his lodestar. But back here in the pleasant variegated pattern of family and social life, with enough duties to prevent boredom, and enough pleasures to provide gaiety, and enough family affection to afford security, and enough attractiveness to ensure marriage when she should desire it, what did she lack that he could offer? Not enough money for the luxuries she took for granted; brief companionship, which he had no reason to think she especially enjoyed, and longer periods of separation; virtually the life of a widow in her family circle; anxiety and loneliness apart from it.

But he loved her. Surely such love counted for something. Surely it must arouse some response; the emotion which affected him so powerfully must have some latent or potential counterpart in her. How could he awaken it?

"Jack tells me" — Polly's voice with that lovely shine in it, that utterly unaffected brightness, was intended, perhaps, to help him — "that you must leave today?"

It was the opening he needed. And I can't go, dearest, dearest Polly, without telling you that I completely worship you. In all my sorrow and sinning — such sinning and such scenes as you cannot even dream of and pray God never will — you have been Beauty to me and the only thing that has drawn me up and out — and back. Humanly speaking, that is. But God used you when I would listen to nothing else. You have it in your power to make this next voyage joyful and brief if I only know that you will wait until I come home. If you but give me the opportunity I shall count the chief business of my life to study what will make you happy; that —

"Polly," he said. "I — you — will —?"

Polly looked at him with faint exasperation, and felt it rather commendable in her that the exasperation was only faint. Really it was a bit ridiculous that a man who had been everywhere and seen everything, who could hold a roomful of people enthralled and laughing as he had done the previous evening, who had been offered complete charge of a ship — Polly did not like slavers but she recognized that they were not entrusted to everybody — should behave so stupidly. Other young men had admired her and told her of their admiration without difficulty, often in set poetic phrases to which it was easy to make a graceful non-committal reply. Mr. Rupert Cleaver, who had obtained Mr. Catlett's permission to pay his addresses, had done so with controlled and praiseworthy eloquence. Momentarily she asked herself again why she had not accepted him. Her father had thoroughly approved and what he had had to offer had been so perfect a pattern of the marriage she wanted — when, that is, she wanted marriage: a fine large house near Rochester, more servants, an equipage with a coachman — Rupert's mother had been "county" and the death of both parents had left their only son so well established that a far less personable young man would have been considered an excellent match. He had a good reputation too. He was not wild — anything but the heartless villain John had feared for her in that letter which she had kept folded away in the great chest in her room — and she could not say why the phrase had flashed to her mind as she listened demurely to Rupert's peroration. But from that flashing recollection her decision to refuse him had been fixed, gently acted upon, and unregretted. Now that the writer of those telling phrases was returned, virtually from the dead, and standing like a great dumb ox in front of her, she felt like asking him why he had bothered to come.

Oh, he loved her, she knew. He had written it often enough. But why, now that she had made the opportunity, couldn't he tell her so, settle this confusion of thought within her, let her know something of him and of what it would be like to call him — she shied back like a young colt from the word "husband" in connection with him. It was all very well for him to arrive unexpectedly after the even less expected visit from Captain Newton, to set all the relatives watching her, to have Aunt Hammond and Mamma pitying the "poor boy who loved her so deeply." She was sorry for his misfortunes, yes. She had cried when that dreadful letter came from Africa, cried in utterly uncomprehending pity and named his name silently for Sundays thereafter when the prayer mentioned those "in any other adversity". But she could not marry everybody she pitied. She really did not want, as far as she could tell, ever to marry him, though his repeated turning up in her life since she was thirteen was most unsettling; and it was certainly asking too much to expect her to take the initiative in a proposal which she did not wish to evoke.

"Mary," John tried again. Her annoyance, faint though it was, had paralyzed him still further. He realized how differently she must see the situation. It was absurd to turn up as from the dead and, because his whole life during his absence had centred around her, to expect her to be ready to respond. What had happened to him in that enlightening moment of first meeting had not happened to her. What right had he to think that his few clumsy attempts, his awkward formalities, years apart, would endear him to her as every adorable glimpse, every graceful act, every gay word, increased her dearness to him?

Now the sound of her sweeter name, the name by which he had always apostrophized her in extremities of sorrow or tenderness, arrested them both. She wished he did not look at her like that, knew somewhere in her disturbed young being that such a look exalted her beyond her power of attainment, and for that very reason feared, not him but what she had become to him. There was not yet any feeling in her to respond, even to compassionate the depth-stirring intensity of his. It was too serious; serious things made her sad and she loved to laugh. The comedies which she saw at the Rochester theatre, farcical and polite even in their glossing over of the fashionable license of the day, were more to her taste than the tragic plays of Shakespeare and even Ford, not because the tragedies did not interest her but because they tore her apart. So the loneliness of winter stars and an occasional splendid word from the Prayer Book and, when she heard Handel's *Messiah,* the heart-stopping minor of the recitative: "He looked for one to have pity on him and there was no man" shook her out of the dear orderly rhythm and inoffensive gaiety of what she considered a normal happy life. And that note, that same note of unbearable pathos, was now in this utterance of her single name. It was upon her, the crisis. She could not avoid it. Her eyes, frightened with the coming of revelation, met his; but John's panic, brought on by his consciousness of her annoyance, was insensitive to this swift change of mood. He could not read their message.

"Mary," he managed from a dry throat, "if I write you a letter, will you promise to read it?"

Mary's quick sense of the ludicrous saved her from anger, her politeness saved her from laughing outright at the anticlimax. Fortunately for her control, at this moment Fancy, who had been confined to the kitchen, burst in upon them and, with a suspicious woof at John, whom he had not placed in his scheme of things, flung himself on his mistress in a frenzy of waggling and panting and insistent devotion that made John

206

envy his freedom of expression. His envy was increased immeasurably when Mary picked him up, held him where he, John, in his most rapturous dreams was only fleetingly held and sought with incomplete success to keep her laughing face beyond the reach of an indiscriminatingly caressing tongue.

"Is a nice dog. Is a beautiful Fancy," she said in a tone which John thought completely wasted. "Thought his Polly had gone for another nasty visit. Well, she hasn't. And next time she is taking her Fancy dog with her." She became apparently aware again of her other admirer's presence. "Isn't he a beautiful dog, John? You like dogs, don't you?"

John liked dogs. In fact he had been almost ashamed of his fondness for little things and of his antipathy towards seeing them in pain. Towards Fancy, as representative of the canine breed, his feeling could at that moment have been warmer. It was at best a violent impulse to dispossess the little monster. He was aware that Mary was offering him the chance to pick up the conversation in a lighter vein but he dared not trust himself to do it.

"Will you read it, Mary? Promise," he repeated tensely.

There was no doubt about the coolness in her tone now.

"I've always read your letters, John. Yes, if you write, I shall read it, of course."

What would she think of it? Would she answer? What would she answer? All the way across the Midlands to Liverpool he had wondered, and his wondering had shortened the journey, as he wrote more buoyantly than he felt to Jack Catlett and derived enormous encouragement from his one slender cause of encouragement: that, though she had it in her power, she had not categorically forbidden his addresses.

It had been so easy to write, so easy except that he could have written forever, so easy compared with the choking aporia which befell him when he tried to speak. He had written by candle far into the night after his ride back to Rotherhithe and he knew the letter by heart, repeating its phrases even as he had stared at his features in the mirror at Rochester, to try to gauge their effect on *her*. The turns of expression were good, but would she think he had elaborated them and miss

207

— how could she miss? — the stark sincerity with which he had tried to write his heart in words?

He had not wanted her to think that he failed to see the absurdity of his conduct. "I am ashamed to acknowledge that where I have most desire to speak I have always been most dumb. . . . though I had a thousand things to say, I let the time elapse before I had determined what to begin with. I should be ready enough to laugh at such ridiculous behaviour in another but cannot help falling into it myself." In extenuation he had pleaded the perplexity of his prospects and an excuse "which I believe your indifference cannot form a just notion of, but, as it is impossible for me to see you without considering you as the object and centre of my chief desires, the reflexion of the improbability of my ever obtaining you makes me continually thoughtful in your presence."

Surely that would arouse some understanding in one who had been moved by the sorrows of unknown slaves?

"I wish you would consider my case," he had written simply, after a quotation and a metaphor which would, he hoped, remove some of her disgust at his awkwardness and silence, "with the good nature usual to you in other things, and bestow a little of your charity, one morsel for God's sake, before I am quite starved." He begged an acknowledgement of his letter to encourage him in "bustling in the world". He had concluded "with begging that you would sometimes in your best humoured minutes bestow a thought on me, and not too precipitately put it out of my power to show to all the world what I have often repeated to you — I mean that I am with the most inviolable regard, dear Polly, your most faithful and ardent admirer and servant

J. Newton."

Now he stood in his room at Manesty's, staring at the missive in his hand. It had come that morning just as he was about to go with Mr. Manesty to meet Captain Hardy at South Dock Kay. He had not dared open it but had thrust it into the breast of his coat where his hand had sought it time and again during the day. There had been opportunities for him to peruse it alone but he had not dared. Now they had supped. It was after nine o'clock and still light enough to read by his open window. He had kissed the letter, wondering just where her fingers had rested as she wrote the address in the studied disjointed hand which somehow belied the smooth easy grace of her outward manner.

But to open it, to know as certainty what he feared more than he had ever consciously feared death, to have the fair hopes, the warmth and cordiality and friendship which had greeted him since he reached England, turned to dust and ashes — that was physically out of his power. So might a man compelled to suicide have his hand paralyzed at the trigger of his pistol.

Ashamed of his weakness, he began to pray, striving for decent rounded phrases: "Gracious God, who hast been infinitely merciful to me in spite of my —". He gave up and leaned against the window muttering brokenly: "O God. . . . Polly, Polly, my dearest. . . . God. . . . God. . . . make me able to bear it. . . . able to bear Thy will."

The six lines did not require much reading. It was the blurring of his eyes, the blurring of his mind, that kept him staring at them for a long time after their sedately expressed, cautious contents had been exposed to his sight.

"My dear John:

It would grieve me to be thought more lavish of pity and compassion to strangers than to a valued family friend like yourself. I wish you Godspeed on your voyage and a safe homecoming. At present I have no intention or desire of making any change in my condition during that period.

Believe me to be, with all good wishes
your friend and cousin
Mary Catlett."

Not a love-letter, not a touch of the spontaneous sparkle of her personality in the stilted and laboured lines. Yet it is doubtful if Heloise's most abandoned outpourings raised Peter Abelard to the first rung of the ladder of ecstasy on the top of which John stood, when their import struck home. The rejection, the veto of future aspirations, which she would certainly have written had that veto been fixed in her mind, she had not written. Apart from that, to write at all was greatly in his favour and, through the careful, uncommitting expression of an uncommitted heart, he realized that she had intended him so to understand it.

The bolt had slipped on the last door of his prison. John emerged into the world, feeling that he was beginning to live indeed, and capable of acting with a spirit and firmness to which he had before been a stranger.

20

MADEIRA, 1748. The first-mate of the *Brownlow* looked across the harbour and the years, new-struck at the change in his circumstances since last his ship was moored in those waters. He remembered the sullen despair with which he had then sighted the island, his ostracized misery while the ship lay in the Funchal Road, the brief agonizing incertitude, then the uncontrolled exultation of his escape from the *Harwich*. He recollected vividly his determination to break loose from all authority — recalled as if it were yesterday the wild days on the *Pegasus* and the nightmare of his enslavement in Guinea.

His mood, which should have been buoyant with gratitude, became progressively depressed. The hopes on which he had been feeding were suddenly deflated by the pressure of present need. Two months since he had seen Mary — twelve more at least until he saw her again — then at the very best, voyage on voyage, separation on separation, and at the worst —

The sigh of his spirit must have made itself audible. He turned at Hardy's laugh, to see his Captain eyeing him quizzically.

"What is the reason for that sigh, Mr. Newton? A fair day and fair prospect surely?"

"I scarcely know, Sir. I wasn't aware that I sighed." John had found the former mate of the *Greyhound* most congenial and had been flattered that Hardy claimed so much of his company. Night after night he was invited to the Captain's cabin for cards and wine. As a result he slept later in the morning and, between the Captain's friendship and his ad-

ministrative duties, the time he had set himself for prayer and
reading was constantly scamped or interrupted so that he
now had no regular devotions. Nor — for Hardy was completely indifferent — were there any religious observances on
board. John kept intending to fix some other time of the
day, to take part of the period he had allotted to the study of
Latin which he found engrossing. He had promised himself
that he would arrange a schedule during the Middle Passage
when there would be more leisure. Just now, with the trading
season at hand and the boat to prepare for receiving the slaves,
any system would be sure to suffer disaster.

"You did. It was the sigh of a man who has been too long
off shore. Fortunately the cure is at hand. However, knowing you, I intend to go ashore with you. I value my first-
mate's services too highly to turn you loose on this island by
yourself."

"I — I don't need —" John hesitated, not knowing how to
frame a refusal or to qualify an acceptance. The word homesick would sound foolish on his lips. Hardy had left a wife
and two sons in Warrington.

"I know quite well what you need," said the Captain drily.
Not at all pleased at Manesty's choice of mate, he had been
agreeably surprised at the change which had come over the
blasphemous trouble-making young passenger of the *Greyhound*. He put it down to the civilizing effect of England,
of prospects for the future, and of a responsible position. He
admired the studiousness with which Newton was attempting
to repair the greatest gap in a gentleman's education, and was
relieved that his subordinate showed no sign of resenting authority. He noticed a greater seriousness, and an absence of
the argumentative tendencies which had characterized his previous conversation. But that the change went further, that it
could extend to chastity, was a fantastic notion for which the
Captain's knowledge of men in general and Newton in particular made him quite unprepared. The type of excursion
on which he was presently bent, and on which he intended to
include his libidinous young friend, had no association in his
mind with his duties as husband and father; still less could
he conceive of any scruples in Newton's. But Madeira was a

strange place and John was strange to it. Better to keep an eye on him.

"Mr. Blodgett will remain aboard while we go ashore. The boat is ready to cast off, I see. Will you come?"

John opened his mouth to speak, closed it again, gave a quick shrug — at circumstance, at conscience — and followed the Captain over the ship's side into the waiting boat. He needed a trip ashore. He had never visited Madeira. As for the other implications of Hardy's words, there would be time to reject them later.

There was time but he did not reject. And, once the body had known satisfaction after its long abstinence, once the stab of the following morning's conscience had been calloused by the new vigour and duties of the day, the next opportunity was seized without demur and the next awaited with avidity. Departure from the island gave conscience a chance to assert itself, absence of possibility making it easier to resolve on future refusal. He composed several plausible speeches, planned several ways of avoiding invitations which, once given, he was powerless to reject.

Unfortunately the enemy varied his strategy. The ship began to trade at Gambia, taking advantage of their early arrival at the end of the rains. They had not expected to take slaves aboard until Sierra Leone and John was left to hasten the building of barricades while Hardy and Blodgett went ashore. When they returned, he greeted the Captain on deck and approved his purchase: four men, two boys and three women. It was to these that the Captain unnecessarily directed John's attention.

"If that buy is an omen, this will be a good voyage," he said contentedly. "Not a flaw in the three — the second is a bit short but still above average."

John assented and began to assign them to their quarters. The men and boys were taken below and he was wondering whom to trust with the women when Hardy interrupted.

"There's no need to confine the women below — yet, at any rate, Mr. Newton. They can be of use to us in the cabins, for cooking, cleaning — perhaps you can think of other services?"

It required no great exercise of John's imagination to grasp the Captain's meaning. So, for daily service and nightly comfort the three were kept above deck, while in the slow tortuous course of trading down the coast the number of their less favoured sisters gradually increased in the barricade below.

Not that John's life was sybaritic. The very difficulties and dangers to which he was almost daily exposed made him, under the less frequent prickings of conscience, more belligerently inclined to regard his carnal activity both on ship and ashore as natural and, if not right, his right. Hardy was fair in apportioning duties. He took a share in the dangerous shore expeditions, but when the long-boat was to be away for a week's trip up the sounds and to the factories, the first-mate was in charge. Sometimes, from the long-boat to shore, trips had to be made in canoes manned by natives. Twice the canoes capsized in the breakers and John, unable to swim, was dragged to shore, the second time scarcely conscious. Once his party had a near escape from a village which had been waiting to avenge an outrage perpetrated by the last ship hailing from Liverpool.

So they came to Sierra Leone, where the *Brownlow* lay at anchor near the Benanoes, while John took the boat to the Plantanes.

When they rounded the harbour point and headed, at his direction, for Clow's landing, John sat in the bow, wry with the pain and relief of memory and contrast. How well he knew the sweep of dazzling sand and low tufted dune and brilliant foliage. Clow's house was just out of view, already hidden by the growth of young palms. He glanced at the blue coat folded on his knees, still fine in spite of several drenchings in salt water, and at his silver-buckled shoes. The last time he had entered the bay — from the other side — he had been a prisoner on Clow's shallop, the very shallop moored ahead to their left. Now he was returning, in fulfilment of the taunt flung at him in utter improbability. Not the master of a ship, true, but next in command. Ah, there was a stir about the landing. Someone, yes it was Clow himself, was coming down to greet the trading-boat. Embarrassed at the thought of the other's embarrassment, searching for the right, the complaisant word to gloss the situation, he remained in his place while his men secured the boat. Then with an unhurried calm he was far from feeling, he disembarked and faced the man who had cheated him, starved him, derided him, and broken his spirit.

"Mr. Clow, compliments of Captain Hardy of the *Brown-low*, trading from Liverpool, Sir."

Clow recovered from the shock with less difficulty than a more sensitive man. Newton met his clumsy efforts at ingratiation with an ease on which he secretly congratulated himself. He accepted his invitation to the house, and the two moved on up to the shady verandah which he had helped· to build. There, while discussing the trade over Clow's best wine, he had a fresh reminder of the reversal of his fortune. P.I. did not appear and an inquiry elicited the information that she was visiting inland. On the whole, he was glad. He would doubtless see her on his next voyage, when his position as Captain would nonplus her even more. Meanwhile he stretched his legs comfortably and glanced at the swaying pattern of fronds against the sky and was pleased with the world and with himself.

Clow went into the house for some papers and John was alone, when he became conscious of a stir at the far side of the verandah. The servant who had brought the drinks was a stranger to him but the faces of the two black women who now stopped and stared were familiar. "Newton," he heard one of them exclaim in blank wonderment, "that's Newton! And look, he has shoes."

"Ay," said the other, "and stockings too!"

Clow's return sent them scuttling off, but John's complaisance was shattered. During his careful negotiations, and his walk down the island to Mr. Williams's house, the thoughts set in motion by the slaves' naive comment were serious and humble. Altogether different he was now, master who had been slave, respected who had been despised, full who had been starving, befriended who had been outcast — and with a reasonable hope of attaining the main objective of his life. Outwardly altogether different, was he inwardly not much the same? True, his blasphemy of tongue was silenced. True, he believed in God and was, yes he was, he told himself falteringly, deeply grateful for His mercy and intervention. But how was he showing his gratitude? The cessation of blasphemy was no credit to him. It had left him, almost involuntarily, with his unbelief and his belligerent desire to shatter belief in others. But in what else could he be distinguished from the religiously indifferent Hardy or the amoral Clow or any untaught, lascivious sailor under his command?

Self reasserted itself, squirming with discomfort. " 'Thou seest I have more flesh than other men and therefore more frailty' " he quoted, and the feeling of satisfaction at being able to recognize his weakness altered the direction of his thoughts. Falstaff's quibble was not literally applicable to his still spare frame, but it assuredly was to his nature. Mentally he was virgin and monogamous. The satisfaction of his lust had no relationship to his passion for Mary. He was doing the women no harm. If he did not take them, someone else would. If — no, when, he dared not doubt — he married Mary, if and when he could give up a seafaring life, he would be different. Still, he would make an effort at continence, if not abstinence.

Mr. Williams's welcome restored the sense of well-being which had been temporarily deflated. He brushed aside John's apologies for his sudden departure from the Kittam factory and was genuinely delighted at his improved status.

"There was nothing else you could have done," he said with more heartiness than John had thought his somewhat dry manner could show. "Mr. McCaig's great fear was that you would not seize the opportunity. Apparently your determination to go black was causing him much concern."

"I had no idea that it mattered to him."

"Oh, McCaig does not show his feelings. But he felt you as a responsibility. And a heavy one, I believe."

"Is he at the factory now?"

"I expect him almost daily, with a cargo. It will spare your boat a trip perhaps. The Bagru factory should be worth a visit. Two tribes are warring there and you are the first trader to arrive. Meanwhile I have a few that may interest you."

John was shown to his room that night in a state of great contentment. His men had been provided for. The food had been better than he had tasted for weeks; his host had been avid for English news and their talk had branched off from politics to literature, where John was able to discuss with an interesting companion, books he had purchased in England.

216

Now, pleasantly but not excessively tired, stimulated by his host's excellent wine, he stood waiting for the servant to leave.

She did not go. Soft-footed, unhurried, she moved about the room, preparing his bed, setting water and light on the low stand beside it, doing what else he did not know, for he deliberately turned away, staring blindly through bamboo shades to keep himself from watching her. He had noticed her at dinner with approval and had brought his eyes back to his host to check the direction of his thoughts. She was a small well-formed mulatto, with features almost European, cast in bronze. He wondered about her parentage, wondered if any child or children were by now bearing his passion and features in their mingled blood on this dark familiar coast or on the far western continent. He wished, at any rate he hoped, she would go quickly while his resolution still held. Surely Mr. Williams could have sent a boy to wait on him instead.

The quiet deft movements had ceased. Presently he would hear the foliage-like rustle of bamboo curtains falling behind her. Instead he heard her voice, soft like the rest of her, almost without expression. She spoke in Sherbro.

"Mr. Williams told me to ask if there is anything else you want of me."

Williams, judging him by former knowledge, was offering the conventional hospitality of the country. John remembered his pricking of conscience. This would be a good opportunity to test his strength. He opened his mouth to utter the Sherbro negative. It might eventually have been uttered, though his voice gave him little co-operation. But the girl spoke again, this time in careful, badly memorized English.

"Malam Williams say for me to ask if I do more for you."

John swung around and saw her in the flickering light, available, waiting.

"Yes," he said.

McCaig came, sharing Williams's pleasure in seeing him and bringing a number of fine blacks. The long-boat had almost its full complement, but the opportunity of making the first selection of Jimson's new supply at the Bagru factory was too good to refuse and the surplus slaves could be left at the

217

Plantanes until the long-boat could return from the *Brownlow* to fetch them.

On the morning set for the voyage, John awoke with a sense of disagreeable association. His brain foggy with the sleep of over-exhaustion, he could not immediately identify it. Then he knew that he had emerged from unconsciousness feeling that he was in P.I.'s power, fever-ridden, helpless, and alone. The sight of his comfortable room was reassuring, and he dressed, wondering a little at the power of such a fancy to make him still feel physically weak.

Not until the breakfast, for which he had been hungry and then suddenly had no appetite, was over did he realize that no mere fancy was responsible for his feeling. The inner gauntness, the terrifying waves of heat, the weakness which would not let him stand, all these were symptoms he sickly recognized. This time there was concern and succour. He was conscious of supporting arms, of cooling applications and fans. Then for an unmeasured, unknown period he struggled feebly, rising and falling through a sea of oblivion.

The waves retreated at last, leaving him spent, like a half-drowned swimmer with their roar still in his ears. He opened his eyes with an effort and found his surroundings familiar. He was alone, although it had seemed to him, whenever he had fought his way, delirious, out of coma, that someone had been standing or sitting beside him. Evidences of care were at hand; a jar of water, fruit, a fan, the cloths which had bathed his head. But briefly he was alone and the house was very still.

Like its stillness was the stillness of his spirit. His body had not quite emerged from delirium; the objects beside his bed wavered and retreated, grew large and small, and the swaying of the curtain sifting the sunlight took on strange fantastic shapes till he closed his eyes against them. His mind, however, had come suddenly into a terrible lucidity, a stark comfortless light in which he saw what he had never seen before.

Was what he saw God, or himself? Or himself as God saw him? Or God as he had never seen Him, terrible and holy with a terror and holiness which had been but names to him at his earlier revelation: God loving with love more awful than wrath because it was love turned back and showing him his sin — no, not his sin, his sinfulness.

There was no rationalization possible against such revelation; no comparison of himself with other men, no defence by accepted standards, no cowardly excuse of weakness. There was no other man in the universe but himself — face to face with God, unable to dwell with the everlasting burnings. He could not plead the weakness of a body which had been redeemed from the power of sin and which he had pledged to the glory of God. Every provision, every care God had taken for him, sparing him many times to live, forcing His Truth on his undesirous, unwilling mind, offering him forgiveness, welcoming him as a son, feasting him at His Table. And like a dog he had turned to his vomit again, like a sow that was washed he had gone back to wallowing in the mire. And of such the Scripture said — his mind recalled the words with cruel exactness — it had been better never to have known the way of righteousness than, after knowing it, to turn back from the holy commandment. It was impossible for him to be renewed unto repentance.

He lay, quiet with despair, and presently felt tears slipping through his closed eyelids. A dull wonder stirred in him. Why was he crying except with repentance? Or was this the torment of the damned, to know and mourn their lost estate? But a reasoning hope had been lighted and sputtered stubbornly in his engulfing gloom. If his case was lost, if there was no forgiveness, why this new respite? For he knew that the crisis was past, recognized the signs of returning health. Why had he not been hurried to judgment? Or why had he not been left to sin undisturbed? Why, except that God was still bending to him?

The room was confining. He must go somewhere to be free from possible interruption and find if there was forgiveness for him, see this greater crisis through, if his hope was not indeed delusion.

He sat up, waiting till the dizziness gradually passed. His outer clothes had been removed and he had not strength to put them on. Sitting on a chair he laboriously pulled his coat around him and made his way to the entrance. Without interception he left the house and managed at last to gain the secluded cove where he had once kept his mind alive with Euclid.

There for a long time he lay prostrate, while slowly, inescapably, he faced a new thing, as surely as though he were lying at Golgotha, looking up at the Figure on the central cross. Christ's death had until now been part of the Creed which he had accepted entire with returning belief, but now it was not merely a theological necessity. The dying agony, the awful vicarious suffering were there before him. More, the One on the cross seemed to charge him with His death. And suddenly he knew that the charge was true. It was his, John Newton's sin which had necessitated the death of God.

Gradually this very conviction which reduced him to broken, undefending humility became the ground of his hope. He was lifted beyond the place where reason with its infantile steps could follow. The spirit operative within him was reason, winged. It did not argue; it declared. And in the light of that declaration, the more appalling his sin now that he saw its consequence, the more adequate its Propitiation. If God's love overflowed in such incredible self-giving, then the sin of the universe, he, the representative sinner of the universe, was far from commensurate with it. To doubt was arrogance.

This sight — so clear that John could not tell whether he was in the body or out of the body, seeing — had a two-fold effect. He saw his own sinfulness as a condition, a state of soul, not as a series of items to be calculated, compared, emphasized or disparaged. Whether his lust was natural or obscene, whether its objects were specifically injured, was irrelevant; the lust which he shared, to which he gave free rein, which was again gaining the mastery of his life, was the despoiler of love, the denial of spirit, part of the great horror which degraded nature and sank its victims, lustful and lusted after alike, in wretchedness and hate and strife. Suddenly he thought of Mary as the victim of some other's lust and knew that if such nefas should occur, *he* would be responsible.

So, too, his growing carelessness, his absorption in diversions and amusement to the neglect of all spiritual exercise: this was not a peccadillo to be corrected and balanced at some future time; it was a share in the frustration of God's redemption, a participation in the cosmic neglect and indifference of His outstretched love, a blow in the face of the suffering Lover.

But the sight of the Man on the Cross had another effect. It drew him, so that for a time he forgot himself. God was no longer — as He had been in the days succeeding the storm at sea — a righteous Judge who, on receipt of satisfaction, remitted the punishment due the law-breaker. He was the Giver, in His own being, of that satisfaction, giving at the unthinkable cost of Himself, granting, not absolution but absorption, so that the sinner might not remain a pardoned penitent but be a sharer in the Divine joy and conquest.

John shuddered with a strange new awe. He turned on his back and sat up, staring out at the cobalt sea, and forcing himself to wonder if the experience were a hallucination of his illness. Instead he was more certain than ever — was it in his mind, or in his heart, or in those deeps of being where one cannot be separated from the other? — that all his trust was in his crucified Saviour. He made no more resolves, put no more confidence in his own efforts, but cast himself completely on his Lord for mercy and for strength. Formerly he had been conscious of transaction; this was transformation, and in his all too carnal person, in his excessively passionate nature, a new principle was coming to birth.

For the first time — he felt its coming with wonder — for the first time, still seeing the Man on the Cross, he felt the stirring of love. A yearning warmth, like that which suffused him when he thought of Mary, stirred in his soul, unlike the reverent thankfulness to which he had risen at the highest stages of his first faith, the dutiful sense of a required return for inestimable favour received. Here too there was a difference. His love for Mary was a projection of himself, his hopes, his desires, his craving for reciprocation. This love was called into being by love which had been already given, which had been poured out on him when he had no quality to merit, no grace to want it. In fact it was not of himself, but part of the strange work which was even now being wrought by God in him.

21

WHATEVER Captain Hardy thought of the change in his first-mate, he had to admit that it made him no less efficient an officer or pleasant a companion. He was glad enough, after the report of his fever had reached him from the Plantanes, to see his right-hand man alive and well, so glad that he made no comment when Newton quietly dispensed with the services of his allotted slave.

It was evidence of the change that John himself, for the first time, was stricken with compunction on the woman's account. It was a subject on which he could not let his thoughts linger; for, with returning vigour, he found that, though he was given victory in his warfare against the flesh, the struggle against each recurring temptation was no less a sore one. The Bible, which he now read with stubborn regularity, grew in interest for him. The prayers which, in spite of wandering thoughts and frequent coldness of spirit, he offered daily as well as in time of special need or conviction, never failed to remind him that he was no longer his own.

He found to his surprise that with the change had come a lightness of heart and a greater zest for life than he had ever known. Instead of a sense of irksome restriction he felt as though he was at last unshackled. Even the slow dragging of month after month at the coast where, as he wrote to Jack Catlett, he had not been ten days in the half-year on board ship in his constant quest to purchase souls "for whom we are obliged to take as much pains as the Jesuits are said to do in making proselytes," could not reduce this new sense of the goodness of living. Jack had engaged him to write at every opportunity and John hoped that Polly would be reminded favourably as he wrote "sometimes venturing in a little canoe thro Seas like mountains, sometimes travelling thro the woods, often in danger from the wild beasts and much oftener from the more wild inhabitants, scorched by the sun in the days and chilled by the dews in the night". Yet he could continue, "I assure you I never was so happy in my life. . . ." He hoped too that Polly, who laughed so easily and adorably and whom he had been too tongue-tied to amuse, would be interested in his account of the monstrous fish which he caught in March at Rio Sesters: "Sixteen foot broad and his liver only weighed near 200 pounds. I have heard some people, who would invalidate the story of Jonah, pretend there is no fish capable of swallowing a man but I believe if this had met one of them in the water he would have convinced him to the contrary, for he had a mouth two foot, three inches wide and a proportionable swallow." He included several Latin tags to let Jack know that he was progressing with his study of Latin and indeed he was, though he wondered, as he struggled through the Odes and Epistles without a dictionary, checking his accuracy when he returned to the ship by an old English translation and a Latin Bible which he had acquired before leaving England, why he should have considered Horace the best author for a beginner. But the labour served a double purpose: often far into the night occupying his mind, and giving him a feeling of achievement in his effort to prove a husband of whom Mary would not need to feel ashamed.

"All ready. Heave away." John took his seat in the long-boat and the men proceeded to cast off the ropes. It was a fair afternoon and, with the pleasant sea breeze, he estimated that they would reach land up river in time to take on their last load of water and firewood before darkness fell. Their last load! Tomorrow was the day of departure for the Middle Passage. Thank God, these eight difficult, dangerous months on the Guinea coast were safely over. Next time he came it would be as captain. Well, he had had his share of these long-boat trips.

"Mr. Newton."

Captain Hardy had emerged from his cabin to the deck above.

"Aye, Sir?"

"Come aboard."

The men stopped in the act of casting the last rope. John, with the unquestioning obedience of ship discipline, but with surprised eyebrows, swung himself back on deck, wondering what addition the Captain had thought of in the five minutes since he had received his order.

"You wished to see me, Sir?"

"Yes." Hardy was non-committal. "I've decided to send someone else in your place. Mr. Blodgett!"

"Aye, Sir."

"You will take charge of the boat this evening, in Mr. Newton's stead. The men know where to get the wood."

"But, Sir —" began John.

Hardy paid no attention. He repeated to Blodgett the instructions he had given a few minutes earlier, and presently the second mate took the vacated seat in the long-boat. It pulled away from the ship's side and hoisted its sail to the following breeze.

John remained standing dutifully at hand. To his surprise Hardy turned back to his cabin.

"What am I to do, Sir?"

"Oh," — the Captain swung on his heel as though surprised — "anything you like."

"But why — I have always gone with the boat."

"I took it into my head to send someone else," said Hardy laconically and disappeared, leaving John staring after him in exasperation. He should, he knew, be glad of a night in the comparative comfort of his cabin, but he was restless, and the activity of the long-boat suited his mood this last night on the coast better than the crowded inertness of an anchored ship. He did not feel like reading Horace. He had devoured all his other books. In the boat at least he would be free of the temptation which came with idleness and opportunity.

He caught himself up sharply. " 'Count it all joy, my brethren, when ye fall into manifold temptations'," he muttered, " 'knowing that the trial of your faith worketh patience —' " Very well. He would try to let patience have its perfect work. He was not so sure that he could count it all joy.

Dawn next morning found the ship astir with preparation

for sailing. The atmosphere was charged with excitement, almost with joy. Except for the two hundred and fifty blacks arranged like books on shelves below deck, those on board felt as if home and pay and rest were already in sight. The dangers of the Middle Passage, the constant labour and vigilance required in a crew already depleted by African fevers, to guard and wash and shave and exercise ten times their number, the ever-present threat of disease among the slaves and its contagion, the storms of the North Atlantic — none of this weighed for the moment with men who had survived the perils of coastal trading.

"Mr. Newton."

"Yes, Sir."

"No sign of the boat yet?"

John, who had been inspecting the barricadoes, where a rumour had reached him of suspicious activity among some of the men slaves, realized that the boat's return was long overdue. He stared up the sound and shook his head. The Captain expressed himself with profane eloquence on the delay, and John diplomatically refrained from reminding him that he had always brought the boat back and had its cargo unloaded an hour before this time.

The sun rose higher. Preparations completed, all but diurnal activity ceased. The slaves, chained in couples, were brought up on deck for air. Even to them, some of the impatience which was fast turning to anxiety communicated itself, and their rolling glances at the land from which they were being raped also scanned the broad waters of the river's mouth for a sign of the boat.

The boat did not come. In the afternoon a long canoe, skilfully paddled by blacks through the ground swell, brought one sailor who had drifted ashore on a piece of firewood when the overused hulk sank without warning in the night. Of Blodgett and the other five there was no trace, although they sent out the punt and yawl and delayed the *Brownlow*'s sailing. "I heard them go down," the survivor repeated dully in answer to questioning and, after several days of unrewarded search, they were compelled to believe him.

Newton, standing beside Hardy when the canoe came alongside, heard the first report of the catastrophe a moment before the personal significance struck home, even as a man sees the smoke of a distant explosion in a moment's silence before the noise reaches his ear. Then he turned to the Captain, who at the same moment turned and looked at him.

"It came into my mind to keep you on the ship," Hardy answered the unspoken query, and again, as though defending himself against a charge, "I just took it into my head to send someone in your place."

For days John walked under a strange sense of destiny and in the attitude of the crew he discovered an awkward respect, as for a man set apart. Hardy alone denied any belief in a particular providence, but he was greatly moved by the occurrence. "It came suddenly into my mind," he said musingly long after they left the coast.

"Dear Polly," wrote John and sat, tapping his pen-point on the table before him until it was blunted and he had to mend it with his pen-knife. Even the morning prayer in which he had committed his disappointment to the Lord had not softened his distress. It was mid-July, over a year since Mary had given assurance that she would make no drastic decision for a twelve-month, and at this rate it would be four months at the least before he could reach England. The orders awaiting the ship at Antigua to dispose of their cargo at Charlestown instead gave little disappointment to the rest of the crew, for whom the liveliest city in America had considerable charm. But John Newton found his philosophy sorely tried. "When I think of you (which is but always)" he went on, restraining the impulse to address her by some of the endearments which he used in his imaginary conversations, "to reflect that the only method I have of aspiring to your favour in a proper manner may possibly render it impracticable for me ever to attain it at all, makes me dull in spight of all my resolutions to the contrary." He went on in studied similes to express his fears and his refusal to give up hope. The letter, re-read, looked as dismal as he felt and he was tempted to tear it up and begin again. Instead he decided to appeal to her sense of humour. "If you could form an idea of my situation while I write this, it would render apology for blunders, etc. quite needless. I am shut up with almost as many unclean creatures as Noah was and in a much smaller ark. I am, with an un-abated passion and regard, your faithful admirer and humble servant — J. Newton."

The comment on his situation was not exaggerated. It was his first experience of the Middle Passage in a crowded slaver and, though it had been a better than normal voyage, the number of blacks had been decimated and three of the crew had been buried at sea. The consequent atmosphere of sick-ness which no amount of fumigation could entirely dispel, the scenes of misery and horror, the occasions on which he had been called to give orders when living and dead had been found in the morning shackled together, he had schooled him-self to endure, as concomitants of the trade in which he was permitted to make his living. He had been counting the days, however, till the sale of their living cargo and the consequent improvement of conditions on board ship. There were other features of the trade which he did not regard as neces-sary and which he was determined to avoid when the authori-ty became his. He would not put the men in iron collars, without very good reason. And he would not, whatever the provocation, resort to the cruelty of punishment which Cap-tain Hardy dispassionately employed.

"It is more economical in the long run," was his laconic reply when Newton ventured to protest the prolonged use of thumbscrews and the killing floggings to which two leaders of an attempted insurrection were subjected. "Make an ex-ample of these and we'll have no trouble with the rest."

They had no more trouble with those two either, thought John, still feeling sick when the event recurred to his mind. One had died that evening, the other was not yet recovered. When he became captain he would treat the slaves as humanely as he could — when he became captain. And when that day came, would a greater day have preceded it? Would he be Mary's husband when he sailed? Else why sail at all? For Mary alone would he undertake the deprivations and dangers and discomforts of his present life, and she alone could reward him for them.

22

WHETHER or not she would was still an undecided question a fortnight and more after he arrived, early in 1750, in Chatham. After the continual discouragement of delay, his homecoming had been most auspicious. The Manestys had welcomed him almost as a son. Joseph Manesty was pleased with his part in the voyage and promised him command of the *Duke of Argyle* the next sailing season. When he reached Rotherhithe, he found that Mary had written to his stepmother — written as her mother's amanuensis, true, but Mary had written — inviting her with him to Chatham. John was not sorry that the three children's recent illness prevented her from accepting, but surely the invitation was a good sign. In the elation of it he had written buoyantly to Mary of his easiness of mind because his former errors and absurdities of conduct had evidently not fixed a dislike in her which he could not hope to remove. Jack, home for the Christmas festivities, had returned to his attorney's office in the City; but their friendship had been cemented by correspondence and Jack approved his noticeable improvement in social grace. On the strength of this John wrote, dating his letter from "Elysium", of his hopes that before long he would be happier than he had ever had a notion of, and asking Jack to purchase for him, against Mary's approaching birthday, an elegant white vellum prayer-book.

Yet of definite assurance, he had to admit when he withdrew from the dazzle of her presence and faced the situation in the cold north light of fact, he had absolutely none. It amazed him that Mary could welcome him so pleasantly, treat him so considerately, and never by word or look betray her knowledge that she, and she alone was the purpose, the end, the object of his visit and presence. Her laughter, her interest in his adventures, the delightful efficiency with which she carried out her share of the housekeeping, or the easy grace with which she performed introductions, arranged the tables for an evening game of cards, or took just the right place at the right moment when the dance was forming: all had the same air of spontaneity free from any touch of coyness. Artifice could not be mentioned in connection with her — unless it were artifice to behave as if she did not know what she had known for years, what she had read in letter after letter, what was obvious to everyone else every time he looked at her. Surely she could give some sign of encouragement if there was encouragement for him and, if not, why had she permitted him to come at all?

John broke off at this moment of pondering, as though his thought were sacrilege. Whatever Mary did was right. Shrewd and critical he was in other matters: recently at Charlestown he had altered his naive view that all doctrine which came from the pulpit must be good, and had forsaken the barren ministry of the Established Church to hear a controverted Dissenting preacher. But he had yet to see one action, hear one word from Mary which did not evoke his whole-souled approval. What did he expect of a girl? To put up with his tongue-tied absurdity and epistolary eloquence for years and then ask him to propose? He had been waiting — or so he told himself — for her to become accustomed to him after his long absence, to see for herself what he had told her brother, and what he felt must be an improvement in her eyes, that he was "more like other people than formerly". Perhaps she wondered what he was waiting for. And, considering the alarming way in which the days of his stay on shore were gliding past, he wondered too. He would propose formally at the very first opportunity. After his past experience he preferred not to give advance notice by asking for a private interview.

His chance occurred the following evening. Mr. Catlett had business which took him to his warehouse after tea; Georgie and Sarah had both taken to bed with a cold and George in particular was a demanding patient.

"Poor Georgie," said Polly, when Mrs. Catlett left the room to fulfil her promise to read to him. "Such a great boy and yet he becomes quite childish when he falls sick. He really is miserable. If he were just a bit ill I should do as nurse. But when he feels quite wretched he must have Mother. It's an infallible test."

"I'm glad he must," said John, recognizing the perfect opening, and seizing it abruptly, "but in my case, well or ill, I should want *you*. I do want you, and have wanted you — always. O Polly" — the name, though dear, was too frivolous for the great occasion — "Mary, dearest, you know, you must know what I have so often and so poorly attempted *to* tell you, that —"

He stopped short. Mary, sitting across the hearth from him, had been smiling into the fire at some recollection connected with Georgie's importunity. Now the face she turned to him was so grave that the words which had for the first time been coming fluently froze on his tongue. Her hand's quick curtailing gesture was peremptory.

"Don't, John," she said and her tone, though breathless, had the same frightening gravity as her face. "I know what you are going to say — and I cannot listen to it. I cannot marry you. You must never speak to me of this again."

Silence fell, the silence of consternation. In terrible dreams this had sometimes occurred but the bleakness had always wakened him to the comparative comfort that it was only a dream. Now it had happened in reality and there was no sequel. Her authority over him was so absolute that even the thought of expostulation did not immediately arise. He must say something, something casual, something reassuring, or she might leave the room and refuse to see him again. But his thoughts, so long focussed on this moment, were shattered and he could find nothing to say among the fragments.

Mary sat very still. The words had been almost as much a surprise to her as to him. She always made an effort to put off things which troubled her. Now suddenly it had come, the often fumbled, long postponed moment, the choice between her present happy self-sufficiency, the sure groove of her little, placid, lovely life and a change, not only of state but of dimension. For whatever life would mean with this strange person, this dumbly adoring boy for whom she felt almost a motherly pity, this thoughtful, increasingly accomplished, unconforming individual, this shy, potentially disturbing man, she knew instinctively that it would be lived on another level, where she would experience great emotion, those heart-tearing moments which she feared and tried to avoid, elemental conflicts and knowledge of vast things beyond the secure limitations of the present. And she could *not* choose it. Why should she? For what compensation? So she sat still, counting on the authority which, even as a child of fourteen, she had realized was hers over him; and her mind was still, almost as formless as his.

John cleared his throat and wished that he had not. The sound was abnormally loud in the quiet room. An instant later a log fell from the andirons, and at the same instant a gust of icy rain blew against the window. He fumbled for the first coherent thought.

"In Sherbro," he said earnestly, "it is very hot at this season."

Mary looked at him quickly, then shrieked with laughter. John laughed too, at the ineptitude of his remark, and with relief at having disturbed her devastating gravity. In the thaw of his dread, his mind and his hope reasserted themselves beneath his surface thought of helpless adoration that any merely human face could look so lovely, whether severely composed or as now, mirth-shaken and uncontrolled. Her features and hers alone, he thought, could be convulsed without distortion, fall into new patterns of beauty with laughter or distress. And either emotion took her quickly, often from causes which his mind perceived more slowly in the wake of hers.

"I am sorry; it was rude to laugh," she apologized contritely a moment later. "I don't know why the — the — climate of Sherbro or a reference to it should seem so funny just then. Mother would be shocked," she went on hurriedly, "at my forgetting my manners."

John was not slow to press his advantage.

"Of course it seemed funny. It was completely irrelevant. But, Polly, that is the very point. There is no relevance apart from my love for you. If I cannot talk of that or hope for that, there is nothing to talk about. Mary, my dearest —"

231

She had recovered her gravity completely now, and with it a suggestion of reproach.

"John, I forbid you to continue. Surely you heard me when I said that I could not listen?"

She rose and for a moment he thought she was about to leave the room. Yet somehow her tone and manner seemed less peremptory than before. He cast about hastily for a topic of conversation to detain her and it was mercifully provided in a snore from the hearth-rug at his feet.

"Fancy is feeling the effects of his walk today," he essayed. "Usually he stirs the very moment you do."

"Yes, silly little dog," said Mary fondly, sitting down on the hearth-bench and leaning forward to stroke Fancy's smooth amber head. Her own curling brown hair fell forward with the gesture and the fire brightened the colour in her cheeks and cast its magic — as if there were not magic enough! — over the curving arm and the deepened hollow where her throat melted into the drooping left shoulder. "He was so happy to get out after being cooped up in the house. I don't wonder he's tired. You and Father and I walked only to the Windmill and back. Fancy must have run five times that distance."

"At least that, I should imagine, if we could chart his course," said John, gathering his courage for another effort. "Similarly, my ship may sail many times the distance on one voyage as when bound for the same port, but with a steady wind. Polly, you are too kind to hurt Fancy who has loved you for scarcely two years. How can you be cruel to me when I have loved you as he never can — and with far less encouragement — for over seven? You must — you cannot be so far ungenerous as to refuse to — let me at least plead my cause this once."

The soft stroking ceased abruptly. She rose again and stood by the mantel, half turned away from him, but said nothing and he continued hastily:

"Don't think that I expect you to feel as I do or to love me at the beginning. Just let me show you, as I cannot in this suspense and uncertainty, what I mean by devotion —"

"But I am not a worthy object of such devotion," said Mary in a cool argumentative tone. "You would soon find that you

232

have been mistaken in me. I have all sorts of faults and am not half as good as you suppose —"

"I am quite willing to take the risk," interrupted John, scarcely believing that she had so far relented as to argue. "I have existed on the mere shadow and idea of love all this time, I am not afraid that the substance will diminish my regard. And —"

"But I am happy as I am now."

"How do you know that you cannot be happier?" said John boldly, his mind groping for a line of poetry that was eluding him. "You surely do not intend to remain unmarried all your life?"

"Perhaps not. But if I marry someone here, I should not have to leave home or to have my husband away at sea for so long, and —"

"Mary, you cannot marry anyone else." She had left the fire now and was walking around the room. He thought of rising but felt less awkward, more able to keep his words in order, if he remained where he was. The line he wanted had come to him: "The Woman Who Deliberates Is Lost". *Gained,* surely, though the turmoil of suspense and uncertainty within him was not yet susceptive of such hope. But it encouraged him to persist. "O my — my *dearest* dear, I know that almost any other man has more than I to offer of money and worldly prospects. But not such love. And not my determination to make it the main business of my life to please you."

"John, I don't deserve —"

"You deserve far better than I or than any man can give you. No, I will not promise what I cannot perform. But all that I can do for you I will and with my whole grateful heart. Mary dear, it is not heroic for me to trade on your pity — but I am no hero, I'm afraid, just the man who worships you. If it had not been for hope of you, though it seemed hopeless, I should long ago have made away with myself. God mercifully restrained me and will restrain. But there can be no happiness apart from you, no —"

He stopped speaking but this time for a different reason. He had heard the soft swish of Mary's dress, as she walked back and forth between the window and fireplace. Now she was before him, facing him and, quite suddenly and simply, she held out her hand.

John never knew how long he sat staring. His heart beat and trembled to such a degree that he could not get a word out. The vital import of this success, the long agony of his suspense, delayed proportionately his grasp of its actuality. But it was true! That outstretched hand, that look on her expressive face as of a game fighter who surrenders, reluctant but relieved, to the inevitable, could mean only one thing.

He took her hand. Though warm it was trembling. Dumbly he reached for the other which was pressed, half-clenched, over the rising confusion of her heart. Tentative, hardly daring to presume or experiment, he opened the imprisoned hands; then buried his face in the palms, not kissing them at first, but realizing their beloved touch as it compensated for the five years since he had last felt it in parting desolation. Then, bolder with one dream fulfilled, still unrebuffed, still not trusting himself to stand, he put his arms around her drawing her close, and with a sigh like a sob his head found its long-desired haven on her breast.

With masculine logic John had anticipated that, since it had taken Mary so long to entertain the idea of marriage, it would require a lengthy interval before she could face the event itself. In this his calculations were delightfully upset. When, later on the decisive evening, he hesitatingly broached the question, Mary's reply had been as unexpectd as her capitulation.

"Since I am going to marry you, it would be foolish to put it off till you are sent to sea again," she said practically. And when, thoroughly in agreement, he had pressed for a definite date, she had put her head on one side and knitted her up-turned brows so distractingly that John could hardly bear her beauty and the joy that it was his.

"I shall have to consult Mother of course — how long Georgie is keeping her! — but I see no reason to put it off for more than a fortnight."

A fortnight, after seven years, was short enough, yet sometimes it seemed to John as long as a Guinea voyage.

Now it was over.

The wedding festivities had been curtailed because George's illness developed into pleurisy, and for some days and nights his life was in danger. He had recovered sufficiently to relieve the Catletts of anxiety, and the small family party had driven to St. Margaret's in Rochester, where Mr. Soans performed the ceremony. Then Mrs. Soans, whom the Catlett children called Auntie, had given the wedding supper. Jack coming up from London rose enthusiastically to the occasion, providing merriment and proposing toast after toast. He reminded John of a letter he had once written promising to drink Polly's health, Roman-fashion, a cup for every letter of her name; and John, knowing his capacity, reduced the number by drinking to "Mary" and making the "cups" very small indeed. Jack had driven them back to Chatham, and it was with difficulty brought home to his bachelor obtuseness that his new brother-in-law, whose enrolment among "Religionists" he deplored, was not in the mood for a dispute prolonged till midnight. Mrs. Catlett had come to the rescue and John was now in the "spare room," which had been converted into a room for the bridal couple. Mary had lingered to say good-night to her mother. Presently she would come to him, his wife.

Suddenly the pulsing blood, the deep strong thudding of his heart, the joyful agony of breathing, were stilled as though under a quiet hand. For him, yes. This was the height of his ambition, the climax of his hope, the fulfilment of those yearning dreams which the sight of a thirteen-year-old girl long years before had originated. This made up for all pain, all privation, all waiting: that Mary was his wife. But what of her? John was not prone to self-deception. The past two weeks had been happy in her graciousness. Once she had given her word, there was no coquetry, no withdrawal. He had relaxed and gained confidence in the sense of belonging, of importance, which her delightful air of possessiveness imparted. But he was quite well aware that the generosity of her nature, overflowing in response to his pleading, had actuated her acceptance, rather than any passion corresponding to his own. He realized now that the prospect which thrilled every nerve in him was to her a mysterious, unsought interrogation mark. He felt quickly ashamed, he who had pledged himself to seek her happiness, that the thought of his own had made him forgetful. Now he remembered the trembling of her arm in the church; and though she had done everything prettily as always, she had been quiet, not at all her usually gay self, at the festivities and on the homeward ride.

He opened the window. The February night was mild and the air blowing from the garden presaged an early spring, balmy as the faint scent of snowdrops which Mary had carried in a nosegay to church. Almost automatically his seafaring eyes sought the heavens and found the constant, unremarkable light of the north star.

"Gracious God," he prayed soberly, "accept my thanks for Thy mercy in giving my dearest Mary to me. When I consider what I have deserved at Thy hands I shall never — let me never cease praising Thee. But make this a happy night too for her. Let me make her happy. Dear Lord I love her so much! Grant that my love be temperate and patient and understanding, so that I desire first her happiness, and am never content with mine alone —"

He awoke the next morning, fully conscious and filled with a sense of complete well-being. The first night after his engagement his sleep had been the sweetest he had ever known, but this was awakening from ecstasy to continued ecstasy. He knew where he was and who was beside him but lay for a moment with closed eyes, too happy to bear more.

When he opened them he found Mary lying on her side facing him. Her cheek rested on her right hand and her intent eyes seemed to have been studying him seriously for some time.

"John," she said as he was about to move, "I want to speak to you."

"Ever since you first came here," she went on, taking his speechlessness as assent, "you have been saying lovely things to me — well, not always *saying* them, I admit," she qualified, her mouth curving into a fondly amused smile, "at least not directly to me. At any rate, I think it is time I said something in return."

John lay very still. She stretched out her free hand and touched his cheek, then drew the other from under her head and cupped his face — such soft hands against the unshaven masculinity of his chin — in the first unsolicited caress she had given him.

"You are very kind and very good, my husband," she said distinctly, though her eyes brightened into tears as she spoke, "and I think I shall learn to love you very much."

It was no surprise to John that he could not speak. But he could now give another answer.

"O my dear," she said presently, "I shall not need to learn. I think I must be loving you already."

23

THE post brought letters for you, John. One is in Jack's writing." Mrs. Catlett took the letters from the beaufet and handed them to him. Mary, who had been half-way up the stairs, turned quickly to look, then went on up more slowly. "You and he are having a steady correspondence these days."

"Yes, Auntie — from Morton to Manby, as he insists on pseudonyms. He has become almost as wordy as I." John tore the letter open, anxious to see what answer Jack had found to his last argument. It was a constant prick to his conscience that his own audacious ridicule had first encouraged Jack to question the casually accepted beliefs of his childhood. Now, although he still adhered perfunctorily to the lukewarm religious observances of the family, he seized on every means to bolster his scepticism, uncannily recollective of John's former statements. So John laboured carefully at his replies, keeping his tone from over-seriousness and endeavouring to present his previous unbelief as baseless in logic as it now seemed to him. He re-read the letter and began to plan his refutation.

Presently, coming out of his musing, he found Mary looking at him tensely from her chair by the window.

"Dearest," he said contritely, "have I kept you waiting? Or what is the matter?"

"Aren't you ever going to read your other letter?" She motioned to the second missive on the table beside him. A glance showed him the reason for her concern. A few minutes later he handed Mr. Manesty's note to her and both fell silent again. So the *Duke of Argyle* was ready and could sail as soon as John saw to her outfitting. She should be away by August. A delay might keep her on the coast until the rainy season and prolong the voyage for months.

That the announcement was inevitable, even essentially welcome, did not soften the impact of its coming. In the marvellous weeks and months since his marriage, every thought of it had been turned aside by some new or recollected or anticipated delight. He had taught Mary and learned from her; joyous experiences both. Never in his crowded lonely life had he been able to share himself; and the interests which his curious mind had stored and considered had come forth one by one, to be re-enjoyed in her enjoyment. Like many town girls, Mary had seen nature only in its trimmed and modified aspect: the gardens and grass, the conventional walk to the Docks or the Windmill, a sight of fields and hills from the not always relaxing seat of a chaise or phaeton. Now with him she climbed the unpathed hills beyond the Medway, and penetrated the heart of spinneys which she had seen from a distance, and discovered the earlier stages of familiar brooks. Once instructed, her quick eyes and mind saw and noted with a sensitiveness of perception which made him feel — though now happily — slow and dull by comparison. And when, one warm May evening, he spread his full-skirted blue coat for her and, as they lay on the grass, pointed out the constellations by name, her thrilled interest made him long to know five times as much, in order to awaken again and again the admiration in her voice.

That was sheer marvel! To be tolerable to her had been his almost eclipsed hope. To be in some measure loved by her, was overflowing grace. But to be admired, to have her take pride in him, think his knowledge and abilities remarkable, that was beyond all expectation. He thought of his degraded isolation on the *Harwich*, his helpless misery at the mercy of P.I., his brutalized weakness under Clow, and was staggered at the contrast.

But the contrast sharpened the edge of this approaching separation. How could he bear to be torn from her for twelve, perhaps sixteen long months? They had only once been more than an hour separated. Now for weeks and months he would not know if she were well or ill — or if she were alive. She could be with child and he would not be with her, die bearing it and he would not hear. With the speed of gloomy thought he had lost her and returned to a desolate existence almost before Manesty's letter had fluttered from her limp hand to the floor.

He heard a strange sound and looked up. It was seldom that they sat apart in their room, but in the depression of the news he had not moved over to her. She was still sitting but with her back to him and he thought —

"Polly, dear," he said, unbelieving, "you're not crying, are you?"

She stamped her foot.

"Of course, I'm crying, silly. Do you think I can marry you and learn to love you and have you go off in a little ship half the world away for years and — I knew this would happen! That's why I told you to stop asking me. But you would keep on. You persisted. And now —"

John sat appalled. Did she mean that she regretted it? Was she angry that he had brought this upon her?

There was the sound of a small tempest as Mary swept across the room, flung herself on his knee, into his ready arms, and rubbed her tear-wet face against his.

"Oh, John, I'm so glad you kept on. Thank God, you didn't do what I told you!"

"You mean," said John rather wistfully when he stopped kissing her, "that you love me even if I spend the money I should use for your support on — on lottery tickets?"

It was a sore point with him and one which he could not quite settle with his conscience. When the thought of separation had forced itself on him during the past months, he had wished to find some way of providing for Mary that would not necessitate his going to sea. During one of these periods, Jack had come down from London, full of grandiose schemes to be carried out with money from a state lottery for which he had purchased a ticket. Lotteries had been growing in popularity during the years John was at sea and the idea was new and fascinating. At Jack's suggestion, John had commissioned him to purchase a ticket. During the period of waiting, he had prayed that the Lord's will might be done in the matter and that he would be content in either case. He drew a blank and maintained a spirit of quiet resignation, until the next opportunity came his way. Then it occurred to him that one failure did not necessarily signify God's opposition. Had he not achieved success with Mary only by persistence? So the purchase of another and then another ticket was preceded each time by specious argument which satisfied his logic but not his conscience. When he had run a few pounds in debt — for Jack showed both a brotherly and a friendly interest in enabling him to quit the sea — he added to his pure resolves regarding the expenditure of the coveted prize, a solemn vow. If he won, he prayed, hoping that the Lord would not consider his promise in the light of a bribe, he would give a generous sum to the poor. Wrapped up in his own concerns, anxious for Mary's comfort, he had not before assumed any responsibility for them.

Alas! they were not to benefit from his belated concern. In this lottery too he drew a blank, and in his final desperate attempt to retrieve all losses, he was likewise disappointed. He had stopped then, seventy pounds — over a year's pay as Captain — in debt. And then he had told Mary, blurting out the story in a mixture of penitence and relief, for only the hope of giving her a glad surprise had counterbalanced his feeling of guilt at the concealment.

She had grown grave at the telling, with the preternatural gravity which moulded her face into pure childish lines. It was foolish to be afraid, he told himself as he waited, but he was, terribly afraid, of disappointing her, of losing the respect and admiration which were unspeakably precious to him. The ticking seconds of silence seemed interminable.

"I don't blame you for being angry, Polly. You have every right," he said tentatively.

Then, suddenly as always, her gravity broke in a wave of laughter, and the clear eyes which looked directly into his were crinkled with amusement at her self as at him.

"Oh, John, what right have I to be angry? What should I have done if you had won a thousand pounds?"

The contrast between this hypothesis and the true statement made him wince.

"I should have said," she continued steadily, "what a wonderful husband you were, and how courageous and persistent you had been in refusing to be daunted by failure, and how it showed your love because you didn't want to leave me. Wouldn't I now?"

"Bless you, my charmer," said her bemused husband, "I suppose you would. But —"

"Well," said Polly practically, "it's just as true. You are the same and you've acted in exactly the same manner. It isn't your fault that you didn't win. So how can I be angry?"

And that, as far as she was concerned, and to John's increasing adoration, was final. The matter for her was closed. Even when John, goaded by something rather more than his sense of failure, re-opened it as he did now, she did not diminish her initial generosity by belated recriminations.

"But I wanted to buy you that new green gown," he persisted ruefully.

"Don't you like me in this one?" She spread the folds of blue sprigged muslin out over his knees. "And I should far rather have it new when you come home. It's to please you I'll wear it, not to please others when you are away."

"Is it any wonder I love you?" asked John with the air of one who demands an honest answer. "I could be unselfish enough almost to be thankful that I love you more because the pain of parting must be proportionately less for you but —"

"Is that true, indeed?" said Mary indignantly. "How do you know you love me more than I do you?"

"Because I've loved you so much longer, in the first place," said John. "You know quite well that it was pity and kindness, not love, which made you consent to marry me."

Her face became dreamy with reminiscence.

"Wasn't it?" he persisted.

"Yes. And yet that is not all the truth. I really had to give in — sometime."

He looked at her wonderingly.

"I suppose I should tell you. I don't understand it. But when I was fourteen, just as soon really as I realized how you felt about me — and long before the thought was at all acceptable — I knew somehow that sooner or later I should be yours. Don't ask me how, or why I fought against it. I can't account for the feeling. I just know it was always there. And as for comparisons, your love has merely continued while mine has been growing —"

"And hasn't mine grown likewise?" John interrupted this heresy. "I thought I couldn't love you more when I married you. But I loved you then, as they say, for your looks — something for which you could never love me! I had none of the endearments, none of the thousand and one favours to be grateful for —"

Mary took his face in her hands.

"You are always so sure, John, that you aren't handsome, that—"

"I'm not," said her husband honestly. "And you know it, Polly. Look at the width of my face. Besides, my hair isn't smooth, yet when I wear a wig in company, I feel that it looks foolish. And —"

"You look like a man, not like a wax dummy," said Polly firmly. "And I'm very glad of it. Your mouth is — it's yours and not like anyone else's. I'm glad of that. And your eyes are the dearest in the world. And there is nothing about you that I would have changed in any particular — except that I wish, I wish you didn't have to go to sea. When you were up in London an hour seemed longer than days or weeks seemed formerly. So please stop this deprecation of a face which is very lovely to me" — she leaned forward and kissed each offending feature gravely, then bent back and surveyed his still imprisoned face with laughing eyes that were not far from tears — "my Pretty Dear!"

"O my Dearest!" The passion which had fed so long on hope alone flourished on such heady sustenance. "If I were not a Christian I should worship you. Even so, I am afraid I do, God forgive me. You were my idol for years and I fear there is still idolatry in my love for you. Pray for me, my precious, that I may not tempt God by exalting you to His place."

"Then you will have to pray for me," said Polly. "Three months ago — even a month since — I should not have known what you meant or how anyone could feel so about another person. Now I understand. And if God is angry with you for idolatry, He will be with me too."

The question was by no means an academic one and kept recurring, as young Captain Newton walked with Mr. Manesty through Liverpool, estimating and ordering quantities of timber for barricadoes, sailcloth for replacements, dry supplies of food for crews and the hoped-for cargo, bales of cloth, kegs of gunpowder, hogsheads of rum, cider, and brandy to make up the "bars" for trading. The agony of his separation from Mary had shocked him out of the honeymoon paradise of their five months together and awakened him to a startled realization of his backsliding. In his gratitude for his married happiness, in the essential goodness of that happiness, he had insensibly made it the main object of his life, rested in it, content as though it were eternally abiding. Now, torn from his idol, realizing not only that his idol could not help him but that he was powerless, in spite of his love, to divert any catastrophe from her, he was thrown back on the Giver whom he had largely forgotten in the gift.

That the Giver did not remain coldly aloof, that He welcomed, pardoned, restored peace of conscience and a sense of renewed communication, drove John further into self-examination. God had forgiven him but he found it hard to forgive himself, harder to trust that he would not again be guilty of the same ingratitude. And the possibility that such folly might deprive him of his idol, or bring upon her the sorrow of his death, made him quail as the imminence of death in a dozen situations had never done.

Not that he dishonoured God by thinking of Him as mean or vindictive. When he considered and feared the possibility that he and Mary might be permanently severed because of his excessive affection, he believed — though with terror and shrinking of the flesh — that God would be dealing with them in love. He was essentially realistic and — for all his depth of emotion — not sentimental. Dim though his spiritual vision still was, he had been given a glimpse of Eternity and of the transience of the present life in comparison. In spite of his adoration he realized Mary's creature limitations. Death was an ever-present fact even in peaceful England, and his calling exposed him to too many varied forms of it for him to consider either her or himself immune. Accordingly the God of love would not allow them to build their lives on quicksand. He who had reached out and snatched him from ruin was not leaving him to sink in the morass of his own deceptive enjoyment. Perhaps, no, surely, that was the reason for the frustration of his efforts to remain with Mary.

Stumblingly he recommenced the pilgrimage which he had temporarily forgotten. But now it was, in a sense, a dual pilgrimage. For though Mary had never been apostate, and though the recollection of his former vileness made him humbly grateful that he had been granted a wife of such essential loveliness of character, he recognized her as a sinner in the sight of God and scarcely nearer the light than he. So in the letters which he sent every post while he was in Liverpool, he tried, faltering at first, then with increasing facility, to talk out the growing conviction of his soul.

The very response of her love to his humbled and reproached him. The surprise and consternation of some of her friends when they learned of the marriage was a theme on which he wrote jokingly to his own disparagement; but it was an unceasing amazement to realize that the "easy and polished" Mary Catlett, who had regarded him with patient exasperation, and had been influenced to accept his proposal largely because she could not bear to cause him pain, was now utterly dejected at his absence. He had made a slow journey to Liverpool because, in her terror of highwaymen, she had extracted from him a promise that he would not ride late. And the poor dilatory correspondent, from whom in seven years he had extracted some seventeen lines in two letters, was now writing every post with an intensity less verbose and more reticently stated but no less real than his own.

This was response to his love, his care, his devotion, for he could not see anything in himself to call it forth. And — the contrast forced itself upon him — what was *his* response to Love which had flowed out to an utterly unworthy object from the absolutely Lovely, the everlasting Lover of his soul? He thought suddenly — while he selected chains and fetters for his anticipated cargo of two hundred slaves — of Mary's discovery of the scars left from his flogging. He had been washing one morning while she lay peacefully in bed, as he

245

thought, half-asleep. He remembered hearing a little cry, and then she was out of bed and he saw her face beside his great bare shoulder in the washstand mirror, startled, questioning.

"John," she had asked, "what is this?" and he felt her hand on his back where strips of raised flesh commemorated the repeated strokes of the edge of the cat.

"Oh, that," he had said lightly, "that is the memorial of my well-deserved punishment on the *Harwich*. You knew about it, my dearest."

"I didn't really know. I hadn't seen it." Scarcely breathing, for every touch, every caress from her was a new ecstasy, he felt her hand, exquisitely tender, then her lips trace the course of the ugly weals. Then, with a sharp intake of breath, she pressed her face against his back, and clung to him, shuddering.

"Oh, John, John, I can't bear it," she had cried stormily, when he took her in his arms to comfort. "It was my fault. You suffered all that for me. You would not have done it except for me."

In a sense that was true, thought John, but only in a sense. He had suffered for his unruly passion, his dereliction of duty, not at all voluntarily or for Mary's benefit. Yet such had been her reaction of sorrow and love. Whereas what feeling had he for the One whom his sins had killed, who had, without sin or compulsion of His own, been scourged and crucified for his worthless and ungrateful self?

"Will that number of collars be adequate? You may have as many as six or seven score man-slaves."

Manesty's voice recalled him from his reverie. He glanced at the fourscore collars which he had — quite deliberately — ordered, and, for fear his employer would consider him impractical, added twenty more.

"It is seldom necessary to put them all in collars, particularly the boys," he explained. "And they are in better condition to bring a good price if they are not chafed when they arrive in the Indies." Secretly he was determined not to use the collars except on the refractory. By leniency and fair treatment he hoped also to avoid the need of using the "bits" or mouth-openers which were regularly carried on board to force unhappy slaves to take their food. The trade in slaves was part of the established order and no easy or pleasant occupation for those who carried it on; but John Newton would carry it on with as little suffering as possible for slaves and crew alike. They would all respond, he was sure, to kindness.

24

THREE years later a more experienced Captain Newton had rather less reason for such assurance. Standing on deck as the pilot guided the *African* — a seaworthy vessel, but "like her master," as he had written to Mary, "rather of the slowest" — into St. Kitt's harbour, he thanked God for a second voyage successfully brought forward, but ascribed praise to Him alone rather than to the co-operation of crew or submission of cargo. True, for the past two months the slaves had been quiet and tractable as children and there had been far less illness on board than on the first distressing voyage in the *Duke of Argyle;* but the lengthy contentious haggling and journeying months of trade on the Guinea coast, the need of constant vigilance, the personal distress of his disappointment with an unruly and mutinous crew as well as with plotting slaves, the loneliness of this ship where there was no one with whom he could have conversation — all had taken their toll. His eyes sought the Basseterre harbour with its quayside as longingly as if it were England, for here within an hour or so he would have letters from Mary — the first word from her in nine interminable months.

A sound, familiar yet alien, diverted his glance from shore. The blacks were being brought on deck for their daily airing, with the slow clanking movement of two walking as one, chained and manacled by the especially hampering usage of right hand and foot across to the right hand and foot of the partner so that absolute concert of motion was necessary to any degree of convenience. The deck was fitted with iron rings to which fifty or more couples could be secured, less than half of this year's slowly, expensively accumulated two hundred and seven, but all still alive. Of the hundred and seventy on his first voyage, he had buried on shore, or committed to the sea, twenty-eight, and a greater proportion of his crew. This second voyage, of the crew only Peter Mcdonald had succumbed to illness, and that illness had prevented the success of a widespread plot to seize the ship, a plot of which he had been the ring-leader. The two other instigators had been put aboard the next man-of-war as had, on his first sailing, several dangerous trouble-makers of the *Argyle's* crew. It had been an action necessitated in each case by a careful consideration of the safety of the ship. With officers ill, and the crew outnumbered at times ten to one by helpless or desperate slaves, the young Captain could not afford the presence of proven and resentful traitors, whose round-robin, circulated among the crew, had marked the first-mate and the doctor for death. His own, he assumed, had been taken for granted. But the action had revived the remembrance of his own misery on the *Harwich,* and the relief of their riddance was counterbalanced by haunting speculation as to their fate.

John tried to shake himself clear of such thoughts, as he had done before, by thinking of the miserable death which had overtaken several of his best men in their pursuit of duty: Mr. Bridson, his first-mate, who had brought the long-boat back from Shebar with half its passengers sick, and died himself of a slow fever ten days later; his friend Richard Arthur the doctor, to whom he had been able to speak of Mary, and who had succumbed to his fifth attack of bloody flux when England was almost in sight.

No, Lees and the others had deserved their punishment. Yet he had felt the treacherous attempts more keenly because of his efforts for the well-being of his crew. Perhaps they understood better the good caning which he had meted out to several offenders for breaking open and stealing the ship's supplies, the two dozen strokes of the cat which he had inflicted on the carpenter for mutinous and insolent behaviour in his absence. He had forced himself at first to administer the punishment, knowing from experience the dividing line between correction and torture; later he had delegated flogging only to trusted officers and only in moderate degrees. Perhaps, too, the consideration with which he had treated them had been despised as weakness. In one of the innumerable letters which he despatched in thick packets to Mary with every home-bound ship, he had mentioned, among the other prerogatives of a sea-captain, that, when he was absent from the ship, the entire crew must remain awake to welcome his return; for which reason he never, if he could avoid it, prolonged that return until midnight. He had also described the boisterous celebrations as they crossed the tropic of Capricorn. Those who had never passed it before were subject to a fine, usually to be paid in brandy and so exorbitant that some fledgling sailors could not afford it. The resultant brutal sport of hauling the victim by a rope to the yardarm and dropping him in the water, fun for the spectators and terror for the helpless half-drowned land-lubber, struck John as so cruel that he always paid for the youngsters unable to pay the fine — doubtless to the resentment of men cheated of their diversion. And on such men the effect of compulsory morning and evening service, by which he sought every Sunday to act the part of minister to his small congregation, had evidently been negligible. That was a sore point, for John was still shy where matters of deep feeling were concerned and conscious of his own inadequacy in performing what he knew to be his Christian duty. It was puzzling too that the worst trouble, both from crew and from slaves, had broken out during the voyage on which, as he recorded in his diary:

"Considering the many extraordinary dangers that they [sailors] are particularly subject to in African voyages. . . I have proposed by the grace of God to set apart a day to humble myself before the Lord in their names, and by fasting and prayer to entreat His blessed will, that the lives of my whole company may be spared to return safe with me to England, or that such as His infinite wisdom shall see fit to dispose of otherwise may, by His grace, have a due sense of their sins and a comfortable hope of pardon through the merits of Jesus Christ afforded them, before they go hence and are no more seen."

And after the heart-searching consequent upon his discovery of the plot, he had been able to say that from "the first day of the voyage I have endeavoured to do my duty by them without oppression, ill language, or any abuse". He had also resolved to entertain no personal hatred or ill will against the offenders, but to pardon them freely as far as he himself was concerned. He would treat them with humanity while they remained in his power, but obviously could not encourage further attempts by passing such an affair over in silence.

Now on the deck below him excitement increased. Ignorant and regardless of what awaited them, the blacks, after the rolling horror of their month on the open sea, were regarding the nearing land with wild enthusiasm. Captain of the ship which had brought them unwilling from their native country, Newton looked down, with eyes in which the growing pity which he now felt for millions of his fellow-creatures obscured his satisfaction. Yet he had reason to feel satisfaction, for assiduous attention to cleanliness, purging their quarters with tobacco and sulphur after sickness, anointing them with beeswax and florence oil, had brought them across the Middle Passage in as good' condition as when they were purchased.

No . . . he hastily corrected his straying thoughts. It was the Lord's mercy and no good management on his part. An epidemic like the one which had broken out on the *Argyle* could have nullified all human effort. Poor wretches! He and they were both longing to set foot ashore, but with what different prospects! For him there would be ease, welcome, that for which he had been literally dreaming for months so that he often woke feeling them in his hands, many letters from his wife. For them, although increasing acquaintance with their life in Africa left him under no illusions as to its happiness, a far darker future.

The detachment was unfastened from the ring-bolts and marched, docile but still chattering, below deck. They must all be securely out of the way by the time the ship docked. Not that any attempt to escape could now meet with success; but men yearning for liberty were seldom prudent in reckoning risk or cost. The Captain did not blame them. In the several attempts at insurrection which had been betrayed or discovered, he had never felt anger with the leaders, though discouraged that the first uprising had been planned by a young man so trusted that he had been left free of irons and in a position of some responsibility. The secrecy and near success with which these repeated attempts were attended — on the first occasion every stantient of the barricado had been sawed through, and on another they had got possession of knives, stone shot, and a cold chisel — made rigid inquiry and punishment necessary. John was sorry for the slaves, but had no intention of proving inadequate to his charge, seeing his crew murdered or set adrift in an open boat, and leaving Mary a widow. It went, however, sorely against the grain for him to be party to such a reversed standard of values that the leaders, who in any historical bid for freedom would have been accounted patriotic heroes, were to be punished and the informers prized, if not rewarded.

Both extracting information and punishing the guilty caused him great concern. At a social evening on a fellow-trader's ship, another captain had described with relish his discovery of an insurrection among the slaves and the pains he had taken to punish all concerned and to make the deaths of the ring-leaders as excruciating as possible. John had been appalled at the callousness which prided itself on such diabolical ingenuity. Yet the flogging, keel-hauling and other punishment for mutiny and less, to which English sailors were even then being subjected, were only less fantastic in that they were part of an accepted routine.

But for him, a redeemed sinner, rejoicing in the pardon and mercy of God? Flogging he used, even with the crew, mainly as a deterrent. Irons meant nothing to those already in them. The thumbscrews, slightly applied and by his own relenting hand, had brought a mercifully swift and full confession. For the first time and for punishment alone he used the iron collars which some captains considered a regular item of the male slave's confinement. But the risk had driven him to another expedient: he had put the fourteen blacks principally concerned on board the *Earl of Halifax,* a large non-slaving ship, and had paid the Captain to deliver them to Mr. Manesty's agent in St. Christopher's; by which carefully calculated move too, he hoped to improve conditions for his own overcrowded cargo. But it had been a wretched business, and even the calm of the ensuing months and the fact that the men slaves seemed entirely to have changed their temper, behaving more obligingly than his whites, only served to fill him with distaste at his office of gaoler.

"Gracious God," he prayed, by no means for the first time, "if it be in accordance with Thy wise will, deliver me from this necessity and fix me in a more humane calling. Until then, and as long as it is the line of life Thou dost allot to me, enable me to bear it as my cross with patience and thankfulness."

At least, his thoughts ran into another channel at the sight of a woman slave very near her time, at least while he was engaged in the traffic, he could check gross misconduct on the part of the sailors. Of course he could not be sure that William Correy's offence with this woman, the more brutish because of its garish publicity and her obvious condition, was the only one committed on board; but he had put the offender in irons for two weeks and had done his best to prevent further occurrences — another reason, doubtless, for dissatisfaction! In this regard crews preferred an easy-going captain. John had sufficient cause in himself to know human weakness on this score. But from lawless and cruel rape in addition to their imprisonment he considered himself bound to protect the hapless woman in his charge. Looking to himself, lest he also be tempted, he had made a resolution which he had kept on both voyages that, as soon as he sighted a point of land where shore excursions and trading would provide illimitable temptation, he would abstain from all meat, and drink nothing stronger than water "to subdue every improper emotion". The emotions were not by this or other means altogether subdued. But by the grace of God operating with the fixed image of his wife in his heart, although desire surged in him strongly, his whole being recoiled from the idea of seeking satisfaction with anyone else.

His consequent abstinence was one of the many points on which the captains of other traders rallied him. During the periods of waiting on the coast it was customary for the captains to entertain on deck or in the cabin and while away the long dark of tropical evenings with cards, drink and conversation. To some, John's previous reputation was known. To all, his present habits were a source of wonder, if not amusement, though they found him no mean controversialist.

He was ashamed to find himself surprised at times into indecent heats of argument when the subject of religion was introduced, and found that the tongue, which was so slow to utter his heart in love, had to be curbed of its propensity to cutting retort. Still it did no harm — "Let your speech be always with grace, seasoned with salt" he quoted in extenuation — to have a salty answer to their personal comments on his philosophy.

"I think you have not the right notion of life, Mr. Newton," said one tough trader, dismayed at his determined sobriety.

"I'm *sure you* haven't. That makes us even," he had retorted equably.

"But what can you see in rambling about an island alone, man?" — this on an occasion when John had refused an invitation to a drinking bout, and spent a soul-satisfying evening in a retired walk around Bence Island — "You must be melancholy."

"To me a man who never wishes to be alone must be mad."

"Because you are married, you would deprive yourself of all pleasure. Why, I'd sooner be dead than such a slave to one woman."

"No, I don't deprive myself of any real happiness. And as for being a slave to one woman, some of you here, if I can judge by your conversation, are slaves to a hundred."

"Well, I wonder at your humour. I have no concept what you mean by happiness."

"I think the better of it on that account," John had retorted.

"Now what does he mean by that?" His latest inquisitor appealed to the company for enlightenment.

"I'll tell you," said John quite pleasantly. "As long as a drunken debauch, such as this is about to become, is your idea of happiness, and while you describe as a memorable pleasure your experience with prostitutes, I should dislike to think that you could form any notion of mine."

"Oh, give over trying to persuade him! A few years of married life will age him. He will realize then that pleasure is where you find it."

"And when I do you can tell me of it. But don't forget," said John as a Parthian shot, for the conversation had taken this turn because of his expressed intention to return early to his ship, "that whereas you have — evidently — never had my experience, I have had an ample taste of yours.   However, if I say I pity you, you'll think me out of my wits.   Yet so would some of the wretches in Bedlam who think their chains are golden ornaments.   Good night."

25

"NO letters?" It was unthinkable that a sailor should play a joke on his Captain, particularly the sober trustworthy individual who had been chosen for the great mission; yet John looked at him sharply, to postpone by suspicion the moment of acceptance. "You inquired at the right place? And there are no letters?"

Mr. Jonas, Manesty's agent, regretfully confirmed the flat negation. The stir and bustle of an unloading ship, details and discussion of market prices, inspection and calculation of slaves, orders and arrangements concerning the home-bound cargo of sugar and cotton: all these kept him moving, talking, listening like a man in a dream; but the waking man stood alone in a cheerless vacuum, every feeling suspended but numbing dread.

When by evening he had a few moments to himself, he went to his cabin and tried to think reasonably. There was a sharp pain in his head and he was reminded of its previous occurrence when, early in his voyage on the *Argyle,* he had been disappointed of an expected letter from Mary. It, or rather they, had arrived three months later after being transferred to six or seven different vessels, and from that happy issue he tried now to take comfort. In her last letter, written on July twelve and received by him at Shebar at the end of October, she had mentioned an earlier despatch, describing her journey home from Liverpool, which had gone astray en route from London to Africa. But letters were regularly arriving here from England. One from Manesty to Jonas bore as date the first of April. From the preceding twelfth of July Mary would have written to him many times and, allowing for the utmost in uncertainties of travel, several of those letters would have arrived at this permanent address — if she were alive.

This possibility, once crystallized in words, was like a cry in his heart. A messenger to the *Seagull,* a Snow, Bristol bound, was to call presently for his packet of letters; and he wrote a post-script to assure her of his safe arrival, keeping the expression of his state of mind by a heroic effort down to a mention of his disappointment.

At this point he glanced at Mary's portrait, staring at him from the wall with the bland, painted eyes so lacking in the lustre and expressiveness of the originals that he could scarcely believe the painter had looked at his sitter. Was this, for the future, all he would have of her to look at or talk of? He had described in one of his letters the visit to his cabin of Henry Tucker, his mulatto trader friend, the one man on the Guinea coast who had never deceived him. On this occasion he had been accompanied by the chief of his half-dozen wives, to whom Polly had sent the gift of a new gown. The first lady, greatly pleased, had promptly put it on over her inadequate native costume and shown off by parading in front of Mrs. Newton's picture. "I pay you no great compliment," he had written, "in preferring *your* picture to *her* reality."

Now he touched it with lingering evocative hands and kissed it, as he always kissed her letters.

"Oh, my Dear, my Dearest, my Beautiful," he said brokenly. "It is my very assurance of your love that brings disquiet. You could not be alive and forbear to write, knowing how I long for your letters. Yet —"

Yet, if she were dead, would not her family have sent him word? But there again the absence of letters from Jack or from any of the Catletts augured as ominously. If Mary were well and her letters had gone astray, was it likely that theirs too had miscarried? It was at least arguable that they would spare him news of her death while he was so far from home. News of her death — O God —

The arrival of his messenger to the *Seagull,* and with him Mr. Jonas's escort to dinner and to shore lodging away from the stifling heat of an anchored ship, interrupted the prayer. In scattered phrases, whenever he was momentarily free from talk, he called on God for help and strength, while questioning whether the dreaded blow had not fallen deservedly and as a direct result of his excessive affection.

That was June the third. By June the twenty-third John, with still more cause to confirm his grim forebodings, came and went about the performance of his duties like a lost man. A week after his arrival a boat had come with a letter from Mr. Manesty; but no word of his wife. A reference in it to the death in childbirth of a ´young woman with whom Mary had made friends during her sojourn in Liverpool before the *African*'s departure, did nothing to allay his terror. About the same time, exploring every avenue, he had dispatched a small boat to Antigua, the *African*'s original destination in the West Indies. Considering how often he had referred to St. Kitts in his letters, it was a slim hope; but the indulgence of it had postponed the sick assurance which was creeping steadily nearer and affecting him visibly, to the anxiety of a large and kindly acquaintance in the busy port.

Had his state of mind been less depressed, he must have been cheered at the efforts of almost complete strangers to help and divert him. "A desire of rendering myself agreeable to you," he had written in some surprise to Mary during his first voyage, "has insensibly made me more acceptable to others." This capacity for friendship, which seemed to grow out of the centrifocal nature of his attachment to her, was rather wonderingly accepted by the young man who had before his marriage made an effort to shake off his "dull rusty gloominess." But he had never in his life been made so much of. His youth, the circumstances and degree of his distress, appealed to the comfortably settled merchants and plantation owners of the island, to whom Manesty's recommendation was the Open Sesame of his acceptance. He was entertained from house to house. Good news from home for Captain Newton was the toast after dinner and supper. If he happened to say, for the sake of conversation, scarce knowing what he said, that he liked any particular thing, it was sure to appear on the table or as a gift, though the whole island had to be ransacked for it. Cags of green and white sweetmeats, pineapples, rare shells, exotic garments, were pressed upon him without payment. Heavy-hearted, he sent them by faster vessels, as fore-runners of himself, to the home which might be no longer home to him.

The slaves were sold and had brought good prices. His fears that the slow condition of trade at Guinea had made the voyage a losing one, were considerately allayed. His own share in the profits was greater than he had expected, and he sent a bill of exchange for a large part of the amount to Mary in one of the letters which he tried to make newsy and, if not cheerful — for that was quite beyond him — at least apparently serene. If — *if* his fears proved groundless, he was ashamed that Mary should know how poorly he had achieved the calm and trustful submission to the will of God which he had enjoined on both of them. Similarly, in the letter which he dispatched to Jack, though he admitted the consternation into which he was thrown, he begged his brother-in-law not to disclose his weakness to others. Deeply conscious of his responsibility as a believer to witness to the power of that belief in his life, he found, like the Apostle Paul, that to will was present with him though not to achieve the good which he willed. And this, his failure of trust, with its consequent inner dread that such faithlessness had rendered the dreaded blow necessary, made his anguish more bitter.

And that was bitter indeed. The broadly built figure, so spare when he first returned to England that Manesty's ship-owning acquaintance, eyeing the prospective Captain, had thought him in a consumption, had once more lost the flesh it had acquired during his months of ease at home. His face, under the weatherbeaten brown of African sun and winds, became more haggard daily. Incessant pains in his stomach made it difficult for him to show even a polite modicum of appreciation for hospitality, and, in conjunction with the pressing pain in his head, kept him in constant fear of collapse. He forced himself to read the Scripture, though much of what he read was lost on a mind which brought every thought around to one thought. He prayed, prayers of intercession, and sobbing cries of penitence. That he continued able to discharge his duties and to assume what he fondly considered an air of cheerfulness in company, he attributed solely to this source of strength; but he felt that his heart was broken, and though he had not previously thought that a broken heart could prove fatal, he trusted — if the desire of his eyes had been taken from him — that the stroke would kill him too.

The *Zanzibar* was weighing anchor at noon for her homeward voyage and would take his letters. John had returned to the *African* for some spare sheets and, alone in the heat of his cabin, sealed the last packet, written for eyes that might be beyond the power of reading. It had been an abatement of his helplessness to adhere to his habit of writing three times a week, but he felt more and more as he wrote like a man calling into the unanswering dark. He pressed his seal into the wax, looked at the name which he never wrote or saw without incredulous gratitude, and dropped his aching head in his hands, beyond the relief of tears.

Outside the cabin the sounds of ship and harbour mingled in the bright hot air: inside it, wrapped in his gloom, John scarcely heard the voices of sailors refurbishing the rigging, the hail of a passing boatman, the untired screaming of gulls. Almost two years before this he had written to his wife: "Nothing, necessary business excepted, seems deserving of my attention but religion and love. For at the age of twenty-five I have seen enough to force my assent to the confession which experience extorted from Solomon in his latter days, 'All is vanity and vexation of spirit.' I mean all that can be possessed exclusive of these two principles; but under their regulation the whole creation blooms with beauty." Now one had apparently been taken from him, perhaps because he had prized it unduly. His faith still held but its comfort was withdrawn.

Not the least instructive part of the school of experience into which his sundering from his wife had thrust him had been the discovery, step by step, of good behind seeming evil. The trauma of separation had thrown him back on the neglected Inseparable One. In all circumstances of his life he saw, with increasing penetration, the amazing grace of God's dealing with him, the preventing Hand which had punished and preserved, granted and withheld for good. As shrewdly observant of others as self-critical, he realized how wretched the two of them would have been, if his desire for her had

260

been granted before he had learned in some measure how to value and treat her. The unutterable ecstasy of their last meeting — a meeting which in one hour repaid him for the seventeen months of separation, and which was but a foretaste of the unclouded joy of their six months together — drove him to an appraisal of the effects of separation in producing the unusual quality of their mutual love, in contrast to the satiety and dissatisfaction of other couples of his acquaintance. Not that his knowledge of seafaring men left him under illusion that separation, qua separation, was a requisite for married bliss! It was he, the individual, on whose refractory and wayward nature this amazing grace was being expended. Similarly the hardships and disagreeable aspects of his employment had deepened his gratitude and sense of responsibility. Loneliness and the comparative leisure of days and weeks on the open sea drove him to study. He became proficient in mathematics and conversant in Latin authors both classical and mediaeval, so that he tried his hand at English translations and at Latin poems in the metres of Horace and Juvenal. They drove him further to a first-hand knowledge of the Scriptures, unprejudiced by controversy or schools of theological division, of which indeed he was still in total ignorance.

With a simple credo he had returned from his first voyage and, during the halcyon months of reunion and the country entertainment in which the Catletts' wide acquaintance spent their time, had been at times guiltily conscious of a moratorium in his spiritual growth. He found that the church services in the vicinity were an instrument little conducive to stir any warmth or interest within him; nor was there anyone who seemed at all concerned with religion, except as a necessary and polite convention. Dread of seeming singular and showing to a disadvantage before Mary kept him reticent, except in argument, and hesitant to share even with her the experiences of his soul.

Yet he had attained some growth. The woods and fields around Chatham afforded the sort of oratory in which prayer and praise came to him most readily. In his reading, Scougal's *Meditations on the Life of God in the Soul of Man* opened new vistas of inner experience, and Philip Doddridge's biography of Colonel Gardiner indicated a step he was loathe to

261

take, the step of public witness to the work of grace being wrought in him.

Of his cowardice in this regard his conscience now reproached him; especially of his failure to speak much of the all-important topic with his adored wife, whose surroundings afforded her no one capable of leading her farther than she had already attained. If she had gone through a lingering illness without the consolation of a working faith, if she had faced death with uncertainty and fear concerning her personal share in the merits of Christ, then he had failed her. He felt that he would give anything for the chance to retrieve one such lost opportunity.

He was still sitting, head in hands, when the messenger came; not the messenger for his letters, but his own boatswain returned with the yawl from Antigua, and smiling as a man smiles who is the bearer of good news.

There were other letters: one from his stepmother, several from Jack Catlett, one from Mrs. Catlett with enclosures from Eliza and Georgie. But the six from Mary (oh, how kind and careful is my dear! as he said in the hasty post-script to his own packet) those six he touched and handled and kissed and carried to his knees in a passion of penitence and thanksgiving; then read and reread with feelings which ranged from delirious joy to solemn gratitude.

When he had finished this — preliminary — perusal he found himself, though shaken and weak, almost restored to health.

26

MAY I never hope to see again this side of hell if I'm not seeing John Newton."

The voice, the West Country accent, plucked so strongly at the chords of John's memory that eight years and their crowding scenes slipped from him in an instant, as did the Liverpool quay where he had just come ashore from inspecting the *African*'s new rigging. The small hirsute man in a blue seaman's jacket was a stranger, or would have been, had not the voice and the outstretched hand made him search beneath the disguise of beard and age and something else which he could not name for his old companion.

"Job Lewis!" he said, and could not speak further for a moment. The recollection of his misery when they had last seen each other, of the wretchedness into which he had plunged, served, as did every such reminder, to re-emphasize the mercy which had been shown him, and his swelling gratitude was almost physical pain. Lewis looked at him curiously.

"Man, it's good to see you. I'd thought you were dead long ago. No need to ask if you've prospered. But let's have a drink and hear how things went with you on the — *Pegasus*, was it? I've never forgotten —"

"Nor do I want to forget." The two men fell in step as they had done on many a shore excursion. "But I am not the only one with news. What of the *Harwich* and her five-year voyage? Is my old friend Captain Cartaret still alive? What news of Miles Cleaver?"

Over John's mug of beer and Lewis's four, talk flowed unstopped. Lewis had failed to obtain a commission but, at the end of the *Harwich*'s convoy duty to the Indies, had been granted a transfer to a merchant ship and was now awaiting his first command of a slaver to Guinea. Miles Cleaver, more successful, was First Lieutenant on H. M. S. *Norfolk* when Lewis had last seen him. He listened absorbed to John's abbreviated account of his mishaps and remarkable escapes.

"So Mary waited for you," he said quizzically. "Well, that was one point on which you were always constant. For myself I'm quite content without marriage."

"You don't know —" began John, and broke off. How could any unmarried man or, for that matter, the majority of married men, possibly know the glory that was his and Mary's ever-enriched experience? Besides, there was something more separating them than years. The brown eyes were friendly as ever — he recalled their rather wistful admiration when he, and not Cleaver, wielded the greater influence — but they no longer gave his face a look of stolid simplicity. On an impulse he said words which came with difficulty.

"God has been gracious to me in that as in everything. I deserved nothing but judgment and He has shown me illimitable mercy."

Lewis stared and, if his friendliness repressed a laugh, there was laughter in his voice.

"I am mistaken after all. It's not the same Midshipman John Newton talking of sin and judgment. Why, man, have you forgotten how you settled my qualms by your quotations from Shaftesbury and Hume? — ably backed by original arguments from John Newton himself."

John had not forgotten. Perhaps for this very reason, he told Mary that evening in their room at Manesty's home, Job Lewis had crossed his path again.

"I would give much to undo the evil I did him — I had almost said anything, but I know to say so would be the rankest hypocrisy," he said, for Mary had come to his knee and he was thinking how charming her face was, even more lovely, if that could be, than he had remembered it when he thought he would never see it again. *That* was the most wonderful and God-bestowed aspect of their love, the excess of realization over anticipated delight. "I would not give you, my precious,

264

nor, I'm afraid, a degree of your love to me. But I must earnestly try to alter his views."

"Are you going to pray for him?" asked Mary suddenly.

"Of course." His prayers were always a source of humiliation to John — so cold, so weak, so wandering, so easily interrupted by chance thoughts, or ugly recollections, or wild and wanton images, or financial calculations — but at all times and on every matter of greater or less importance he prayed. He could not live now, he knew, without prayer.

His wife withdrew the arm that had rested around his neck, took his face between her hands, shook her head slightly to prevent the kiss for which any such caress was more than adequate excuse, and looked straight into his eyes.

"John, why don't you ever pray with me?"

He thought of his good intentions at St. Christopher's, only partially put into practice.

"Because, God forgive me, I've been too cowardly to suggest it."

"Are you so afraid of me?" she asked soberly.

"No, my Dearest, not really. Just afraid of disgusting you, of seeming 'singular', of not sufficiently impressing you — I don't know what I am afraid of, God help me for a poor inconsistent wretch who knows what is right to do and is afraid to act on it."

"Then I think you had better begin. Hasn't it occurred to you that I may need it, need it very much?"

Once again the hinge on which his life turned, she had opened a door at which he feared to knock.

But their combined prayers and his most serious efforts left Job Lewis unaltered. In vain John used the answers which seemed so unarguable to the arguments he himself had once propounded. Lewis was no great controversialist. If debate was forced upon him, he did little more than parrot the most trite statements of the Free-thinking school. His friend was sorrowfully convinced that freedom from moral restraint, rather than intellectual conviction, kept him a stubborn adherent of unbelief. More than once, with no answer to John's evidence for the truth of Christianity, Job tacitly admitted as much.

"You were the first person to give me an idea of my liberty", was his adroit retreat, and beyond that John could not move him.

In matters unconnected with creed and morals he still deferred to Newton's judgment, and was especially glad to avail himself of the latter's greater experience as commander of a Guinea ship. John shared freely the knowledge he had painfully acquired and, as his friend's sailing time preceded his own by more than a week, devoted to him all the leisure he could spare. He would not scant any hours he could spend with Mary, but shared those hours with him. Secretly he hoped that closer acquaintance with his wife and the sight of their happiness together would effect what his words could not in disgusting Lewis with his loose and irregular conduct, and making him yearn for deeper satisfaction. Job was a model of courtesy to Mary, deleting from his speech the commonplace oaths which he used neither more nor less than most sailors, and was so obviously impressed by her gaiety and grace, that he repeatedly congratulated her husband on his "good luck." After such entertainment he made no secret of the fact that he sought one of the port's many brothels on his way to his lodgings; and John, from his own self-knowledge, could not reproach but could only try to reason with him.

His ship, the *Terra Nova,* was due to sail on the fourteenth of October. On the evening of the twelfth Mr. Manesty came home with news which set the town buzzing next day, that her owner had gone bankrupt and that ship and cargo must be sold to pay off outstanding debts. John sought out Lewis and found him in a tavern stoically drinking away his losses. They spent the day trying to hear of a suitable opening for him, but all ships were manned for the season. Lewis had no dependents and his state was not desperate, but John foresaw what idleness and disappointment might do, and thought he saw more clearly than ever the reason for their reunion.

"Mr. Manesty," he said, addressing the man who had been a second father, and indeed whom he approached more easily than he had ever approached his own, "my friend, Mr. Lewis, has been left in a distressing situation."

Joseph Manesty nodded.

"I might say that my friend, his erstwhile employer, is left in an even more distressing situation. But that does not alter the truth of your remark."

"And I have been wondering, Sir —" he had discussed the matter with Mary, whose quick brain had hit on the idea now at his tongue's end — " if you would permit him to accompany me on the *African.*"

"In what capacity? Your officers are all engaged."

"That is true. I suggest, in view of the incidence of illness on board, particularly during the trading months, that Mr. Lewis might travel with me as a supernumerary — without portfolio, if you like! I scarcely know under what title. Captain's Commander might express his rank, while not interfering with the status of the first-mate. Perhaps Volunteer Captain's Commander."

"Are you sure such an arrangement would prove satisfactory to you?"

"I should be most happy about it," said John, delighted that Manesty was falling in with his plan to have Job Lewis at once indebted to him and under his eye and influence. "You had mentioned the possibility of putting him in command of a ship next season. In this way he can gain much experience of the coast which he now lacks and without which I had fears for his success on the *Terra Nova.*"

John had expressed himself as most happy and Job Lewis, with Manesty's promise confirmed of a ship of his own next season, was touched and pleased with his appointment.

"Mr. Welch?"

The first-mate paused.

"Aye, Sir?"

"Is Captain Lewis below?"

"He is still ashore, Sir, with the punt. Mr. Cary is with him, Tam and William Jordan rowing."

"Thank you, Mr. Welch. You may turn in. I shall watch till the boat returns."

The mate went off and Newton began to pace the deck, glad of the silence and coolness of the night to hide and calm the anger which possessed him. In the two months of an otherwise unperplexed voyage, Job Lewis had proved a thorn in his side which pricked more frequently, now that shore excursions provided almost daily opportunity for offence. John's persistent hope that he could influence his once pliable companion had died hard. Circumstances had permitted them frequent, lengthy periods for discussion. Weather and seas were so favourable that it had taken only three days to get out to open water, instead of three weeks' dangerous tacking and manoeuvering as on his first voyage, and a following wind had given them a quick passage to the Coast. But within the limits of cordiality Lewis grew steadily less receptive to John's argument and exhortation. More, as if goaded by an imp of perversity, he was not content with passive resistance, but subtly at first, then more openly, studied to undermine the Captain's efforts to improve the crew. His peculiar status on board, his punctilious good humour, and the regard, as genuine as could obtain under the circumstances, which he felt for his friend, made John's position singularly difficult. Again and again he asked himself how Lewis could have so little gratitude; again and again he was disconcertingly shown his unregenerate self in the glass of his friend's conduct, himself when leniency, favours, and kindness issued only in presumption, and disrespect. On such occasions he was driven to his knees to thank the God who had saved him in spite of himself, and to intercede with him for his fellow-sinner.

But if he had conceded that regret for a good action was consistent with his profession, he would have admitted many times the regret he felt at bringing this burden upon his own head. Job was never openly insubordinate; but to be forced to enjoin a command at all made John uncomfortable. He attended the reading of morning and evening prayers on Sunday; and John's efforts to lead a solemn and meaningful service were not assisted by the presence of one whose expression of cynical boredom was as patent as open ridicule. John attempted to restrain the men from blasphemy; Job's language grew daily more profane. John was stringent in his treatment of drunkenness; Job had brought his own supply of liquor on board and was able to consume enormous quantities without losing the required control. With more leisure than John could fill up for him, he was gregariously friendly with the crew. Unwilling to spy, the Captain could only suspect that the nature of talk and laughter which was quickly hushed to

268

decorum at his appearance did little to impress the men with the importance of their spiritual concerns.

Since their arrival at the coast, John had made his task of instructing Lewis in the mysteries of trading an excuse to keep him under his eye. Now for the third time he had taken advantage of the Captain's pressing business to go off alone — yet unfortunately not alone. John had no illusions — his own experience was his instructor — as to the nature of his employment; this unseasonably late return was probably to give the carpenter and the sailors time to sober up; and how could they be punished for intoxication when in charge of the Captain's Commander?

The tranquillity of sky and star-reflecting ocean, the two noblest objects of sight, his sea-loving heart thought fondly, were used, as often, to calm the rage which distressed him by its intensity. Control of his temper had been one of the miracles of his conversion, and heated words or actions he considered inconsistent in a Christian. But the problem remained, and after a few moments in which he kept tryst with Mary by looking, according to their honeymoon agreement, at the north star and offering up prayer on her behalf, he set about finding a solution. By one o'clock when the prodigals returned, the crew extremely silent and the Commander speciously garrulous on the subject of mistaking the location of the punt, he was satisfied that he had found it.

"Captain Lewis?"
"Captain Newton?"

The conventional exchange was made in John's cabin. The *African* was anchored at the Plantanes, and nearby lay the *Racehorse*, a forty-five ton ship which John had lately purchased at Shebar. Job Lewis, in high good-humour, had come for his final instructions before going on board as Captain. In charge of some 3200 bars, with the small but seaworthy vessel he was to trade for other products in the off-season, while the *African* made its homeward voyage.

"We shall meet in mid-March when I return to Shebar. By then you will know how your affairs prosper," said John, with the awkwardness of a man who wishes to say much more.

"I'd not have you think, Captain Newton — John," said Lewis with more affection in his tone than he had used since their first day of reunion, "that I'm lacking in gratitude for what you have done and are doing. I promise I shall use every effort to further Mr. Manesty's interests and to justify your trust."

On his return to Liverpool from the previous voyage, John had given his employers a frank opinion that trade was overdone on the Windward coast and that, if they sent him again, they might have to stand a loss. When, despite this advice, the *African* had been despatched within six weeks, Manesty had added the proviso that it should not remain at Guinea during the rainy season. April had been set as the date for John to leave Africa, with or without his full complement of slaves.

By December, after consultation with Clow and his mulatto friend Tucker, he had surmised that by the assigned date he would still have a thousand pounds of goods on his hands — a loss to carry back, a risk to leave. It was then that he had conceived the idea of letting Lewis remain to trade with a small boat. Responsibility and work would, John trusted, counteract his tendency to dissipation, and the Liverpool ship owners would be spared the additional loss of wasted goods. Perhaps, too, the advice and example which served only to irritate the young infidel when he was present might recur and be enforced in his absence.

"Job," he said honestly and with deep feeling, "nothing I have done, nothing I can do for you can balance the harm which I did you once by my perverseness. I shall not weary you, as I have done, by preaching. But for your welfare I am urging you to consider where your present course is leading. Had I not been like you — and far more hardened — did I not know from experience the difference between what you call pleasure and true happiness, if I did not see you posting to eternity there to answer before God for rejecting His Son and His love, I should not dare speak — nor should I care to, for, believe me, it is not easy —"

He broke off suddenly, with tears in his eyes, and was surprised to find Lewis so much moved that he could only grasp his hand and turn away with a muttered word of thanks. The next moment he was gone and when John emerged on deck, the two Captains saluted and parted.

Rio Junque, March 1

My dear, sweet, precious, beautiful Polly:

I still continue in health, and all is well excepting one late circumstance which has given me, as you will believe, much concern. Not to keep you in suspense, I must inform you that all my schemes in favour of Captain Lewis are at an end. I told you in a former letter that I had bought a vessel upon the coast and had given him the command of her. He went from me in good spirits and with high hopes, but was seized with a fever before he had left me three weeks, which proved fatal to him in about eight days. I have been much affected by this sudden stroke. . . .

John broke off. Not to Mary, certainly not by letter, and probably not at all — for why should she grieve, as he knew her warm heart would? — could he relay the description which eyewitnesses had given him of the month which his decorously worded sentence had covered. Lewis's emotion at parting with him had been powerless to effect any change. The sudden freedom from restraint, the prevalence of opportunity, had acted on his passions like an intoxicant. Fever had resulted from his unbridled plunge into vice and had acted speedily on a body weakened by indulgence and the unwholesome climate. But to John the awful part of the revelation was that, on his death-bed, conviction of the truth had struck, but struck without bringing repentance or hope.

In delirium he had raged and blasphemed against the God whom he had once believed and, coming out of delirium into the stark gloom of sanity, he had cried with a rage and fear which John's informants could not describe without a shudder:

"I am lost for eternity. Damned. So be it. God, I have not asked you to save me, curse you, I don't now." And with that he died.

John fell on his knees beside his half-written letter.

"Gracious God, why not me? I deserved no more," he said.

27

THE *African,* the owners decided on its return in late August, was too slow for a trade in which conditions were unpredictable, and speed in collecting and delivering the cargo immeasurably lessened expense. She was accordingly transferred to another branch of trading, and Mr. Manesty kept her Captain in Liverpool to choose a swifter vessel.

Not that the *African's* voyage was considered a failure. On the contrary, Captain John Newton found himself much congratulated for achieving an enviable record: his ship had been brought to the home port without the loss of a single man, white or black. The circumstances of Job Lewis's death set him, of course, outside the number of the crew. It was rather the opinion of the ship-owners that a commander whose intelligence and dependability could wrest moderate success from losing circumstances should not be hampered by an inconvenient ship. The successful trading of Mr. Welch, Job's successor in the *Racehorse,* had amply justified that stroke of policy in their eyes. So John could not be spared long to Chatham, and Mary returned with him to Liverpool to crowd an aeon of joy into the brief interlude between voyages.

"But where has the time gone?" she demanded plaintively as John, coming in from the November dusk, stirred up the fire before taking the seat at the tea-table. "You sail the day after tomorrow, John. I can't believe it. And then every day will seem like ten."

"Polly, dearest," John began, and broke off. He knew he should repeat his cautions about their duty of submission to the will of God, but for the moment his heart was not in it. He came instead, drew her up and held her fast, his face buried in her hair, as if to create a union inseparable by time or space. Then very gently he put her back in her chair, drew his chair closer with his left hand and sat down, still holding hers with his right. Presently, with the smile which she seldom allowed to be long subdued, she took her kerchief, leaned over and dried his eyes.

"I didn't know I was crying. You are too," he said. "They are really joyful tears."

"I know."

"Sweet," he said earnestly, for to realize that her suffering at their separation was now no less than his doubled his own pain, "is it not much better to know such joy, even if it occasions sorrow, than to know only the placidity or dreariness which makes many married couples of our acquaintance long for any diversion?"

Mary looked unconvinced. She poured his tea and hers without immediate reply.

"I suppose you mean that if you were with me all the time you would find it dreary?" she said perversely.

"Rather, I'm afraid I should mistake it for heaven," answered John. "To do everything in my power to please you seems now as natural as breathing. Yet I might change. I know very little but evil of my own heart. And when I am fit to be so indulged, when God sees that it would be good for both of us, He will bring it about. Surely," he went on, persuading himself no less than her, "we have every reason to trust Him. When I remember at Basseterre my fears that I should never see you again. . . ."

She nodded quickly.

"Or when I think of your letter just last April when you had fever and wrote to me as if — as if it was your last."

"I thought it was." He remembered what he had said, words which he found it so much easier to write to Polly than to utter: that he was quite peaceful at the thought of death, and asked to live only for her sake, and because, as his former wretched apostasy was known to hundreds, he should like to show as many what God had wrought in him. And then —

"But don't you see," she burst out in another passionate

273

digression, "that if you were ill at home, at least I could look after you? You never look after yourself. Why, you admitted then that there was no fresh food on board because you had given it all to the men who were sick before you. Oh, I know you'll say the Captain must care for his crew. But who is to care for the Captain?"

"Polly, Polly, let us not return ingratitude for what God has done. My health has been a wonder to many. And as for preservation through dangers! Do you know that I never heard of so many being lost through illness or insurrection or shipwreck as on this last voyage? And both this and the previous sailing our greatest danger — as far as we could see — came when we were almost within sight of land. And when I consider Job Lewis's end and that of Miles Cleaver —"

"You never told me about him."

"No? I think, so short a time after the other, I could scarcely bear to write of it. He was swept overboard in a storm on the Bay of Biscay. His ship, H. M. S. *Norfolk*, weathered the storm and put in at Madeira where my informant had the news. Dearest, if I had my deserts, I should have met some such fate years ago. Surely we have cause to trust God for the future. He has not favoured us thus far to part us without reason. All that we meet *must* work for our good, if we love Him."

"Ah, but you are good, John. I'm not. I have a dreadfully rebellious heart. But I'll try to be better" — she changed her tone swiftly — "or you'll quote your Captain Clunie at me."

She could always make him laugh.

"Now you are being contrary. You will love Captain Clunie when you meet him, as I do. He taught me more while we were at St. Kitts together then I could have learned by myself in years."

"He sounds frighteningly *good*," said Polly, deliberately exasperating, "I suppose I mean serious. Now you are good but you don't frighten me with it. Ah, my pretty Dear" — she broke off, setting her tea cup aside and shifting her chair closer so that she could rest her head against his shoulder — "I'm just being troublesome. Forgive me. John, will you tell me something truly?"

"Do I usually tell you something falsely?"

"Indeed you do. Such as that you are not good enough for me, and that I am the loveliest creature in the world. Dreadful falsehoods." The forced lightness left her voice. The hollow of restrained tears was in it as she said almost abruptly, "John, are you sorry because I haven't — yet — had a child?"

"Are *you*, Polly?"

"I should love to have children. And perhaps I shall. I have thought maybe it was a mercy that I hadn't when you are away so long and so far, because it would be something else for you to worry about. But recently I have wondered if I ever should. And then I thought that you might be disappointed. Tell me."

"Didn't I write about it once?"

"Yes. But that was years ago. And you were frightened for me when you wrote."

"I'm afraid I shall always be frightened about you, unless God gives me greater grace. As I told you when news reached me of my father's death — and I grieved because I truly loved and revered him — there is only one such event, at the very thought of which I tremble. Dearest dear, I can say now what I said then, when I had just heard of Mrs. Marvin's death in childbirth. I shudder to think that I may be the cause of exposing you to that terrible risk. I could not bear it, I think, if I were the immediate, though innocent, cause of your death. I own that children, from the consideration of their being *yours,* would be very acceptable to me. But I hope, unless God sees fit to grant them, I shall never be so mad as to wish for them. I know I am already happy without them. Happier than I ever dreamed of being. Why —"

"What is it, John?" she asked, sitting up, for he had withdrawn the enfolding arm, and the sudden tenseness in his last word communicated itself in the sudden stiffening of his figure.

"Nothing, nothing, that is —" In the lamp-light she saw his face, surprised, bewildered. Then with no other sound he swayed away from her. The chair crashed above the thud of his body which carried it sideways to the floor.

Mary sat motionless in the suddenly silent room. During that immobility, whatever had seized her husband seemed to

275

fasten upon her too, so that her body grew deathly cold and a tearing sensation reached from her paralyzed limbs through her vital organs to her throat, where it strangled the cry which she knew she should give for help. Then Mary Catlett took control of Mary Newton, forced her to rise, ring the bell-pull by the fireplace, kneel beside the strangely peaceful figure on the floor, and, instead of throwing herself hysterically upon it, loosen the cravat, feel for an almost indistinguishable pulse, fetch some brandy from the cupboard and try with cold steady hands to force a spoonful into the rigidly closed mouth.

So they found her, the frightened maid-servant, Joseph Manesty, his wife, and the physician hastily summoned. So for an hour without outcry, without words except in answer to questions, she remained, her eyes straining to catch the slightest alteration in her husband's lifeless face.

For an hour there was none. Dr. Hadley had feared to move him even to the bedroom next door; so a pillow had been slipped under his head — her arm had lifted the head — and a blanket tucked around the recumbent form. Restoratives, massage, heat compresses, bleeding — all were tried. Mary Catlett was no stranger to death. A baby sister and a brother had died in her childish arms, and already she had been summoned to the dying bed of more than one girlhood friend. But never had she seen death more certainly written than on the still face of her husband.

"He breathes," the doctor said after holding a mirror to his face, "and his heart beats."

But how slowly, and how fitfully. And the breath — if indeed he breathed — came and went without visible rise and fall of his chest. His hands and feet grew cold in spite of their ministrations. And Mary, who had suffered torments of dread and anxiety in his absence, was now made brutally aware of the difference between imaginary and real fear. She had complained at his projected absence for fifteen months. Now she would gladly face twice the time, if she could see the closed lids open and hear him say her name once more.

So desperately did she wish and pray, in a confusion which could not distinguish between wish and prayer and vow, that the desired event passed as though in a dream. The others,

276

the Manestys and the physician, breathing their excited relief, had to gesticulate and touch her gently before she could believe that John's eyes were actually open and that his long impassive hand had moved in an instinctive gesture towards her.

28

THAT hour lost from John's life, unexplained and unrecurring, was big with consequence. Though he was hardly restrained from getting up as if nothing had happened, his admission, that evening and the next day, to dizziness and pains in the head made the physician shake his own and inform Manesty that he was not fit to sail. Mr. Welch, his excellent mate of the *Greyhound,* was given command, and the *Bee,* after a few days' delay, set out on her voyage, leaving her erstwhile commander standing on the quay beside his wife, joyful at the unhoped respite but wondering not a little what the future held.

Mr. Manesty had promised him a ship next season. Meanwhile, seven or eight months of idleness, added to the interval already spent on shore, would drain away much of his savings. He knew a moment's regret, and rebuked his lack of faith in feeling regret, at the mischances which had deprived him, first of a marriage settlement, then of a modest legacy from his father. But his sun could not long be clouded by fears merely financial. It was easier for him to say "The Lord will provide" than to overcome the new anxiety which was sending them with all possible despatch from Liverpool to Mary's home at Chatham.

The strange fit which had seized him had passed, with no apparent injury to his constitution. Perhaps, in view of his many hair-breadth escapes, the periods of sleeplessness on every voyage while the ship battled storms or her Captain battled the thousand perplexities of his trade, the intensity of his passions and anxieties: all these working on a physique which had survived long months of ill treatment and attrition, it was less wonder that nature had taken toll than that the price exacted was so small. But within two days John became aware that the stroke had not fallen on him alone. Though not robust, Mary had seldom since childhood had a day's illness. When John returned to consciousness she had maintained an iron control, watching by him till he fell asleep, and the next day looking after him and anticipating his needs with a gentle insistence which her adoringly submissive husband added to the treasury of his indebtedness. But two nights later, when danger seemed no longer imminent, her control suddenly snapped; and, as she lay in his arms, she was seized with shuddering so violent, so uncontrollable, so prolonged, that he would have risen and sent for the doctor had she not clung pitifully, assuring him that only he could do her good.

He had quieted her at last, but the next morning she was too weak to rise; an excruciating headache set in, which resisted all efforts to assuage it until bed-time. Since then she had been better, though with little appetite. The doctor and the Manestys confirmed John's opinion that a winter in the softer climate of Kent would benefit them both.

Once his battle with worry over his worldly prospects had been fought and won — his battle with worry over Mary was permitted armistice but never victory — John regarded the waiting months as a grant, an opportunity to be exploited to the full. Recently his periods ashore had been intervals of more or less stated duration. Now he had leisure to explore and expand, to test and rectify the ideas which he had beaten out to the rhythm of the lonely ocean. The Clunies lived in London. Mary, proudly exhibited to them, forgot her fear of the Captain's "seriousness" and was mothered by Mrs. Clunie, while the two men renewed the fellowship which had, for the younger, made his last stay at St. Kitts as brief and pleasant a period as any period away from his wife could be.

At Chatham he set himself to discover more of such edifying companionship. In the Catletts' immediate circle there was none and, in spite of Clunie's blunt declaration that he must be ready to witness to the redemption at work in him, John was not prepared for the raised brows, the discomfiture and amazement, which such a breach of good taste would occasion in any conventionally "Christian" home. So he went hopefully to St. Mary's in Chatham, to St. Margaret's and to Rochchester cathedral, walked eight miles to Maidstone for little better fare, tried the Baptist assembly, where the preaching disappointed him, and recorded sadly in his diary that had he not a duty to attend for the sake of example, he might better have worshipped privately, as he did daily, in the fields and woods around home. There he knew again those periods of communion with God which had steadied and empowered him on his voyaging.

He did not come to this conclusion or remain in it without self-examination. At first he blamed his sleepiness at afternoon service (not unjustly) to over-indulgence in the Cattletts' excellent Sunday dinner, and tried to attribute his dissatisfaction with the sermons to a carping spirit. But fasting and determined intercession for the preacher could not make the dry bones of an imitation Ciceronian discourse or a ranting invective against other schools of theological thought palatable or nourishing to his soul. And what grieved John was that the glorious gospel was thus withheld from those whose need of it was as great and as desperate as his own. Only at the Methodist meetings on Sunday night and during the week did he find encouragement and blessing.

Captain Clunie was a Dissenter; and though he had not concealed from Newton the lethargy which had succeeded generations of heroic struggle against persecution in Dissenting circles, he had spoken warmly of his own Stepney minister, Mr. Brewer, and of David Jennings, to whom, as his mother's pastor, Newton had written diffidently for advice before his initial command on the *Argyle*. So, with and without Mary, he made several trips to London, attending in brief weeks more religious services than he had attended in any two years since his regeneration.

From his first visit to Charlestown, which still buzzed with the stir of Whitefield's visit, he had been curious about the great evangelist, ostracized by most clergy of his own church, and resented — though less than John Wesley — by Dissenters. At St. Kitts, Captain Clunie had given him a not unbiased account of the Whitefield-Wesley controversy and now, in the great Moorfields Tabernacle, John had the opportunity, secured by ticket, of hearing Whitefield preach. After the three-hour sacrament service which commenced at five a.m., Newton, who had never before had such a "foretaste of the business of heaven" went morning after morning. As no Methodist services were conducted at church times, he could proceed on Sunday straight from Moorfields to Stepney for morning and afternoon services, and return to hear Whitefield again in the evening.

Between services he visited. His widowed stepmother still lived at Rotherhithe, where there was little more to make him feel at home than in the days of his truancy. Mrs. Newton evidently regarded his religiosity as another phase of the temperament which had strangely allowed her husband's difficult son to develop into a capable man. His half-brother Billy, who held a position procured by his father's influence with the Hudson's Bay Company, was at twenty-two a citified and respectable version of the infidel debauchee that he himself had been. He had a fund of unsavoury stories and, failing to elicit from his journeying brother anything of the more lurid side of his adventures, turned a deaf ear to the latter's invitation to Captain Clunie's or to various lectures, by which John hoped to lead him into a religious atmosphere. Young Harry was at sea and his sister Kitty, a quiet girl of eighteen, was glad to see him and eagerly accepted an invitation to Chatham.

With Jack Catlett, now absorbed in surmounting the difficulties of establishing his own law practice, John found himself on equivocal terms. The attraction which had made the younger man his ardent admirer, even when there was least to command admiration, showed itself in strange resentments. John's rejection of Free-thinking, Jack had tolerated, so long as *he* was the chief recipient of his correspondence. When, after marriage, letters to him were neither as numerous nor as long as to his sister, and when John dropped the "Morton and Mamby" pseudonyms because — sufficient reason to him! — "Polly does not like Morton and Mamby," Jack's consequent sulkiness had been quite incomprehensible to Newton's straightforward mind. The letter which he was sure would rectify matters had somehow failed to do so.

"When I am with her," he had written simply, "I am a little negligent of everybody else just as, if you will allow such a blazing comparison, the presence of the sun makes us bear the loss of the stars without regret. I believe," he had continued, mindful of Jack's hyperbolic flights over several inamoratas, "you would consider such an expression fort galant if applied to a mistress, and why it should require an apology when meant of a wife, I cannot tell. But I am determined to stick to my unfashionable humour as long as I live . . . for the rest, nothing but your sister will stand in competition for the regard I bear you."

This handsome assurance had not succeeded in removing Jack's peevishness. He had taken for granted that marriage would cure his friend of the devotion, excessive indeed if excusable in a lover, but ridiculous in a five-years-married man. It would completely spoil any girl but Polly, Jack thought, for his affection for his older sister was not diminished by his opinions of what was due her as a wife; and he was concerned both about her present ailment and about the seizure which might incapacitate John for his profession. He could have understood a great deal more anxiety than his brother-in-law showed for the future, and would have enjoyed diverting him at Vauxhall or Drury Lane, or in long inconclusive debate with friends at a coffee-house. Now, however, John always brought discussion around to Christianity — not pleasant, patronizing discussion showing the discrepancies and hair-splitting squabbles of religious teaching and religious men, but a personal and pointed application of what, with most unphilosophical assurance, he called revelation and the word of God. And when he consented to accompany Jack to the theatre — Jack wished afterwards that it had not been a revival of *The Female Rake* — his disapprobation was so evident that it quite spoiled the evening.

"I never thought to see you a censorious prude," he said, when they had jostled their way through the crowd and were walking along towards Lincoln's Inn Fields in the flickering light of links running ahead of coaches and sedan-chairs. "You might as well be a Methodist."

"If to be a Methodist is to consider that play filthy and attendance at it an unfit pastime for a Christian —" began John warmly; then altered his tone. "Tell me, Jack, do the attitudes and situations you laughed at tonight represent the conduct you would care for in your mother and sisters — or your wife and daughters when you have them?"

"Of course not! But it's a farce, man. You take it too seriously."

"Perhaps I do. Perhaps I have cause to take it more seriously than you. Perhaps you find no temptation in the conduct and conversation on the stage. They will not recur to your mind or keep you from living either in action or thought according to a strict moral code."

Jack flushed and said nothing.

"But I cannot believe that it is equally without effect on all the audience."

"Oh, come now. No one is going to change his scheme because of what he sees on stage. The play simply satirizes society as it is and we can't do anything to change it."

"We can refuse to condone it," said John.

"Be logical. You quote Shakespeare with approval. Do you consider that the sight of Macbeth and his wife planning a murder will make the audience go and do likewise?"

"It's your logic that is at fault and you know it. There is not the slightest similarity between the feeling with which Shakespeare leaves us regarding murder and that which this play induces regarding fornication and adultery. To see evil and face its consequence is one thing; to condone and laugh at it is quite another."

"Your hands will be full if you intend to reform the world."

John shrugged.

"Reforming the world is not in my hands; but I can desist from what will deform me and others. As I wrote once to Polly, 'A reformation could be effected swiftly in our sex, if women who have regard for honour and virtue would treat with contempt men who live in open defiance of them. Yet, as long as they are sufficiently genteel, they are received with a smile, while poor young creatures who have been duped and ruined and abandoned are considered unworthy of pity.' "

"Lud, man! Do you mean that you'd expect Polly to be friendly with a whore?"

"Why not, if she is friendly with the man who makes her one?"

"Egad, John, you'll turn society upside down. What unfashionable humour will you adopt next?"

It was early June when he met Whitefield, who had recently returned from America. John had ridden to London in great excitement to post his answer to a letter from Mr. Manesty which had suggested that he might be able to procure for him a land-waiter's position with the Customs in Liverpool. Mary's condition had been much better since the coming of spring, and the prospect of an appointment in England for her husband seemed to complete the cure. On the strength of this improvement, and because it might be his last opportunity for some time, John remained almost three weeks in the capital, listening and questioning on points of doctrine and scriptural interpretation.

On his return to Chatham, the benefit of his spiritual feasting was put to an immediate test. Mary had lapsed into what the local physician described vaguely as "a consumption" accompanied by periods of violent gastric disorder. John was thrown into consternation, the more poignant because his conscience told him that his idolatry was bringing its necessary punishment; that, despite the goodness and mercy which had prevented and followed him, his first thought — concerning the future, concerning his appointment, concerning any plan — was for Mary and their happiness together; that submission to the will of God came a belated second, and long after both, desire to seek and do that will, to testify to His glory.

"But Thou art God, and not man," he pleaded one night, when his wife had finally sunk into a fitful sleep. "And even as I pray, I know how much this praying differs from the cold wandering thoughts of mine which often pass for prayer and praise. I know, too, that separation must come sometime. But, gracious God, not yet. She has been my idol, I confess. Yet Thou hast so ordained that if I had not loved her, I should not have been brought to Thy love. I speak as a fool. Thou knowest my weakness. Give me grace to bear whatever Thou seest fit to send in love. But, I pray, lay not my sin to her charge. Abate her pain. Strengthen her, comfort her as I cannot, my dear, my dearest. . . . Enable us both to say: Thy will be done."

With the continuance of alternating days of indifferent health and anguish, John decided that the faith which employed insufficient medical aid in Chatham was justified in seeking greater skill elsewhere. The Brewers in Stepney had spoken very highly of their physician and there were others in London to consult. Mary, who tried to make light of her illness, except when helpless with pain, faced the journey as gamely as she had offered to come to meet him on his first return from Guinea. The Catletts' anxiety overcame their dismay at parting with her in her present state. Fortunately Mary's aunt would welcome them in London, and Jack would be close at hand.

In arrangements for the journey John spared no expense. As swiftly and painlessly as possible a comfortable chaise carried them to London where the Brewers' doctor, frankly mystified at her symptoms, called in a specialist. The resultant treatment of purgatives threw her into an agony during which John felt that months of separation would be a light price to pay to ease her pain for a minute. During this period too his love underwent refining. Mary's elegance, her grace, her gaiety and self-possession, the daintiness of her person and the expressive beauty of her face: all these charms were stripped individually or together from her in the feverish distorting spasms which racked her thin body and made her briefly insensible even of her ruling passion, to spare him anxiety. But John knew, watching the pitiful inroads of sickness on mortality, that his love, which had begun as desire, now so deeply encompassed the essential Mary that if he could never touch her again, it would suffer no abatement.

Something of this he was trying to put into words and, as usual, falling short, during a blessed lull in the pain, when her aunt brought him a Liverpool letter forwarded from Chatham. It was early August and, in the larger issues of Mary's life-and-death struggle, his increasing assurance that Mr. Manesty had not succeeded in his effort had scarcely cost him a pang. Now, as he broke the seal, the two were tensely silent. Had the appointment come through after all? Or was this his summons to another sea-voyage?

"Neither," he explained huskily, giving her the gist after a hasty perusal. "The land-waiter's position was filled. But there is a better appointment as a tide-surveyor, for which I am nominated and which I can have if I come at once."

"At once?"

"The present incumbent has died suddenly. Mr. Manesty

does not write clearly about it but there is another applicant, the mayor's nephew. And the position cannot lie idle. If I want it, I must enter upon my duties Monday sennight."

"If you want it? John!"

Her husband turned a haggard face to her.

"Dearest, I cannot part with you like this. What does a position, any position, matter compared with leaving you in weakness and pain, not knowing —"

"It matters very much to me," she said with a faint attempt to speak lightly, though he could hardly hear her weak voice. "It means being with you, on land — I hate the sea! It means a home of our own and — my pretty Dear, where is your faith? Do you think *you* are going to cure me, or God?"

"God, of course." He knew her argument was true, "But—"

"And He can do it in your absence. You must go, John. I shall do very well, if you promise not to worry. I think the very prospect will cure me. I feel better already."

The brave words confirmed John in the duty which warred with his inclination. Fortunately for his resolve, in the next few days his wife had longer intervals of ease, though the doctors were unwilling to make any hopeful pronouncement. On Saturday, after he had paid his Customs fees in London and booked a seat on Monday's coach for Liverpool, the pain returned and kept her all night in sleepless agony. The resultant exhaustion of Sunday made his last day with her — perhaps his *last* day with her, said commonsense loud and blatant over the weakened whisper of faith — one of the most trying he had yet endured. Torn between the need for a position to support her and the fear that she might not need that support, forced from her in order to secure a dubious future with her, at the time when his heart cried to seize every moment together, he made himself talk calmly, arrange for her removal home as soon as she was fit to travel, and falteringly say more to her of his personal trust and experience of his Saviour than he had ever done before. When at last he tore himself from her arms, he walked blindly downstairs not daring to look back. He took his seat in the coach, counselling Jack to tell Mary how easy and comfortable he was in his mind, and on the first stage of the journey wrote her a tender letter to reiterate what was certainly a misleading statement.

Yet, paradoxically, it was not misleading. Compared with the serenity of trust which should, he felt, characterize so signal an object of his Lord's grace and protecting care, his distress and anxiety and fear were deplorable; but the old John Newton would not have had the power to perform his duty, the control to chat amiably with fellow passengers in the coach. He would not have been able to submerge his panic in cheerful letters and, on arrival in Liverpool, to accept congratulations and enter upon his tasks, with a composure which gave strangers no inkling that heart and mind were in another part of England set on the beloved object, apart from whom the genteel, potentially lucrative employment, and the pleasant social circle open to him, was less than nothing and vanity.

Then, mercifully, the sharpness of his trial was over. Jack Catlett's letters, either deliberately or carelessly reassuring, kept from him until later the acuteness of Polly's illness after his departure. But miraculously, when physicians held out no hope, the periods of pain slackened and then ceased. Within ten days she was able to sign her name beneath Elizabeth's on her sister's letter. Her first short, shaky-handed, note, written a week later, moved him to fearful rapture. And two months after he had left her to all appearances dying, she was able to set out for Liverpool.

From the coach at Stone, forgetting in his joy that he had strongly advised her to travel more expensively and easily in a hired chaise, he received her as one brought back from the dead. What her letters had told him — he held her at arm's length briefly to see — of her improved appetite, health, colour, was all true. She had never looked lovelier. But, though every reunion with her had been more glorious than the last — what charm had Mary that he could never anticipate the fulness of satisfaction or the merry variety of endearment which each successive meeting included? — they had never come together before with so much confessed unanimity.

That Mary had endured, even enjoyed, the moralizing and meditative passages, by which with ever greater freedom he clarified in writing the convictions he could so poorly utter, was to a great extent, he knew, because she loved him. Almost two years before, she had asked him to pray with her, but

287

it had always been he who prayed. Apart from the dutiful repetition of childish verses and Our Father, she had never acknowledged that she could pray. His assurance, wondering and humble, that he was accepted by God through the merits of Christ, sometimes seemed groundless arrogance when he realized that Mary, whose life and thought were blameless in comparison with his, was apprehensive of judgment, and unaware of any personal communion with the Deity whom she had ceremonially worshipped since childhood.

Since his departure from London, however, her recovery to health was, in John's view, not the only miracle which had occurred. Letters every post kept her amused by anecdotes or incidents which he could turn to entertainment, kept her acquainted with his serious activities. These latter were of a sort to alarm any easy-going, respectable family; and the Catletts, their anxiety for Mary's health relieved, became anxious and by no means covertly anxious, for her social future. On the topic of John's desertion of St. George's fashionable church and his edification among the Baptists, Polly kept discreetly silent. She was personally thankful that the latter group had barred John from fulfilling his wish to join them, by their insistence on his baptism by immersion as a condition to membership, "to which," he wrote "as I do not see the necessity myself, I cannot at present submit," though a little later he admitted himself deeply impressed when he first witnessed the ordinance. But she shared with her news-loving family the story of Whitefield's visit to Liverpool, of her husband's attendance at his preaching, of his friendship to the extent of entertaining him for dinner, of his consequent nickname of "Young Whitefield" by wags of his acquaintance; and was sorry she had done so when she saw the resultant disapproval. Letters of protest, covert from Polly's aunt, blunt from Jack, reports softened in Polly's account to him, made John aware that the steps he had taken to identify himself with the serious Christians in Liverpool were exposing him to censure from the very people who had hitherto been his warm supporters. He felt the criticism, reviewed his actions and motives, resolved, unless principle were at stake, to give no needless offence by any appearance of "singularity or sourness," and was chiefly concerned with its effect on his wife.

288

Polly's reactions were never calculable. At twenty-one, though less giddy than the younger Elizabeth was now at twenty-three, she had been contented as the petted darling of her family and acquaintance in a round of gentle dissipation — cards, games, dancing — from house to house, with plays and assembly rooms on formal occasions. Dresses and mild gossip and family concerns had been her chief interests. Serious she could never be for long, and had shared unthinkingly the attitude of her milieu towards what was vaguely called "enthusiasm," as hypocritical and in bad taste. She had had before her marriage a hazy, a very hazy, idea of what John meant by calling himself a "profligate and libertine" and was very glad, if he had been one — he could never possibly have been really bad, she thought — that he had changed. When, in his first letters, he had suggested that their correspondence might tend to their mutual improvement she had been rather piqued — after all, had he not praised her as perfect? — and had drawn a swift apologetic explanation from him. But she soon found herself so many fathoms deep in love that it was a comfort to pore over his letters until they were almost committed to heart. At first the multiple endearments "my dearest charmer," "my precious beautiful Polly," the infinite variety of adoring assertion, with reference and reminiscence and gratitude which called the blood warmly up her spine and through her head merely to peruse: these were the parts on which she dwelt. Then, because it was all John and she yearned to know him thoroughly, she found herself wondering and trying to think with him through the rest, agreeing and approving with her mind where her heart could not follow.

That mind, always alert but largely ignorant, except of home management and trifling current knowledge, was happy to enlarge its scope. Mary had never been to school, although Elizabeth Churchill had learned Latin at the select academy attended also by John's mother. Her eldest daughter had been such a help during Mrs. Catlett's frequent childbearing, and so quick to acquire social grace that George Catlett saw no need of a formal education for her. "Being with her mother will teach her more than a schoolmistress," he had said easily. Mary had found her native wit quite able to hold her own in the general or gallant conversation of the dinner-table

289

or the tête à tête. She had a shrewd ear too for the difference in quality of the conversation of husbands when with their wives and when with other men. She had watched the gradual settling into good-natured apathy of most, even of the love-matches, of her acquaintance. John's unabated ardour, his increasing and grateful devotion were not to be taken for granted. If they were somehow related to this religion of his which was so different, so much more personal than any she had ever met, then, though a bit fearful of the serious strain of his writing, she found it of great interest. She was deeply impressed, too, by his learning, and flattered that he thought her capable of enjoying references to Pliny and Aesop, to the systems of heathen philosophers, to prophets and apostles, who had never been real people to her until described by his lively pen.

When they were together, the lover in John overcame the moralizer, and the tongue which had mastered its difficulty in telling her of his love was still reticent, though less than formerly, about religion. Mary was incapable of pretense and, though his prayers comforted her, she could give him, even to ease his desperate anxiety at their recent parting, no indication that she had found the peace and joy for which he earnestly besought Heaven on her behalf.

Almost before he left the room, however, keener than her physical pain, the upsurge of anguish that she might never see him again, the conviction that if she died she would *never* see him again, and a queer interplay of desolation at the thought and of responsibility for his distress, unstopped a hidden spring. She found herself praying, wildly, sobbingly, beseechingly, not for herself, but for him, yet therefore for herself; and for the first time had comfort in knowing that her prayer was heard. During her convalescence she had gone to hear Mr. Brewer and was immeasurably strengthened by an apt sermon on the Great Physician. Then, restored beyond all expectation, she surprised herself by answering Jack's annoyance and her mother's distress with pointed, though equable, statements of confidence in John's balance and good sense. Meanwhile, without drawing attention to it, she decided to find out for herself; and from the Clunies' house began to acquire "a fine set of Methodistical acquaintance" as her elated husband wrote her, finding among them, not the unsociable sour rigidity she had feared, but a happy warmth and concerned interest quite different from any she had known before. Some of this experience, clearly but reticently stated, she set forth in her letters to John, together with an altogether new note of personal concern over her shortcomings: "I delight, admire, and love to hang upon every sentence and every action of my dearest John," she had written in a burst of candour never previously attained in writing, "yet how wanting and how cold am I to the gracious Author of all our mercies, to whom we owe each other, our happy affection, and all the satisfaction that flows from it!"

When, in corroboration, one of John's Dissenting ministerial friends wrote to him: "God has been pleased to give her a great measure of your spirit. She is neither afraid nor ashamed to own her profession," he felt that his greatest wish was fulfilled. And when Mary, privately a little less confident of John's prudence than she professed to her family, and doubtless goaded by Jack's jibe that she would have no friends in Liverpool but washerwomen, cautioned him that there was "a *way* of doing things," he allayed her fears by assuring her that he did not expect her to consort with washerwomen in this world — though he reminded her that they would probably be glad to have fellowship with them in the next. The same letter told her frankly that in Liverpool any serious interest in religion would bring upon them the name of singularity, and that their home must be one where God was worshipped and where nothing was practised or permitted out of keeping with their Christian profession.

Undismayed by the prospect, she had come. And the rapture with which she was greeted, the preparation which her husband had taken to make his rooms agreeable to her until they could find a house, the excellence of the dinner which his landlady had prepared — she who had scouted the idea of hearing Mr. Whitefield and then unexpectedly been one of his converts — the warmth of their fire and the beauty of flowers which John had taken pains to supply in profusion for her flower-loving eyes would have reassured a much more apprehensive mind than hers.

29

THE pulpit reached by a spiral staircase was as high as the gallery which faced it in the small Congregational meeting-house in Leeds. John, ascending slowly, wished more than ever that Mary were present to hear this, his first formal sermon. She had heard him speak in public: on the momentous occasion almost two years before, when for the first time he expounded the Scriptures to his family and a few friends after Sunday supper; several times since, when he had repeated the experiment; and at an informal gathering during this same visit to Yorkshire. But this was his first public sermon and it was a sore trial to him that one of Mary's fits of unpredictable illness had prostrated her at his sister Kitty's home. He always felt awkward without her.

He was in the pulpit now. The congregation, serious and attentive as he had observed them here where the gospel was flourishing as in few other provinces, settled down after a chanted psalm, expecting the sermon of this visitor from Liverpool, this Customs official who had leanings towards the ministry. He knew that he was presentable, because Mary had inspected him, smoothed his hair — he still wore his own — adjusted his full cravat, and pronounced him her "Pretty Dear" with the smile which her migraine made only a trifle wan. He had worked carefully over his sermon and was so familiar with its gist that he had no notes. Read discourses were the general diet even in Dissenting churches, but the masterly oratory of his friend Whitefield, the penetrating quality of Wesley's preaching, he attributed to their freedom from manuscript. With earnest assurance he gave out his text:

"I have set the Lord always before me. He is at my right hand; therefore I shall not be moved."

The words vibrated in his own ears. Had he spoken too loudly? Mary had complained of a visiting preacher in Liverpool that his bellowing delivery kept the sense of his words from affecting her. He knew his voice lacked modulation — shouting orders on a ship was poor training, and not to be undone in four years.

The moment's speculation drove his carefully planned opening sentence from his mind. If he repeated the text it would come to him. Dropping his voice to something like a whisper he began again slowly: "I have set the Lord always before me. He is at my right hand."

There was a movement under the gallery which he interpreted as a craning of the congregation to hear. Hastily he raised his voice and the conclusion of the text was almost a shout:

"Therefore I shall not be moved."

The ludicrousness struck him but without mirth. He had sat in silent criticism, sincerely repented, of many ungraceful speakers — he was now, he realized, leaning far over the pulpit. And still the words would not come. The tremendous text hung on the air. He, John Newton, once a servant of slaves, an ingrate and a blasphemer, had thought to exhort a congregation with it. The arduous self-instruction of the last three years in Greek and Hebrew and Aramaic, his periods of prayer, waiting upon the Lord for guidance, his day of fasting and preparation before his momentous decision to risk Mary's future and the world's opprobrium: all led to this moment. He *must* be adequate to meet it.

The silence of the people appalled him. They were waiting for speech and once again, when speech was most necessary, he was powerless to command it. Words, phrases, sentences were jumbled in his mind until he feared that whatever he said would be incoherent.

"A great text," he essayed. "I spent long in deciding," he tried again. "The Book of Psalms differs. . . ." As when his bursting heart could salvage nothing of the fine speeches he had composed to win Mary, so now words were dried up by the very exuberance of his preparation.

"Mr. Newton," said his friend, Mr. Edwards, encouragingly from the seat he had taken in the front pew, after conducting the earlier part of the service, "do not be distressed. We are waiting with you on the Spirit."

But these well-meant words completed the rout. Till then he had hoped against hope that his confusion was being exaggerated in his own mind. Now it was patent to the congregation, patent that he must be encouraged like a child, he who had fifty people under his direction in Liverpool, and had been master of a ship containing more than two hundred souls. Shame filled him and a desolate indignation.

"I," he muttered, "I. . . ." whether or not he said that he was sorry he never knew, nor did the congregation.

They saw him turn and disappear as he groped his way down the stairs. Mr. Edwards, not a little shaken and disappointed, for he had issued the invitation, rose, and giving out Dr. Watts's hymn: "Am I a Soldier of the Cross?" exhorted the people briefly on the words before asking them to sing it. Meanwhile John had taken himself out through the door at the foot of the pulpit and was walking almost blindly towards his sister's house.

"Of course you will preach again," said Mary soothingly. He had tried all the way home to devise some means of concealing the devastating fiasco which, he was afraid, would distress her unduly in her weakened state. But even if an explanation which did not violate the truth had been possible, he could not hide his feelings from her. "You have preached — or at least expounded the Scriptures — wonderfully time and again to almost as many."

"How do I know that the same thing will not occur next time? Perhaps I am wrong in thinking that the Lord has called me into His service. Who am I to be so honoured?"

"You are the best and the cleverest man I know. And a great many people think as highly — well not quite as highly — of you as I do," she answered stoutly. Then an irrepressible twinkle came into the gray eyes as she looked at him sitting at her bedside. "Do I not remember an occasion when all that you

294

could manage of an eloquent speech was: 'If I write you a letter, will you read it?' words that I don't think you intended at all. Yet I've heard you say that your mouth has been somewhat opened since."

John laughed, and kissed her until he remembered her headache. Then he sat with his big hand on her broad white brow and spoke soberly.

"There was a 'need-be' for this, I don't doubt. Mr. Self needed his comb cut. O my Dearest, your husband is a poor creature — yes, Precious, he is! — vacillating between utter humility at what I was, and pride at the state to which God has raised me. And, may He forgive me, in that pride when friends praise me, I tend to forget that it is all grace. Today has taught me that I cannot of myself even exercise His gift. If I ever preach again my dependency must be utterly on Him."

30

REMEMBER that the progress of faith to assurance is gradual. Expect it not suddenly; but wait upon the Lord for it in the ways of His appointment. As it depends upon the manifestation of the Holy Spirit, let this engage you to constancy and earnestness in prayer; and as it arises from a knowledge of Jesus, be assiduous in searching the Scriptures which testify of Him. If you persevere in this path, you will be helped forward by the experience of every day; and every dispensation of Providence as well as every exercise and frame of mind you pass through will be sanctified, to give you an increasing conviction that you are nothing, and that Jesus is All in all.

"As you cannot see or maintain a sight of your interest in the covenant, but by the light of the Spirit, beware of grieving Him. If you indulge a careless, trifling disposition, or venture upon known sin, you will find dark clouds raised between the Sun of Righteousness and your souls. Assurance is not so invariable, but that it may be affected, weakened, and perhaps for a season quite suspended, by unfaithfulness and backsliding. If you have a persuasion of your interest in the love of God that remains always the same, though prayer is restrained, the ordinances slighted, and watchfulness intermitted, take heed lest this, instead of assurance, should be vain confidence and presumption. The hope that maketh not ashamed, endears every precept and ordinance to the soul, weans the affections from low and trivial pursuits and strengthens the exercise of every gracious principle.

"As it is thus possible and desirable for a believer to 'know that he is of God' so a concern for many here present will not suffer me to close without desiring you to consider if you have not cause to conclude that you are *not* of God. 'Whosoever doeth not righteousness is not of God.' 'If any man have not the Spirit of Christ, he is none of his.' If your love and dependence are not fixed on the Lord Jesus Christ, if your tempers and practice are not governed by his commands, you are not of God. Whom then do you belong to? The whole world is divided between two masters, and ranged under opposite banners. A neutrality is impossible. If you are not of God, you belong at present to Satan. You are his captive; he leads you blindfold; he meditates your destruction when you shall have worn out your lives in his miserable service. And will you continue fond of your bondage and follow him like an ox to the slaughter? There is a redemption price paid, there is an arm of power revealed in favour of such helpless perishing specimens. Jesus whom we preach is able to take the prey out of the hand of the mighty. O may he incline you to believe and be saved. If you reject Him you seal yourself to an aggravated condemnation. 'But if you hear his voice and call upon his name, he is able,' as I can well testify, 'to save to the uttermost'."

John, looking from the pulpit over the crowded Olney church, felt the warmth which rose to meet him from his people and from the strangers who came in increasing numbers to swell his auditory. Three years before when, after the disheartening rebuffs and six-year delay in attaining his ordination, he had unexpectedly been appointed in the curacy of Olney, the church had been comfortably attended for Morning Prayer at least. Within a year the attendance had so taxed the capacious fourteenth-century building that his patron, Lord Dartmouth, had added a gallery down one side of the nave; now two thousand often crowded in to hear him. His success mystified John, for he never considered himself a pulpit orator, though he had progressed far from that wretched day in Leeds — he still dreamed of it and of the ensuing week, when he was sure if two people were chatting on the street that they were discussing his failure — or for that matter his next attempt two years later when he had taken his book into the pulpit and, being near-sighted, had kept his head down and droned steadily on to the uninspiring close. He had learned to prepare carefully when possible, but to speak "warm from his heart" and if, as on occasion he found it necessary, he caught at a text as he went up into the pulpit, the Lord had never failed to supply his need.

He pronounced the benediction and made his way down the aisle. The figure under cassock and gown, a gift from Martin Madan, the famous London preacher, was a trifle heavier at forty-three; the business of his week, and frequent riding and walking, kept it vigorous. His eyes met Mary's as he passed, with the joyfully communicated sense of rightness that never failed him. His passing had been too swift to catch more than a glimpse of their new house guests but Mr. Cowper had sat throughout the sermon in rapt attention. How many would accept the invitation to dinner at the house, extended to all who walked six miles or more to the service? Mary managed wonderfully with Phoebe and Martha but the incessant round of company taxed her strength and he wondered if he would be justified, when they moved into the rebuilt rectory, in getting another maid or even two. Mr. Thornton would not object. How amazingly God had provided when he had ceased worrying about money and employing questionable means to increase his store. He could *not* have done otherwise than acquiesce in Moses Browne's wish to retain twenty pounds along with the title of vicar of Olney; but how would he have managed on thirty pounds a year? Well, the Lord's answer was the rich London merchant and philanthropist, John Thornton. "Not *many* rich are called," he quoted silently, but some certainly were, and of those, his friends Lord Dartmouth and John Thornton were not least.

The congregation, moving through the north porch, filed past, scarcely any willing to miss his greeting. The few who did — he must remember to pray more earnestly for them! — were well-to-do farmers and merchants who resented many things about their parson: his plain speaking on worldliness, his methodistical preaching, by which they meant a personal application of the gospel with no respect of persons, his prayers that the Lord would "disappoint those who make a real scarcity, disappoint those who grind the faces of the poor." These were equally uneasy, having long been the important members of the congregation, that their minister attracted strangers of evident learning and position; and that he was so unimpressed by respectability that he spent no time in social visiting at their houses but went in and out — praying and singing hymns forsooth! — the miserable cottages of the lace-makers. He was above himself, that was all; this book of his — more than one, they were told, but the strange story of his life — its success had gone to his head. Yet it wasn't a story to be proud of certainly; in fact, it wasn't proper to make so much of his wife as he had done and still did, referring to her in public on all sorts of occasions; and at the same time being so mealy-mouthed and humble, calling himself the chief of sinners, yet always in a way to make them feel that they were too. And now — shaking hands with that notorious Molly Mind who should be ashamed to show her face in church after the life she had lived — and to do her justice she hadn't until the last few weeks. Thick as thieves with Baptists and other Dissenters too — why didn't he go among them if he didn't know what a Church of England clergyman owed himself and his parishioners?

When the empty church echoed thinly to his last greeting John walked through the porch from the stone-preserved coolness into the warm mid-September air. The fields sloping down to the Ouse beyond the churchyard were lush with grass, and half a dozen cows huddled with chronically moody enjoyment in the shallows. Slipping the gown from his shoulders, he proceeded in his cassock for the longest walk he ever took in these clerical garments, the few hundred yards or so past his rectory, which was being conveniently enlarged and modified by Lord Dartmouth, to the old house which served him meanwhile. He felt more comfortable out of clerical dress and had even attended the bishop's visitation at Newport Pagnell without it until he found it the subject of comment. He rather hoped that their dinner guests would be few today. Mary had thoughtfully suggested that Mrs. and Miss Unwin and Mr. Cowper might dine upstairs, but they had refused to cause extra trouble. From what he had seen, Mr. Cowper might not be happy in a crowd. He was glad that Mary had taken so instantly to Mrs. Unwin. It would be good for his Dear to have a congenial companion nearby during his periodic absences. The whole village loved her — the place looks "so unked" when Madam is away, they complained when she had visited Chatham the previous winter — but there were few kindred spirits.

His pleasure at the outcome of an apparently fortuitous — but nothing was fortuitous with John — consolation visit became more marked during the days which passed before their guests could move into Orchard Side, the house he had procured for them on Market Square. Dr. Conyers, whom the Newtons had visited that spring in Yorkshire, had suggested that he call on the Reverend Morley Unwin, and John, visiting nearby, had ridden the intervening miles to Huntingdon. He had found Mrs. Unwin bearing the shock of her husband's sudden death — he had been thrown from his horse a few days before — with quiet fortitude. "They cannot have loved as we do," had been Mary's instant and decided comment when she heard of it, and he was inclined to agree, although the cheerful decorum of her behaviour was, as he reminded his wife, the way a Christian, in fact, Mary, should face the world if *her* husband was taken. Mary had looked at him with her demurest, most docile expression, but her upturning brows were quizzical. "Should I, John? Should I?" she had asked meekly and when, unable as she knew he would be to resist, he had taken her in his arms, she had returned his embrace with a sudden passionate strength and burst into tears.

Susannah Unwin, a girl of twenty-two, was at the Huntingdon home. Her brother had returned to Cambridge, where he was studying with the intention of taking Holy Orders. For William Cowper, a gentleman of aristocratic connections who had come to live with the family two years earlier and remained almost in the relationship of a son to Mrs. Unwin, though only seven years her junior, Newton was unprepared. An hour's talk had discovered such mutual attraction and so much common ground to two men outwardly and experientially dissimilar that his invitation for a visit to Olney was eagerly accepted. Mr. Unwin's death had left them unrooted at Huntingdon and they decided to rent a house at Olney to be under the evangelical ministry which they both desired.

"He was delighted that I knew Mr. Haweis. I told him that, without his interest in showing my letters to Lord Dartmouth, I should probably not have gained Dartmouth's patronage and my ordination — nor would the *Authentic Narrative* have been published. I find that he was at Westminster with my Lord and is a cousin of Martin Madan," John reported after his visit.

"They are greatly attached to each other," said Mary on the night of their arrival at Olney. "Miss Susannah is of less consequence to either of them than the other. Do they intend to marry? I mean when her period of mourning is over, of course."

Her husband pondered this in some surprise that the idea had not occurred to him.

"He regards her as a mother, I think. Remember, he is two years younger than you."

Mary considered.

"Mrs. Unwin is forty-three, she tells me, but she looks certainly no older than I."

"Nonsense, Dearest. She looks a middle-aged woman. You never will. You are ageless, and altogether beautiful in my eyes."

"Ah there, that spoils it! In your eyes! But when I say that in *my* eyes you are my Pretty Dear, my Golden Image — very well, John, I won't say it again. But to Mrs. Unwin. Does it seem a — an ordinary arrangement to you?"

It was John's turn to be quizzical. "It would not be an ordinary arrangement for me — if you were Mrs. Unwin! But I think Mr. Cowper's circumstances are extraordinary. And Mrs. Unwin's care seems to be exactly what he needs. He tells me that he is sure God directed him to their household, just as he is sure he has been directed to my ministry. He is a Calvinist like me," he added smiling, "in fact a much more rigid Calvinist than your poor husband, who is considered a speckled bird among his Calvinist acquaintance."

"How did he come to stay with the Unwins?"

"Young Unwin noticed him in church and sought his acquaintance. He is a charming person — you think so, don't you, Polly? Probably it was the only place in Huntingdon where he could feel at home. The others of his social standing there did not share his religious views. He could not share their employment of their time, though he had earlier

301

been completely frivolous. In fact, he tells me he had only a polite interest in religion before his second terrible lapse into madness. He does not talk much of it. Dread of the oral examination for clerkship in the House of Lords threw him into a melancholy derangement and he tried repeatedly to destroy himself. For two years after, he was confined in Dr. Cotton's establishment for the insane at St. Alban's."

"John," said Mary with sudden recollection. "It comes jump in my head that he is the nephew about whom Mrs. Madan expressed such concern when we were at the Lock several years ago. Her son had been called to pray with a cousin, demented and sure that he was damned."

"Of course, it must have been," said John. "The times coincide exactly. Mr. Cowper tells me that Dr. Cotton's personal faith and teaching gave him for the first time relief from his fears and a glimpse of the glory of the gospel. From that time he steadily improved in health until he was dismissed from asylum."

"Has he independent means?"

"Very little. I believe that his connections contribute to his support."

"Well," Mary summarized the situation and signalized her intention of going to sleep by curling up under his protecting arm, "both of them think highly of *you* and that qualifies them for my approval. Mr. Cowper may well think himself a fortunate man to have the opportunity of your friendship."

"Most impartial judgment," said John contentedly. "I have no desire for you to think otherwise. But you are prejudiced, Sweet. A few minutes of his conversation assures me how much I can learn from him. And the depth and warmth of his spirit shames me with my wandering and coldness. I count it my privilege that he has come to stay in Olney."

In this humility there was, as Mary in wonder and occasional exasperation knew, no touch of hypocrisy. Her husband's dealings with others were characterized by complete absence of self-importance. Consciousness of his own evil heart prevented him from passing stern judgment on individuals, even while, with fearful earnestness, he preached their danger and their glorious opportunity. In the crowding friendships of the past few years, friendships with not a few distinguished

302

men, he was so genuine an admirer of the good qualities of others that he viewed their regard for him with naïve surprise.

So the arrival of these new friends, primarily for their spiritual welfare, was regarded by him in the nature of a benefit conferred. Not, he would have confessed, that he ever felt the need of other company when Mary was with him; but the radiant warmth of their relationship flowed out to others without diminution, grew rather in intensity by expending interest and affection upon more and more — and miraculously neither disliked any friend of the other. Jack Catlett for whom, in spite of their religious differences and diminishing companionship, he had retained strong affection and determined hope, had died quite suddenly soon after their settlement in Olney. Now the friend that Jack might have been was given him in this keen-faced aristocrat, with the large, too mobile eyes, a friend sharing his literary tastes, his sense of the ludicrous, but also his beliefs, his passion in the service of God. Cowper had, a year or so earlier, contemplated Holy Orders. And for his Dear's comfort when he was forced from home, the quiet humour and patient kindliness of Mrs. Unwin would be invaluable.

He had not anticipated the eagerness with which William Cowper — soon called Sir Cowper in the squireless village — threw himself into the work of the parish. As if he had discovered the field in which unofficially but really, he could fulfil the desire to "turn many to the truth in a private way" of which he had written some years before to his cousin, he sought avidly the occasions which John accorded him.

Compared with his retired life in the Unwin family at Huntingdon, where day flowed into day of sermon-reading, singing, gentle conversation and more reading aloud, always intermitted in fair weather by a walk with Mrs. Unwin, the life into which William Cowper now plunged was one of bustling activity. John's week of services was staggering to the connections of the late Morley Unwin, who had so successfully delegated all parish duties to his curates that he had not even performed a marriage or baptismal ceremony or officiated at a funeral for years. In addition to morning prayer and evensong, a meeting was now held after tea in the new rectory for prayer and hymn-singing and, the number of attendants rising to seventy, tickets were issued to exclude the merely curious and social-minded. Monday evening John conducted a Bible class for men. Tuesday evening was devoted to the prayer meeting, and recently another prayer service, well-attended, had begun without his instigation, early on Sunday morning. Wednesday he held classes for young people and enquirers. On Thursday afternoon he had a children's meeting, ostensibly to teach the catechism but really, as he told his friend, "to reason with them and explain the Scriptures in their own little way." The same evening his weekly church service with sermon was attended by people from many of the villages around. And on Fridays members of the Society, a group of earnest believers, met for devotions and study.

Amid this demanding array of meetings, time was found for reading, for visiting his people and ministering to their very real, at times desperate, need.

"Mr. Thornton gives me two hundred pounds a year for charity and hospitality," he explained during one of the walks on which Cowper now habitually accompanied him. "Else I should have to choose between helping that woman procure the next meal and seeing my Dear, who never knew hardship or inconvenience until she ventured her all with me, straitened and struggling with duties beyond her strength! And whereas she would urge me to the latter choice, I thank God He has spared me the necessity of making it. The Lord saw to it that Mr. Thornton's bounty came in good time. I had scarce removed to Olney when my kind friend, Joseph Manesty, went bankrupt and with him all my savings were lost. Perhaps few other circumstances could have made my personal loss so insignificant." He was silent suddenly. Manesty's death, close upon the shock of his failure, and Mrs. Manesty's subsequent collapse into insanity was a still fresh grief, kept alive by correspondence with their daughter. Cowper's voice recalled him.

"Yet you were offered the better living of Hampstead — and rejected it."

John smiled. His eyes rested affectionately on the broach spire of his church, clear against the washed green sky above the river meadows.

"Yes. My Dear's mother, in particular, was eager to have

her near. Yet would it not have seemed that I came into the church solely for profit if I had left Olney almost before I was settled here? And after all the business of attaining ordination!"

"That I cannot understand," said Cowper vehemently. "Considering the vast majority of the ordained, the ignorance and worldliness, in some cases licentiousness, of William Unwin's companions at Cambridge, I should have expected that your qualifications would be immediately recognized. On what grounds did they reject you?"

"I had not been at the University," said John simply, "and though I had prepared myself adequately in all branches of study, the lack of a degree was held as sufficient bar. It was, I fear, rather a handle to use against the suspicion of Methodism which I had incurred. On the first occasion Mr. Crooks had recommended me and that was enough for the Bishop."

"Yet if you prattled scandal, were familiar with a round of Ladyships, never at your books, seldom scrawled more than a card, you would be eligible!"

"Well, I confess that I had quite given up and, had not Lord Dartmouth exerted himself on my behalf, would have accepted a call among Dissenters or Presbyterians. In fact I should have done so long before, except that my Dear was against it and I would not, apart from an assurance of the Lord's will, take such a step without her full concurrence. She has been the hinge on which my whole life turns."

"I suppose you know," said William Cowper, absently but vigorously using his stout stick to clear a fox's earth which some sport lover of the neighbourhood had stopped with stones, "that it is a remarkable experience to observe your mutual affection, and a little difficult to realize that it has survived the honeymoon?"

"Survived it by eighteen years. I know. 'Omicron and his Inamorata', Mr. Thornton calls us. I cannot help it. I have no desire to change. But I confess to having had some concern at one time on hearing that my references to her were thought excessive, lest discredit be brought on the gospel."

They had paused by the Ouse where its meanderings described an incomplete parabola in the lush flats. John's chin was more set than usual. His love for Mary he made no attempt

305

to conceal, because he was as incapable of concealing it as he had been at their first meeting. The years of marriage had given him, were daily giving, so many additional causes for affection that he would be, he told himself reasonably, more than ungrateful to God who had made her so altogether love-ly for him, if he felt less than he did. Yet he was acutely conscious of the danger of idolatry in their love, evinced in the pain of their partings, the restlessness of their separations, their fears for each other's safety: all warring against that glad trust in the Lord, that swift submission to His will, which should characterize his attitude. On one passage in Scripture he had never spoken, nor would he ever speak, though he read it through wistfully time after time. When — if — Mary was taken before he was, then, if God's grace was suffic-ient — no, the grace *was* sufficient, but was he faithful enough to avail himself of it? — he would preach from that text. Till then he dared not, for he did not *know*, he could not be sure.

So his conscience was sensitive to criticism which his growing popularity and influence in Evangelical circles made inevitable. His jaw relaxed suddenly from the set grimness which from early boyhood had masked shyness or hurt.

"Mr. Wesley comforted me much on that score," he said reminiscently. "I shall always be grateful to him."

Cowper glanced up in surprise.

"I should not have expected to hear you speak favourably of John Wesley," he said, and only the admiration which never saw flaw in its current objects of admiration kept a shade of disapproval from his voice. John regarded him whimsically.

"So at one time I thought, being a supporter of Mr. White-field and the doctrines of Calvinism. Mr. Wesley shamed me out of myself by sheer graciousness. His reassurance, on read-ing my *Narrative,* that he did not see how I could speak of Mrs. Newton less or other than I did is only part of the debt I owe him. His book on the *Nature of an Oath* informed my conscience so that I could no longer accept gratuities in the Customs' House. Perhaps I had never learned what holiness of life implies had I not been forced — for in Liverpool there was such dearth of gospel preaching that I dared not stay from his when he visited — to hear him."

"Holiness, yes. But this mad insistence on sinless perfection — and as an essential, dying without which believers go straight to damnation — what is this but salvation by works? Martin will have none of it."

"Nor, from what he has written to me, will Mr. Wesley. Surely the man has been greatly slandered and, I fear, by some of the very men who should most rejoice in his work."

"I cannot conceive that Martin Madan or Thomas Haweis would slander."

John melted instantly. Martin Madan, the encourager of his early efforts, for whom he now preached on occasion to the important audience which gathered in the gallery of the Lock Hospital Chapel; Thomas Haweis at whose request he had written in letters the now famous account of his early life: they were imperfect but they were men of God, his friends, and his loyalty to them was unwavering. Yet, characteristically, he did not find it incumbent upon loyalty to praise or condemn at their decision.

"I love them both too well to think so. But Mr. Wesley merits no less my love and honour. Not that I cease to uphold — neither of us will dispute — my conviction upon Particular Election and Final Perseverance. I could not be easy without those doctrines for an hour." He shuddered suddenly. "Were it not all God's electing grace, what could have brought a wretch like me to see salvation? And as for perseverance, I know enough — not all — of the perverseness of my own heart, the helplessness of my will, my ungovernable imagination. . . . Ah, no! If it depends in any sense or degree upon me I am lost indeed."

"But," he went on, smiling reminiscently again, when Cowper's fervent agreement had established their unity of view, "it was in this very matter that Mr. Wesley turned the tables against me. His writing, like all his communication, is apparently effortless, but crystal-clear and happily phrased. I had stated my belief that it was my duty to oppose Perfection as a dangerous mistake which is subversive of the foundations of Christian experience, and which has given occasion to the most grievous offences."

"Good," said Cowper, pleased. "Like your sermons, plain and neat. I cannot give anything higher praise than that. I

307

hate circumlocution and adornment. How did he answer?"
John laughed.

"More plainly and neatly still. He quoted with approval
my own words, distinguishing opinion from essential doctrine.
The former I had defined as something 'compatible with a
love to Christ and a work of grace.' He said he and his
brother had reasoned thirty years ago, in my very vein, that
they must oppose Predestination as a dangerous mistake, subversive and offence-causing. Then, after bluntly stating that
he could vouch for the offences which holding that doctrine
had occasioned — and I fear I have seen them also — he continued, 'But another fact stares me in the face: Mr. Haweis
and Mr. Newton hold this and they *have* real Christian experience. Then this is only an opinion, *not* subversive of the
foundations but compatible with a love to Christ and a genuine
work of grace.' After which," John went on in a lower voice,
"he knocked the ground from under me by saying, 'Yea, many
hold it at whose feet I desire to be found in the day of the
Lord Jesus. If, then, I oppose this with my whole strength, I
am a mere bigot still. I leave you in your calm and retired
moments to make the application'."

"Touché." Cowper relished the delicate thrust of the words.
His long well-cut mouth curved into an appreciative smile.
"I begin to understand your respect for Mr. Wesley."

"He explained," continued John, "what he means, not what
his detractors say he means, by Perfection: the belief that even
in this life Christ can and will redeem a believer that he may
love God with all his heart so as to pray without ceasing,
rejoice evermore, in everything give thanks. And though, as
I told him, I still believe, if I am saved, it will be as a sinner,
not as a saint, I would rather pray for and press to nearer
advances towards his view than fight and dispute against it.
Again to quote Mr. Wesley: 'Lord, if I must dispute, let it be
with the children of the devil; let me be at peace with Thy
children'."

"It must be evident to all that this is your aim," said Cowper,
leaving the subject of Wesley without reluctance. "Your refusal to be controversial with Mr. Balfour in Newport when
he criticized you for exhorting sinners and inviting in your
sermons —"

"My strict Calvinist brothers who would plead with no one, because pleading is wasted on those not foreordained to eternal life! They must do as they see fit. I own, if I try nicely to reconcile two opposite texts, I begin to bungle. I cannot reconcile certain texts of Scripture even with the scheme I believe to be most consonant with its general teaching. Therefore, if a Christian hold but the essentials — and to them I came with no man as teacher, at sea and alone with my Bible — I care not to dispute. Mr. Self too easily plumes himself on such occasions. But observation and experience have shown me which type of preaching is blest by the winning of souls. And so, since I have Scriptural warrant to declare 'Whosoever will may come', I declare it."

They had reached the bridge and paused upon it for the prospect of which John never tired: the uninhabited Great House, which Lord Dartmouth was allowing him to use for the weekly meetings which had overgrown their present accommodation; the distant mill; nearer than either, its spire reflected in the widened river which flowed past the churchyard, his Olney church. He was conscious of his friend's eyes upon him and turned, apologetically.

"Sloth is not the least of my besetting sins. I was sincere in the reasons I gave Mr. Wesley some seven years ago, when he was kind enough to concern himself with my rebuffed attempts to obtain ordination in the Establishment and suggested that I become an itinerant —"

Cowper shuddered.

"You would have no need to give me reasons for your refusal. The very prospect appals me. How a man of any sensibility —"

"I could scarcely offer that to Mr. Wesley, whose sensibility and refinement far surpass my own," said John dryly, "but I had to search my soul to make sure that I was not rejecting a call of God from self-indulgence."

"What did you reply?"

"Mainly that my constitution, on which considerable inroads were made during my years in Africa, would not sustain the life. Indeed a ride of thirty miles a day, or to ride in the rain, unfits me for anything."

"I see no evidence of sloth," protested Cowper. "Your life

in the town itself is a constant round of activity, stimulating but exhausting for one of my temperament to behold. And your coming and going from here to Yorkshire, to Liverpool, to London — your house open at all times to everyone — you can scarcely imagine what impression of business Mrs. Unwin and I derive from it."

John became uncomfortable. He had not intended to solicit defence or approbation.

"My observation sprang from this prospect, which always fills me with gratitude that my lot has not been cast in the city. I never go to London without delight at return here — even if my Dear accompanies me," he added to stop the teasing remark evidently on Cowper's tongue. "I never tire of the sounds and sights of the country. And to live so, yet have a field for my labour at hand — it is all part of the Lord's kindness in dealing with me."

Cowper turned from the sky which had folded a gray blanket close above the town's thatched roofs. His face, which reflected every mood, often with startling suddenness, was troubled as at the recurrence of unwelcome memories.

> " 'Visionary scenes and voices,
> Flames of Hell and screams of woe' "

he muttered. "Mr. Newton, I have been surprised — I cannot say disappointed, for one would willingly forget . . . if one could — but surprised that your preaching contains little of damnation, little of the terror of hell. And though I have meditated question, I feared that you would think me critical or presumptuous. Do you never feel that you may, in that, be neglecting your duty to awaken the fear of God in the careless? I do not ask by way of giving opinion. I earnestly desire to be taught of you . . . as I have reason daily to thank God, I daily am."

John's gravity was equal to his. He hesitated, as always fumbling in speech when he wished to say anything of particular importance.

"I used to feel it my duty," he began slowly, "particularly in the early days of my Christian experience. The sight, the realization of men posting every hour to eternity, careless, evil, blasphemous even as I had been — though far less so — how should this not be a burden to me? But I cannot say that I was blest with success among the very ones I sought most to influence, by pointing out their danger and the imminence of unexpected death. But Mr. Howard told me of his experience, as he wrestled to bring a condemned criminal to repentance. All his threats of judgment, all his warnings of hell left her unmoved, more sullen than before. Then, he said, he was impressed to tell her of God's love for her, His desire that she be reconciled to Him, the life and suffering of Christ on her behalf. She was at once interested, moved, then converted. She went to her sentence of transportation a changed soul. That story altered my whole attitude in preaching, for not only is it scriptural, but it is confirmed by my own experience. When I was hardened in my sin, I was again and again on the point of death and quite unaffected. Such threats as many preachers feel they must utter, I should have laughed to scorn. No, I am convinced that it is our concern to preach the gospel, and the gospel is Good News. More, I am convinced that love and fear, like sun and moon, are seldom seen together."

They had reached the rectory walk and Cowper, who had been pacing silently beside him, halted irresolutely. "Have you forgotten that you are coming to tea today? Mrs. Unwin and my Dear will be awaiting us."

William came out of his reverie with a sigh and, once the broad gracious door had welcomed them into the hospitable hall, regained his former cheer.

Cheer was the predominant note in temporals these days, thought John when, a few moments later, Mary entering with a covered muffin dish put an end to the sense of incompleteness which he always felt in a room devoid of her presence. While Cowper responded to her welcome with the shy eager courtesy which seemed to make all women yearn to wait on him, while she presided at the tea-table, and the talk flowed gently with ripples and eddies of laughter — for Mary Unwin was second only to his Mary in love of laughter, though more apt to join in than to provoke it — he stood on the hearth, his surface participation in the immediate no less acute because of the wave of retrospective gratitude which almost overwhelmed him.

The house itself: would he ever become accustomed to it?

the graceful front, the light and spacious rooms. His eyes roved lovingly the length of this, the great room, as large as the whole ground floor of his Liverpool cottage, with its two front windows giving a view of the church and distant meadows, the equally generous fenestration at the back opening to his walled garden and the field stretching to Orchard Side. He would never have asked for such a rectory, luxurious and convenient beyond the usual appointment for a village parish, nor did its possession increase his sense of importance. Rather his whole fearful joy was rooted in the amazing grace which had provided him, the bare-foot, despised outcast of the Guinea coast, with such a home. To prevent any upsurge of pride, he had painted above the mantel of his study on the top floor:

"Since thou wast precious in my sight, thou hast been honourable. But: thou shalt remember that thou wast a bondman in the land of Egypt, and the Lord thy God redeemed thee."

And his friends: his gaze rested fondly upon these two — he did not include Mary for she was exclusive, the single inenarrable blessing, but on these close friends — who had come to epitomize all the others given to him: Cowper in his unconscious elegance of manner, his winning mixture of aristocratic ease, polite learning and grateful humility, Mrs. Unwin in her reposeful strength of character, her intelligent piety. The amazing and ludicrous grace which made them — and Mary, and Mary — turn naturally for spiritual leadership to him, the foul-tongued libertine, whose sleep and waking hours even at prayer were still periodically haunted by scenes and recollections which, if he could bring himself to clothe them in words, would puzzle, rather than horrify their incredulous ears!

His heavy lids hid a flash of amusement. Mr. Cowper had taken his large silver snuff-box from the velvet pocket of his jacket — Mrs. Unwin always brought his jacket when they were to have tea at the vicarage — and was performing his inevitable ritual, offering it first to Polly, who abhorred snuff, then to Mrs. Unwin who took it and applied it delicately to her nose. Then after a token move in John's direction, he took the sensuously exact pinch himself, with an air of exquisite unfailing enjoyment. How he detests my pipe, thought

John affectionately, and how it solaces his disappointment that I don't smoke it here or in the presence of ladies!

"The post left a packet of letters for you, John, and two for me," said Mary. "Sister Elizabeth writes that Jackie is growing almost visibly from hour to hour. Mamma says that Elizabeth cannot take her eyes from him for long! Georgie's wife has been to visit. But I forget." She turned to Mrs. Unwin. "These family matters cannot interest you."

"Indeed they do," protested Mrs. Unwin. "You show interest in my William and Susannah."

"Ah, but we *know* them. Now if Eliza fulfils her promise to bring Jackie to visit in the summer, I shall spare you no news, however tiresome, thereafter. I hope she comes while her James is absent. I know what it is to wait for a husband away at sea."

The husband in question would have responded at length had they been alone. As it was, he thought how lightly the years had dealt with her, how girlish her figure — compensation, doubtless, for the children which had been withheld from them. Mrs. Unwin's fine oval face with its delicately arched brows and high-bridged nose, her queenly figure with the white lace fichu folded across the bosom of her full-skirted black gown, emphasized his Dear's vivacious charm.

"My other letter was from Thomas Jones," she continued. "He tells me how great blessing he received on his last visit and what source of strength your *Six Discourses* and *Omicron* have been to him and his friends in Oxford. I shall make you read his letter, John, for he says that if he wrote to you half as warmly of all you have done for him, you would disclaim all the praise and accuse him of exaggeration."

"That is true," murmured Cowper. "Any attempt to voice appreciation gets no encouragement from our humble friend here."

"Nonsense!" retorted John. "How little you know me! One such remark is enough to make me say, like the fly on the axle of a coach-wheel: 'My, what a dust I raise!' As for young Jones — he came to study Greek and Hebrew with me before going up to Oxford — he and his friends stand in need of encouragement, if the official resentment of their Methodistical activity should become more determined."

"Are they of Mr. Wesley's persuasion?" enquired Mrs. Unwin.

"One need never have heard of Mr. Wesley to be called Methodist," said John dryly. "It is a general term of opprobrium to cover all — Dissenters excepted — who preach and approve the doctrines of the gospel, and it operates with almost a magical force, the very sound of the word sufficient to fill the minds of many with prejudices against the truth. These young men are all aiming at Holy Orders. Yet, because they meet for prayer and Bible study, and sing hymns, there is such criticism and opposition that I much doubt if they will be ordained. And even if they are, not many such receive a benefice — unless, as in my own case, by private patronage."

"The Establishment has great cause to be grateful to Lord Dartmouth," said Mrs. Unwin.

"I have great cause," corrected John, gently, "though I feel he was but the instrument of God. For had his appointment come a week later, I should have been committed elsewhere. My talent and temper are best adapted to the Anglican Church, and I see a larger sphere of usefulness here. But I had strong leanings toward Dissent and had, as I was frank to tell the Bishop of Lincoln, some reserves regarding certain expressions in the Liturgy. Our Reformers, though they did great things, only made a beginning; the rubric tells us gravely that those who die in infancy may be saved, if baptized; I believe they may be and are saved, whether baptized or not; for I cannot think that the salvation of a soul depends upon a drunken minister who cannot be found to baptize a dying infant. However, I seem unable, without compromise, to adopt any system or party, and pray that I may live at peace with all — all who hold fast the Head."

"Even the Baptists," said Mary mischievously. Her persistent annoyance with that body because it regarded her adored husband as a "disobedient believer" was a recurrent theme of difference between them. "If you would keep yourself to yourself as they do, I should like it better," she had written recently, adding that he would not scold her because she was so far off and would forget it by the time she came home. Mr. Wesley's warm commendation of her husband had endeared him, even more than his nice courtesy to herself; she had friends among the Congregationalists, and her new brother-

314

in-law, Scottish James Cunningham, was a devout Presbyterian, "but," she had fired as her final shot, "I would much rather be a Methodist than a Baptist!" It was a never-ending topic of teasing that John, genuinely distressed at an attitude which he felt must both harm her and grieve the Lord, had concluded his affectionate remonstrance with unconscious assurance: "We must try to bear with each other upon this point until the Lord gives us to be of one mind about it, and *when He does, I think the change will be in you.*" But before others, even such dear friends as these had fast become, they never aired their few differences. So the challenge went untaken.

"With some Evangelicals we are suspect on this point too," said Cowper presently, as Mrs. Unwin took her seat at the harpsichord and the others gathered round her for the hymns which introduced their informal family prayers. "Cousin Martin has suffered severe rebuke on occasion for his composition of hymns and his inclusion of Mr. Charles Wesley's and others at the Lock services. 'God does not bless the singing of human compositions in His Church,' Mr. Romaine told him."

"There, as in his espousing of Hutchinsonianism, I believe Mr. Romaine to have the wrong of it, though I revere the man himself. Scripture speaks otherwise. Even if we grant the psalms and hymns enjoined by St. Paul to refer to Old Testament verses, the spiritual songs must surely have been current composition. And experience confirms Scripture, for I have been greatly blessed by such singing at worship."

"I too." Cowper's face lighted as with incandescence. "Sometimes while I sing, a sudden light surprises me, like a season of clear shining after rain."

John started.

"That is poetry in prose. I wonder—"

"Yes?" said Cowper as he hesitated. The two Marys waited, Mrs. Unwin's hand arrested as she turned the pages of the well-worn book of Dr. Watts's hymns.

"I have a scheme very dear to my heart, but one that I am not capable of compassing alone: to compose hymns, Scriptural and experiential, not perhaps for the Lord's Day services but to enforce the theme of my talk or sermon on week-days. I have conceived the hope that it might be a joint understaking, and at some future date be published. Placed beside yours, much of my verse is doggerel —"

"John, I won't have you say that," cried Mary. "You've written verses to *me*. Doggerel indeed!"

"Not *all* my verse, my Dearest. But I know when I have met a master." He was watching his friend's mobile face anxiously, trying to read the success of his project. He had spoken sincerely; but at least half his interest in Cowper's cooperation was the hope that such creative exercise might benefit a mind which was still an occasional prey to melancholy.

"My idea in part," he continued tentatively, "is that we go through the Scriptures, composing a hymn to paraphrase or spiritualize whatever verses seize our imagination. Then for special seasons and functions, for our children's meetings —"

Sir Cowper's meditative face cleared in its peculiarly candid smile.

"By the grace of God, I shall try. 'Hymns by an unknown writer in collaboration with John Newton, well-known author of *An Authentic Narrative, Six Discourses, Review of Ecclesiastical History* —' "

"Not yet finished *or* published," interrupted John. "What shall we sing now? My Dear, will you choose?"

31

SIR, Mr. Newton, Sir." It was Phoebe's voice, breathless as always when she forced her plump, middle-aged body to run up the stairs, but urgent with excitement and distress.

John had been lying in comfortable somnolence, feeling slightly guilty of self-indulgence in sleeping past seven and thereby losing the early morning hours which John Wesley still, and he once had, devoted to prayer. On this occasion, as on many, his conscience had been mollified by the consideration that Mary, who had for some weeks laboured under one of her unclassified periods of illness, had suffered a restless night and was now sleeping soundly against his shoulder. He tried to draw his arm gently from beneath her, but her eyes opened even as he moved.

"Is anything wrong? Somebody called."

"Mr. Newton, Sir. I'm sorry to wake you, but it's Mrs. Unwin's Lottie. She says will you please to come presently to Orchard Side. The poor squire's taken very bad."

"Mr. Cowper!" cried Mary as John began to dress with haste. "I've felt something hanging over him of late. I know that he has been under a cloud since his brother died, but this has been deeper and gloomier. Shall I come with you?"

"No. I'll return as quickly as I can. Judith will bring up your tea. Take care of yourself, Precious. I grieve over Sir Cowper but everything hinges on you. I'm as much a child in all that concerns you as ever I was."

He stopped to tuck the coverlet under her feet, for the

January morning was cold, and bent for the kiss without which he never left her. Then he was gone.

Almost two hours later he returned, coming as he had sped by the well-worn path through the gardens and across Guinea field. Mary, who had kept watch at the great back window, met him at the door, question arrested on her lips at the bewildered grief of his face. She untied his muffler and unfastened his old seaman's jacket when he showed no disposition to remove them; then drew him to the dining-room fire where the servants set out his delayed breakfast. Not until he had drunk the coffee she poured for him and eaten a toast, was the silence broken by more than the eliptical, homely, soothing phrases of a wife, proving herself a helpmeet with woman's simple faith in the efficacy of food.

"Tell me, John," she said at last; then, when he twice opened his mouth to speak and fell silent, she left her chair and came to his knee. "Don't try to spare me. I'll find out sooner or later. O my Pretty Dear, you look so unked, as Phoebe would say."

"Poor William!" It was seldom that, even with the warm affection and daily intercourse of six years, she had heard her husband use "Sir Cowper's" first name. "I am glad you did not come, Polly. He had tried to do away with himself. She — Mrs. Unwin — heard him fall and rushed into his room in time. By the dispensation of Providence, he had not bolted his door. And the knife had slipped so that there was only a flesh-wound. But his rage and despair are horrid to behold. He is convinced that God has finally rejected him. I said little and might better have said nothing. But I dared not leave until he was calmer. And so he became a few minutes since. And full of apology for being a trouble — like himself, yet pathetically like a child."

"How *can* he think that?" asked Mary, her attention focussed on one sentence of her husband's statement. "If ever a man loved God — except you of course, but you will not admit the exception — it is he. Think of his conversation. Think of his hymns.

> 'Tis joy enough, my All in all,
> At thy dear feet to lie;

318

or
*'One view of Jesus as he is
Will strike all sin for ever dead'."*

"I know. I know! Many times I could have coveted the
depth of his thought, the facility and grace of his composition."
Mary, who thought that only a few of Cowper's hymns could
match, much less excel her John's, knew the genuineness of
his humility too well to begin an argument. "And when he
prays, in spite of the trepidation he tells me he feels beforehand, he speaks as if he sees the Lord face to face. It is a
terrible and mysterious dispensation, Dearest. Yet we dare not
doubt that the Lord will work in it for his good."

"Poor Mrs. Unwin! She was looking forward to their marriage. Somehow — John, am I mistaken? — I never felt that
he was."

John did not immediately reply. What he had jokingly said
to Polly almost six years before was still true, that to live
under the same roof with a woman as dear as Mary Unwin
was to William Cowper, in a relationship like marriage in every
way except in physical union, did not seem ordinary or even
possible to him. And though he by no means coveted the
quality or lack of it which made such a relationship satisfying
to his brilliant friend, he felt that Cowper's nature must
be finer and more spiritual than his own.

"I think it was more by way of concession to convention
— with Miss Susannah's marriage imminent."

"Not so imminent, Miss Unwin tells us, unless your Mr.
Powley can find a living. Has Lord Dartmouth mentioned him
lately?"

"No — but he has his curacy, and she cannot be quite penniless. I had not thought — surely he believes that the Lord will
provide?"

"Yes. He probably does," said Mary demurely. "But I think
he isn't sure that *what* the Lord will provide will be quite
sufficient for Miss Unwin."

John, surprised into a shout of laughter, sobered quickly and
looked at her as she knelt, toasting-fork in hand, by the fire.
His expression, after almost twenty-three years of marriage,
made her feel still a bride.

319

"Precious, I've always thought that your greatest act of grace was in marrying me from sheer kindness and compassion. But every time I realize what you faced in the way of straitened circumstance, if not downright poverty and deprivation, I marvel how I succeeded at all."

"Oh," — she held the toast out to him on the fork and turned away from the fire, her face glowing — "it was your letters, I think."

"My letters?"

"Of course. You know perfectly well that writing is your forte. Mrs. Unwin said of you the other day that she never in her life knew one who seemed so much at a loss as you for expressing your feelings by word of mouth — out of the pulpit, that is. And though I couldn't agree entirely, for I've sometimes known you almost eloquent, I wanted to say to her: 'Ah, but you should see his letters!' And every time I was thoroughly exasperated, because you wouldn't or couldn't speak, I received a letter which spoke so beautifully that I couldn't bear to put away the possibility of receiving another!"

"So I won you by post?"

"Instead of the lottery prize you used to watch for —"

"My so much-to-be-preferred prize!" he said, drawing her up again to his knee. "But, my Dearest, here we — I am jesting when I should be praying for our friend . . . and casting about for other ways to help him."

"Has the doctor been called?"

"Yes. I doubt he will prescribe anything but bleeding. If this state continues, I shall ride to St. Albans and consult Dr. Cotton. I wonder if my electrical machine —" he stopped, catching Mary's eyes.

"You and your electrical machine — for everything from Phoebe's rheumatism to my migraine."

"It helped *my* rheumatism," said John stoutly. "And Mr. Wesley has reported some success in nervous cases."

"Dear, I'm just teasing. There is no harm in trying — if you can prevail upon him."

It was some months before he could be prevailed upon, and then the treatment was ineffective, as was the Olney physician's and later Dr. Cotton's prescriptions. The first alarm had taken place on January the second, and on January the third

320

John was again summoned to Orchard Side to prevail over a brief period of violence, which subsided just in time to let him go, shaken and confused, into his pulpit for morning worship. A few days later William consented, though indifferently, to accompany John on a walk; but the apathy of the one, and the concealed efforts of the other to win him from apathy, divested it and subsequent walks of pleasure.

So began the prolonged trial under which John, not yet forty-nine, for the first time felt the approach of age and a premonition of failing strength. . . . "Dear Sir Cowper's" state, second only to the health of each other, was the barometer of the Newtons' mental condition; and all their optional concerns were made subservient to their devotion to him and Mary Unwin. Public duties still had to be performed. Whether at home or by invitation abroad, John's rise to popularity and leadership among the minority of Anglican Evangelicals and his friendship with Dissenters assured him of five or six preaching engagements a week. His house had become a Mecca for his growing circle of religious acquaintance. The Vicarage was seldom without guests. Not only personal friends, the Thorntons and their relatives the Wilberforces, Mr. Brewer, Miss Manesty, but others, attracted by John's published letters and sermons, came to meet him, sit under his ministry and, sometimes, with their servants, stay for days or weeks. The number of correspondents, too, who wrote for help, advice and comfort was exhaustingly large.

But in the work of his parish he suffered a double disability. It must continue complicated by personal charities and dispensed philanthropy, individual visits, calls of the humble and not so humble poor who, having become slowly assured that their pastor cared for their temporal and spiritual needs, brought them to him with increasing frequency; and it must now be performed, not only without the eager aid of his Curate's curate, as William had styled himself, but with hours of his time and attention diverted to the help of his erstwhile helper.

So winter wore into spring; and with spring even the precarious occasional privacy of their home was violated. On the evening of the Spring Cattle Fair, which took place in Market Square opposite Orchard Side, Cowper declared himself unable to bear the noise, and begged refuge at the Vicarage. To the Vicarage accordingly on Easter Monday he and Mrs. Unwin moved. Miss Unwin had gone to visit her brother in Essex and protracted the visit when she heard of her mother's departure, although Mary wrote warmly, inviting her to share their hospitality. Perhaps it was fortunate that she found the atmosphere of her home, where everything centered around the invalid, depressing, for once William had settled at the Vicarage, he refused to depart. The situation had to be explained and many other visitors put off.

Mary thought it was characteristic of John — he thought of it as characteristic of Mary — that no amount of inconvenience, weariness or distress made them question the validity of Cowper's claim on them. His advent and Mary Unwin's had been, in John's words, productive of pleasure and good for them; to do everything in their power to help was axiomatic to their concept of friendship. Accordingly they took him for rides in a hired chaise and walks in his once-loved country. The two Marys, who shared Cowper's love of gardening, tried to interest him by asking his help and advice in their spring planting; while John, to whom a cowslip gave as much pleasure as his wife's auriculas or carnations, admired hugely and injudiciously whatever was done. As the periods of wildness became less frequent, periods in which he was convinced that everyone hated him and, though he would not let Mrs. Unwin out of his sight, was darkly suspicious that she was trying to poison him, John sought to revive his interest in reading and, failing that, in composition. He reminded him of the rhyming riddles which Mary, in particular, had loved to solve, and on one occasion delicately hinted that the work of their collaborated efforts was at a standstill. "God wants no hymns from the one He has rejected," said Cowper sternly.

Meanwhile the world, which seemed to stand at a melancholy twilight with their guest, went on with sunrise and sunset for others. John's first indication that the strain was telling on him was an almost complete failure of hearing, which for its week's duration debarred him from conversation. It vanished mercifully as it had come, without warning. Mrs. Catlett, whom Mary had visited every spring unless prevented by her husband's affairs or her own illness, had been failing perceptibly for some time. Every letter that came from Chatham without the fatal news brought a flurry of spirits in her daughter, from trepidation to almost tearful gaiety. Yet when the expected word arrived, Mary, who had been in the best of health, was immediately prostrated with torturing migraine, for which John could give her no relief except in the laudanum prescribed by her physician, which she heartily loathed and refused to take. The post which brought the news had been delayed, and by the time Mary was well enough to travel the funeral was over. Almost upon the heels of this came tidings of the death from consumption of Georgie's young wife. The double bereavement, the daily depression of Cowper's unsmiling company, and her determined suppression of her malaise before her guests, produced in Mary a series of ailments from feverish spasms to a mild case of shingles; and leeches applied to her leg resulted in serious though temporary lameness.

So when requests came in October for John to visit Warwickshire, and William Cowper's distress had softened into a settled but milder melancholy, John insisted that Mary accompany him, and for ten days of glorious fall weather their travels resembled at once a honeymoon and a triumphal tour; for John's preaching was heard with warmth and Mary basked in the glow of it. Not even to each other did they suggest that their elation was sheer relief. Sir Cowper and Mrs. Unwin were remembered in prayer several times each day. And when a message arrived that he had again become 'tumultuous and troublesome', both hurried home.

Mrs. Unwin met them at the door and, forgetting her usual serene reserve, sobbed with relief on Mary's shoulder.

"I had so hoped that I might not need to summon you. Mr. Cowper was for some days more open and communicative than since this dispensation came. Then suddenly he became another man. I could prevail nothing with him. He —"

"Did he —?" inquired John, as she broke off shuddering.

"He insisted that God required him to sacrifice himself — we were preventing God's will. The three of us could not hold his hand. By mercy, Mr. Barham arrived for the preaching in time to aid us. But he is angry with me. It is as if he waits his opportunity."

Thereafter, John and Mary decided, they must not leave

Olney together. Winter came with its enforced confinement. Daily fireside companionship which had once provided gay recreation from external pressure was now an additional strain, for Cowper, even at his nearest approach to normalcy, never smiled; if he made any comment on the parish talk it was as an outsider; and his sad but punctilious dissociation from family worship, singing, even grace at meals, had a dampening effect on the other three. When guests came he kept to his room and Mrs. Unwin waited on him there, afraid to leave him day or night in the inspissated gloom of his solitary imaginings.

The habitual absence of laughter altered the atmosphere of the familiar house so sensibly that John wondered how merriment which had been only occasional should effect such a change by its cessation. It was, he decided, not that William laughed so often, though his geniality had increased amazingly in the years of their fruitful association — those years which he had frequently called the happiest of his life — but that the calamity which had stilled his laughter had stifled their mirth in deference to it. Mrs. Unwin had no heart to laugh. His Mary, whose irrepressible cheerfulness was seldom submerged, after trying vainly to cheer Sir Cowper by some amusing anecdote and meeting with a sorrowful haunted glance, reserved her efforts for her husband. Even then they hushed themselves lest the invalid misinterpret the sound. "Come, dear Madam, stay with us awhile. My Dear will make you laugh a little for your health's sake," John had written Mrs. Plaice in the midst of her domestic sorrows. Now such willing therapy was suspended.

More than by anything else John was dismayed by William's obsession: his unshakeable determination that God had cast him off. His own faith was too deeply rooted to be swayed by the tempest of his friend's illusion, but of all the difficulties he had encountered, this was the hardest to reconcile with the sovereign grace of God. That there was a 'need be' for every apparent evil and affliction: this was essential to the nature of God as Scripture, illuminating life, had revealed it to him. In the larger scope of history and in the microcosmic histories of himself and his friends, he rejoiced at every post-eventum justification of this confidence. Where the puzzle was insolu-

324

ble he had been encouraged to await eternity for the apocalypse. Evil was the inevitable result of sin; or punishment was permitted in love for reproof, correction, guidance; or good was withheld that greater good ensue; but always there was acceptance for the repentant, discovery for the seeking, an open door for the humble knock. Yet here for no committed sin, here in spite of glad tremulous service, here compatible with unimpaired faith, continued belief, heart-broken love, was a fixed gulf, a closed door, an awful sense of eternal rejection. In his quieter moods Cowper would talk — talk freely — of God's love, of mankind's undeserved redemption by Christ Jesus, of the Calvinistic doctrines of particular election and perseverance which he had learned from Dr. Cotton and held far more positively than John. In vain did John reason against an unreasoning conviction, show evidences of God's love at work in the very nature and attitude of the one who believed himself hated, urge him to regard it as a physical ailment which would be removed with returning health. In vain. Cowper's insistence was fierce to the point of resentment; the dream of that fateful night had been revelation; the awful words: "Actum est de te. Periisti" were the words of God to his own soul. To refuse them would be rebellion. He had been elected by God, alone of men who loved Him, to be eternally and agonizingly damned.

The assumption, which John felt utterly dishonouring to the God he adored, was so painful that he seldom attempted to shake it unless some comment plunged him unwillingly into discussion. Religious controversy he now always avoided, both because of Mr. Self's determination to have the last word and because of his slowly reached persuasion that no good was so achieved. When, in spite of his love for Cowper and his almost unremitted distress, he discovered in himself twinges of exasperation, moments when he yearned to suggest that his friend's insistence on the uniqueness of his fate bordered on egotism, he repudiated the thoughts with shame. The Christmas Day alarm which precluded Christmas festivity, the New Year's which William approached with darkening dread as the anniversary of his visitation, the slow coming of spring which seemed to bring a faint lightening of the gloom, John sought to regard as precursors to the day when, in Mary's words, "the

Lord will shine upon poor Sir Cowper and then he will own that he has had rich amends".

Meanwhile he found some relief in writing. He had always turned to verse for amusement and Mary seldom passed an anniversary without a diffident tribute, 'a something', which he never dignified by the title of poem. Going up to his attic study early in April, to find out why he had not come down for tea, she discovered him, head in hands at his table. He looked up as she came over to him, his face, as she had often seen it, at peace after a long struggle.

"You shouldn't have climbed those stairs, Dearest," he said gently, and noticing that she was carrying letters stretched out his hand to take them. Then she saw that the paper in front of him was verse, written, crossed out, and emended in his fine careful hand.

"May I?"

He handed it to her without speaking and watched her reading. Before she had read a few lines, her tears could not be blinked away and when she finished, she put her arms around him as he sat and clasped his head almost fiercely against her breast, sobbing above him.

"Don't grieve so for him, my Dearest," he said earnestly.

"I don't. Or rather I do. But it's for you I'm crying," she protested, and pointing to the paper, "Are you going to show it to him?"

"I think not. Not now at any rate. It isn't finished and must be polished before anyone but my Dear sees it. If — no when — his madness is over, it will not be necessary. If it should persist I may let him see it. But it has cleared my mind a little. And I believe it to be as true as — as your existence, my Delight — the truest and greatest of all demonstrable facts to me."

She returned his embrace and looked again at the verse.

"Has it a title?"

"Not yet. What do you suggest?"

" 'The Meeting'? 'The Re-union'? I have it! 'The Supposed Meeting of Mr. Newton and Mr. Cowper in Heaven'!"

"No — of Cowper and Newton," he corrected, and inserted her last suggestion above the lines:

My friend, my friend! And have we met again
Far from the home of woe, the home of men?
And hast thou taken thy glad harp once more
Twined with far lovelier wreaths than e'er before?
And is thy strain more joyous and more loud
While circle round thee Heaven's attentive crowd?

O let thy memory wake! I told thee so!
I told thee this would end thy night of woe.
I told thee that thy God would bring thee here,
And God's own hand would wipe away thy tear,
While I should claim a mansion by thy side.
I told thee so — for our Emmanuel died.

. . . Did I not turn
From brighter scenes these mysteries to learn?
When thou didst mourn the loss of heavenly grace
And deemed that God had turned away his face.

That could not be! His oath was firmly taken:
"My people shall not, can not be forsaken.
Their earthly sorrows make them doubt my love.
They will not doubt it in my Heaven above."

"I don't know anyone else who can say: 'I told you so' as nicely," said Mary a little tremulously. "Look, John, I brought the post up when you didn't come because I don't like opening letters from home unless you are with me. Let us read them here."

They opened the one postmarked Rochester and read it together.

"So Elizabeth is going at last. I knew it would come."

"Scotland is not Guinea, Precious. And Mr. Cunningham has waited long and patiently for this appointment which will clear him of the sea. On May the second they sail, does it say?"

"Yes, but Father is unwell too. I feel that I must go when he is express in saying that he wishes to see me. This parting from Betsey and the children will be a sore wrench so soon after . . . and though Auntie Soans is there I feel that something is wrong with Georgie. Since Sarah died his whole disposition seems altered. Perhaps I could have some influence over him. He was always fond of me. But I hate to leave you — never more than now."

"Of course, you must go. As for me, I shall manage. I am never quite the thing without you, as you well know. But the Lord will care for us both."

"And give us a happy meeting," murmured Mary. "John, if — if they were back at Orchard Side you could come with me."

"But they aren't, Dear. And you heard Mr. Cowper when Mrs. Unwin suggested leaving before Miss Unwin's wedding. It was pitiful to hear him weep and beg to be allowed to stay. I am thankful *that* event is over before you are called away."

"Mrs. Unwin feels keenly the drain on your purse, John. She has repeatedly asked me to beg you —"

"Dearest, I cannot, I will not take payment for hospitality. The Lord has seen fit to give him a comparative feeling of safety in our house and He —"

"I'm not arguing, my pretty Dear! She made me promise to speak to you and I have. Your other letter is from Mr. Thornton. That is sure to be pleasant," she added, for the remittance in many a letter from Mr. Thornton had come just when her confidence in John's favourite saying: 'The Lord will provide' was wearing thin.

Her husband, who had recently had a conversation with his benefactor which he had not seen fit to mention to her, was not quite so sure. And a swift perusal of this friendly, but positive epistle justified his prognosis. John Thornton had at last taken upon himself the distasteful task of voicing the wide-spread criticism of the unconventional Cowper-Unwin menage. Briefly, and obviously desiring that the Newtons should not share the censure, he spoke of William Unwin's distress and the new Mrs. Powley's embarrassment regarding their mother. Comment, being whispered, he remarked, was well circulated and all shared his opinion that the situation should not continue.

"If they will not leave the Vicarage we should move to Orchard Side!" repeated Mary, aghast. " 'If Mr. Cowper was a woman Mrs. Unwin would not attend him as she does. All appearances of decency are sacrificed.' John, that isn't true. And if it is, what can we do about it?"

"Nothing," said John, so unhesitatingly that she looked at him in surprise. He laid his cheek against hers.

"Would you do anything, Polly, other than we are doing?"

"No, but I thought you would dislike to disappoint Mr. Thornton."

"Mr. Thornton will be reasonable. He knows that I would disregard no suggestion of his except for the sake of principle. Remember the Cottenham affair."

Mary did, and for that very reason wondered at her husband's assurance. Cottenham was one of the Newtons' anniversaries. John had not remained a curate in Olney for lack of better opportunities. He was scarcely settled — in fact Mary had not yet joined him — when Mr. Soans had offered him the living of Hampstead, a little village north of London which he had, to Jack Catlett's annoyance and her mother's sorrow, felt compelled to refuse. Several years later, Lord Dartmouth had offered him the presidency of his new college in Georgia, together with the living of Savannah. This John had earnestly weighed, trying to keep a balance between the opportunity to do the work of God and the inducement of honour and profit. But his ministry among the poor Olney lace-makers constrained him, and Mary detested the sea; so he refused. The next offer of the Cottenham living was less easy to reject. Mr. Thornton, having busied himself to procure it, would hear of no objection and only Lord Dartmouth's intercession extricated John from the most difficult of predicaments: refusing to accept a benefactor's benefaction. But when he thought of the need at Olney he had not hesitated to offer opposition to his millionaire patron. Nor did he now.

"Even if he should prove otherwise," he continued simply, "I cannot either try to separate them or follow his counsel. First, I think Mrs. Unwin's attention vital to Mr. Cowper. No man could ask for such devotion but, since she gives it, I dare not deny it to him. Secondly, we, more than any, are in the position to know the true state of affairs. To dismiss them or to depart ourselves would be equally a tacit denial of the innocent relationship which exists between them. How could we live with ourselves if we betrayed them so?"

But the weeks of Mary's absence at Chatham he found sorely trying. Her management of the house and of him — so complete that he did not even buy his own stockings — when removed, left a dozen decisions a day devolving on him and he marvelled anew at the way money flew, despite Peggy's conscientious attempt to keep accounts. Callers from near and farther often required a room for the night. Although all were deeply sympathetic with Mr. Cowper, and heartfelt prayers went up for him throughout the town — he wrote to Mary of another prayer-group which planned meetings in the cottages of several earnest men and women — he had been rendered sensitive by Thornton's letter to a score of remarks made or reported to him. The criticism was not always levelled against Cowper's domestic situation, though ribald remarks had often been made by the cruder sort; for William's strong, well-proportioned frame, his former pleasure in swimming, riding and walking and Mrs. Unwin's mature grace and beauty did not readily suggest a platonic or maternal-filial affection. Other talk was abroad which John was less able to refute. His successful ministry, as he well knew, was still a minority ministry and had stirred deep resentment and opposition in the polite worldly Conformists, the irreconcileable schismatics, and the openly lawless, irreligious elements of Olney. The Church might be full on Sunday both morning and evening. Its bell-ringers withstood their parson's efforts at reform and were frequently drunk in the performance of their duty. The Sunday night meeting at the Great House might be crowded to capacity. Raucous shouting and singing of riotous young people, while a girl's body was being carried to burial, forced John to halt and rebuke them — a rebuke repeated in mimicry as soon as the procession recommenced its sorrowful way. People of all classes and ages might apply to the Olney curate for assistance and advice; his published letters and sermons had already gone into several editions and were being read in far-off, trouble-torn America. Unruly children at home, whose families were helped by his charity, defied his efforts to instruct them, and imitated their elders in calling 'Methodist' after the youngsters who responded. The town as a whole had taken some pride in the minister who, with unclerical garb, sea-faring experience, and assiduous devotion, had made Olney a centre of religious attraction. But after ten years the novelty had worn off, and resentment at his uncompromising sermons made his detractors seize eagerly on Cowper's illness to justify their opposition. That he preached people mad, that

Cowper's collapse was the natural results of 'enthusiasm', that the gentleman himself had been harried against his will into a round of religious duty; this was tea-table talk among the well-to-do farmers and gentry who had resented 'The Squire's' indifference to their social life.

The facts so completely contradicted this explanation that John regarded the unfavourable light in which he was placed as part of the 'evil report' through which all who would live godly in Christ Jesus had to pass. He was given strength to perform his public duties with some liberty and warmth. But his 'evil heart of unbelief' under which, he told Mary, he expected to go mourning to the grave — told her in letters, for he still was often more tongue-tied in speaking to her about spiritual things than to anyone else — made him fear that the criticism might have some effect upon her. It was the same charge of enthusiasm which Jack and Georgie had made years before. Years before, it had been the subject of the one criticism which she had allowed herself to voice; and though his answer had silenced her, the objection recurred to him sometimes.

"John, I don't want to be presumptuous," she had said, returning from a visit with her brother Jack in London, "but do you think you gain by putting some reference to — to Jesus in every letter? I mean, may it not do more harm than good? Jack knows what you believe."

He had looked at her silently for a lengthy moment, feeling a return of the clumsiness, the owlish gravity, which had reduced him to speechlessness in front of her during his courtship. Polly, seeing his expression, had come and snuggled her head against him to take the sting from her words. But she had not retracted them.

"You may be right," he had admitted slowly. "I know, of course, that you are thinking of Jack and that you want him to admire me as he used, as he still might if I did not add a religious postscript. Polly dearest, I *must* do as I do. Only too easily am I drawn aside, and in conversation I am too often prevented from seizing any opportunity of testifying to the Lord's grace. Perhaps it seems monotonous, even redundant. But we never know when the Name of Jesus will take effect. And I cannot forget that once I blasphemed that Name in

331

every speech I uttered — nor feared to be thought monotonous. The least I can do is to speak well of it as often."

And perhaps, he meditated now, the Name had wrought on Jack, though no word to him had revealed it. There was only the garbled story to which Polly and he clung, the unexpected tale of Jack's weeping landlady, that "the gentleman" had asked her, two nights before his death, to find a Bible and read to him; that, and his last ambiguous message to his family that it was "all well" with him.

He turned off the Newport Road and followed the meadow path to Mr. Wiggin's home where he was breakfasting. Not till the friendly, leisurely breakfast was over, and he had taken his leave, lifted in spirit by the prayers which they had shared, did he return to his consideration of her spiritual state. It was an enigma which he found baffling, usually when she was away. One moment of her gloriously reassuring presence, one embrace of her unfailingly responsive arms, one charming shake of that pretty head — ridiculous that she could be forty-five! — and his gnawing worries on her behalf, and briefly on all other counts too, would disappear. But he wished — he assembled his straying thoughts long enough to turn the wish into a prayer — that she had a steady assurance of her salvation, an abiding, fear-removing conviction of her acceptance with God.

I have no doubt of it, he thought, his spirits responding perceptibly to the wayward gleams of April sunshine from a noncommittal sky. But I may be prejudiced, in spite of adoring the inscrutability of God's electing grace, into feeling that He cannot fail to think Polly as lovely as I do. God forgive me if I blaspheme! At times she seems sure. When she had that bad attack of fever in '66 something took place in her heart, I know. She had quite suddenly a calm and a cheer, a fearlessness of death — not just assumed to spare me, as she has often tried to do — and a liberty in prayer that I never knew in her before.

He mounted the stile, then changed his mind and straddled it, giving himself up to the sights and sounds of a day which had finally decided to be May instead of April. Young lambs were calling their mothers in the field beside him; a medley of bird song from the distant spinney was so mingled that he could not distinguish the several calls. A return to the Vicarage meant the accentuation of Mary's absence, the re-assumption of his burden of distress and warfare for his friend. Here, briefly, in the healing countryside he could give thanks, as he did on every remembrance of his Dear, and gain assurance that his intercession for her was accepted.

"Each sweet Ebenezer I have in review," he murmured and realized that the words had fallen into his favourite metre. "Confirms His willingness — no His pleasure — His good pleasure
To see me — to help me, perhaps — quite through."

He jotted the words down in his note-book. The time he had spent in writing hymns had been largely pre-empted since Cowper's illness but he endeavoured to compose at least part of one each week, and used it as a theme for his informal talk at the special Sunday evening service, where it was first sung.

His thoughts returned to Mary and the superabundant indications of the Lord's special providence in designing her for him. Even when there was least evidence that she was willing to be his, he had been certain that she would make him the best of wives. But how far beyond any imagination she had proved. Yet to be what she had later become, the wife of a clergyman: that required still other qualities which the event had demonstrated her to possess. He marvelled again at her conduct from the beginning of his concern, through the chequered years of self-preparation, encouragement, and rebuff. Few if any of her sex, as he had told her gratefully, could equal it. To give up, after years of uncertainty, a genteel position in Liverpool society and risk the vicissitudes of a profession where worldly security was dependent upon patronage, to do this against her family's wish and advice, had required no persuasion. But though her admiration of him, her desire to see eye-to-eye with him in everything was a more precious amazement to him than the favour or approval of anyone else, she had still a mind of her own and a shrewd acute judgment. "I am always glad when I think as you do" she had written recently when their letters, crossing, gave evidence of their oneness on a casual topic. But she had *not* thought as he did and had persisted in her difference in face of one of his most powerful and pleading letters, when he had desired to abandon his attempts to gain ordination in the Established Church, and to begin preaching independently in Liverpool or to accept a call among the Dissenters. If he had seen no medium between grieving her and acting against the light of his conscience, she would have, he knew, complied and suffered in silence. But, lacking conclusive assurance, he had listened to her reasoned plea for a little more patience, though no other consideration would have prevailed with him.

He thought back further to the social gaiety, thoughtless if not entirely godless, of her youth and her environment. To what but to the grace of God working within her, could he attribute the readiness with which she had become mistress in Liverpool, then here, of a house where cards and dancing were eschewed, where the theatre went unvisited, where she attended a number of religious meetings for which there was scarcely a precedent in the kingdom. Nor was this interest assumed or compelled. In Chatham she was now attending several services each Sunday, and he had known her, unaccompanied by him, to hear five sermons among varied denominations in a week's stay in London. Her letters were full of frank, discerning comments which amused and informed him:

"Mr. Venn preached an hour and a half. He is a good preacher and seemed much alive but the people seemed weary at the length of the discourse."

(Ah, thought John, I'm glad I stick in the main to the old-fashioned hour-glass!)

"Mr. Stephens spoke very well on 'I will bear the indignation of the Lord'. There was bones and flesh, but I think there wanted life."

"The vicar, I believe, left the congregation as he found them, for there was a great deal wanting."

"I heard Mr. Romaine Sunday morning from Luke seven — a sweet discourse . . . had some plumb-cake in the chariot, so drove to Stepney and heard dear Mr. Brewer. He was very excellent. Wednesday evening I heard Mr. Elliot. I believe he preached the truth, but I did not much admire him, the fault was chiefly in my self I believe."

Then there was her whole-souled interest in the work at Olney, repaid by the loving concern of the people. Even in her absence they were not forgotten. "Would you offer to lend old Mrs. Andrews some money and make her promise, if she wants, to ask of you? You will know how to do it and do not mention my name. It came jump in my head the other night when I was in bed." What other wife would receive his host of expected and unannounced friends, taking the endless contrivances, the rapid alteration of plan, the adjustments in kitchen and pantry, with a gaiety and graciousness which gave no indication of the volatile nature of her spirits?

And surely the tranquillity with which she bore her disappointment of children was a work of grace. Not for years had she even spoken of it, but he was aware of a fleeting shadow over her sunniness when Elizabeth, only a year or so her junior, bore a son and two daughters, and when Georgie and his young wife had a little girl. Her natural outflowing love for children made her especially solicitous of these youngsters, and they eagerly anticipated her visits to Chatham and Rochester.

John knew that the love which his unbounded passion had awakened in her had grown to match his own. The knowledge gave him delight and unease. For when he was sure — almost sure — that his love was no longer idolatry and that he could — some day — endure the ultimate test of his faith with equanimity, a trifle like the delay of a coach, or his detention by an over-long service in a nearby village could cause his Dear to fall sobbing into his arms on his return. "I've been thinking what a poor creature I should be if the Lord (as He justly might) should take you from me. I've loved the creature more than the Creator. John, will He pardon this sin also?"

And John, whose sin had been described so accurately, could only hold her close and pray that they be spared to each other until they were given more grace. As for him — he had recently refused an invitation in Bedford, since to delay there would have meant absence from Olney on a post-day when he expected a letter from her. But whereas he recognized his excess as a net by which he was ensnared from the fulness of the Lord's blessing, an Achilles' heel vulnerable to constant darts of fear and pain, she regarded hers as an indication of unbelief and unworthiness.

335

Yet there was the little book which he had recently discovered, the book in which she had begun — and, like Polly, had presently ceased — to jot down texts of Scripture, prefacing them with a prayer such as he had never heard her utter, even in the most unfettered moments of their private devotions. But her next letter might contain the sort of strangled cry which sometimes she voiced, to his swift dismay, in the darkness of their room just when he thought her certainty complete. "Your hymn talks about hearts being harder than stone. Mine must be harder than the hardest or it would have been broken many times over! John if I were a child of God, would I not be sure of it, as you are?"

John sighed, swung his leg over the stile to resume his walk and glanced in dismay at a fray, almost a rent, in his breeches. So his next letter must request Mary to buy material for a new pair, as well as for the waist-coat which he should have for the sake of decency. His coat, he had realized when he put it on at Mr. Wiggins, was more nearly thread-bare than shabby. He would not ask for another now, or Polly would forego the new gown and bonnet which she craved and which he had urged her to buy in London. Mary's weakness for pretty clothes — weakness! he reproached himself for the word, thinking how resolutely she repressed it and how little it was indulged — was partly occasioned by the delight with which he saw her in them. He pictured to himself exactly how she would enter his study, move casually to the window, turn to straighten something on the mantel, and then, unable to dissimulate longer, pose in front of him with arms clasped behind the new headgear to show it and the dress off to the best advantage, or whirl about with a swish of the skirt and drop in a full curtsey at his feet: "D'you like it, John, d'you like it?".

Mary, Mary. He did not know when he had felt her absence more sorely. "How my eyes will delight to see you, my ears to hear you speak, my arms to enfold you," he repeated the words of yesterday's letter, as if she were within hearing. "You will be as welcome as on the happy night which first made you mine." That night! And the ever-increasing tenderness and unabated delight of their love since.

John shook himself from the shivering holy joy of the recollection and strode into Bridge Street. Dare he tell Sir Cowper Mr. Wiggins's anecdote of the runaway chaise? He was not as adept as Polly, who could turn a small incident into laughter by the delicate shade of her narration, and who saved every such to make him laugh. Perhaps, if he did not make his desire to amuse too obvious, he could bring a smile to that drawn, hollow-cheeked face. It was the very sort of tale in which he had once revelled.

His effort failed. His friend listened with remote courtesy and shook his head sombrely. "With His presence God has taken away all relish in mirth," he said.

It was not until May the twenty-first, some time after Mary's return, that John recorded the great event in his diary:

"To-day my dear friend smiled for the first time."

And a week later, with a mixture of emotion in which he hoped that joy at his friend's betterment completely outweighed any other feeling, he recorded:

"My dear friends Mrs. Unwin and Mr. Cowper, who have been our guests since ye 12 April last year, returned to their own home. This is a proof that he is in some respects better, for till very lately he could not bear the proposal of going home. The Lord has graciously interposed in this business. Reports and misconstructions have sometimes made me uneasy. My friends were willing to blame me. I endeavour'd to satisfy myself that, however chargeable with blame before the Lord in many respects, yet in this point my heart was upright in His sight. I could not relieve myself, but He has mercifully relieved me."

32

IN the world, wars and rumours of war. '74, '75, '76, '77. The firing of cannon in America re-echoed in an England as divided on the issue as the Colonies themselves. Her western dominion came apart in England's hands: Germans and French fought her battles in the New World; Spain and France threatened war in the Old. Statesman, philosopher and preacher, drawn into the national crisis, fulminated for and against their brothers overseas. And in the trail of war, economic distress cut fortunes from the rich and sank the poor deeper in their poverty.

In Olney the shattering events which were reshaping a hemisphere were discussed and regarded against the background of personal, poignant issues: summer and winter, spring and fall: a bitter winter with snow clogging the roads and stopping the stages; a damp spring with water lying on the meadows and flooding into cellars. Lace-makers from the youngest to the aged could scarcely make their purple hands thread the intricate maze of bobbins. Many of them, according to their pastor, "starve with cold even when abed". With prices high and the tale of lace low, a gang of men gathered outside the Bull, set upon and overturned a wagon loaded with flour. Putrid fever took more than its usual toll and together with consumption saw to it that families had to rear only a quarter of the children they produced.

On the whole Olney was no worse off than it had been, and better tended than most parishes in the kingdom. The hungry sheep looked up and were fed spiritually; their shepherd was also concerned with their material food. While he had money by him he was liberal; when that failed, he had no hesitation in applying for needy souls to his wealthy friends. In and out of dark, reeking cottages, where sometimes three funerals followed one another swiftly in one family, he went with what aid and consolation his compassion and not untried faith could proffer. Individual joys and problems, as well as sorrows, he took upon himself. Individual sins and the larger sins of mob violence and unruliness caused him twofold grief, both for victim and culprit.

At the Vicarage, against the steadily glowing background of unchanged love, many changes took place: young George Catlett's strange obsession of covetousness and fear ended in an early grave . . . John and Mary, disregarding her father's fears that his middle-aged children would not be able to understand a child, immediately adopted five-year-old Betsey, who became the pet of the household and of Orchard Side. . . . Mr. Catlett himself grew gravely ill and Mary, called to his side, found herself three wintry months away from John, enmeshed in the problems of persuading her father to come to Olney, of selling his business and her childhood home, making arrangement after frustrated arrangement to convey the sick man across three counties in the depth of winter. . . . Then John went up to London to have a tumour cut out of his thigh . . . on his return Mary, weighed down by this last pressure on long over-wrought emotions, collapsed and kept her room for a month with the most serious attack of her undiagnosable illness since they had come to Olney . . . nor did it entirely lift, but left her liable to seizures brought on by any extreme noise or unusual alarm. . . . Mr. Catlett, having survived his uprooting for a tranquil eighteen months, died in a state of happy faith, which had in his later years been increasing so that his children scarcely recalled the hard-headed Conformist, scrupulous of appearance and suspicious of John's Methodism. . . . Betsey was sent to school in Northampton. . . .

John's circle of influence and acquaintance grew, indifferently including all parties and denominations. Five publications had already made his name known and respected and detested as far as Holland and America . . . one of these, the *Review of Ecclesiastical History,* in spite of Cowper's preference for his style to that of Gibbon, he considered himself incapable of completing and produced unfinished . . . the hostile increased in hostility but the sincere found their hostility melting beneath his disinterested candour . . . a lifelong friendship was commenced with the Congregational minister of Newport Pagnell, Reverend William Bull, of whom Mary, who liked everyone to look up to her dearest John and saw no reason for John to look up to anyone, said: "I think Mr. Bull is your pope" . . . from a very different origin came his friendship with the unbelieving incumbent of Weston, Reverend Thomas Scott, whose contempt and dislike of John's views was unwillingly coupled with admiration of his pastoral faithfulness; for John had several times walked miles to visit a dying couple in Mr. Scott's parish, whom he had neglected. Failing in a deliberate attempt to involve John in theological dispute, he was much later driven secretly to seek his companionship and advanced under his instruction to conversion and to a powerful Evangelical ministry. . . .

With Orchard Side there was still almost daily intercourse. William's violence had not recurred and apart from his obsession — which he never forgot nor let his closest friends forget — his reason was clear and incisive. He smiled often if he seldom laughed: at Betsey, his Laughing Lady, for whom he made nonsense rhymes and child's furniture; at the antics of his two guinea pigs and later his three tame leverets; at Mary and Mrs. Unwin during their eager conferences about their respective gardens; and at John who lent him books — Cowper never bought any and owned no more than half a dozen — discussed news current in the political, social and literary world, and, while he waited for the cloud to lift from his friend's spirit, was glad of anything which took his interest. It was he, too, who encouraged the indifferent Cowper with suggestions for poems, and urged him to take up painting; he who made repeated efforts to break through his curtained life by enlarging his circle of acquaintance. . . .

In October of '77 the worst of Olney's frequent fires broke out a few hundred yards from the Vicarage and, had the night been windy, most of the thatched village would have been destroyed. The Newtons, who were in London, hurried home. John raised, largely among his London friends, a fund of two hundred pounds to help the families of the twelve demolished houses. The catastrophe was serious enough to alarm the thoughtful, and Newton thought that an opportunity for which he had waited had arrived.

"Should you not be wise to cancel the preaching service this evening?" asked Cowper, as John, pulling out his watch, waited for Mary to take that signal for leaving the Orchard Side tea-table.

"Because Thursday falls on Guy Fawkes' Day?" asked John, with rather forced surprise.

"You know how they celebrate in Olney," said Mrs. Unwin quietly. "The excitement has been growing all day."

"Yes." He knew. The year before, a drunken mob had raped a poor woman till she died on the street. Their milder pleasure was to roam the town, breaking windows in the houses where the regulation candle failed to show. "Especially for that reason I intend to hold the service, though in any case I should not feel justified in cancelling it for fear of man. But some of the weak of my flock may come who would otherwise be induced into the gin-shop. And the very service may act as a restraint. Besides, I carried out the wishes of Council in proclaiming on Sunday a ban on candles in the windows. And I think the recent fire has sobered them sufficiently to give heed."

If his wife and his friends thought him over-sanguine, they saw no point in discouragement. Attendance at the service was thinner than usual, but early darkness kept away those who came from neighbouring villages in the spring and summer, and doubtless prudence had restrained some of his regular parishioners. Besides — John faced the fact — the attendance at all his services, including the children's meetings, was not what it had been. Curiosity to see and hear him had brought many indifferent, in the early days of his ministry. Curiosity had kept them coming to see one change after the other and to gape at the strangers who crowded around their strange parson. But curiosity had been sated and replaced by resentment at the plainness of his preaching and at the consistent rebuke of his public life, so different from the negligent, fox-hunting parsons of many parishes.

Still it was a good service, and the streets, when the congregation dispersed from the church doors into the dark familiar ways, were still fairly quiet. John and Mary gathered the members of their menage, Sally and Peggy and Phoebe, and crossed Mill Road to the Vicarage.

Supper was almost over when John heard the first sounds, the first distant unmistakeable sounds of a gathering mob apparently emerging from the village's many public-houses. He raised his voice slightly and knew that he had given away his design, knew too that his wife had heard, by the swift response and the brighter than her usual brightness of voice. Their habit of family prayers furnished an excuse for music, and in the presence of her three maids Mary rose to the occasion, playing the harpsichord and kneeling composedly beside her chair. John, who had vigorous opinions about overlong prayers which he considered more blameable than overlong sermons — "a weariness of mind in prayer and the thought still returning: 'When will you have done?' is worse than unpleasant" — was sure that his fellow-worshippers were not wearied by this one. His petitions, punctuated by distant bursts of laughter more ominous than the shouting which followed, by unintelligible song, by crashes and thudding, voiced their fears to the Father, prayed for their misguided townsmen, thanked Him for past mercies, and placed themselves and other believers in His care.

The noise had dulled by the time they rose from their knees. The rioters had apparently swung to the far end of town on some nefarious errand. John, whose memory had reminded him that, with his natural propensities, he would have been a ring-leader in such mischief, smiled at the sober women.

"Sally, Phoebe, it's time for bed. You too, Peggy. My Dear, if you will go up I shall watch here for a while."

"Mr. Newton, Sir," said Phoebe, "mightn't you let I put a candle in the window — to be on the safe side as it might be?"

"They don't like you speaking against the candles, Sir," contributed Sally, "and that's a fact."

"Now how can I put a candle out when the Council decided against it?" asked John gently. "It has never been my practice and this year less than any other should I do it. Was that a knock?"

"Go to the door, Peggy," said Mary.

"I'll go myself," said John as Peggy hesitated; but when he

reached the hall doorway he saw that his wife was close behind him. "Why, Richard, what brings you here at this hour? Come in."

Richard Stamford removed his hat, came in, pulled his forelock to Mary, and burst into swift agitated speech.

"It's to warn you, Parson. They're coming here. 'Let's go for Vicar', they said. 'He'll put a candle in his window or pay for the smashing of them', they said. 'Lots of windows to smash at Vicarage', they said. They're worse'n I've ever seen 'em, Sir. Satan himself might be at their head only, God have mercy on him, it's Tom, my own half-brother. I'll help you, Parson, whatever you do."

The fighting blood which had staked his life against drunken mutineers and insurgent slaves coursed unexpectedly in John's veins. This time, he felt, more than physical life, more even than *her* life, was at stake. This mob of his own parish should not think that a man of God was afraid of them, he who talked about the Name of Jesus as able to drive away fear.

"I must go out to speak with them," he said.

"John, you won't!" She never called him John in front of servants and strangers. The omission indicated her intensity of feeling even more than the almost angry cry which did not sound like her voice at all.

He spoke reasonably.

"My Dear, I shall be in no danger. Individually these men know me and in some sense respect me."

"These aren't individuals. And they're drunk, mad with drink. John, if you love me, you won't go."

"Madam is right, Parson. These chaps are beside themselves. They'll do in a mob what they'll never believe next day."

"Are our friends at Orchard Side safe?"

"Orchard — oh, yes, Sir. I never heard mention of them. The Squire keeps himself to himself, you see, and they feel a bit queer about him, seeing he isn't quite — They'll be all right. Listen. They're coming this way now."

The scattered sounds were welded into a bar of sound — the sound of a steady roar coming nearer. They had crossed Market Square, John thought, and come into Bridge Street; they were nearing his corner.

"Mary." She was clinging to him and he dared not look at her, for he knew that those piteous eyes would shrivel his resolution. "The Lord will protect me. You have heard of the angry mobs Mr. Wesley has braved. You would not have your husband a coward?"

"My head, my head," she cried suddenly and leaned heavily against him, shaking so violently that she would have fallen, if he had not caught her. "John, it will kill me if you go. Promise."

John carried her into the drawing room, praying silently. His eyes, as he laid her on the sofa, met Richard's.

"I came with a thought, Sir, if you'll take it. Tom, he won't hurt me, even if he does call me Methody and St. Dick. Now if you was to send me with a message like and a shilling, it'd buy his protection."

John's heart revolted. A soldier of the Cross buying protection from the enemy!

Mary had heard. She was lying quietly enough, but he knew her state by the long shuddering which shook her and by the knuckles of her small hand which she held to her mouth, biting to counteract the pain in her head. Her voice was a sob.

"John, for my sake, for my sake, please."

Down the street there was a call of "Parson's next", a wild shout of laughter at some indistinguishable remark, and the beginning of a hymn tune, raucously bellowed. Moaning, she flung one arm over her face and groped blindly for John with her other hand. Richard Stamford nodded.

"I'd do as she says, Sir. It'd really be best." Then, with a touch of inspiration, "You'd not like them to do something they'd be transported for may be — or worse?"

John capitulated. The money changed hands.

"You are sure you'll come to no harm? What shall I say to them?"

"I'll think up a word, Parson. Just leave it to me."

He was gone. Sally had flown to bring sal volatile to her mistress but, as if at a signal, all movement was arrested, and they waited, silent in the silent room, for the message of noise without. The hymn tune, a bit uncertain, a bit defiant, with parodied words blurred in drunken delivery, moved un-

344

steadily nearer. John, with ears which had heard many mobs, estimated the crowd at fifty. His other senses were numb. Even when the noisy approach was halted, when voices were raised in question and explanation, when a single voice, obviously Tom Stamford's, called: "Cole's: all to Cole's," and apparently emphasized his leadership by dealing a crushing blow to one or two who complained bitterly at being diverted from the parson to the constable; even when comparative silence surged back into the street and the room became noisy with the maids' relieved weeping; even when Mary's hand pressed his in trembling gratitude, his resident feeling was soreness of heart, shame as at an opportunity unavoidably fumbled.

33

S T. Mary Woolnoth and St. Mary Woolchurch-Haw, the parish church of the Lord Mayor." John raised his eyes from Mr. Thornton's letter, and Mary, who had been listening with rising excitement, saw the 'Africa look' in his far-away gaze. "Such a settlement at my time of life might be desirable but — Dear, what do you say?"

She rose from the bench and came over to him. In the walled Vicarage garden, her garden, September sunshine deepened the enchanted summer silence. John's eyes, returning in time and place, travelled lovingly from the flower beds, the house, the little gate through which they walked to Orchard Side to the dreaming, cloud-sailed sky above the water meadows. She slipped her arm through his in a gesture of unconscious symbolism and said nothing.

"I love this people," he said as if to himself and therefore to her. "I have wished and prayed to live and die here. If other thoughts of late have sometimes occurred, they have been transient and involuntary. May the Lord not let me be deceived in thinking this *His* call. I can so easily be pleased by being thought Somebody — hateful!"

Mary raised her head and stopped him with a reproving kiss.

"You did not deceive yourself when called to Hull — or to Halifax."

John smiled wryly.

"Perhaps I did, in a different way. I could not but notice, when I stated my apprehension of being removed to Hull, that, though those who prayed prayed affectionately for me, they

346

did not put up one direct petition for my continuance. And that was two years since. There was enough rejoicing when the scheme fell through to be reassuring. But the work declines around me. Consider how the number of children has dropped off, how thin the attendance at the Great House and at the Thursday lectures."

"John, you have never had so many write you or express gratitude for your works and letters."

"But my work at Olney, Sweet. I have buried the old crop and there are not enough of the new to make up. Perhaps I have erred in over-gentleness, perhaps in over-familiarity. I don't know."

"Shall we talk with Sir Cowper and Mrs. Unwin?"

It was an odd conference, John thought a few minutes later, as the sitting-room at Orchard Side, where they had fore-gathered in every state of emotion from merriment to bleak distress, saw them now in earnest discussion of their projected separation. Cowper they had found in his garden and his pleated linen cap, usually neat and precise, was pushed back over one ear. Mrs. Unwin, disproportionately worn by her constant vigilance, was composed and selfless as ever. But the centre of interest had shifted for both of them to the invalid and his state of mind; so their consideration was disinterested and therefore valuable — as it could not have been ten years earlier.

"Our loss will be deeply and sensibly felt," said Mrs. Unwin sincerely. "Yet I should not feel justified in urging you to refuse what seems a position of honour and service."

"Were I able to benefit by your ministry as in happier days," said Cowper, "I could be selfish to beg you to stay. Nor do I doubt that some who fail to realize their blessing in you today will be awakened to it when you go. Perhaps they can be awakened in no other way."

"I should wish above all things that Mr. Scott might succeed me." They were John's first words. In the soreness of his heart at the possibility of leaving his dear flock to a careless shepherd he had almost forgotten the waywardness of the sheep. "He has already got before me in the gospel and could perhaps, being new to them, effect where I have failed."

"John —" protested Mary.

"But how can we not believe that God has called you to this?" said William earnestly. "In all the Establishment in London there are not more than two Evangelicals — in fact Martin and Mr. Romaine are the only two I know."

"You must not talk of failure, Mr. Newton," said Mrs. Unwin seriously. "No man has served more faithfully and your service has borne much fruit. I have cause to thank God daily for your ministry, as well as for your unfailing kindness —"

"And I, before the door was bolted against me," said Cowper, and the veil, suddenly drawn over his face, brought the conversation to a close.

"What shall you do, John dearest?" asked Mary, when their silent stroll across Guinea field (John paid a guinea a year to keep it as a throughfare between the Vicarage and Orchard Side) had brought them almost back to their own garden.

He stopped and looked wistfully across the fields beyond the mill.

"If I were to choose for myself, London is the last situation I desire." Mary knew that the statement was sincere. "I am glad to visit it, and always most glad to come away. Nor would I have anything of pique affect my decision. What does my counsellor say?"

"You always tell me that I must not let my partiality influence me," she began gravely, though a quick glance up at him was a reminder of the many occasions on which his rebuke had been disregarded. "So I must not speak of being angry that the Olney people do not value you as they should. I love it here. We have many friends. I prefer the country to London. But I think you may be used greatly of the Lord there. . . ."

"Don't mistake that the gospel will be received more readily in London than in Olney. I shall meet opposition there too."

"Then you must go or stay as you believe the Lord would have you. It's all one to me, as long as it does not mean separation from you. Perhaps in London we should have less of that. Oh, John, I feel very ungrateful when I think that you might have gone on for years making Guinea voyages, but I want us never to be separated again as we were that dreadful winter I was in Chatham, for months and months —"

She broke off, so near to tears that John, with more wit than tact, tried to divert her.

"Oh, come now, Polly," he said. "I recall one letter in which you suggested that you might stay till mid-summer. Surely you haven't forgotten!"

That she had not forgotten was evidenced by the scarlet face which she turned on him.

"John, how horrid of you to remind me! I thought you were too kind to mention that shameful letter of mine. You promised to forget."

"I know I did. And I have — almost. Forgive me," said John penitently, overcoming her half-hearted resistance and kissing the top of her head so that she would not see his amusement. They both knew that it was not in his power to forget that childish outburst of frantic exasperation, which had made him want at the same time to comfort his wife and shake her. Mary's letters, unlike his own purposeful screeds, were unpremeditated reflections of her mood. "I always write as I stand affected," she had expressed it candidly. And on this occasion, when John's repeated attempts to come to Chatham had been frustrated by a great snowstorm and when he had taken advantage of a friend's necessary journey to London to suggest that her father might come to the City alone, then travel to Olney in his care, her disappointment had vented itself in almost incoherent phrases:

"Your letter of Tuesday has put me quite in the dumps to think that I have been waiting all this time to get my Father sent to Olney that I may get the house clear and come after him and now . . . you say you must leave it to me or rather to the Lord to take care of us. I do not know that I dare undertake it, so then we may stay till Midsummer, for I cannot well spare Sally and I know not but I may be careless and stupid enough not to mind it. I am sometimes as if I cared about nothing (everything seems so contrary I wish I had never come). You have repeatedly said you would come and fetch him. I am very far from desiring you to undertake such a disagreeable journey. . . . The frost is very severe. I know not what to do tho my Father thinks he shall not mind the cold. He is watching my looks all the while I am writing. (I know the people want us gone, the man wants to sell the

349

goods. Nothing can be done till my Father is gone and no step can be taken towards it) . . . . I hope I shall say no more about fetching or carrying . . . perhaps we may meet sometime. May the good Lord keep *your* mind in perfect peace trusting in Him. Perhaps I make difficulty where there is none. Father, Aunt, Sally, all join in Duty and Love with your most affectionate wife

M. Newton."

And the pathetic postscript in which her usual self struggled towards the surface.

"You must not mind if I write peevish; perhaps I shall be better next time, but I meet with so many disappointments that I know not how to behave as I ought. If I could look to the Lord everything would be well."

Two days later the cloud had lifted.

"My own best Dear," the remorseful letter ran, "On Friday pen, ink, paper were all miserable and I worse than all. I looked around and could see no way to escape, thought I must be here always. Know not what I wrote but am ashamed of myself."

That was his adorable wife, capitulating unconditionally even when she had real cause for distress. She raised her head now and he knew that she had recovered her advantage.

"When did I write that letter?" she demanded. "When I had been almost ten weeks from you, of course. Doesn't that prove that I cannot be trusted away? Besides, is it quite fair to quote that letter and not my other? Wasn't it during the same period that I wrote: 'I should like to live together and die together and the Lord grant we spend an eternity together.' For without you, Dearest, I become very husband-sick, and the only good of that separation was to make me worship my Golden Image the more. So —" she ended half-tearfully before he could interrupt, "if separation is less likely in London, I hope you will be led to accept Mr. Thornton's offer."

If John sought a sign, the small company at the Great House for prayer meeting the following Tuesday seemed an indication that his influence, if not his usefulness at Olney had waned. He wrote a brief, grateful consent to John Thornton, and felt, when he sent it, that he had signed away his life. He wrote lightly to William Bull that he was on the point

350

of forming a connection for life with one Mary Woolnoth, a reputed London saint in Lombard Street, but he felt as he wrote, that the divorce from Olney would be painful. When the anti-Evangelicals in Parliament opposed Mr. Thornton's nominee and the appointment hung in the balance, he almost rejoiced. The matter was settled in his favour, and the weeping occasioned by his announcement of departure at the Thursday service wrung his heart.

It was well for both of them that matters moved swiftly. His formal farewell brought the largest attendance that the Great House had ever housed for his Tuesday meeting. All day they had called and by evening Mary's headache was violent and his own head ached with sympathy and strain. Scarcely one shook his hand who did not recall, sharp-etched and poignant, some name, some interview, some incident engraven on the records of his mind, perhaps inscribed with accompanying prayer in the pages of his diary: Mr. and Mrs. Robythen whose grief-stricken faces had kept him from "improving" the opportunity at the funeral of their elder son, who had died, old at twenty-five, from drink and dissipation, while his brother spent the very day of his death in an ale-house; Judith, their maid, whose marriage to a much older man he had at first opposed, later giving the wedding party at the Vicarage; Molly Mole at whose cottage the first Mole-Hill prayer-meeting had been established in the rich days of his middle ministry; little Eliza Asprey, who at eleven on her presumed death-bed, had expressed a comfortable hope in the Saviour and, being raised from it, was growing in grace; the Cooks, whom he had gone to comfort when their fourteen-year-old son was thrown under the wheels of an overturning cart and instantly killed, who had "often wished that something would bring him to their house" and had since found comfort in his ministry; Molly Mind, notorious even in Olney, who had dreamed a warning visitation from her dead father, ventured out to church, sent her current paramour packing, and was still evincing in herself the power which had cleansed Mary Magdalene; Tom Davis, brother of the Davis who had once been a professor, had backslidden and had finally been hanged for strangling young Anna Hughes who was with child by him; Cissy Jones, one of his converts, who had turned and sped down a side

351

street to avoid meeting him one day, . . . she had been running away to meet a soldier and had returned a week later, heart-broken and unwelcome in her father's house. . . . John had talked with the family, Mary and Mrs. Unwin had given her employment, and she was evidently reclaimed as well as grateful; Richard Stamford and William Clifton and John Nicholls, who were fighting a good fight against the pressure of steadily increasing, violent dissipation among the hardened young sinners of the streets; Elihu Knight, one of the obstreperous bell-ringers, who had taken his crippling, while drunk, by a descending bell as a warning; the Higgins, the Rabans, the Robinsons and others who had aided him and Mary with their loving help and hospitality.

John saw Mary into the Vicarage and walked in the starlit October night through the gate into the churchyard. He would return to Olney — there would be a farewell Sunday in the Church some weeks hence, before his final settlement in London; but this was the real end of his first pastorate which he had hoped and believed would be his only one, for he knew his call and talent to be that of a pastor and teacher, not of an itinerant evangelist. He wanted, he needed, to review the past before his Lord and to rededicate himself for the unknown future. His heart was burdened too for William Cowper, who believed that he had been providentially guided to his ministry, yet who was no longer advantaged by that ministry. How strange that the hymn-book, that memorial of their friendship, had arrived from London just before this removal, as if to perpetuate his connection with Olney: his Olney Hymns. Perhaps his absence, the letters which William had begged him to write, would be more valuable than his presence. Thank God, William Bull, whom he had introduced to his obstinately retiring friend, had made an instant bid for his confidence. "A man of letters and a genius though a Dissenter," Cowper had declared, and had welcomed Bull's promise of a weekly visit.

About to enter his church, he turned instead and found his way to the corner where he had buried his father-in-law. "I would give thanks for Thy mercy to him and to all those whom I have buried here who died in Thy faith and fear," he murmured. It was easier to keep his thoughts from straying if he prayed aloud. Would he ever reach the place of sanctification where he would not be plagued by wandering thoughts, by wild imaginations, even at the most solemn moments? "I ask Thine upbuilding power on all these sheep and lambs of Thine whom I am leaving. Lord, Thou knowest how I have failed Thee and them. Yet what a mercy that I am used at all! Not one corruption of my vile heart is dead, though some at times seem to sleep. But through Thine enabling I am given some liberty to preach, and strength not to disgrace my profession in my daily walk. My enemies see Thy standard over my door and dare not enter. If Thou shouldst leave me, they would make an end of me in a moment. What a wretch I am and what a God do I serve!"

The headstone glimmered in the starlight. He knew the inscription: George Catlett . . . of Chatham, Kent. Recollection flooded his mind: George Catlett questioning him about his non-existent prospects; George Catlett by the garden sundial, forbidding him the house; the months and wretched years that followed. John fell on his knees, his still aching head pressed against the cold stone. "O my Lord, how hast Thou dealt with me," he whispered. "I am a poor creature, once a slave in Africa, but Thou hast honoured me with many honours and art now about to place me in a still more important situation. O teach and enable me to abase myself. And do Thou provide for my poor people and sanctify this breach to them."

34

MARY, looking up at the great canopied pulpit almost immediately above her, thought how much more clearly she could see John's face than from the distance and against the east window light of Olney Church. So much smaller, so utterly different was the ponderous English baroque masterpiece of Wren's brilliant pupil, with its Corinthian pillars, its narrow gallery and centre clerestory. Mary, brought up in the dim Gothic distances of Chatham and Olney, felt that the bright blue, star-studded ceiling was almost irreligiously gay, but John, she knew, liked it. If he could have his way he would always worship under the open sky. Even now, at sixty, he walked in the pleasant country near their Hoxton home every day, unless the weather and the calls on his time absolutely prohibited. He would miss it, and their lovely garden, when they moved presently into the City. So would she, although she had neither time nor strength now to work in the garden or to walk with him as she always did — when she could.

Her eyes filled with quick tears. It was good to be out again, at church again for the first time since dear Eliza's funeral. John had, in spite of his love for the child, taken her death so much better than she; but then he *was* much better than she, for all his saying to the contrary. But though Eliza's life had been forfeit to consumption when she came to them two years before, her departure a question of time, yet the maturity of her mind, the almost surprised delight with which, coming from school to them as to strangers, she had returned their affection, had swiftly made a place for her in their hearts equal to that occupied by Betsey. Or almost equal — Mary's hand went out instinctively and rested on her dear child's arm. Next to John — such an immeasurable distance behind, but still next, in spite of or perhaps because of those faults, those tempers and moods, beside which Eliza's angelic tranquillity had showed in disconcerting contrast — she loved the niece who did not remember calling anyone else Mamma and whose childish shouts and tears and quick laughter had made her feel the mother which she had yearned to be.

Not that John did not feel Eliza's death; he did intensely. But his assurance of glory beyond the grave, his experience of the pain and distress and uncertainty of life, made a Christian's death to him in reality what it was to many only in theory. Her death alone he feared, as she well knew, praying daily to be delivered from that fear. And *his* death, her inability to survive him was her great fear, though she had felt of late, with a suspicion which so far avoided confirmation, that she was the one who would be spared that sorrow. But this latest death, her niece's death, apart from its proper grief, had swept her with the desolating thought that, of their entire happy family of her girlhood, she alone survived; not only was the Catlett line cut off, but only one of the second generation left. In four years death had claimed Elizabeth's husband, her son, her elder daughter, herself, and now so recently Eliza. Odd! At twenty she had hesitated to marry John because of her contentment in her family. Now at fifty-five she had lost them all, but because he was spared she was still happy.

Betsey's gloved hand had moved to clutch hers in grateful response to the caress, and presently Mary saw a tear fall upon the hymn-book on her lap. The child was like her, she thought, all feeling and impulse, as easily moved to laughter, but much more quickly depressed — and completely Catlett in appearance, pretty, where Eliza had been long-featured and beautiful, resembling her blond Scots father. Betsey had been secretly afraid that her cousin's coming would endanger the place which had been solely hers, jealous of Eliza's ease of manner, of the good impression which she made instantly on all strangers, while she herself swung between childish audacity and agonizing self-consciousness. The doomed girl's genuine sweetness had conquered her suspicion; the grief she felt at her death had been tempestuous and sincere. But after that grief-stricken October day six weeks ago, she had confessed the feelings which John and Mary had seen and tried by letter and attitude to nullify, and her conscience still reproached her with them.

Mary, whose shrewd critical mind was following every sentence of her husband's sermon, while recollection and emotion ran undisturbed and undisturbing beneath her surface attention, did not wonder that Betsey's conscience was stirred. That was her John's great gift: to stir the conscience of believers; his great wish: to break a hard heart and to heal a broken heart; but he did the latter more often than the former. Because his own conscience was never satisfied, she supposed, he challenged others; and woe to the comfortable, the self-assured, who listened to that kindly, honest voice tearing the veils of pride, self-righteousness, self-deception from his own heart and theirs. She was glad that she could hear this last of the fifty sermons he had preached on the text of Mr. Handel's *Messiah*. Polite society had been affronted, but the sermons had attracted an attentive, strangely mixed crowd — there was not even standing room today in the church — and John, regardless of criticism, had pursued his appointed design. It was *like* John, she thought happily, to turn people gently to the Scripture, while Mr. Romaine thundered denunciation, and dear Sir Cowper vented his disapproval in caustic verse. None of them had approved turning Westminster Abbey into a concert-hall for the commemorative production of Handel's Oratorio, the suspension of worship, so that thousands of careless dilettantes might admire and criticize the musical rendition and accompaniment of words which fell on unheeding ears. Mr. Cowper, who had become quite well known, now that John had launched him as an author by seeing to the publication of his first poems, had animadverted satirically upon it:

> Man praises man. Desert in arts or arms
> Wins public honour; and ten thousand sit
> Patiently present at a sacred song,
> Commemoration-mad; content to hear
> (O wonderful effect of music's power!)
> Messiah's eulogy for Handel's sake.

But John, never content to sting where he could hope to heal, had taken those pregnant texts which many lovers of the Oratorio disbelieved and most disregarded and brought the implications to their startled or wistful attention. He was concluding now. Long familiarity with his methods made her as sure as if he had given a signal. No — she was wrong. He was repeating, for those who had not been present at the early sermons delivered a year ago, the summary of his reasoned quarrel, not with the Oratorio but with the strange phenomenon of its popularity. His face, under the full formal wig which he now always wore, was all earnest absorption.

"I represent to myself a number of persons involved in one common charge of high-treason," he was saying. "They are already in a state of confinement but not yet brought to their trial. There is not the least doubt of their guilt being proved, but they are entirely regardless of their danger and wholly taken up with contriving amusements that they may pass away the term of their imprisonment with as much cheerfulness as possible. Among other resources they call in the assistance of music. They choose, amid a great variety of subjects, to make the solemnities of their impending trial, the character of their Judge, and the awful sentence to which they are exposed, the groundwork of a musical entertainment . . . their attention is chiefly fixed upon the skill of the composer in adapting the style of his music to the very solemn language and subject with which they are trifling. The King however, out of his great clemency and compassion prevents them with his goodness. Undesired by them, he sends them a gracious message. He assures them that he is unwilling they shall suffer. He points out a way in which their submission shall be accepted, and in this way he offers them a full and free pardon. But instead of taking a single step towards compliance with his goodness, they set his message likewise to music and this, together with a description of their present state and of the fearful doom awaiting them if they continue obstinate, is sung for their diversion to the sound of cornet, flute, harp, sackbut, psaltery, dulcimer and all kinds of instruments. Surely, if such a case could be found in real life, though I might admire the musical taste of these people, I should commiserate their insensibility."

The young man in the pew ahead stirred and leaned forward, intent on the words. His handsome face, even more — for she loved fine clothes — the not-quite-foppish elegance of his dress, had drawn her attention before the service commenced, though he had taken his seat unostentatiously.

"But is not this case more than a supposition? I should insult your understanding if I judged a long application necessary. My supposition *must* already have led your thoughts to the subject of the *Messiah* and to the spirit and temper of at least the greater part of the performers and of the audiences. Mr. Handel has been commemorated and praised in a place professedly devoted to the praise and worship of God. But alas! How few are disposed to praise and commemorate Messiah himself! The same truths, divested of the music, are heard by many admirers of the Oratorio with indifference, too often with contempt."

John leaned out over the pulpit. He had returned now to his concluding sermon.

"It is probable that those of my hearers who admire this Oratorio may think me harsh and singular in my opinion, that of our musical compositions this is the most improper for a public entertainment. But while it continues to be equally acceptable whether performed in a church or at a theatre, and while the greater part of the performers and of the audience are the same at both places, I can rate it no higher than as one of the many fashionable amusements which mark this age of dissipation. Though the subject be serious and solemn in the highest sense, yea for that very reason, yet if the far greater part of the people who frequent the Oratorio are evidently unaffected by the Redeemer's love and uninfluenced by his commands, I am afraid it is no better than a profanation of the name and truths of God, 'a crucifying the Son of God afresh.' You must judge for yourselves. If you think differently from me, you will act accordingly. Yet —"

His earnest appeal ended in a church as still as death. The young man in front was staring at him as though transfixed. It wasn't eloquence, Mary thought. He never played on the emotions, and in preaching largely extempore he avoided the balance and period which drew attention to composition rather than to matter. It was, she supposed, his directness, the fact that he knew the human heart, felt both what he said and what his hearers were thinking when he said it. Her John, her Golden Image . . . wonderful to know that he was being valued and loved, in spite of opposition . . . wonderful to see this attentive auditory. In Olney Church she had almost unconsciously checked off the townspeople who attended Sunday by Sunday. Here few of the hundred families of parishioners came at all regularly, but their place was filled with strangers of every sort and of every party. It had distressed John at first: the absence of the wealthy merchants whose tithes paid his stipend; the departure to other churches of those who resented his Methodism and innovations — how some of them disliked congregational singing! — the vexation of those who, arriving late, could not be accommodated in their customary pew, so that a church-warden had urged John not to let it be known when he was preaching. He had printed and sent to them that most gently reasoning document "A Token of Affection and Respect to the Parishioners", and some few had responded. But in general his congregation was as little parochial as John Wesley's at City Road Chapel. And, having delivered his soul, he was content, if not satisfied, to have it so.

They were singing now, her favourite of John's after-sermon hymns, his paraphrase of the conclusion of Hebrews:

> *"Now may He who from the dead*
> *Brought the Shepherd of the sheep,*
> *Jesus Christ, our King and Head,*
> *All our souls in safety keep."*

Mary and Betsey settled back in the pew after the Benediction while the church emptied into the chill December air, the unusual Sunday hush, of Poultry and Cornhill. John would come as soon as he could, but his vestry was usually crowded. Her eyes followed the broad-shouldered, gowned figure past the chancel with its great baldaquin behind the Communion table, the baldaquin which always reminded her of their four-poster bed. He had gained the south door leading to the Vestry.

The young man in front had not moved except to let other worshippers pass to the aisle. Head bowed, he remained apparently in devotion, but not too absorbed to watch his opportunity. When, according to Mary's reckoning, her husband would be disposing of his last consultant, he rose, slipped on the heavy dark cloak which seemed designed as a disguise, so little did it suit the richness of his wine velvet breeches, took his tall hat from beneath the seat and made his way, with rather affected casualness, to the south door.

"Nuncle," said Betsey as the hired coach rattled up Bishopsgate Street towards Hoxton Square. "Who was the dandy who called on you last, just before you came out?"

In John's momentary hesitation his wife felt embarrassment and was about to relieve it by a gentle rebuke, when he spoke:

"I am sorry I cannot tell you his name."

"Didn't he tell even you?" inquired Betsey.

John smiled.

"When I said I could not tell you, I meant just that. He desired me to keep his confidence."

"But you'll tell Mamma," said Betsey with the suggestion of petulance which Mary knew so well and always tried to prevent John from seeing.

"Euphrosyne!" said John, using William's pet name for her. "What would Sir Cowper say of his laughing lady now? Betsey, I shall make you a prophecy — no a promise. When you have lived as long as your mamma, have proved yourself a thousand times to be wise, discreet, helpful, worthy of confidence, as she has done since I knew her (and she was then younger than you), your husband, if he is the right one, will tell you things he can tell no one else . . . and if I am alive by that time, which is most unlikely, so shall I. Is that fair enough?"

Either Sir Cowper's name, or her uncle's gentleness, or a recollection of how Eliza would have behaved in like circumstance prevailed over Betsey's disappointment. She threw her arms around him and kissed him with the impulsive sweetness which was her usual reaction from any show of temper. Then she sighed.

"I'll *never* be like Eliza. I can't see that I become any better!"

"We don't want you to be like Eliza," said John, as Mary's eyes filled with tears. "We want you to be Betsey. And if you thought you were better it might not be a good sign. When we first enter the Divine life, we propose to grow rich; God's plan is to make us feel poor."

"Do you mean that the great saints were poor sinners?"

"They were poor saints, indeed, if they did not feel that they were great sinners."

"Then you must be a great saint — and Mamma too," said Betsey with sixteen-year-old logic, "because I've often heard you say what great sinners you are."

"I never said that was the sole criterion of the saint." John gave up the useless argument. "Only remember, my child, that if the Lord loves you, Satan owes you a grudge. He is always ready to fish in troubled waters and to assault believers under pressure of trials. But remember that he is a conquered enemy and cannot go an inch beyond the length of his chain."

In his study before dinner John gave Mary the letter which the young man had handed to him. It requested an opportunity for serious conversation, stressed rather nervously the need of privacy:

"I have had 10,000 doubts in myself whether or not I should discover myself to you," it stated; then with disarming simplicity, "but every argument against has its foundation in pride"; and it was signed in a bold, sensitive hand

"William Wilberforce."

"You talk of answers to prayer," said Mary. "His aunt has remembered that boy at least daily, since his people cut him off from her."

"Whether they actually cut him off or no, they have certainly done all they could to eradicate his early 'Methodism'. Apart from a comparatively decent and moral behaviour, rare in a young man of fortune, I should have said they had completely succeeded. The Thorntons were saying regretfully the last time his name came up — and with his friendship with Pitt and his influence in the House he is very much in the public eye — that he has no interest left in religion. Scarcely any wonder, surrounded and petted by everyone from the Royal family to the Archbishop of Canterbury. He gambles recklessly, sings well, has the gift of mimicry which can be a curse to its owner — as I have some reason to know — and is completely absorbed in politics and pleasure."

"But this letter," said Mary, putting a remindful finger on it.

"Ah, there the unpredictable Factor is at work. Dearest, I was not relaying gossip. And what they say at Clapham and

Wimbledon is said in sorrow, not in criticism. But let us pray for him, and pray too that I may be adequate in this interview.   For this young man as an instrument of God could reach a class and accomplish a work that no one else is circumstanced to do."

35

I WONDER, thought John, if with an infinite distinction this is how my Lord felt towards the rich young ruler, whom he loved at sight. William Wilberforce, seated across from him in the study at Charles Square, was unhappy and ill-at-ease; but his deportment in unease was composed and graceful enough to make another man look awkward, and his unhappiness gave a fine seriousness to the handsome features and the remarkable eyes. "Shrimp" might be his pet name to his burly Yorkshire constituents, but the perfect harmony of frame and limb made the body seem a norm, deviation from which in size or shape was fault. More, the voice was genuine in its beauty, the eyes straightforward in spite of reticence. John's heart warmed as he waited.

"I said I was restrained by pride," he began abruptly after the opening remarks. "The word 'evangelical' is an impolite one among my friends, as you are too well aware, and to consult one, even so honoured and revered as you, Sir, filled me with such repugnance that — well, pride 'o'erleaped itself and fell o' the other'. So I came."

"But why —?"

"Why to you? Or why at all?" Wilberforce's smile made his face quite wan when it faded. "To you, Sir, not certainly because you are a friend of my Methodistical aunt and uncle. Rather because my friend and tutor, Isaac Milner, has spoken highly of your honest and friendly dealings with him in a matter of religious doubt; spoken of you as a man of learning, but chiefly as one who knows the human heart and who is free from party or selfish spirit."

"I shall not contradict your friend's kind opinion to assume modesty," said John quickly. "God is my judge and he has a truer picture of me. But tell me — what you came to tell."

The story, so different from his own, had the same framework, though the lurid colours of his own sins and adventures were supplied in delicate pastels of peccadilloes and omissions. In both cases boyish piety had given place to unbelief. In both cases a constraining hand had been placed on an undesirous, contented sinner.

"I went with Mr. Milner on vacation to France. For want of anything more enlivening I picked up his copy of Doddridge's *Rise and Progress of Religion*. From our discussion of that we decided to read the Greek Testament together. And there begins my — misery."

He glanced at John as though he expected expostulation, but meeting his understanding unaffected gaze — as if it were a natural thing for him, the darling of the House, the playboy of London's most glittering social set, to be pouring out his heart to this queer original, this minister who had more private homes than Churches of the Establishment open to his preaching — he felt somehow comforted, and continued:

"It's hard to explain, Sir. It was dull work at first, but I had perforce to continue. Having heard it most of my life, I was unimpressed. Yet I knew that there was a word for me and I must find it. I came on Luke XI:13: 'If ye then being evil —' you know it, of course?"

Involuntarily John had moved at mention of the verse. A ghostly ship blown into ghostly seas by a capricious wind; a wretched, hungering, muttering, fearful crew; and another young man arrested and driven, fumbling through dark Scriptures in a cold dark cabin, till suddenly, like a key handed to him, these words had unlocked the door of his understanding.

"'God moves in a mysterious way'," he murmured and smiled at Wilberforce. "Yes, very well I have reason to know it. And then —"

Then had come conviction, repentance, good intentions, a return to England where everything was as before and none of his friends recognized, or expected, or saw any reason for change. Engagements filled his days from his daily breakfast with Pitt to prolonged evening parties for dancing, gaming, plays. An attempt at regular, early morning devotion resulted in a cold stupor at the time, and weariness later in the day. Renewing his church attendance, he found nothing to feed or stimulate his spirit.

"I've given up gambling, much to Gloucester's surprise because I've taken a small fortune from him. Great sacrifice," he told John with wry self-contempt. "My friends think I am dull because I had some talent for mimicry, which I put to no charitable use much to their delight. And I felt it was not becoming. But I can talk to no one. After dinner one night where everyone was more or less hilarious except the Archbishop, I tried to converse with him, to ask his advice. Mr. Newton, he was not only uncomprehending; he was embarrassed."

John believed it. He recalled his ordination, twenty-one years before, and the flippancy of almost all the fifteen who had been ordained with him. He thought of the indecent contempt of the first neighbouring clergyman on whom he had called to request, according to the custom, his signature to the testimonial for priest's orders; remembered how furious he had been until he realized that it was an honour to be publicly insulted for the gospel's sake. He envisaged the next consistory where, with the most charitable will in the world, he would find himself, as he always did, among men serious about trifles and trifling about the most serious matters. He suppressed a smile at the thought of the Archbishop, leaning urbanely forward with an appropriate quotation from Horace, probably

> "... *dissipat Euhius*
> *curas edacis*. ..."

and his well-bred horror at being met with an earnest, if diffident, request for spiritual counsel.

"But what am I to do?" Young Wilberforce had risen and was pacing the floor. "Already I wonder if what I thought God had done for me was self-deception, a flash of enthusiasm. I have no strength to resist the pressure daily brought to bear on me. I am unhappy now but what I fear most is that I shall cease to be unhappy, that I shall lapse back into contentment with what I considered pleasure. And yet with all my doubt and unbelief I *know* that God has . . . that nothing

365

else can ever satisfy me again. I am trying to serve two masters. Shall I give up the House? Am I, like the rich ruler, held back by my great possessions? Should I 'sell all that I have' and retire to a life of poverty and prayer? At least it would be free of this constant struggle. Or should I study for Holy Orders? When I heard you on Sunday you cannot know how I coveted your serenity and assurance of heavenly things. 'A man on earth devoted to the skies' I thought and I felt I should give anything to attain to it. But by Monday evening —"

He broke off with an expressive shrug and stood on the hearth-rug, slim legs in their velvet breeches slightly apart, his white shapely hands clasped in an unconscious gesture of appeal.

John regarded him with a calm he was far from feeling. There had been a time when he deplored the fact that the friendship of titled or prominent people pleased him, though primarily as an other instance of the contrast with his early slavery, brought about by God's grace alone. The increase of his wealthy and influential acquaintance, the honours heaped upon him, had removed any element of surprise or disparity from such an interview as this. Besides he was genuinely unconcerned whether his dealings were with a member of Parliament, a periwig-maker like young Jones whom he had coached in languages, a baronet like Sir Harry Trelawney who had come to Olney to prepare himself for Holy Orders under his instruction, the servants whom he treated, to the amazement even of the Thorntons, as personal friends, or Sir Charles Middleton to whose dinner-parties he and Mary were frequently invited. But he knew his own limitations and recognized in this twenty-six-year-old dilettante, as he had recognized in the brilliant and successful playwright Hannah More, instruments ready to God's hand for work in fields that he could not touch. "A knock on my study door is a message from God," he had said the day before to a friend who bemoaned his frequent interruptions. Surely the hopes that had sprung up in his heart as Wilberforce told his story, the joy he felt, signalized a very special message. "You have mentioned alternatives," he probed gently. "Is there any one of them to which you feel led?"

The hands unclasped and were spread out empty.

"No. None. But *something* I must do. I cannot continue as I am. I cannot lead a becoming Christian life — a Christian life at all — in my present environment."

"Is it your own power or that of God which you doubt?" Wilberforce frowned, questioning.

"You cannot continue as you are. True. God in mercy will not allow it. But does that mean that you must desert the post in which He has placed you?

"In my case, for instance," he continued, as his companion re-seated himself and leaned forward attentively, "the Lord left me for six years, though engaged in a business which I now regard with loathing. Yet in that station he was pleased to teach me many valuable lessons which I could not have learned, considering my background and disposition, in any other situation. Then when His time came, and not before, though for selfish reasons I had often prayed for it, He removed me and provided a position in which — though again I had no idea of it at the time — I had leisure to prepare myself for the ministry."

"You refer to the slave trade? I had forgotten, though I heard of your connection as a child, when I was a frequent visitor at Wimbledon."

"Yes." John forgot for a moment the business in hand. "The Lord leads us step by step as we can bear it. Had I thought of the slave trade then as I have thought of it since, no considerations would have induced me to continue in it; for though my religious views were not very clear, my conscience was very tender, and I durst not have displeased God by acting against the light of my mind."

"There is much sentiment against it, but I fear mere sentiment can prevail little against so well entrenched a source of revenue. Lord North recently declared it an economic necessity."

" 'Mere' is not a word I should use to describe sentiment," said John smiling, "and the darkness of the times may well be the hand of the God raised in judgment against us for resting our prosperity on the sufferings of fellow human beings. My friend Mr. Latrobe is of that opinion. He —"

"Latrobe?" inquired Wilberforce, "Dr. Johnson's friend?"

"Yes. He has discussed the matter at our Eclectic Society. But to return to your case: It is a dangerous thing to run before God. If he wishes to remove you from public life He can, and I believe will, make it plain. Until that time the safe course is to go softly looking up to Him."

"But my Christian life. You — forgive me, Sir, but you can scarcely imagine the distractions, the dissipations."

Can I not? thought John, and some that have not entered your imagination, much less your experience. Aloud he said with perfect gravity:

"Were there not saints in Caesar's household? Are the riches of His grace in Christ Jesus sufficient for the supply of all others' need except those of William Wilberforce Esquire? No, my dear young Sir, I am not advocating a continuance in evil or unbecoming indulgence. Already God has revealed certain practices as wrong for you. He will doubtless show you more if you seek earnestly to do His will."

"You mean *you* will not advise me?"

"I shall gladly give you my honest opinion on any question which you consider open to doubt, but your orders come from Him alone — and if I am any judge, Mr. Wilberforce, you will take them from no other authority. I have been thirty years forming my own views. Some of my hills have been sinking and some of my valleys have risen. I do not expect this to take place in you in the course of a year or two. No older Christian should say to a young one: 'Stand in my evidence': it is like a man on the top of a house crying to one at the bottom: 'What a prospect. Come up at a step'."

"But my faith is not increasing, Sir. It requires food."

"Ah there I can make suggestions. You must find gospel preaching, preaching which, wherever you find it, speaks the Word to you, and attend it faithfully. Through mercy there is more abroad, much more, than in the days when I began my search. This cannot take the place of a daily season of Scripture reading and prayer. I know something of the temptations which will assail you to keep you from this, and at your very devotions. I can also testify to God's blessing on the poorest of our weak efforts."

"My time —" began Wilberforce.

"No one of us can say 'my time'," said John gently. "What

time we have is the gift or the loan of God. If you place it
at His disposal He will use it to your best interests. But to
that end I should, if I were you, talk frankly to Mr. Pitt."

"I wrote him. He could not understand why Christianity
and action were incompatible. We talk usque ad aras. He
will think me mad."

"Perhaps. Perhaps not. But you are friends and it will
help your position if he understands — let us say recognizes
— your change in view. Then — but perhaps you think me
officious?"

"I should not have sought if I had not wished an answer."

"You need judicious Christian friends. And surely the
very kind you need are most advantageously placed for you:
Mrs. Wilberforce, her brother — and his son Henry, a young
man of your own age whom you cannot help liking, unless you
determine on it beforehand. I think a visit to that house will
effectually dissociate religion from dulness in your mind."

"May I come again, Mr. Newton?" Wilberforce presently
rose from prayer, his face tranquil, his voice for the first time
touched with humility.

"If I can serve you at all in the things of God, it is my
privilege." On an impulse John put his hand on the boy's
slender shoulder. "In the words of Mordecai, mutatis mutan-
dis, 'Who knoweth whether thou art come to the kingdom
for such a time as this'?"

When next the young M.P. appeared in Charles Square,
having in the meantime sat rapt through John's Wednesday
sermon, he had read *An Authentic Narrative*. Doubtless convinced by that document of John's knowledge of temptation,
he spoke more freely to him of his failures and sense of guilt. In
particular he had found comfort in the slow growth of sanctification and the recovery from backsliding so candidly revealed
in the *Narrative*. His attempt to witness to Pitt had been a
failure; affectionate, high-principled, and worldly, his friend
could see no sense in William's spiritual concern, though he
made the courteous effort at understanding which is almost
more dampening than expressed annoyance. The visit to his
parish church had likewise proved unfruitful. He had yielded
to his besetting temptation to show off and had come from the

unremarkable service quite forgetful of the God of whom he went in search. Altogether he was in a bitterly upset state of mind when he found his way to the Charles Square study; and Newton, feeling that perhaps the Lord had denied him sons of his own that he might play a father's part to this young man among others, sent him away after an hour or more, comforted.

John had not been mistaken in the deep joy of his assurance that God's hand was effectually upon the boy, whose defection from all religious influence had been mourned by the Methodistical branch of the Wilberforce family. Fluctuating between self-disgust and hope, contemptuous of his own snobbery, and deeply moved towards righteousness, the young politician had that implanted within him which would not be denied growth. Losing the dread that he be termed 'enthusiastic' he came more often and more boldly to St. Mary's, and was rather relieved than apprehensive when a friend met him out walking with John — enough to brand anyone as a Methodist. In Holy Week that year — he had come to Newton the preceding December — he received the Sacrament for the first time; and though, as with his mentor to whom he referred affectionately in diary and letters as Old Newton, the battle with self was not over, he had thenceforth the assurance that Christ had won the victory.

The change soon made itself manifest in his public life. At the Thorntons he was introduced to a set, small but fearless, of which the very existence was unknown to his society friends: people of wealth and taste whose Christian hospitality took little account of class, and whose philanthropy left neither time nor interest for the glittering fripperies with which his other set whiled away their leisure. The contrast in temper struck him no less than the contrast in occupation. John's quotation from the book of Esther had never long left his mind. For this time he had perhaps been brought to the kingdom, but for what purpose? What was the need of the hour in England which he, uniquely situated, could by the prevenient help of God, fulfil? The brutal, ignorant viciousness of the unchurched masses, still abounding, was increasingly feeling the impact of Wesley and his untiring disciplined host of itinerants, his organized classes and bands. *The Gentleman's*

Mazagine contained frequent letters about the new Sunday Schools by which a man named Robert Raikes was setting about to redeem vagabond children, many of whom would otherwise briefly terrorize the populace, before ending their short unhappy lives at Tyburn. Old Newton's influence by person and publication ramified in many directions and was spreading the Evangelical cause in the Establishment. Wesley and Whitefield and he reckoned among their converts some of the great, and there was a slow rising of a moral tide to cover, at least with a wash of seemliness, the blatant excesses of the Restoration and post-Restoration ebb. But little had seeped into the frivolous degradation of the upper classes, the custom-hardened, profligate mockers of seriousness and virtue.

Perhaps it was his task to set in motion a reformation of manners and morals. A bold scheme, its outlines inchoate, its method of fulfilment unformed. Yet Newton, when he confided it to him, strengthened his confidence, for it was such a concept that had taken form in his mind when first the young stranger talked in his study. That — and who knew where it might lead?

It led, by the almost casual steps which a man who seeks God's will is led to take, first to a deepening, then to a sharing of his devotional life. When he came to St. Mary's now, he seldom came alone. If few of his fashionable friends were converted, there was less laughter at 'fanatic enthusiasm' in his immediate set; for his spirits were high as ever and his wit — "as much wit as if he had no piety", was Hannah More's approving comment — had a rapier edge, clean-cutting and unpoisoned.

It led, while he was still meditating a book on his projected reform of manners, to association, through Newton, through Latrobe, through his cousin Henry Thornton, with the 'sentimentalists', bent on a reform that spelled economic revolution. It led, well within two years of that memorable Sunday at St. Mary's, to his representation in Parliament, first unofficial, then recognized, of the far-flung, amorphous, uninfluential group working for abolition of the slave trade.

36

THESE interviews with Wilberforce were only one incident in John's crowded life. The pattern of parish duties as minister of St. Mary's was less exacting than that which he had set for himself in Olney. Always learning, never dogmatic of opinion, always eager to adapt himself to the will of God as revealed in events and circumstances, he had realized the impracticality of setting up in his metropolitan living such a graded series of meetings as the poor and populous parish of Olney, bereft of other instruction or diversion, had required. Less than half of the hundred families who made up his spiritual constituency attended St. Mary's. Those who did came on Sunday morning when, as he candidly admitted, he kept his sermon to forty-five minutes and fed them with milk instead of meat. Then, and in the afternoon for his more profound exposition, the church was crowded. When he came, it had been the custom to read prayers on Wednesday and Friday — apparently in an empty church. John, who saw nothing God-honouring in this ritual, discontinued the Friday observance, and made Wednesday a preaching service which soon attracted a large congregation. "My hearers are made up of all sorts and my connexions are of all sorts likewise," he wrote to a Baptist friend . . . "I mean of those who hold the Head. My inclination leads me chiefly to insist on those things in which all who are taught of God agree. And my endeavour is to persuade them to love one another, to bear with one another, to avoid dispute. I preach my own sentiments plainly but peaceably and directly oppose no one. Accordingly Churchmen and Dissenters, Calvinists and Arminians,

Moravians and Methodists, now and then I believe Papists and Quakers, sit quietly to hear me. I can readily adopt 'No Popery' for my motto: I dislike it whether it be on a throne, as at Rome, or upon a bench or at a board as sometimes in London. Whoever wants to confine me to follow his sentiments, whether in doctrine or order, is so far a papist. Whoever encourages me to read the Scriptures and to pray for the teaching of the Holy Spirit, and then lets me follow the light the Lord gives me, without being angry because I cannot or will not see with his eyes, nor wear his shoes, is a consistent protestant. The depravity of human nature, the Deity of the Saviour, the influences of the Holy Spirit, a separation from the world and a devotedness to God — these are principles which I deem fundamental; and though I would love and serve all mankind, I can have no religious union or communion with those who deny them. But whether a surplice or a band be the fittest distinction of a minister, whether he be best ordained by the laying on or the holding up of hands; whether water-baptism should be administered by a spoonful or a tubful, or in a river, or in Jordan (as Constantine thought) are to me points of no great importance. I will go further. Though a man does not accord with my views of election, yet if he gives me good evidence that he is effectually called of God, he is my brother. Though he seems afraid of the doctrine of final perseverance, yet if grace enables him to persevere, he is my brother still. If he loves Jesus, I will love him."

This determined effort to walk in love with all brethren did not meet with unqualified success. His friendship among Dissenters, his acknowledged debt to Dissent, the unpopularity of his Evangelical position in the Establishment, gave some ground to Nonconformists who said in effect — and in public: "What do you here?" His increasing prestige, they knew, would have been a bulwark in the fortress of hard-pressed Nonconformity; it was neither needed nor wanted by entrenched Anglicanism. So, to answer repeated criticisms, perhaps to clarify his position to himself, he published, four years after coming to London, his *Apologia,* in his favourite epistolary format, four candid letters to an imaginary minister of the Independent Church. With disarming frankness he had justified his choice as an individual matter, a question of guidance through events to the situation most suited to his temper and ability, most useful as a sphere of service. Point by point he dealt with objections to the Anglican Church, conceding imperfections in rubric and liturgy, but gently suggesting that no other church or party, however assured of its Scriptural position, was free from error. He deplored authoritarianism which had resulted in persecuting spirit and action in former centuries; but hinted that similar authoritarianism was not unknown in Dissenting bodies and, rather naively, suggested that the present latitudinarianism of the State Church gave him greater individual liberty than he could enjoy elsewhere. The objection to set order and printed prayers he recognized, countering humorously that it was not outside the bounds of possibility for hymn-singing to become formal and thoughtless.

> *Crito freely will rehearse*
> *Forms of pray'r and praise in verse.*
> *Why should Crito then suppose*
> *Forms are sinful when in prose?*
> *Must my form be deem'd a crime*
> *Merely for the want of rhyme?*

His summum, far from suggesting any apostolic pre-eminence of his branch of the Church over others which he had once desired to serve, was a plea that his right to minister where his conscience directed be conceded to him, as he conceded the right to others; a wry admission that the paucity of gospel preachers in the Establishment made their position more precarious, financially and socially, than outside it; a grateful recognition that the Holy Spirit had again visited the Anglican Church, which He once seemed to have left, and that the parochial fields were white to harvest.

Somewhat to John's amaze, wholly to his sorrow, these gentle letters did not put an end to the matter. An answering publication, entitled *An Apology and Shield for Protestant Dissenters,* took his arguments apart piece by piece, with such devastating reference to historical injustice and contemporary iniquity in the Establishment, that John squirmed with the truth of it, though his personal consciousness of vindication remained unshaken. Unfortunately for its influence on him, or on others who might have been won by the incisive logic and the appeal to Scriptural precedent, the document breathed a spirit of vituperative bitterness and deep resentment. Failure to admit fault in the doctrine, order, or practice of the Independent bodies and preachers contrasted strongly with John's candour and humility. The not too carefully veiled suggestion that Newton had chosen the Establishment for the sake of a good living left his withers unwrung. Of many sorts of vileness he accused himself constantly before God; but he had rejected too many opportunities of ease and advancement to feel concern at this charge. He resisted the temptation to reopen the controversy either in the press or pulpit, and obtained grace to pray for his exasperated brother.

Perhaps that exasperation had been intensified by the admiring reciprocal friendship which existed between the unabashed Anglican and many leading Nonconformists. The same year which saw Newton's *Apologia* in print saw also his "Plan of Academical Preparation for the Ministry." This Utopian letter, written at the request of his friend William Bull, was used as the foundation scheme of the New Independent Theological College at Newport Pagnel. The Taylors of Southhampton, whose hospitality to him and Mary at Portswood House had made them fast friends, were Congregationalists. As the Anglican Church in Southampton was closed against his request to preach, he worshipped with his hosts at theirs. Mr. Taylor had built a private chapel to accommodate about three hundred; and here, several times a week during every visit, John preached for what he referred to as his 'Portswood living'. It was there that Mary had so recently taken Eliza for the proposed cure of sea-bathing.

"If you should be asked to stay at the Sacrament," he had written from London, "I should like you to do it. My wife and any of my people have my full consent to 'eat of that bread and drink of that cup' with Mr. Kingsbury and his people and he shall be heartily welcome to share with us at St. Mary Woolnoth. I should . . . be glad if such testimonies of mutual love and consent in the great truths of the Gospel could take place amongst those . . . ranked under different denominations."

Such house-preaching on a smaller scale, at the Wimbledon home of Mrs. Wilberforce, in Clapham at the Thornton's, in the homes of parishioners and adherents, partially took the place of other Olney meetings. So did his Thursday breakfasts and his increasing number of personal interviews. To make himself more available for these, he and Mary regretfully gave up the country atmosphere of Hoxton for the convenient location of Coleman Street, a few minutes' walk from his church. The group of young men, which at his suggestion had begun to meet fortnightly at the Castle and Falcon for tea and discussion, had finally achieved the name of Eclectic Society. Eclectic it was indeed: Richard Cecil was a member, dilettante poet and musician who, repenting after an irregular youth, took Holy Orders and became a more sanctified Boswell to Newton's Johnson. Similarity of nature and disposition, his predilection to the same sins, John knew, accounted for young Cecil's devotion. He was too well aware of the danger of dependence on any creature to encourage it; too conscious of 'Mr. Self's' enjoyment of praise to bask in it; too often reduced to humility by his own weakness and indwelling sin to feel more than uncomfortable when he realized that Cecil, regarding him as an 'original', was keeping a notebook of his conversation and mannerisms. "I want none of these sweetmeats," he said with unwonted sharpness, when a fulsome acquaintance commented effusively on the 'pretty wit' of an anecdote he had narrated. John Bacon was a member also, the genius apprentice in a Chelsea factory, who had risen to national eminence as a sculptor. Discussions ranged from: 'Why do Ministers' children so often prove to be bad?' to 'How far may Music be subservient to true devotion?'.

As by his writing he had first come to public notice, he found his books so popular that he was constantly urged to publish. Even the little memorial, which on the death of Eliza he wrote for Mary and their many friends, found its way into print, though only on Thornton's urging, and with the stipulation that all proceeds go to charity. Too many had paid tribute to the blessing received through his personal letters for him not to realize that the talent which had won his unwilling Mary was perhaps his greatest means of usefulness. *Cardiphonia*, for which apt title he was indebted to Cowper, was received with instant and continuing acclaim far beyond the boundaries of Britain. Through its reading the Dutchman Van Lier was greatly helped. Through its reading Hannah More, whose clear head had not been turned by the fact that she was the darling of London's intelligentsia, and who had been saddened into temporary retirement by the death of her friend Garrick, had sought John's ministry and acquaintance.

On one topic, however, John had refused to publish his writing, one topic, the talk of the town from court to coffee-house, the scandal of the Evangelical party; the brilliant, honest, warm-hearted and wrong-headed *Thelyphthora*: A treatise in Female Ruin.

Martin Madan's ill-fated volume followed hard upon John's arrival at St. Mary Woolnoth and became notorious overnight. Cowper's cousin, whose poetic mother had been immortalized by Pope, and who was generally conceded the golden-voiced orator of the day, had for years made the gallery of his chapel the most fashionable centre of Evangelical preaching in the kingdom. In the body of the chapel the congregation was composed of inmates of the Lock, a hospital devoted to sufferers from venereal diseases. Years of ministry among them had acquainted their pastor with many women whom trustfulness and a solitary moral lapse had driven, as social outcasts, to a rotting death-in-life, while the man responsible or equally culpable occupied a respectable and affluent place in society. Searching pitifully for a cure, Madan had produced his thesis, and supported it by a literal application of Old Testament Scripture, combined with a searching examination of the history of the marriage tie before and during the Christian era. Polygamy was the cure, by which a woman used for sexual purposes, and the children produced by such unions, had legal rights and status; by which also the innumerable cases in which a young man's affection was subordinated in marriage to financial or family interest would no longer enjoy social sanction.

John read the voluminous treatise when it came from the press, unwilling, as he usually was with a book, to put it down until completed. The close-knit deduction from Scripture fascinated him; the theme appealed to him, for in individual conversations with women whom his preaching at the Lock had affected he had been deeply moved by tragedies in which his early sins gave him more than a general sense of personal guilt. Before its publication, having some rumour of Madan's design, John had written a cautioning letter and received a reply which seemed at once to anticipate disapproval and to desire to forestall condemnation. Madan's deep concern for this section of human wreckage had, as John reviewed his arguments, distorted the teaching of Scripture; he had either deliberately or of conviction erred in giving the Old Testament equal authority with the New. The glory of marriage with Mary made it impossible for John to consider such unions as were advocated in *Thelyphthora* true marriage at all; and he was apprehensive of the danger that a scheme promulgated from lofty motives would be debased in vulgar conception, apprehensive also that harm might be done to the cause of gospel preaching.

As he discussed the book with Mary, for she shared his friendship with the Madans and his present concern, a wave of indignation from righteous and unrighteous alike threatened to inundate the man who had hitherto escaped most of the opprobrium through which ministers of his persuasion had to pass. The King, according to rumour, expressed a wish that such an author could be punished by law. There was a movement to secure suppression of the printing. The bishops were supposed to be meditating action against the offender. Angry letters appeared in the press. Dr. Thomas Haweis, Madan's friend and one-time associate, published a scathing indictment which made no separation between author and work in its condemnation. Such pressure indeed was brought to bear that Madan was eventually forced to retirement in the country. Of the most prominent Evangelicals two refused to publish against *Thelyphthora*. John Wesley, by whose ministry Madan had been changed from a dissipated young lawyer to a devout clergyman, and who had been deserted by him in the lonely days of his own abandonment, was one. The other was John Newton.

The insistence of many friends that such a work on his part was a sacred responsibility failed to persuade him. Indeed he was dismayed that William Cowper, who was bound by relationship as well as long friendship, had instantly turned his undoubted talents into a harsh, poetical *Anti-Thelyphthora*, which he requested John to send to his own publisher. To explain his own reluctance, he wrote gently to the poet, whose views on every subject, from the divine right of kings to Sabbatarianism were much more rigid than his own.

"Heaps of folk would persuade me that I can attempt nothing so seasonable, needful, and with equal probability of usefulness, as an answer to *Thelyphthora*. I am not yet of this mind. Mr. Indolence uses all his influence, which is considerable, to keep me quiet; Mr. Prudence cautions me against meddling with one above my match; and Mr. Delicacy says, Surely you would not write against your friend. Notwithstanding, I must bear my testimony against *Thelyphthora* tomorrow viva voce. In the course of sermons I lately began on relative duties, I must enter on the relation of husband and wife tomorrow night; and it would be misprision of treason against the truth, when expressly preaching on the subject of marriage, to leave the dangerous and novel doctrine of the present lawfulness of polygamy unnoticed, because I have a love for the person who presumed to broach it."

To Martin Madan, he did write privately, stating his own refutation of the *Thelyphthora* thesis firmly, but expressing his belief in the purity of his friend's motives. The brief ensuing correspondence, stiffly defensive on Madan's part, restrained on Newton's, left the situation unchanged and John, rejecting suggestions that he publish it and fearing that it might find its way into less reluctant hands, burned all the letters. Beneath the argumentative rancour of Madan's replies, he detected the bitterness of disappointment at his friends' desertion and, as the storm gathered around his head, he felt too much distress for his former benefactor to add to its fury. Sir Cowper, Dr. Haweis and the rest must do as their consciences directed. He must do as his conscience directed. But had not Martin Madan done the same? And would the book with the difficult Greek name and the preposterous suggestions have done more harm if its author's Christian friends had saved their public attack until it was clear that it was actually doing any?

37

OUT of the sorry situation John salvaged one bit of comfort. William Cowper now yielded to Mrs. Unwin's insistence that he publish the stray poems in which his mind had for years found occupation, if not escape, from its misery. To John anything to relieve that pitiful depression, anything to bridge the cheerless present (when, as his letters revealed, an apparently pleasant day was bounded on either side by a night of horror) was to be encouraged. Accordingly, at Cowper's request, he advised him on certain debatable lines, made arrangements with his own publisher, Johnson, and solicited a subscription among his friends to defray the cost. At Cowper's request again — "you can draw a hair-stroke when another man would make a blot as big as a sixpence" — he wrote a preface, acceded amiably to the publisher's judgment that it be deleted from later printings as too religious, and did the work of Cowper's London agent as diligently as if he had not a thousand calls on his time and energy.

This first venture, its sales promoted also by Mary's wholehearted co-operation and by the efforts of William Unwin, met with moderate success. Considerable additional stimulus was given the poet's talent by his new and exciting friendship with the beautiful, fashionable sister-in-law of John's onetime protégé Rev. Thomas Jones of Clifton. This charming titled widow came to shop in Olney with her sister, was seen from his window by Cowper, who with unprecedented initiative urged Mrs. Unwin to ask the two to tea. Lady Austen came, saw the interesting, courtly recluse, was conquered and conquered simultaneously. Desire to settle near her sister and to sit under Mr. Scott's ministry — for he had at last succeeded briefly to the Olney curacy — gave discreet purpose to her decision to take the adjoining half of the building which contained Orchard Side; from that time the poet had two devoted companions, the trio dining alternately in one or the other's house. It was Lady Austen's gay recital which inspired the writing of *John Gilpin;* in more serious vein she set him about his first blank verse on *The Sofa* which extended into the grand discursive work *The Task.*

John Gilpin, published anonymously, swiftly became the rage of London. John let its authorship be known and sent William news of its success: the uproarious effect of its recitation by young Henry Thornton at a Charles Square gathering; the approval of Mrs. Siddons; the acclaim in far-off Scotland; the parodies and imitations which were the sincerest form of flattery. He liked Lady Austen whom they had met years before and, with his usual singlemindedness, rejoiced that his friends had been sent a congenial and diverting companion.

It was Mary whose demurity, when he so expressed himself, made him wonder a little, though he could elicit no comment from her more committal than: "Very nice indeed. I know they have been lonely since you left." Likewise it was Mary who did not share his surprise at the sudden news that the two-year, inseparable companionship had broken up and that Lady Austen had permanently retired from Olney.

"My dearest John!" She shook her head at her obtuse husband. "I don't know who knows less of women, you or poor Sir Cowper. I am amazed only that it has lasted so long."

"But he regarded Lady Austen as a sister."

"No one could see them together five minutes without realizing that Lady Austen did *not* regard him as a brother," retorted Mary. "And to do her justice, Mr. Cowper's manner and address to her, as well as the poems he wrote, were more gallant than brotherly. She showed me one, when she visited, written about the exchange of a lock of hair. I can't repeat it, — something about

> *The star that beams on Anna's breast*
> *Conceals her William's hair. . . .*
> and
> *The heart that beats beneath that breast*
> *Is William's well I know.*

John, I never exchanged locks of hair with Jack — or poor Georgie either. Oh, I know he is quite unconscious of the effect of it. But he should have realized that there is only one Mrs. Unwin. As I am sure Mrs. Unwin did."

"Do you think she raised objection?"

Mary put her head on one side to consider, in a gesture evocative of so many memories that John momentarily forgot the matter under discussion.

"I think she is far too sweet to wish to deprive him of any pleasure," she said loyally. "The situation must have been different for her from the beginning. Lady Austen is young — comparatively — and beautiful and much more vivacious and stimulating. But I should think the Lady herself probably brought matters to the place where even Sir Cowper realized that he was no brother to her — and took fright."

"Well, we shall never know," said John, accepting his wife's acute diagnosis as probable. She was usually right in such matters; "but his description of a daily walk with one or the other, his evenings reading aloud to the two, or holding yarn, 'like Hercules and Omphale' sounded so content that I pray he may find other things to amuse him."

The other thing came as a shock that same autumn. Cowper's letters continued. They described the election at Olney, his green-house and garden, the books he was reading, the state of international affairs and occasionally, in deep depression, his own spiritual isolation. Then one, dated October 30, informed John that he was again in the hands of his (John's) publisher with a magnum opus, of which this was his friend's first intimation. The preliminaries, the conferences, the receipt and despatching of proof-sheets had all been entrusted to William Unwin.

John felt as though his alter ego had struck him. In vain he told himself that he was relieved of a burden; that with his two publications that very year, with Mary's fluctuating health, with his own recent recovery from fever, with Betsey requiring his letters and Eliza declining fast at home, Cowper had kindly spared him the labour. In vain he realized that young Unwin's expressed hurt on the occasion of the first publication had influenced Cowper, as well as a desire to please Mrs. Unwin. John thought of the fourteen months when the Vicarage had been Cowper's chosen asylum, its master and mistress at his service, while William Unwin had let embarrassment at his mother's conduct colour the views of John's friends. He thought — and ashamed of the thinking, prayed for grace to prevent the thoughts lingering. But what to do? His first impulse, to show only casual interest, he dismissed as unworthy. His second, to write an affectionate letter, urging Cowper for more information about the great work or a glimpse at the proof-sheets, met with a positive refusal of the latter and a partial satisfaction of the former request. The next exchange was as little satisfactory. By that time Christmas was upon them, and with the New Year John, asking his conscience how he dared be angry with a friend who felt himself denied any access to the God he loved, resumed his correspondence with an apology for its interruption. Cowper responded and the breach was healed.

When *The Task* had established Cowper as a literary figure, his circle of correspondents and acquaintance expanded so that the Newtons could feel relieved of the necessity to minister constantly to his cheer. In the first years of their settlement in London nothing but the weightiest concerns ever kept John from answering William's weekly letters, though at that time his correspondents outnumbered Cowper's twenty to one. Mary sent seeds and garden information, barrels of oysters and crated lobsters, cocoanuts and other edibles unobtainable in Olney. The two took Betsey down to visit. John sent books, news, anecdotes, exerting himself to write lightly and amusingly, making much of the gifts of Mrs. Unwin's poultry and of William's rhyming riddles. "I have a laughing friend at my elbow," he wrote, stopping to caress her hair, "always disposed to do your wit justice. The five-toed, feathered inhabitants of Olney arrived safe in London but had not been long in town before they went to pot." He reminded Bull of his promise to visit. He introduced Cowper by letter to the sculptor, Bacon, who sent him an excellent sketch of his designed memorial for the Earl of Chatham in Westminster Abbey. The correspondence from Cowper contained versified thanks for oysters, a rhymed dialogue between a pipe (John's) and a snuff-box (William's) and several John and Mary poems. Each friend had sent the other anything "to raise a smile".

Now long-silent relatives began to communicate with the newly discovered poet. His cousin, Harriet Cowper, at whose home in London William had been at home while he studied Law, and for whose sister Theodora he had cherished his first romantic love, the love forbidden by her father because of his mental instability, was now the widowed Lady Hesketh. Her descent on Olney had all the pleasurable consequences of Lady Austen's without any of its risks. Not only did she settle in the vacant Vicarage, shower the household with gifts, whisk the secluded pair about the country in her coach, but within a comparatively short time had moved them into a much more convenient and pleasingly situated house a mile away at Weston Underwood. Their new home adjoined the park and gardens of the Throckmortons, who gave them the freedom of the estate and library and prevailed on Cowper to see more society in their home than he had consented to do in twenty years. Several young men, charmed by his poetry, sought him out, and basked in the quiet gaiety which never betrayed to strangers the abyss of melancholy over which he lived and moved.

Yet none of this, nor the success of his third publication *Tirocinium,* nor the self-imposed, absorbing discipline of his translation of Homer prevented a severe nervous declension, which kept him for six months from writing. For eight he saw no one except Mrs. Unwin, who, scarcely recovered from the sudden death of her only son, and a narrow escape from burning, watched over him with customary selfless devotion. Mary, learning of his illness from her friend, offered to go and help her as she had so often done in the Olney days. Her offer and John's were gratefully declined, but as soon as William had emerged from his mental imprisonment he resumed his correspondence with an added warmth, to which the Newtons found the key in the significant sentences:

"I return to our correspondence in one respect better qualified than before: I mean by a belief in your identity in which for thirteen years I did not believe. The acquisition of this light, if light it may be called which leaves me as much in the dark as ever on the most interesting subjects, releases me, however, from the disagreeable suspicion that I am addressing myself to you as the friend whom I loved and valued so highly

384

in my better days, while in fact you are not that friend, but a stranger. I can now write to you without seeming to act a part and without having any need to charge myself with dis-simulation."

They finished the letter at the same moment.

"Poor Sir Cowper," said Mary softly; then "Poor John! But remember, Dear, whatever has happened, whatever else happens, you haven't to go through it, as he does without —"

But does he? John asked himself in the midst of his pity, does he? He thought of the letter he had written, commenting on certain religious observations which Cowper had made.

"How strange that your judgment should be clouded on one point only, and that a point so obvious and strikingly clear to everybody who knows you! How strange that a person who considers the earth, the planets, and the sun itself as mere baubles compared with the friendship and favour of God their Maker, should think the God who inspired him with such an idea, could ever forsake and cast off the soul which He has taught to love him! Though your comforts have been so long suspended, I know not that I ever saw you for a single day since your calamity came upon you, in which I could not perceive as clear and satisfactory evidence that the grace of God was with you as I could in your brighter and happier times. In the midst of all the little amusements, which you call trifling and which I would be very thankful you can attend to in your present circumstances, it is as easy to see who has your heart as to see your shadow when you stand in the sun."

Yet the only occasions — apart from that rift regarding *The Task* — on which Cowper ever wrote or spoke with asperity was when John so answered a gloomy letter with re-assurance and a reiteration of his belief that William's conviction was delusion, a physical illness that would pass.

If he had not so insisted? if he had continued to identify himself with worshippers at church, at family prayers? if he had gone through some form of prayer, meaningless though he might feel it?

John shook his great head. These were deep waters. Who was he to presume to tell a Christian like William Cowper how he had erred?

"You need not urge me to feel less, Sweet," he said earnestly when she put up her hand to stroke his head. "It is my shame that I feel so little for others, as long as *you* are spared to me. Even the poor wretches at Bridewell to whom I spoke today — God forgive me, how easily my grief for them passes if you are well, and how quickly I forget all His mercy to us, if you are ill for a week."

"Then be thankful I am much better now," said Mary cheerfully. "Put Sir Cowper out of your mind. I have written to tell Mrs. Unwin, that, all being well, we shall accept their invitation to Weston next summer. Come and see how Phoebe and Crabb and I have laid Mrs. Taylor's new carpet — Phoebe and I, I should say, for Crabb was seized with her asthmatic cough when it was half done and I sent her from the room."

"Polly, when will you stop performing tasks beyond your strength? Why did not Sally help you, or Betsey?"

"How could I perform them if they were beyond my strength? Betsey and Sal were on errands for me. You know the pheasant I had for dinner? It came jump in my head that Mrs. Taylor might like a piece. And as she is just able to leave her room, I thought she might accept the shawl Betsey just finished making for me. The dear child says she will presently make me another. So I looked at the clock and saw that if they were packed off at once Mrs. Taylor would have them in the morning. It is so little we do for them in return for their kindness. Oh, I forget. A load of your favourite lignum vitae arrived from Portswood today and I had Sal lay the fire in your study with it."

"Have I ever told you," asked John, when he had duly admired the carpet, "what a marvellous manager you are?"

"I think so. I'm sure I've heard it from someone. But you are to write the peppercorn letter for all this. I enclosed a note with the pheasant but it's not a proper letter."

"You must tell about the carpet — how it fits and looks. I am no good at that."

"Then leave me space on the cover. Now while you drink your tea I'll tell you the rest of the news. Betsey has gone to drink tea with Mrs. Wilberforce. I did not feel equal to it — besides I wanted to be home when you came."

"It isn't home unless you are," said John simply. "And although to know that you are about the house, even confined to your room, gives a certain peace to my mind, to have you downstairs here in your parlour —"

He broke off abruptly. Mary looked at him, her brows contracting as a sudden pain. Then suppressing whatever thought had caused the spasm, she resumed lightly.

"First, Mrs. Thornton called. She says Mr. Thornton thinks that you should publish your lectures on *Pilgrim's Progress* just as you gave them at Wimbledon."

"I cannot possibly. Much of it was extempore."

"I doubt Mr. Thornton will be satisfied with that answer — bless him, he thinks almost as highly of all you publish as I do," said Mary, with the comfortable faith of a poor writer that good writing is somehow self-creating. "He says that your comments, bound together with Bunyan, will make *Pilgrim's Progress* intelligible for this generation."

"Intelligible! If they can read at all —"

"I know, Dear. I'm just telling you what he says. And he has talked your publisher into his mind. Then there is your invitation to the Goldsmiths' dinner after your annual sermon."

"Oh, dear!" John borrowed Mary's favourite phrase. "When all the noble statements I made in 'Christian Feasting' will rise and rebuke me. I could almost wish that the Lord had not created me with a disposition so 'richly to enjoy'."

"There is an invitation for you to preach at Colchester, and another at Reading. Half a dozen letters from strangers, which I left on your desk. Mrs. Hannah More sent me a note asking if she could come for a chat on Friday at tea-time. And a special messenger brought a note in Mr. Wilberforce's hand." She produced it from the bosom of her gown.

"He wishes me to write against the slave trade," said John, glancing down the letter. "Pitt has suggested that he give notice of a bill next session. He asks if I will be willing to testify before the Privy Council, which will be conducting its enquiry in the New Year."

"You will, of course?"

"Of course. Thank God our deliberate sins, much less those committed in ignorance, are not held against us. But I am grateful for any chance to atone for participating in that iniquitous business. What I could do in a private way I have done. But the Lord is good to grant me this opportunity of making a public retraction. And though the fight remains for young men like Wilberforce and Henry and Clarkson, and though much abler pens than mine will serve — Miss More's for example — yet I think Wilberforce is right that my experience will give an unusual turn to my testimony. Few, if any, will write, who have known the trade from my point of view."

38

SO by February, *Thoughts on the African Slave Trade*
was published. And shortly afterwards, members of
the Privy Council witnessed a scene unique in recorded
history. Perhaps its wonder escaped them. It did not escape
the chief actor, who felt in the sharp, mysterious ambivalence
of personality the two shockingly contrasted characters which
were united in him.

"The Reverend John Newton." The name was one of many
in the long list of witnesses which Wilberforce and his Society
had assembled. But it was familiar, though by no means popular, with every member of the Council and, had it not been,
the immediate effect would have roused their interest. There
was a stir in the front seats. The Prime Minister left his and,
unhurried but with nice deference, advanced to meet his friend's
adviser, accompanied him to the witness stand, and after a
brief complimentary introduction, left him.

"The Rector of St. Mary Woolnoth and St. Mary Wool-
church Haw, eminent for learning and piety, endeared equally
to the great and the humble, author of renown whose writings
have carried his name through Europe and to America, scholar,
philanthropist, divine: Gentlemen, we are honoured. . . ."
John stood under the roll of words uttered in the voice which
played on the House of Commons as on an instrument, stood,
his clergyman's wig, his rector's silk gown impeccable, under
the eyes, lazy, amused, curious, intent, of his interrogators. He
answered their questions, expanded and verified references in
his pamphlet, commented tersely on statements quoted in con-
tradiction. But he saw vividly the spare boy's figure in seaman's shirt and loose trousers, weals on his back still livid, glad

to escape penal servitude on the *Harwich* and caring little what trade engaged the *Pegasus*. He saw the dissolute young manager, pursuing his quest for pleasure and slaves to the point of going black on the coast. He saw the serious young Captain, battling for survival and for livelihood in the one job open to him; saw him gathering curious, fumbling impressions, seeing in the sufferings and misery of blacks even as in the sufferings and misery of whites, part of the lot of fallen humanity, but seeing them with an increasing, compassionate determination to add nothing to that misery which he could prevent.

He saw entry after entry in the Log of his three voyages which he had consulted for his manuscript:

> John Bridson, 1st Mate: deceased, January
> Robert Arthur, Surgeon: deceased, 17th August
> Andrew Corrigal, Carpenter: deceased, 11th January

I find whites, blacks, and mulattoes all double-dealing alike. Believe I have lost the purchase of more than 10 slaves for want of the all-commanding articles of Beer and Cyder. Ansak Selavakos, one of the African princes, came aboard and spent the evening with me, much to my satisfaction, being master of a great deal of solid sense and a politeness of behaviour I seldom meet with in any of our own complexion hereabouts.

Five whites not able to help themselves.

Cleared one side of the boy's room for a hospital . . . having the melancholy appearance of a sickly ship.

Visit from Mr. Clow and my quondam mistress P.I.

Found King of Charra on boat with a goat as a present, but had to salute him with 8 guns, costing twice the amount.

> Slaves obtained marline spike; 20 had broken irons. Secured all men's irons again and punished 6 of the ringleaders. They still look very gloomy and sullen and have doubtless mischief in their heads.

Can hardly keep slaves warm in rooms.

There was a scare about poisoning. A fetish had been put somehow in a water-cask to 'charm us to death'.

Perhaps it was this element of recollective impartiality which made both his oral witness and his written account effective where more impassioned pleas failed of their purpose. Miss More wrote powerful pentameters on the rape of Africa, solemn appeals to the tribunal of Heavenly justice; William Cowper wrote sardonic or passionate jingles to be sung, and noble idealistic sentiments, couched, however, in the terms of a man never faced with the alternative of starving or doing a distasteful job. Others, equally high-minded, devoted themselves to an aim that seemed unrealizable, for which they paid a high price in time, health, popularity and prestige. Ramsay, a Jamaican parson, died of attacks launched by infuriated planters against him. Clarkson was nearly drowned in the Mersey by a gang of paid roughs. Wilberforce himself had worked against such discouraging odds that he was only now recovered from an illness in which his physicians gave him three weeks to live.

On the other hand, to millions of Britons the slave trade was respectable with use, remote from daily experience. There were enough disagreeable sights and painful sounds near at hand to make the bizarre sufferings of an exotic people unreal. Some were sincerely convinced — perhaps anxious to be convinced — by the economic evidence of Makettrick's *Unanswerable Arguments against the Abolition of the Slave Trade,* or by the religious force of *Scriptural Researches on the Licitness of the Slave Trade.* But many thoughtful and pitiful people, willing to pay more for sugar and rum, even to forego dividends from money hazarded on the trade, were left unconvinced by impassioned speeches and writing which denounced as vile and villainous, without excuse, enemies to God and man, all traffic in slaves and all who had any share in that traffic. They knew sea-captains who had risked their lives or lost them in the trade, kindly, respectable merchants who made and outfitted ships, worthy divines who held services of thanksgiving in harbour churches when local ships and men returned from the dangerous coast, slave-owning planters in the Indies or America as decent and family-loving as themselves: none seemingly with any conscience about the righteousness of using something which they had not begun and which they had no power individually to stop, as a means of precarious and hard-won livelihood.

So did John: his Basseterre hosts, his honoured bencfactor Joseph Manesty. Thought of them, thought of himself — wrong and utterly unenlightened as he now believed them all to be in this particular — kept his writing temperate, with the result that his reasoned arguments were unanswerable and the damning indictment carried more weight from its very basis on averages rather than on extremes. From the opening confession which identified himself with the many who had felt no guilt in their activity, the candid admission of possible inaccuracy of memory which had determined him to make only such statements as he would willingly confirm upon oath, the lucid description of the locale and circumstances in which the trade had been conducted, the first-hand, experiential nature of his writing gripped attention and commanded credence.

Without apparent adroitness he dealt first with the evil effects of the trade on their own seamen: the appalling loss of Britons, at least fifteen thousand yearly from exposure, tropical and epidemical diseases, violent death; the pejorative effect of its necessary discipline upon the minds and dispositions of commanders and crews. The very reticence which cited one or two horrible examples of callousness, the laconic frankness which set forth the plight of female slaves, the autobiographical references which ripped away any white assumption that the blacks were deficient in humane sensitivity or innate principle: all prepared for the tremendous pathos of his account of their inevitable sufferings and mortality. "I have lived long and conversed much among these supposed savages. . . . And with regard to the women, in Sherbro, where I was most acquainted, I have seen many instances of modesty and even delicacy which would not disgrace an English woman." The splendid assemblage, bewigged and arrested by his colloquial interlude in the very act of passing a jewelled snuff-box, faded; he was again lying, gaunt with hunger and frustration in his hut, feeling the gentle touch and generous insistence of his small benefactress — where was she now? To what depersonalized hell-on-earth had the nefarious commerce doomed her? He saw again resigned quiescence warring with restive modesty, instinctive as his Betsey's, in his young bride under her father's proposal of her assets. "Yet such is the treatment which I have known permitted, if not encouraged, in many of our ships — they have been abandoned without restraint to the lawless will of the first comer.

"When I have charged a black with unfairness and dishonesty" — he flicked the pride of his hearers — "he has answered, if able to clear himself, with an air of disdain, 'What! do you think I am a white man?'."

He passed to the methods by which the slaves were acquired, the guilt of European nations in offering desirable goods in exchange for human beings, and thereby fomenting bloody wars between native tribes anxious to obtain the requisite commodity.

"Some people suppose that the ship trade is rather the stealing than the buying of slaves. But there is enough to lay to the charge of the ships without accusing them falsely. The slaves, in general, are bought and paid for."

Such casual concessions, his refusal to include all ship-captains in brutality, all natives in virtue, served to emphasize his ensuing description and statistical calculation.

"Their lodging-rooms below the deck are sometimes less than five feet high . . . the slaves lie in two rows one above the other on either side of a ship, like books upon a shelf . . . sometimes so close that the shelf would not easily contain one more . . . the poor creatures, thus cramped for want of room, are likewise in irons, for the most part both hands and feet, and two together, which makes it difficult to turn or move, to attempt either to rise or to lie down, without hurting themselves or each other. Nor is the motion of the ship, especially her heeling . . . to be omitted as they lie athwart the ship. . . . The heat and smell when the weather will not admit of the slaves being brought upon deck, and of having their rooms cleaned every day, would be almost insupportable to a person not accustomed to them," he continued; and the select members of a society beginning to pride itself on its daintiness suddenly realized that the immaculate parson before them had long been accustomed to them. Taking a low average, John computed that one fourth of the whole purchase (that is fifteen thousand slaves) perished annually before setting foot in the Americas. He left Wilberforce to calculate the mortality of *healthy* negroes before the sales were completed as fifty per cent. He conceded the existence, during his trading-days, of humane masters whose slaves were comparatively happy; but from his own observation he had been left with no doubt that the condition of the majority was wretched in the extreme.

"The gentlemen to whom my ship was assigned at Antigua in 1751, himself a planter, told me that calculations had been made, with all possible exactness, to determine which was the preferable, that is the more saving method of managing slaves:

"Whether to appoint moderate work, plenty of provision, and such treatment as might enable them to protract their lives to old age? or

"By rigorously straining their strength to the utmost, with little relaxation, hard fare, and hard usage, to wear them out before they became useless and unable to do service; then to buy new ones?

"These skilful calculators, he said, had determined in favour of the latter mode as much the cheaper; and he could mention several estates in the island on which it was seldom known that a slave had lived above nine years."

John's voice broke. Mindful of his determination not to endanger the force of his argument by emotion, he controlled himself to continue in a tone harsh with effort:

"I hope it will always be a subject of humiliating reflection to me that I was once an active instrument in a business at which my heart now shudders. If this, my testimony, should not be necessary or serviceable, yet I am bound in conscience to take shame to myself by a public confession which, however sincere, comes too late to prevent or repair the misery and mischief to which I have formerly been accessory. I have spoken voluntarily, without other motive than feelings of humanity and a regard for the honour and welfare of my country. There is a cry of blood against us: a cry accumulated by the accession of fresh victims, of thousands, of scores — I had almost said of hundreds — of thousands from year to year.

"Though unwilling to give offence to a single person, yet in this cause, in such a cause, I ought not to be afraid of offending many by declaring the truth — if, indeed, there *can* be many, whom even interest can prevail upon to contradict the common sense of mankind by pleading for a commerce so iniquitous, so cruel, so oppressive, so destructive, as the African slave trade."

39

"MY Dear —" wrote John, and paused. How many times, how many hundreds or thousands of times had he written that phrase? It was his almost inevitable reference to her in letters and in his diaries. But inadequate . . . so inadequate that he put his pen to the paper again and wrote: "Sweet —" The word was true of her, far more true than he had dreamed even in the early days of marriage; sweet with the genuine, unforced sweetness of a heart that stored no dregs of bitterness or jealousy. Yet 'sweet' had a suggestion of insipidity, of cloying, which was far removed from the effect, at once stimulating and restful, of his virtuous woman whose price was above rubies. Price — he added "Precious," and then, remembering how she protested, yet loved the adjective — "at my age, John?" — "Beautiful".

But it *was* appropriate, incredible though in his youth he would have thought it. How arrogantly the young spoke from their ignorance. He had never before experienced what it was to be sixty-three. Therefore he could not have known that a wife of fifty-nine could look as beautiful as when they first came together. "We are now far advanced in the thirty-ninth year of our joint reign," he had written recently to Mrs. Taylor. "My Dear's health continues precarious." But how remarkable that the frequent and painful periods of indisposition made no more inroads on Mary's loveliness. Perhaps they refined it, kept it from the placidity, the impassive, kindly mask which age drew over the faces of many women. Mary's *difference* had always been a thing of expression, of vivacity, of laughter bubbling up at unexpected moments, and this even her pain, even nights when she had lain trembling with the agony of her head until dawn brought fitful sleep to both of them, even six months confinement at a time to her upstairs room, had not quenched. Nor had age altered the delight which she derived from every effort to please her, so that even the pleasure which she took in making herself attractive — pleasure which he felt he should deplore yet could not help encouraging — became a reciprocal joy.

"Doesn't God give us all things richly to enjoy?" she had inquired when John, being asked to choose, had selected the more flattering colour for her new gown and was introspectively questioning his motives in the choice.

"I can't contradict Scripture on that point," he had admitted smiling, "but —"

"And don't you enjoy seeing me look well — as well as I can, considering age and infirmity?"

"You know that I do! But —"

"But you are afraid I shall become vain . . . as if what you have written and said to me for forty years hasn't undone me completely long ago! But have you considered that *if* I deliberately chose dull material and a plain style, I should presently look censoriously on every woman who dresses prettily? And that censoriousness could spring from envy? And I don't really spend much time curling my hair. But if I didn't, I **might spend more time wishing I had. So —"**

It was one of the many points on which she had given him a balanced perspective, so that, when he wrote for the *Evangelical Magazine* an article on Female Dress, it had distinguished nicely between essentials and matters of little import. Doubtless the success of the correspondence which he carried on with women of all ages and classes was due in no small part to the liberal education which Mary had unobtrusively given him. Mary, his own —

Gratefully he added the possessive and brought the greeting full cycle with two final words: "My Dear Sweet Precious Beautiful Own Dearest Dear" — the letter now read. He had risen early to put it in the post before his full-day's programme began.

"I had a safe and pleasant journey, agreeable chit chat company and by the Lord's goodness arriv'd here in safety at 3 o'clock. Much and earnestly have I been importuned to stay till Saturday but my desire of seeing you, and my promise to you that I would return on Friday have prevail'd. . . ."

John paused again for a brief review before the Lord of the events since his arrival on Monday in Colchester. This sort of prayer, arising from business in hand, he had learned to employ whenever impulse and opportunity offered; for he had frequently mourned the fact that he was seldom more a prey to vain and evil thoughts than when on his knees; and though, of late years, the thoughts and imaginings which pestered him were idle rather than vile, he had too much knowledge of his own heart to attribute the change to improvement in that organ, rather than to increasing age. Yet such was the mercy of God that he was enabled to preach and write with acceptable power, even while most conscious of his weakness — perhaps *because* most conscious of his weakness, most dependent upon his all-sufficient Saviour.

Yes, he felt justified in refusing to comply with the Routleys' urgency that he stay to address the Society on Friday evening. Before that he would have spoken three times in the morning and as often at house or Chapel meetings in the evening. His interview last night with young Sandwell had convinced him — if he needed convincing — that there had been leading in his decision to accept the invitation to Colchester rather than to St. Alban's. And his fund for Ellis William's destitute family had been unexpectedly doubled. The burden which he had assumed to assist the poverty of that devoted young Devonshire curate, and the sorrow with which he had heard of his death were lightened a little, now that over four hundred pounds would somewhat alleviate his widow's difficulties. Thank God he had seized the opportunity to speak of it at yesterday's dinner table, little knowing that the response would be so generous. He must be more ready to buy up opportunities in future. Mary would be glad. He wrote a brief account for her, describing the new acquaintances whose hearts had been touched and whose purses had been opened.

"I have paid earnest to return by the same coach which brought me," he continued. "I long to see you already. It seems as if I was coming home from the East Indies."

Why had he written the *East* Indies, he wondered, when he

had never been there? Had his mind reverted unconsciously to the great dread of his life, those weeks and months on the *Harwich* when he was being forced from Mary to the East Indies, when anything seemed preferable, any risk worth the taking, even the mad risk which had plunged him in misery?

As always, recollection of those days was enough to send him into a mood of fervent gratitude. "O to grace how great a debtor" was he, the African blasphemer and profligate! Not least of his blessings was the powerful, almost reproductive memory, which awoke again and again, to keep him from being lulled into complacence at his present state.

"I have only to mix a little Plantane sauce with my meals" he had written to Mary, on the first occasion of dining off gold plate at Lord Dartmouth's. So now, glancing from the window as the October morning sun slanted on the roofs of this ancient city, he gave himself up to the general thanksgiving occasioned by his last sentence.

Never had a man been so blest in temporals as he, especially in these last few years. Nor, surely, had any man been raised from such unmitigated degradation to such honour, from such loneliness to such love. Few of the trials which had clouded his Olney ministry, the presumption and opposition of his own flock, were met in London. The offence of the cross had not ceased, but its manifestations were more subtly expressed. The debt which his share in the slave trade had impressed upon him in the more-than-quarter-century since his conscience had been made tender on the subject, was not paid — it never could be paid — but the mercy of God had opened a way for him to make some compensation. Young Wilberforce, meeting Betsey in Cambridge recently, had mentioned the beneficent work achieved wherever any of his thousands of pamphlets had gone. The struggle would not be short or easy; but John did not believe that William Wilberforce had been called, fired, empowered, to no purpose.

And Betsey — there was another cause for thanksgiving. Always sensitive and volatile, she had recently displayed more control of her feelings, more steady cheerfulness, and was becoming at nineteen an intelligent companion and a great comfort to his Dear. The Venns whom she had visited in Cambridge had written an admiring account on her return and he had wondered if real parents could have glowed more warmly than Mary and he when they read it. She had gone with them to visit Mr. Cowper at Weston in August and —

Another cause for thanksgiving! The love and regard, the admiration which had led him to subscribe himself 'fidus Achates' to his friend was, like John's other affections, unabated by time, distance, honours, or newer friendships. He had loved William Cowper when he was unknown to the world; he had loved him when the love cost dearly and paid no returns; he had loved him and thought constantly of his cheer and welfare when separated in distance and sphere of interest; he loved him still, now that he had become a poet of some renown and largely independent of him. But he was not unaware that the discursive gaiety, which had once been part of William's letters to him, now found its way into other letters, while the dark and gloomy disclosures were reserved for him; not unaware either, from Lady Hesketh's attitude, that his influence was blamed for the course of life which her cousin had chosen and in which he had experienced joy and usefulness, and that this course of life was held responsible for the recurrence of his malady. John knew the facts and forbore the defence and justification which Cowper alone, he felt, could offer. But the happy weeks at Olney and Weston, their first visit in years, had restored much of their former rapport. The lifting of Cowper's hallucination concerning John's existence had almost renewed the union of soul which nothing now impeded but his gloomy obsession. They had chatted interminably, discussing the international situation on which, as on the revolt of the Colonies, Cowper was much more conservative than John. William had consulted him about some vexing lines in his translation of Homer, conceding that his previous suggestions had been the most valuable criticism he had received. Mary and Mrs. Unwin had resumed their relationship and his Dear had exerted her usual friendly charm on Sir Cowper. That too was blessing, her continued health all during this summer for, as late as June, she had been so frequently indisposed that their visit to Weston was almost cancelled.

Mary, *Mary*. Wherever he began his intercession or thanksgiving he always came back to her. Other blessings, health, life itself, had value — that is, as far as they afforded him satisfaction — only with her to share them. He had been enabled for many years to endure her absence, to take pleasure, as once he had not known pleasure, in other things: in beauty of scene or friends' conversation or reading, even when he knew that days or weeks would elapse before he saw her again. He hoped, fearfully, that he had learned to value the gift in due proportion to the Giver; but next to Him —! He had written during one of their now infrequent separations that the passion of love had grown into an inexpressibly tender friendship; but he realized suddenly, as he re-read the last words of his letter, that young Cecil's recent wondering exclamation was a truer estimate: "A lover's passion, Sir, lasting unabated through life!" He picked up the pen and wrote at his heart's dictation:

"I shall think of you and dream of you till I hold you fast. I am by twice ten thousand ties your most affectionate and indeared —

John Newton."

A fire burning warmly in the grate; late asters on Mary's sewing table; the supper things cleared away by Phoebe, Sally and Crabb, who took unnecessary turns with the serving "just to show how glad they are to see you" — his peaceful happy home! Betsey was spending the day and night with an old school-friend near the Knights' Bridge and the arrangement suited John admirably.

"I can wait to see the dear child till tomorrow," he said happily, as Mary settled herself on a low chair beside him. "Now if she were here and *you* had gone into the country — that would be very different. I yearned, but scarcely hoped, to have the evening alone with you."

"I wanted it too." She said nothing more for a moment and John, who felt that he had spent five days in talking, let the communion of silence rest unbroken. They had told each other the items of news and interest. His letters could wait. There were no knocks at the door, no pressing parish call to answer. His body was not tired but his mind was almost asleep with relaxed contentment.

"John," said Mary.

400

Something, he could never say what, for her voice was quiet and she did not move the head on which his hand rested, startled him into alertness, even as years ago at sea he had sometimes awakened for no perceptible reason, to know that something was wrong on the ship. Suddenly he remembered his feckless gaiety as he had swung along the Tor Bay road, approaching the bend around which he was to meet doom and anguish. So — and in the moment between her utterance of his name in the voice that was hers, yet not quite hers, and his unbetraying answer — he felt that he had reached a corner that must be turned, and that some unknown danger lay around it.

"Dearest?" he said, and waited.

"I wonder how many times," she began almost lightly, though he noticed that her hands were clasped, not folded in her lap and that their close interlacing had made the fingers white, "you have written or told me that we should — that we would — that there would come —" She broke off her effort at circumlocution and turned slightly so that he could see her face, composed, even serene, though she did not look up at him. Her next words were a shock; they brought dread, but not enlightenment.

"I went to see Mr. Warner yesterday."

"Mr. Warner of Guy's?" The surgeon who had operated on John's thigh twelve years before was a friend and had become eminent for his skill. "But —"

"Do you remember the little lump I had after I fell on the garden stake in Liverpool?"

White-lipped, John remembered. She had suffered occasional recurrence of pain for some time afterwards, but it was years since she had mentioned it, and pains in various parts of her body — nervous disorders, the doctors all said — were so frequent that he had given it no specific thought. Now, meeting her loving, revealing eyes for the first time, he slipped his great hand gently beneath the stays which supported her left breast, felt what he found with shaking fingers, and drew back his hand, shivering.

"Dearest, how long has this been? How could I not notice? Why did you not tell me?"

401

She took the hands which he held out to her in a blind, pitiful appeal and answered quite calmly:

"I haven't known myself for long. Before we went to Olney this summer I felt a pain there and noticed that it had grown larger. As for telling you — that was the reason I went to Mr. Warner yesterday. I asked if he would operate while you would be away at Manchester so that you would not need to know until it was over."

His Dear, his Mary, lying conscious on the operating table, as he had lain, but with the knife cutting, not a comparatively small tumour from a relatively insensitive place, but that most delicate flesh near her beloved heart . . . and he away . . . not knowing. . . . The frantic cries of John's mind were scarcely prayer; yet somehow they enabled him to articulate from a closed and aching throat.

"He said —?"

"He said" — the strange note, the note of effort, was in her voice again but the effort was to spare him — "that he dares not attempt it. The — the growth is now the size of half a melon."

"But what is to be done? What of the pain?"

"He recommends quiet and ease of mind," said Mary, smiling slightly for the first time. "And he says that if the pain is bad, it may be relieved by laudanum; which you know I dislike, I think, more than the pain."

Silence closed over them again but a silence like the stillness at the heart of vortex. The clamour of John's spirit, the groaning of his heart was so loud that he dared not trust himself to speak. Besides his grief he felt utter shame. He should have words, he should be comforting her, he should be rehearsing the many prognostications he had made of this crisis, of their need for submission and trust. He should quote the strong comfort of the Scripture, as he had quoted it, sincerely, feelingly, not glibly, to many in similar case. And he could do nothing but sit, dumb and faithless, his only claim to manliness the sheer dogged will which pent his emotions within him that their uncontrolled expression might not add to her grief.

She knew. The cry of his heart reached her as though it had broken on her ears. Ultimately it was she who gave what comfort he was able to receive. He had not ventured to touch

402

her lest the touch unman him. Now, to bridge the gulf of un-uttered fear between them she left her chair and stood before him, taking his face in her hands and looking into his eyes with an expression which he never forgot.

"Remember, my Pretty Dear," she said, and the brave voice shook slightly on her favourite endearment, "this need not be incurable just because the surgeon cannot cure it. But if it is — if it is — oh, John dear, always remember that the Lord is being very kind to me. I would so much rather die than be left without you."

He drew her to him at that and they cried together, cried until tension departed and he was able to speak almost nor-mally. She fell asleep early that night; he doubted if she had slept the night before, while waiting alone to break the news. But John lay staring into the dark, battling his anguish and striving for coherent prayer.

It would come some day. He had always faced and — as Mary had tried to remind him with laughter which she could not quite achieve — had repeatedly urged *her* to face the all-but-inevitable prospect that one of them would be left. More, in spite of various illnesses and accidents, he had been fairly sure, except during the fever on his last African voyage, that he would be the survivor. Many, many times in Mary's sud-den violent seizures and long periods of weakness he had thought the time was at hand — and thanked God for delaying the blow until he was able to bear it. In some sense — he realized it, as he lay staring into thick darkness — he had lived all his married life in the shadow of this long-suspended sword.

But he was not able yet. He caught frantically at phrases from his own hymns, hymns that he had written in the fulness of faith, hymns that were true — and if true for others, surely for him, if in all other circumstances, surely in this.

> *"Since all that I meet must work for my good*
> *The bitter is sweet, the medicine food."*

But it isn't, Lord, it is bitter. And the more bitter because I acknowledge it just. I deserve to lose her; I never deserved to have her. I should have lost her long ago if Thou hadst marked iniquity. . . . I have always perverted Thy best gift, making her a cause of fear instead of trust, letting thoughts and concern for her come between Thee and my heart. But how could I love in measure, when it was the immeasurableness of my love for her which Thou didst use to bring me to Thyself? Wilt Thou blame —?

He broke off, aghast. Was the clay arguing against the Potter? such clay as he against the Maker who might long ago have cast him aside as useless and marred? He tried to recollect his mercies, to stir his soul to gratitude. Even in what she had said there was mercy: whatever she suffered — and sweat broke out on his whole body at the prospect — in a sense he would suffer more. He recalled the agony of her face as she had watched the doctors adjust the bone dislocated by his last fall; recollected the complete alteration of her whole constitution which had come about from her mental stress at the time of his apoplectic fit, thought of her desperate anxiety when snow had delayed his journey to Chatham, and knew that he should feel grateful that she was spared the final blow.

But he could not feel gratitude. He could not feel anything but mad, raging, fearful, desperate, pitiable chaos.

> *"It soothes his sorrows, heals his wounds*
> *And drives away his fear."*

My sorrow, my wounds, my fear, Lord! Is this what poor William feels, deserted by Thee, unable to approach Thee? The things I have written to others, the sermons I have preached, the hundreds of mourners whom I have enjoined to cheerfulness! What a hypocrite! As if death is not inevitable and bereavement the common lot. As if pagans without hope and without God in the world have not faced it with dignity. The shame of knowing all this, and of being helpless to apply it!

> *"Amazing Grace, how sweet the sound*
> *That saved a wretch —"*

Do not let me disgrace my profession, Lord. Do not let me bring shame upon the Name. And Lord, Gracious Lord, do not let me fail her, when her faith may be assailed in her weakness. Do not remove Thy grace from me. For without it I can do nothing. Thou seest I can do nothing, but toss, toss like a wild bull in a net.

40

IF thou hast run with the footmen and they have wearied thee, how wilt thou contend with horses?"

This disconcerting question, a favourite text of John's, recurred frequently to his mind in ensuing months. After the bleakness of that first night, resumption of normal life with its compelling duties, absence of any alarming symptoms in Mary's health, induced a brief suspension of dread, a sort of emotional twilight in which Dr. Benamer's pronouncement that the case was not hopeless — such growths had been known to disappear or at least to remain static — shed a pre-dawn flush of hope.

They had not intended to tell Betsey. For a season of her school-days she had passed through a period of morbid fear which John had met with frank discussion and wise encouragement to diversion. Small wonder that the thought of death had obsessed her, when at thirteen she had seen ten of the relatives dear to her childhood claimed by it and when at fifteen she had watched the dissolution of her play-mate and cousin. Recently her spirits had risen and fallen perceptibly with Mary's illnesses.

Somehow, by the sensitiveness of affection, by the whispers of servants, by John's unconscious watchfulness, by the additional care which Mary now allowed without protest, the girl's suspicions were aroused. Under her pathetic questioning John told the truth, grateful that he was enabled to speak cheerfully and to forget himself in assuaging her passionate grief. But the redoubled efforts which they made for her entertainment, her own desperate efforts to hide her feelings, could not prevent loss of appetite and fits of secret weeping. In a weakened condition she was attacked by a nervous fever which tossed her for days and nights in melancholy delirium. And while it was still raging, she contracted the typhoid, epidemic in London that winter.

The rest of body and peace of mind enjoined for Mary were summarily snatched away. She rejected John's first suggestion that she go to stay with friends in the country ("How could I rest there, John?") and could not accede to his urging that she leave the nursing to the servants and himself. "Our child, John. She's calling for me," she pleaded, and with truth, for Betsey clung to her in delirium, though she was covered with remorse when sense returned. But the anxiety, the broken sleep, and, during the slow convalescence of an illness which lasted most of the winter, the attempts to cheer her daughter took a visible toll. Against the doctor's gloomier hinting, Betsey recovered as spring drew on, but John's relief was light in the scale against the wordless anguish with which he watched his wife, her figure wasted, her eyes hollow, her smile a tattered banner flaunted above a besieged citadel.

By her growing restlessness he had been sure that the pain in her breast was increasing, though his questions were put off with evasive replies. One April night, roused out of fitful sleep the third time in as many hours by her pathetic effort to turn without disturbing him, and asking if he could do anything to help, he heard her control break in a sob.

"Oh, John, dearest John, I'm sorry, so sorry," she cried, while he held and soothed her and felt that his heart would break with helplessness. "I hate to distress you but it hurts so that I cannot lie still. John, pray for me. I can hardly pray for myself."

All other petitions that John had ever offered seemed weak by comparison with this outpouring of his soul. No stranger to bodily pain, he would have suffered the worst of it again and counted it the easier alternative to his present suffering. He was not given the alternative; but perhaps the willingness made his prayer effectual. Next day, having asked the Lord's blessing on any means that were attempted, he applied again to Dr. Benamer for relief. There was none known, his sorrowful friend stated plainly, but if he was willing to try a new

406

unproved analgesic some good might come. John was. To his unspeakable gratitude, gratitude so overwhelming that it was almost joy, prayer or the medicine took effect — *and* the medicine he had no doubt, for the improvement exceeded the doctor's most sanguine expectation. With the blessed release from pain, his Dear experienced a renewed lease of strength. In late August, John, beginning the General Thanksgiving, looked towards the pew where for the first time in nine months his wife sat, with Betsey and the three maids beside her; and the General Thanksgiving was particular indeed.

Encouraged by the convalescence and by the doctor's buoyant hazard that a complete cure was not impossible, John left his new curate in charge of the parish and took Mary and Betsey to visit the Taylors at the seaside. September was an idyllic month. The sight and smell of the sea — as long as neither John nor she had to venture on it — a few short strolls with John in a wood which he loved, long hours in the sunlit garden, the presence and visits of friends, the opportunity of hearing her husband preach again in Mr. Taylor's chapel where an easy chair was brought for her, the restoration to health and gaiety of Betsey: all created an atmosphere almost of inter-calary days, inserted between the uncertain past and the certain future.

"Safely home," said John's diary on Saturday, the third of October. Still warmed with the halcyon air of holiday, Mary insisted on going to service the next morning; on Wednesday she announced her desire to attend that service also. But before the following Sunday it became evident that the surge of nervous energy had ebbed. No, she assured John, it wasn't pain, there was scarcely any pain, but a little exertion brought on a feeling of collapse and to stand or sit upright for very long distressed her. So John declined the invitations which came for her, as he had often done before, but this time with the foreboding that there would be no rallying, that she would never accompany him again. At her insistence he went alone on occasions which she deemed important, treasuring up anything of interest and amusement to tell her on his return.

Yet she was more likely than he to supply diversion. Even when her appetite failed, when she took a strong aversion first to meat and fish, then to fowl, so that he was forced to depend on friends to supply him, out of season, with the small birds for which alone she briefly retained some relish, even when she wasted, almost before their eyes, for want of the nourishment which she could not force herself to take, it was she whose brightness shamed their flagging spirits.

During the winter and spring and summer, whenever she admitted the possibility and the weather was fair, she went for an ever-shortening ride in a coach. Friends called to cheer and found themselves cheered by an invalid who spoke little of herself, and took a lively interest in their concerns. Wilberforce and Hannah More carried on lengthy, vigorous, witty, earnest discussions with John in her presence. She revived her long-unused skill at dominoes and chess to play with Betsey, over whose health she kept surreptitious watchful eyes, planning excursions, and insisting that she accompany John on any suitable occasion. For Sally and Crabb and Phoebe, whose devotion was baffled by the paucity of means to express it, she invented foolish little games: guessing contests as to the exact time of the post's arrival, John's return home, the number of steps to run a certain errand, the number of letters received on any particular day, the number of carriers passing the window within a given time; and held a solemn prize-giving each evening, apportioning comfits to the daily winner.

Jaundice attacked her, and with it a loathing for almost any food. "My Dear can sometimes eat a little fruit," John wrote Mrs. Taylor. "If your walls can afford a few peaches and you can spare a pine apple. . . ." and when a fine basket of peaches and pears arrived from Portswood in the care of a London-bound friend, he admitted: "She saw the letter I sent. I put down the fruit postscript afterwards without her knowledge." But even jaundice did not daunt Mary's courage. She quipped bravely about her colour; and only John, who knew the innocent care which she had taken in sun and wind to preserve her cream-white skin, guessed at the wistfulness under her provoking question.

"You used to say that if I hadn't called you home from Africa you would have had a black wife. Should you have come, if you had known I should turn yellow?"

And it was a point of pride with her when, a year after

408

their return from Southampton, she could do little more than lie all day on her sofa by the window facing Swan Alley, to walk back to her bed, once they had set her on her feet, without any aid.

"See how well I can walk, John," was her customary remark and once, to the complete destruction of his self-control, she raised her arm, took a gliding step, and executed the shadow of a curtsey. "I declare, I could still dance! Do you remember our first Assembly in Rochester, Dear?"

But, for John's great steadying and comfort, whatever amusements she planned, whatever diversion she admitted, nothing was allowed to interfere with her stated time for Scripture reading. The place of family prayer had followed her failing strength, from study to parlour, from parlour to bedroom. But her own Bible became daily more worn with her reading, daily more marked by the gentle pressure of her pencil. Her prized copy of the Olney Hymns — the first copy received from the press with a loving inscription in her husband's hand — was similarly marked, as verse after verse of his or Cowper's hymns suited her need or spoke to her heart.

Meanwhile the outside world in which John carried on his work, while its pleasures and its duties failed to remove from his mind for five minutes — except during his preaching — the heavy absorbing cloud of anxiety, had more than its usual share of important events. The first bill for Abolition came before the House. John, in the gallery of the Commons, heard his young friend, white with strain and emotion, deliver himself of a masterly speech lasting three hours and a half. "I mean not to accuse anyone," said the voice, beautiful in speaking as in the singing which had once so attracted the Prince of Wales, "but to take the shame on myself. We are all guilty. . . ."

But in spite of his eloquence, which compelled praise from the veteran oration-taster Burke, only one hundred and sixty three were won against opposition of one hundred and eighty three. Events in France were looming larger in British minds than belated justice in Africa. Two months and two days after Wilberforce spoke, the Bastille crashed, and the rapid strides of freedom once seized by serfs were little reassuring to those who entertained forebodings about granting it to blacks.

America praised the Revolution, claiming it as a result of her own precedent, and continued to develop her resources with slave labour. John rejoiced in the fall of the Bastille and shook his head as the pendulum began to swing from the cruel excesses of the rulers to the brutal license of the liberated. In the enthusiasm which swept many Evangelicals into political preaching he refused steadily to abandon the proclamation of the gospel for a programme of social reform which would leave sinners unredeemed, unchanged, but more comfortable sinners. "If all the brethren have preached according *to the times*," he wrote to a clergyman who rebuked him for not using his pulpit as a political sounding-board, "may not one poor brother be suffered to preach *to eternity?*"

The result of such preaching was making itself felt on the times, however. Hannah More sent him an inscribed copy of her first volume: *Thoughts on the Importance of the Manners of the Great to General Society* which went into seven editions; and followed it with *An Estimate of the Religion of the Fashionable World*. These books, soon found in the library of every fine lady and of many fine gentlemen, disappointed their authoress, who saw only their failure to convert many of the fashionable for whom they were written, and had little concept of their effect in producing attitudes in which conversion would take place. "Ladies read me but do not heed me. The duchesses say they adore but do not mean business. They fail completely to grasp what is meant by plucking out the right eye," she said ruefully, and was cheered when John replied:

"There is a circle by which what you write will be read and which will hardly read anything of a religious kind that is not written by you."

"Read, yes! Because they have seen my *Percy* at the theatre or read my *Bas Bleus*. Even admit 'How true!' to my most depreciative comments on their attitudes. But change —"

John smiled at her animated, expressive gesture.

" 'I planted, Apollos watered, but God giveth the increase'," he quoted. "I once knew a gardener who boasted that he could sow salad and have it ready when the meat was roasted. God seldom works at that speed."

"Oh, how I wish that my Mendip hermitage and your ministry lay nearer to each other, Mr. Newton. Failing that, I should love you both to visit me this summer." She broke off, suddenly sensitive to the look on John's face, glanced at his wife's frail form on the sofa, and was at a loss to continue. Mary's quickness of wit saved the situation.

"*Dr.* Newton and I thank you very much and shall put your invitation first on our list," she said with demure emphasis. Her husband squirmed.

"Dearest, I have asked you not to mention —"

Hannah More turned to him with relieved interest.

"Dr. Newton? Please tell me. I have been at Gloucester House where one hears everything except the thing of importance."

Mary smiled triumphantly.

"Tell her, John. Or I shall. And if I do, you will like it very much less because I shall put on airs."

"The College or University of Prince-town in New Jersey," complied her resigned husband, "has seen fit, for some inscrutable though well-meant reason, to confer on me an honorary degree of Doctor of Divinity. And since the newspapers apprized the public, I have been the recipient of a shower of letters addressed to a Dr. Newton with whom I claim no acquaintance."

"If it were anyone else," said Mary, as the visitor looked at her in surprise, "I should believe him insincere. No, he means it. I have seldom known him so annoyed as when the post brings another letter."

"But surely, my dear Sir," said Hannah More warmly, "it is a matter for congratulation. The Americans are also to be congratulated on their perspicacity. I think I can safely say that I have never known a Reverend Doctor who had better claim to the title."

"Not having a pocket glass I cannot see if I am blushing," retorted John. "Nor, I think, should I need to protest to you, my dear Madam, further than to say simply, as I have already written to the College and to my misguided friends: I have neither the pretension nor wish for honours of this kind. However the University may overrate my attainments, I must not forget myself. I am determined not to assume the title of Doctor, unless I should receive a diploma from a college in

411

the New Settlement of Sierra Leone. The dreary coast of Africa was the university to which the Lord was pleased to send me, and I dare not acknowledge a relation to any other."

His feeling on this subject was, as Mary had said, deep and consistent. It led him to write to a Scottish correspondent who persisted in using the title, in terms much stronger than his courtesy normally permitted, stating that he would be forced to return unopened any more correspondence so addressed.

Similarly it was under protest that he let Bacon's friend Russell sketch him at this time. "There are faces better worth the commemorating," he insisted, wishing that such an artist had captured his Dear's face for him before illness had made her unwilling and unable to undergo the effort. Only when Russell offered to make the sketches during their friendly visits, did he agree, and the resultant pastel, his lips parted in conversation, an ironical deprecatory look in his eye, convinced him at once of its honesty, and of the years which Mary's illness had added to his appearance.

41

OHN raised himself gently on one elbow. The clock
of St. Stephen's had struck seven long before but he
had been unwilling to awaken Mary by stirring. She
slept fairly well these nights, but lightly, and usually awoke
before he was ready to rise. Now, however, her breathing
was even and, though in the curtained October dawn he could
dimly see her face, it seemed quite unconscious.

With long-practised control of movement remarkable for
his slowly increasing girth, he eased himself out of the bed
and went into the small adjoining dressing-room. When his
toilet was complete he returned and, drawing the curtain of
the great bed carefully aside, knelt beside his still sleeping
wife. They always prayed so before he left the room and this
morning he must breakfast downstairs with a young minister
who had come to him in desperate trouble. During these last
months he had discontinued the Thursday breakfasts, which
had become a vitalizing, often gay institution for Evangelical
clergymen in the City. Mary had protested, but yielded to his
argument that the extra labour was an unfair tax on the
servants and Betsey. Frequently, however, when no other
time served, he used the breakfast hour for interviews such as
this. His home had become an asylum, particularly for young
people in trouble: Betsey's friends, strayed members of his
Olney flock, distressed acquaintance of the servants, young
men away from home whose families persuaded them to get
in touch with him. He had become unwontedly indignant when
Richard Cecil ventured to take him to task for consoling where
— according to Cecil — he should have rebuked. "Christ is.

413

the only one who can cast a stone," he had said, sharply for him. "And the Holy Spirit alone can rebuke effectually. It is not for such a worm as I to break the broken reed or add to the sorrow of a disconsolate sinner."

Still Mary did not stir. There was no cause for alarm, though almost any unusual circumstances caused his heart to feel arrested in its beating. If it had been possible to entertain the idea he would have thought that she was deceiving him. Years ago and rarely — Mary never let custom stale her infinite variety — she had pretended sleep and he had watched until the flutter of an eyelid betrayed her, then kissed her into laughing wakefulness. But now —! He put the absurd notion from him with a sigh, prayed silently by her side, and with a last backward glance left the room, asking Betsey, before he descended the stairs, to watch for her mamma's awakening.

By the time the young man had unburdened himself and departed, Sally and Betsey had Mary ensconced on her sofa. She seemed much as usual, they had brought him word during breakfast; very quiet, Betsey said as he went upstairs.

Very quietly too she greeted him, answering his solicitude almost perfunctorily and showing an unusual lack of interest in his replies to her also perfunctory questions about his visitor and his programme for the day. At a loss and casting about to elicit the reason of her altered manner — perhaps a heroic effort to conceal some new pain or discomfort, although she denied it and he had never known her to lie — he noticed that her special pile of books was not at hand on her table and moved to place them closer.

"Don't bother, John. I don't want them."

"I'll put them there, anyhow," he said, anxiously cheerful. "Are your poor eyes tired? Shall I read to you?"

"No. My eyes aren't tired." When had he heard Mary speak fretfully to him? "I'm just tired of — of everything, I think. And I see no use in reading the Bible. It doesn't mean anything to me."

How wilt thou contend with horses? The words rang ironically in John's ears a few days later when, coming from another painful interview, he shut himself up in his study and paced the room, trying to master at least the outward appearance of his tearing grief before facing his Sunday afternoon congregation. Viewed from his present acme of agony, the long months of trial and apprehension seemed soberly tranquil. Mary's state had rapidly worsened. She made no efforts to appear cheerful and dully resented theirs. From a contradictory confusion of statement regarding her own share in the promises of Scripture, she had reached the point of declaring — though she spoke little of anything — that she could not believe that the Bible was true, or that truth existed. She had always been timid and hesitant about claiming her salvation but her whole-hearted interest in the Evangel, her identification with believers, her earnest desire to labour in the Lord's work, as well as many remarks in prayers and letters, carefully stored in his memory, had made him happily certain that only deep spiritual humility kept her from the assurance which some asserted so easily. Now she said — indifferently — that she had never had it; that if she ever had thought so, she was mistaken; in fact that she had probably thought herself into such a state in order to please him.

Such remarks were made to him in private, but the others could not fail to notice her change of habit and attitude. Seeing the puzzled pain with which Betsey watched her mother, he had obtained an invitation for her to stay with Mrs. Wilberforce. During family prayers — he did not see how he could omit a custom so long established — she preserved an aloof demeanour which almost incapacitated him for conducting them. The simple, heartfelt petitions, with which he brought every one of the household to the throne of grace in need or thanksgiving, sounded stilted and awkward to his now acutely listening ear.

But to stand calm in public when he was tossed and torn in private; to preach consolation when he felt that his grief if Mary were so taken was inconsolable; to assure his hearers of the God whose people proved even down to old age his unchangeable love, when at the very time of her need all consciousness of that love seemed to be withdrawn: this was beyond his power. God could not expect of him strength which He failed to supply. . . .

He broke off abruptly, realizing as if another had spoken, to what point his personal grief had led him. So far — just so far, but that was as far as he had come — he had been enabled, he had not disgraced his profession, he had, under the watchful eyes of friends and critics — and critical friends who had thought his affection excessive and extravagant — been able to fulfil his office.

"Yes, Lord, yes. I would not be ungrateful; I would not be faithless. But how can I go now to preach? I am tired, so very tired! I have no feeling for the truth I must proclaim. I should be little better than a hypocrite. I trust in Thee. I know Thy promises must be true. And yet —

Suddenly, with unusual force, the thought struck him:

The promises of God *must* be true. I have proved too many, too often, to doubt now. He has promised to help me. Surely He will help me, *if I am willing to be helped.*

He stopped pacing the room, and realized, when his eyes cleared, that he was staring at Mary's picture, the same picture, poor but precious, that he had taken to sea and stared at on the long-ago occasion when he was afraid he had lost her. What he would have given then to be assured of thirty-seven years of her loving presence, and what an ungrateful wretch he was proving himself in return. Yet self-recognition and self-denunciation were very far from cure, as he had often proved. His eyes filled with yearning tears as he gazed and turned away, forcing his attention from grief back to the thought which had arrested him.

"Lord," he said aloud, for he could not command his thoughts long enough in silent prayer, "I am helpless — need I tell Thee? — in myself; I cannot even say I am willing, but I *hope* I am willing. Make me willing, without reserve, that Thou shouldest help me."

A few moments later he left the house, walked slowly but firmly down Coleman Street and along Lothbury to Poultry. Half an hour later the congregation saw their minister ascend the familiar pulpit.

" 'Fear not, thou worm Jacob, and ye men of Israel'," he read and no one present could have known from the sermon which followed that he had caught at the text as he made his way up the steps; " 'for I will help thee, saith the Lord, and thy Redeemer is the Holy One of Israel.' "

So, with no sensible elevation of feeling but with the simple assurance that God had engaged to support him, John con-

416

tinued outwardly unperturbed during the period which seemed every day to set a new high-water mark in his affliction. Mary was noticeably weaker. The difficulty which she now experienced in walking from bed to sofa and back was not solely due to her present inertia. It was terrible for John that at the very time when the doctor said daily that it was doubtful if she could survive the night, she could not bear the mention of death and kept weakly making plans and giving instructions for Christmas, talking of making a visit in the spring, and showing almost her sole interest in long-unused dresses, which she insisted that Crabb bring out of the press and prepare to alter for her future use.

During this time the wife of the Reverend Thomas Scott, his convert and friend, died suddenly. Mary had known her for years and they had often exchanged visits. Divided between desire to spare her pain and a great yearning that she might again realize and speak of her own imminent dissolution, John broke the news. She looked at him, her eyes clouded with rebellion.

"Poor Mrs. Scott," she said; then coldly, "I suppose you think there is good reason that she should be taken, while out there —" she made a feeble gesture towards the street — "hundreds are spared who do no good to anyone and do harm when they can."

In all the bewilderment and bitterness of a trial which stretched in unrelieved sorrow, so that he could scarcely believe that little more than a fortnight had passed, John found his one ray of light in something which at first seemed not the least dark aspect. Not only towards God had his Dear's attitude changed; her whole relationship with him had altered. That she could utter, without softening or apology, words which, however true for her, she would once have suppressed to spare him: that might have been consonant with a desire to be honest. Complete cessation of all endearment, her lack of response to his touch, her indifference to his presence or to his departure: only the experience would have convinced him that he could find consolation in this. He did, though it was comfort a step removed from desperation. Her realization of acceptance with God might — from her hesitance in constant assurance — have been in doubt; her love for him had been spoken, written, amply demonstrated over forty years. Therefore, he argued with fearful logic, it was not his Mary who disclaimed faith and renounced God. It was the power which tempted her through the weakness and pain of her long-tried flesh. And if she should die in this state, it would make no difference. "Ask me not how a man died, but how he lived," he had answered a curious inquirer regarding the death-bed utterances of a friend. And he believed it.

"But for my sake, do not let her die in this state," he cried silently, towards dawn on the sixteenth night of her aberration. Betsey had insisted on returning home but he let her spend little time in the house, employing her as she loved to be employed, with visits and practical assistance to the poor who lived in the alleys and attics of his wealthy parish. The three maids and he had divided the night into watches and he had been wakened at four to find his wife sleeping quietly.

It was dark in the street but the candle threw enough light to let him see suddenly that Mary's eyes were open, and in the dimness he knew that they were meeting his again without that intangible veil obscuring their gaze.

"My poor Dear," she said and John felt, at the faint but familiar warmth in her voice, that he was awakening from a horrid dream, "how much sleep have you lost, sitting up to watch me? Come back to bed at once. I shall do very well."

In his relief, his gratitude that she was *his* again, restored from a state which made him realize what he had always known, that death was little to be feared in comparison, John was enabled to bear almost with equanimity the touching, trying weeks which followed. Whatever constitutional change had been taking place during that gloomy fortnight, the results were soon apparent. One or two days more, supported on either side, she made the little journey from her bed to sofa. The next morning they found her utterly unable to move. The cancer, Dr. Benamer said, had affected the spine, but, though her legs and body were incapable of motion, her breast was so sensitive that the slightest touch distressed her. When it was necessary to move her from one side of the bed to the other, Betsey and he with the three servants, working with cautious tenderness and breaking off till her next faint assent allowed them to continue, accomplished the feat in two hours.

The books which she again tried to read were too heavy for her hands to hold. But the eagerness with which she listened when John and Betsey read to her, the close attention with which she followed his prayers, the gentle protesting gratitude with which she acknowledged their efforts and their vigilance: these were Mary. The whole household felt as if a heavy curtain had been drawn back to admit the light.

That is why Thou forbiddest idolatry, thought John looking down at her one morning, not to deny, but to spare us. When this can happen to an idol, when I, her idol, am powerless to help her, what would be our wretchedness if our dependence were solely on each other? Pity my poor sufferer, I beseech Thee. . . . Aloud he said, as she stretched out her hand with a welcoming smile:

"You suffer greatly."

Mary's brows, still upturning at the corners, knit in consideration.

"I suffer indeed, but not *greatly*," she contradicted. "Nothing as I thought a year ago I must suffer. And, thank the dear Lord, I am still able to use my hands."

John did and nearly broke down doing so. He had some painful news to tell and cast about to spare her the shock.

"Precious, you know whose illness has been much in our minds of late?"

She knew. Since the death of her family, and outside her household, no one occupied so dear a place in her affections as their beneficent friend, John Thornton. Her eyes spared him the necessity of making the announcement, and he went on:

"I think I should not have told you now, except that I am asked to act at his funeral and if I do I may be absent almost five hours."

"Go, by all means," said Mary, her eagerness restoring energy to her voice. "My Dearest, you know that I would not have you stay with me on any consideration. Oh, John, is that —?"

It was the funeral ring, enclosing a lock of Thornton's hair. Her eyes filled with tears.

"His last favour to us," she whispered, kissed it, and held it, as she had always done with anything dear, to her eyes before giving it back to him. "Dear, you must go, but while I am able, may I ask you something?"

He nodded.

"I shall not survive him long. And, my Dearest dear husband, remember what I told you, that the Lord is kind to me in this." Her voice became faint with longer speech. "I used to think I should like to be buried in Olney — you know, where Father is. I don't care at all now, as long as you will lie near me when God brings us together again. But my ring" — she held up her left hand where a guard kept the wedding-ring from slipping from her wasted finger — "I've never taken it off since you put it on — remember?"

Remember! As if it were yesterday.

"When I am gone, I want you to put it on and wear it. I know it won't go on the same finger!" She kissed his left hand which clasped hers. "That's all. You needn't speak. I am quite happy now that I have told you."

She knew that he could not speak. He left the house fearing, as he always feared these days when he went out, that he would not find her alive on his return.

Yet he did. As though to offer proof that grace was sufficient for prolonged, as for sudden trial, that the strength on which he relied was made perfect in absolute weakness, as though to fulfil his prayer that to a sceptical or wistful world he be displayed as an example of his Lord's sustaining power, another month was allowed to take its exhausting toll of Mary's person and of his endurance. Her friends — she had always made herself loved — called, inquired, sent gifts. John relayed their messages and soon ceased even to do this, for her ever susceptible head became so affected that the lightest foot and the softest tone were almost unbearable, and several times they had to leave her lying for more than a week in the same position. But the smile with which he was greeted, the sigh of contentment when she opened her eyes and saw him at her bedside were enough to keep him there, even when he could only sit and look at her, offering at times no more than the prayer of tired trustful silence.

Throughout the days and nights of watchfulness — for he could scarcely bear the thought that he might not be with her at the last, that she might call and not find him near —

420

he carried out his church schedule regularly, preached his annual sermon to the Guild of Goldsmiths, forgot no correspondent who was in need of a letter, and, particularly with Betsey and the maids, tried to make up in cheerfulness for the sadness and strain of their prolonged vigil.

Sunday, December twelve, seventeen-hundred-and-ninety. John, preparing to leave his study for the morning service, glanced down at the date of a letter which he had just begun. December twelve, that forty-eight-years-gone December twelve, and scarcely later than this in the morning, he had first met Polly. Recollection flooded upon him and he sat down, a bit unsteady with the poignance and sweetness of it.

"It's dear Madam, Sir." Phoebe, whose turn it was with Sally to stay from church, knocked and opened the door almost simultaneously. "She wants to see you."

It was farewell, John knew when he entered the room, though nothing had changed since he left it. He took the hand which she held out to him — the hand which she had extended in friendly courtesy on that long-past December day, which she had held out in half-unwilling capitulation the night of his proposal — and knew that he was taking it at her giving for the last time. He knelt beside her and, once again, when words were most wanted they would not come. Tears did and choked his utterance but, though hers were flowing, she pressed his hand with a last summoning of strength on his behalf and stroked his face.

"My Pretty Dear," she murmured gently, and again, "My Pretty Dear."

Then John found his voice and prayed, though he never knew what words formed the last of spoken prayers to commit her to their Father's keeping, their Saviour's mercy. He remained kneeling until the gentle pressure of her hand aroused him.

"Church time." He could scarcely hear the words. "Goodbye — my Pretty —"

Her voice failed, though she tried feebly again to bring out the last fond word.

He kissed her then, rose stiffly, and with his hand on her forehead, whispered her favourite benediction: " 'The Lord bless thee and keep thee. The Lord make his face shine upon

421

thee and be gracious unto thee. The Lord lift up his countenance upon thee and give thee peace.' "

He reached the door but could not bear to pass through it. Until her strength failed she had often, when he prayed or as she lay beside him, murmured: "Lord, Dear Lord, Dear Saviour, Almighty God," with a familiar tenderness which he had never before heard her use in prayer. Now he longed, with longing which exceeded physical pain, to know that he was not leaving her lonely.

Her eyes had followed him. They met his when he turned and walked back to her bedside.

"Dearest Mary," he said, and prayed that he might speak steadily, "I know in Whom you have believed. But if your mind, as I trust, is in a state of peace, it will be a comfort to me if you can signify it by holding up your hand."

There was a moment while his words found their response. Then Mary raised her hand, but, like Mary, went further and waved it feebly several times to and fro.

EPILOGUE

December. I know it is December but what date? They have been talking of Christmas, Crabb and Betsey. It must be near Christmas: Christmas 1807. Old Eighty-Two to pass another Christmas here? If it be Thy will, gracious Lord, let me pass it with my Mary . . . in Thy presence. Yet not as I will but as Thou wilt.

Seventeen years since she left me. In some sense I have been dead for seventeen years too. The world died for me on that day. Apart from Thy service I had no wish to live. Yet through mercy Thou hast chosen otherwise and in measure I see the need-be for it.

How strange to be here and yet not here, conscious of friends and yet scarcely in communication with them, able — still able, thank God! — to move and not be a complete burden, yet scarcely hearing, scarcely seeing, dependent and most conscious of their kindness. I am closed off, shut up, like a package sealed and ready for the post . . . to be opened and put to use at a new address. Once before I was shut up and closed off like this, but how differently! That was on the *Harwich* in seventeen-forty-five, awaiting my flogging. How dark, how imprisoned, how hateful I was. This is a different seclusion. Here I have light and love and liberty. But oh, *what* light and love and liberty shall I yet know when I open my now useless eyes on endless day!

> *"Till then I would Thy love proclaim*
> *With every fleeting breath;*
> *And may the music of Thy Name*
> *Refresh my soul in death."*

423

Perhaps it is a sign of approaching death that I can no longer publicly proclaim His love — how long? over a year, I think, since I last preached in St. Mary's — and privately only on occasion, when the world around and the world within me run together in sudden focus. Yet that, too, is part of the need-be. "Yea, even if Thou shouldst see fit to lay me aside from public service, so that I may honour Thee by a willing submission," so I said after she died. And Thou hast shown me that here too Thy grace is sufficient. But I was always impatient and a slow learner, gracious Lord, in Thy school. How often when I was coming home to Mary, I have gone to the window long before the time, to see if the coach was coming. So now I keep peeping out at the window, impatient for Thy coach. . . . Odd that I never feel as if my ship is coming . . . when I awaited a ship it was always to take me *from* Mary.

Seventeen years . . . how mercifully the Lord hides the future from us. I never believed that I could live seventeen years without her. I did not think I could bear to stay in this house, sleep in her room, in her very bed. All cries to me "She is not here". Yet I have not spent one uncomfortable night. I should gladly at any time have relinquished life; yet I was able to live pleasantly. While I was active in the world there was a constant sense of void; but Lord, it drove me to a closer walk with Thee.

Every year, I can see looking back, every year has shown me something of the Lord's goodness to me in the land of the living. Every year till now, and how can I question His wisdom when I have proved it in all else? Even until last year I could preach. They suggested I stop — before I find myself obliged to stop. That was young Cecil! Perhaps they were right — I know I wandered of late. But while people came to hear me — and the church was always full — I thought I was bound to stand before them, if I could do nothing else, as a testimonial of what the Lord can do, in His amazing grace . . . to the chief of sinners. And when I am taken, I have made certain that they will not falsify me with eulogizing epitaph. Mr. Wesley also wished to prevent it but his loving people had their way. Well, all that is said on his tombstone is true, though very different from the "God be merciful to me, an unprofitable servant" which he once wrote for himself. My case is different — infidel, libertine, servant of slaves in Africa — restored, pardoned, appointed to preach!

To preach in the parish church of the first magistrate of the first city in the world . . . why, that is no greater wonder than to be allowed to preach at all the faith I once laboured to destroy. But it writes large the grace of God to others and so I rejoice, yea and will rejoice. But I rejoice more that my name is written in the Lamb's Book of Life — with that of my dearest Mary.

Only my eyes and ears and strength failing made me desist. My memory, they say. How strange that we should call it *failure* of memory when the memory recalls, as if it had just happened, every great event — and so many small ones — of my life. I know, I know. I remember as a young man so criticizing Mr. Bradbury when he had preached sixty years. It was at Pinner's Hall before I commenced tide-surveyor. . . . His discourse was not so connected as those of other speakers or as his own had been before extreme old age weakened him. How much kinder my hearers have been to me, yet doubtless many felt proud and dainty also.

Yet I did not always forget. They thought I was wandering because I repeated "Jesus Christ is precious". I knew I had said it twice and I said it again. I cannot say it too often. When I think of His longsuffering while I blasphemed and insulted His Name. Indeed "To you who believe He is precious" . . . the Greek says "is the preciousness". What it will be to know — fully know — the meaning of that word!

Still I may have more to learn here. To learn how to be laid aside is a great thing. I prayed and must still pray to be kept from the sins of old age which have distressed me in other men — alas, other Christian men: impatience, fretfulness, jealousy, arrogance, a dictatorial spirit. I prayed that I might rejoice to see others coming forward to do the Lord's work. The times are awfully dark. So all say. So I have said myself. But to the eye of faith they are much brighter than when I was a boy, when all was peace and plenty with us at home and abroad, but all was ignorance and wretchedness. Many church doors were seldom opened even on the Lord's day; three-quarters of the children could not tell their letters, the official shepherds neither fed nor cared for the flocks. Many, perhaps the great majority, still do not. But now, through village and open-air preaching, the Gospel has been spread. It has been revived in Dissent where it was then but low, the Methodists have been signally blest of the Lord, and He has been pleased to visit the Established Church with some power. No, these are rather bright times.

Bright times, too, in that Thy glorious Gospel has softened men's hearts towards the oppressed. Wilberforce cared nothing for the enslavement of blacks until the Lord broke his own chains. That I should be spared to see the success . . . yes, realization may be far away but now the Commons of England have at last declared for Abolition, and it must come. I thank Thee, Gracious Lord, for permitting me to add my mite. I thank Thee for preserving and leading that young man far beyond me. I thank Thee for his friendship. I thank Thee for using me as a friend to him.

For all my friends. How many and how kind they have been. And still they write, though Betsey must read me their letters and I cannot write to them. Mrs. More . . . her little hermitage at Cowslip Green . . . is my pipe still there? . . . she said nobody would disturb it. . . .

> *"In Helicon could I my pen dip*
> *I might attempt the praise of Mendip. . . ."*

Cowper does that sort of thing so much better than I. Dear Sir Cowper. I was sure, so very sure, that his delusion would be dispelled before he went hence to be seen no more. Yet his last sad letter to me — the very last letter he wrote to anyone — and Johnson's word, assured me that he died believing it. O merciful Lord, though I cannot understand, I adore Thee. Had I been in his case I could not have stood for a minute. I should have brought shame to Thy Name. He never did. Yet what anguish he suffered; for in his bright days his communion with Thee, his lively communications of Thy Spirit were deeper, more constant than mine. What a glad surprise he must have had after his long night. Holy surprise — that was his Johnnie's word for the expression of his face at death. How I shall delight to say: I told you so. It won't annoy him in Heaven!

Mrs. More . . . I must write to her. No, surely I wrote long ago; I hope to her comfort.

> *"The heirs of salvation, I know from his Word,*
> *Through much tribulation must follow their Lord."*

She is finding that true. What an evil thing is the human heart that her efforts on behalf of the poor rouse such calumny and hatred. But Thou canst preserve her. She is Thine, one who knew much of the world's applause until she separated herself from it. So did Wilberforce. They were both like men intimate with one whom they at length discovered to be the murderer of their kind father. Then they broke the intimacy. O Lord so are all Thine who are much in the world. I thank Thee for bringing them unscathed through it. Polite, elegant people . . . the good sort of people . . . to me their company is enchanted ground. . . . I seldom entered it without fear or retired without loss.

So I wrote to her . . . or think I did. I cannot well distinguish now between what I wrote in letters or preached in sermons or recorded in my Journals. Yet I did all — I remember dates clearly — until 1805. . . . Since I ceased writing I seem to have slipped

> *"'into the lean and slippered pantaloon'."*

No, certainly not lean, but neither does my voice pipe and whistle! "O that this too too solid flesh would melt", Shakespeare, like Pitt, had *the* word for every occasion.

Thank you, Phoebe. Shall I call her back and tell her I know she isn't Phoebe? I buried our dear Phoebe ten years ago. How good my servants have been to me and to all mine. I'm glad Miss Hillier was led to leave them a legacy. They will not want when I am gone. I'm sorry I called her Phoebe. She is Jean, Crabb's niece. I know quite well . . . as I knew the other day when I called Cecil, Bacon. To think that Bacon is dead so long and I am still spared. I could wish that . . . Lord let me not form a wish . . . I have never been wise enough to carve for myself. I heard Mr. Wesley preach at eighty-two. . . . Wilberforce tells me he wrote to him from his death-bed. Ah well . . . the marvel is that this vile body has been spared so long. And that my name is known — and has been honoured of Thee, my gracious Lord — from India and New Holland to Labrador. That is grace indeed.

I thank Thee too that of recent years the abominations of my heart disturb me less. I pass for righteous among men

427

but Thou knowest! Never did I think to get out of the seventh of Romans! There again Thy wisdom is shown. Had I done, I should have taken credit to myself. Always there is pride in my humiliation, in my repentance, self in my most spiritual desires. All is wrong! But Christ is made my Righteousness. I need not *feel* righteous to know that I am accepted in Him, even on the same grounds as Wesley was . . . and Whitefield. I thank Thee for both, and what I learned from them. Lord, forgive Thy people. That two such men should be sundered for a time and thousands sundered with them by disputes about hard sayings. I could so easily have had a party spirit. Increase, Lord, the number of true Bible Christians who will see much to approve in a variety of forms and parties, but who, even if led to connection with anyone of them, will not confine their spirit and affection within these narrow enclosures. When a house was afire in Olney I never heard men ask of one coming to help: "Are you a Methodist, Baptist, Dissenter, or of the Establishment? What is your opinion of the Five Points?"

That is the spirit in which our Society for Missions has been founded. Lord grant its continuance! I thank Thee for permitting me in that, too, to make some amends. Prosper my dear young friend Buchanan as he goes to India, and William Carey . . . and Johnson in the Antipodes. If St. Paul were alive he would choose his position in Botany Bay rather than a polite curacy with me in London . . . or the pulpit in St. Mary Woolnoth.

The surprise of my little blackbirds at Clapham when I spoke to them in Sherbro! Dear Lord, make them thine and send them back to convert their brethren. Surely this work is the first colony Christians have planted with no motive but to do good. And, of thy goodness, it is in Sierra Leone, the very country where I sold myself to do evil and where later I sinned in ignorance against my fellow-men. Sinner such as I! The condemned men whom I have visited week by week in Newgate . . . hanged for no greater crimes than I perpetrated in deed or in desire. I shall not live to see it, Lord, but bring about a softening of our laws, so that a wretch who steals five shillings to buy his family bread, or a poor miner who smuggles some commodity from a wrecked ship is not hanged with the man who murders or rapes.

"Is it you, my dear child? What, dinner-time? It seems — Thank you, Betsey. Thank you, my dear."

I do not want food. But she has brought it to me . . . always carefully prepared. The least I can do is make a pretense of eating. Accept my thanks for Thy bounteous provision, Lord. Remember in mercy the poor, raise others up to care for their needs. The dear child does for them what she can, I know. I thank Thee again for Thy mercy in giving her to my comfort when my dearest earthly comfort was removed, and for restoring her to me from that place of sadness and horror.

His thoughts blurred into a kaleidoscope of images: Betsey's sorrowful, eager, young face when she came after Mary's death to ask if she could be of any use to him; her daily presence as companion, housekeeper, secretary; coaches, post-chaises as they had travelled on holiday in those first years of his loneliness to Cheddar, to Rochester, to Southampton, to Olney; her usual cheer and her shamed remorse when nervousness overcame her, as when she was found hiding in Hannah More's cupboard after a thunderstorm; Betsey asking him shyly his opinion of the quiet young optician, whose shop was near the Royal Exchange and who came so regularly to St. Mary's; Betsey's face wild and haggard, as she cried that her religious profession was hypocrisy and that she was marked out for God's special vengeance. Betsey's handkerchief fluttering from her window at Bedlam as he waited her signal daily, rain or shine, even though he could not walk unaccompanied to his station near the hospital during that awful, trying year of her incarceration.

A sigh of thankfulness broke from him. Thou hadst pity on us both, in giving her back. Bless her now and her husband. Make them as happy — I can wish them no greater temporal — as my Dear and I were; but keep them from the inordinate affection which caused us so much needless anxiety and pain. There was a need-be in the trial, I know. It is the only one I have had since *she* went from me. Perhaps without it, the peace and success of my ministry would have made me forget what a poor creature I am. And her restoration seems to have removed all the hurry of mind, the groundless fears which she had from childhood, and which I tried so hard to eradicate. Why do people put alarming books into children's hands? I always told her to avoid uneasy thoughts, to be sure never to indulge a hard thought of her Saviour as being severe and stern and ready to take advantage of her. Her mamma and I urged her to diversify her interests, to read in French and English, to write, to play her guitar and harpsichord.

I seem to have received my training in a sort of nervous school. At least I have had an unusual number of nervous patients consult me. If they could take a journey to Land's End or John O' Groat's, I advised them to go, instead of worrying about their souls. Some of my brethren were shocked that I sent Betsey out of hearing of hymn-singing and prayers. Why not, when they only served to distress her? Some would not have had me consult doctors. The cure is of God, but He uses the skill which He has given men. I thank Him — I thank Thee, O Lord, that her distress is past. I thank Thee, too, that she has a husband to care for her, but most that her reliance is upon Thee and that she knows the joy of Thy salvation.

The joy of Thy salvation. I thank Thee, my glorious Lord, for proving to me that it endures when all earthly joy departs. I have never, since the desire of my heart was given me, seen another man with whom I would exchange places; and for a quarter century was happier in temporals than most men. Yet without Thee nothing is worth the gaining. How palpably true it is that except a man be born again he *cannot see* the kingdom of God. Heaven is not like earth. There are no routs, assemblies, playhouses, horse-races there, no business to be managed. How then should they whose hearts are entirely set on these things possibly be happy in Heaven? Heaven must be Hell to an unhumbled, unsanctified sinner. The company, employments, enjoyments are what he despised on earth. Admit a pig into the drawing-room. He will have no pleasure there. He would rather be wallowing in a ditch.

As I wallowed, as I would still have been wallowing, for such, O Lord, was I.

"Thank you, my child, but I cannot eat more. Tell me,

whether you have already told me or not, what day this is. December twenty-first and a Tuesday. Great House night. A preaching day. Nothing more. Thank you, my child."

December. It was December when I met my Dear. It was December when she left me. Shall we be reunited in December . . . but there is no December in the Lord's presence. Sixty-five years . . . and she has not been a waking hour out of my thoughts. Perhaps I was too much the egoist in writing of her, every anniversary of her death. Strictly speaking, I needed no anniversary as reminder, for her idea has not been absent from me, I think, five minutes since that night. . . .

Why could I not rest in Thee, accepting Thy gift as a loan with gratitude and submission? Why did I provoke Thee, deserving every day of my life to lose her by my sinful fear and anxiety and idolatry, placing her too near Thy throne? Yet now, knowing Thy pardon, I would not have it otherwise. For otherwise I should not have learned so much of Thy grace, Thy forbearance, Thy sustaining power. I could not have preached Thee to sinners or aided those in temptation, had I not discovered by the folly and weakness of my own heart what Thou canst do. I might have come to ascribe some goodness, some strength to myself, and have been proportionately harsh with others.

How harsh we are on each other, Lord! Some were shocked that I was seen on the street and visited friends next day; they accused me of insensibility when I dared not stay home for fear of indulging my grief . . . how much more lightly men view a breach of God's commands than a breach of established custom! Others, since my Mary was no longer young and we had lived together forty years, thought I made too much ado. Too much ado! But let me praise Thee now and through Eternity that Thou didst demonstrate in power that I *could* live without her, that I could prove the truth of what I preached to others, that the gospel is a catholicon.

Jesus my Shepherd, Husband, Friend, my Prophet, Priest, and King, accept my praise for the assurance of Thy care those three nights and three days of watching; of Thy care for my Mary that she lay all the while as in gentle slumber; that even her dying groans did not ruffle the peace of her face. O my Lord — why am I crying now when I was strengthened not to

431

give way to unmanly sorrow then? When I could take the ring from her dear finger, and give thanks before the servants for her peaceful deliverance?

When I could preach three times while she lay dead in the house? And see her laid, see her laid. . . .

The text, the text I marked when I began to preach, for this, for no other occasion. Now the time has come. The Lord has heard my prayer. It is worth standing in the fire to experience His power and faithfulness. My friends would spare me; they mean well; do they not know I *must* preach now or never again? Not to preach would mean that I am an idolater still. The church is very crowded, though it is Christmas Day. How silent they are! Sanctify this occasion to them in their afflictions. For this Jesus was incarnate. 'Tis His love His people raises over self to reign as kings. Truly this is Thy work, that I can at last, with composure, echo Thy prophet:

"Although the fig tree shall not blossom, neither shall fruit be in the vines; the labour of the olive shall fail, and the fields shall yield no meat; the flock shall be cut off from the fold, and there shall be no herd in the stalls" . . . in other words, all earthly joy, comfort, sustenance is utterly removed . . . "*yet* I will rejoice in the Lord, I will joy in the God of my salvation."

Will — yea I *do* rejoice!

O gracious and merciful Lord! Surely — surely — the coach has come!

JOHN NEWTON

CLERK,
ONCE AN INFIDEL AND LIBERTINE,
A SERVANT OF SLAVES IN AFRICA,
WAS,
BY THE RICH MERCY OF OUR LORD AND SAVIOUR
JESUS CHRIST,
PRESERVED, RESTORED, PARDONED,
AND APPOINTED TO PREACH THE FAITH
HE HAD LONG LABOURED TO DESTROY.

HE MINISTERED
NEAR XVI YEARS AS CURATE AND VICAR
OF OLNEY IN BUCKS,
AND XXVIII YEARS AS RECTOR
OF THESE UNITED PARISHES.

ON FEBRUARY THE FIRST MDCCL, HE MARRIED
MARY,
DAUGHTER OF THE LATE GEORGE CATLETT,
OF CHATHAM, KENT,
WHOM HE RESIGNED
TO THE LORD WHO GAVE HER,
ON DECEMBER THE XVTH, MDCCXC.

BIBLIOGRAPHY

JOHN NEWTON:
An Authentic Narrative
Cardiphonia; or, The Utterance of the Heart in the Course of a Real Correspondence
Forty-one Letters on Religious Subjects
Six Discourses Intended for the Pulpit
Twenty Sermons Preached at the Parish Church at Olney
Letters to a Wife
Olney Hymns
Thoughts on the African Slave Trade
A Review of Ecclesiastical History
Messiah: Fifty Expository Discourses on the Series of Scriptural Passages which Form the Subject of the Celebrated Oratorio by Handel
Ebenezer: A Memorial
Notes on Bunyan's Pilgrim's Progress
A Sequel to Cardiphonia
Miscellaneous Papers
The Christian Correspondent

BERNARD MARTIN:
John Newton: An Autobiography
The Ancient Mariner and the Authentic Narrative
John Newton and the Slave Trade

DONALD DEMARAY:
Amazing Grace

JOSIAH BULL:
John Newton: A Biography
Letters by John Newton

RICHARD CECIL:
Memoirs of the Rev. John Newton

MRS. DAWSON:
Life and Writings of Mrs. Dawson of Lancaster

435

J. Callis:
    John Newton: Sailor, Preacher, Pastor, Poet

J. Campbell:
    Letters and Conversational Remarks
    Essay on the Life of Newton

Archdeacon Lindsey:
    The Church's Song

A. W. Parsons:
    Great Christians, Vol. 11

M. B. Cropper:
    Sparks Among the Stubble

L. H. Dalton:
    Singing Slaves

Thomas Wright:
    The Loved Haunts of Cowper, with Newton's Poem "The Supposed Meeting"

T. Williams:
    The Early Life and Conversion of John Newton

F. Hamilton:
    Autobiography and Further Particulars

Mary Seeley:
    The Later Evangelical Fathers

Oliver Ratcliff:
    The Newton-Cowper Centenary, 1907

Sir James Stephens:
    Essays on the Evangelical Succession

Thomas Scott:
    The Force of Truth

A. Skevington Wood:
    Life of Thomas Haweis

Thomas S. Grimshawe:
    Works, Life, Letters, Poems, and Private Correspondence of William Cowper

Robert Southey:
    The Life of William Cowper, Esq.

Gilbert O. Thomas:
    William Cowper and the Eighteenth Century

Hugh Fausset:
    Life of William Cowper

LORD DAVID CECIL:
  The Stricken Deer

C. DILLY:
  An Apology and Shield for Protestant Dissenters

A. S. TURBERVILLE:
  English Men and Manners in the Eighteenth Century

LORD SHAFTESBURY:
  Characteristics

TOBIAS G. SMOLLETT:
  Roderick Random

MARTIN MADAN:
  Thelyphthora; or, A Treatise on Female Ruin

WILL DURANT:
  The Age of Faith

SACHEVERELL SITWELL:
  Spain

ETHELREDA LEWIS, ED.:
  Trader Horn

WILLIAM WILBERFORCE:
  Private Papers

MRS. CENTLIVRE:
  Plays

JOHN FORD:
  Plays

WILLIAM LAW:
  A Serious Call to a Devout and Holy Life

JOHN WESLEY:
  Journal and *Letters*

W. H. FITCHETT:
  Wesley and His Century

M. PIETTE:
  John Wesley in the Evolution of Protestantism

M. R. BRAILSFORD:
  A Tale of Two Brothers

ABRAM LIPSKY:
  John Wesley, A Portrait

J. BOSWELL:
  Life of Johnson

M. ESTHER HARDING, M.D.:
  Woman's Mysteries, Ancient and Modern

437